MATED TO THE

WEREWOLF VILLAIN

PART 1 -6

BEATRIX ARDEN

Images: @Canva @shutterstock: Serge Lee

Author Website: beatrixarden.com

Other Hot Stories by Beatrix Arden

Chained Omega

Werewolf Breeding Academy

You're my Omega

Omega Harem Lost

The Village Omega

Alpha Hates Alpha

Subscribe to Beatrix Arden new release notifications!

Get notified of new stories by email and get free ebooks.

sub.beatrixarden.com

CONTENTS

PART I

CHAPTER 1

A muffled scream echoed through the sewer system, followed by a dull thud. Deepa clenched her jaw as she hurried through the dark tunnels. Her black hair was tied back in a tight bun, sweat dripping into her eyes as she moved swiftly between the rancid puddles and ancient pipes. The stench of waste made her want to gag, but she fought past it with every breath.

There was a glimmer of light up ahead. Heart racing, she approached cautiously, silver gun raised.

As she rounded a corner, she found a gruesome sight, a teenage boy trembling against the wall, blood dripping from the bite mark on his hand. Tears poured down his face as he rocked back and forth.

His eyes met hers, filled with panic and terror.

"Please," he begged, scrambling away. "I don't want to hurt anyone."

His pleas were cut short when he collapsed to all fours, retching bile as he began to shudder and change. His bones cracked and reformed as black fur spouted from his skin.

He was turning into one of *them*.

The gun trembled in Deepa's hands. Her heart thundered, drowning out the boy's whimpers as his humanity was stripped away.

In a matter of seconds, he'd become a six foot long monstrosity with black fur and glimmering teeth. He snarled at her, his fangs bared.

"Fuck," Deepa hissed under her breath, raising her gun and firing off several rounds that ripped through its body.

The werewolf fell to the ground with a pained howl, blood spraying across the concrete.

It twitched and then lay still, lifeless.

"Sorry kid." She wiped her brow and holstered her weapon, feeling the adrenaline slowly drain from her veins. "You didn't deserve what they did to you."

She momentarily let her shields down, which turned out to be a fatal mistake.

Two more wolves emerged from the darkness, their yellow eyes flashing as they stalked towards her.

Deepa gasped, reaching for her gun. But before she could raise it, one of the wolves pounced, knocking her to the ground. She struggled against the creature, trying desperately to break free.

A gunshot rang out, and the wolf slumped over dead.

Deepa looked up to see a large man standing above her, black hair neatly cropped and yellow *Infection Control* jacket gleaming in the darkness.

"Parker," she gasped, relief washing over her as he riddled the second wolf with bullets.

Parker grinned, extending his hand to help her up. "I thought I was the only one allowed to put you on your back."

Deepa rolled her eyes, brushing herself off. "Very funny. How are the other tunnels?"

"All clear. Ran across a few homeless that must have been their lunch, but nothing else."

Deepa suppressed a shudder. Newly turned werewolves had little control of their bodies, easily succumbing to the virus that had taken hold of their minds. Without easily available prey in the tunnels, they soon turned to snacking on humans.

Deepa brushed the grime from her *Infection Control* jacket, then smoothed any stray hairs back into her bun.

"Come on," Parker urged, lacing his fingers through Deepa's to pull her away from the bodies. "I think we're done here."

The gray hallways of Infection Control stank of cheap sanitizer and blood. Deepa and Parker passed a trolley carrying several wolves in cages, one of them transforming back and forth from his human form like he couldn't control the process.

"Please," the werewolf begged as he rattled the bars, but no one stopped to help him.

It was just another day at the office.

"There you are!" called out Varn as he came jogging towards them, curly blond hair plastered to his forehead with sweat, werewolf blood splattered across his jacket and shoes. "Craig wants everyone to report to him before heading home."

Deepa groaned, she was dying for a shower, but she knew better than to keep their superior waiting.

"Where is he?" Parker asked.

"Interrogation room five," Varn replied. "They just brought in one of the turned ones that's been laying low for decades. Craig hopes that he can make the guy spill the location of more."

Deepa nodded, the three of them falling into line as they made their way through the facility. They passed by a few other teams, all looking equally tired and beat up, before coming to a halt outside of a heavily fortified door.

"Good work out there," Varn said as he placed his thumb on the scanner, granting them access.

"Thanks." Parker clapped Varn on the back as he headed inside. "Drinks later?"

"Wouldn't miss it for the world." Varn waved and jogged back down the hall.

Parker shook his head, turning back to Deepa with a grin. "What do you think, babe? Can I talk you into going for drinks with the boys tonight?"

Deepa arched an eyebrow at him. "You can try. But I make no promises."

He laughed, taking her hand in his. "Fair enough."

They passed by an examination room, the harsh lights glaring off the metal surfaces. Craig was hunched over an iron table, his dark gray hair ruffled and unkempt. There were large bags under his eyes like it had been a busy evening.

Deepa and Parker took a seat on a bench outside the room, watching in through the clear glass.

"How's it going?" Deepa asked Sadie who was sitting on the next bench, furiously writing notes while chewing on the end of her long auburn braid.

Sadie shrugged, her green eyes darting to the haggard man opposite Craig. "It's been a slow night. This one doesn't seem keen on handing over his secrets."

Parker snorted. "Why are they always so stubborn?"

"Don't ask me," Sadie said. "I'm just here to record."

"If anyone can crack him, it's Craig," Parker said with a grin.

Craig's steely gaze bore into a weathered man in his fifties. Long strands of gray hair cascaded over the werewolf's stained flannel shirt and his wrists were firmly clasped in shackles. Restraints held each ankle together.

"Scott Morris," Craig said as he flipped through a file. "It's a miracle that you've managed to stay sane for this long after being infected. We both know that it's only a matter of time before your mind and body succumb to the disease."

"It's not like that," Scott protested, tugging at his restraints. "We found medicine that can help we-"

"Medicine that only prolongs people's pain," Craig retorted. "We both know that the werewolf infection is incurable."

"But people can have normal lives!" Scott insisted. "I've seen it dozens of times! You can help-"

Craig slammed his hand on the table. "Until what? They lapse and bite another innocent victim? Spreading the infection even further? Do you know how many children I've had to console because their parents were ripped apart by monsters like you?"

Scott hung his head. "No," he murmured. "We're not all like that."

Craig snorted, "We all know that the only cure is to eradicate the source."

"Please," Scott begged. "You can't just kill all of us. We're people too!"

"Then tell me the location of your friends! Isn't it better to grant them a quick death instead of suffering for the rest of their lives with a rabid animal lodged in their brains?"

Scott shook his head. "No, you're wrong. It's not like that. You don't understand! We can live together!"

"There is no together. Your people have made it more than clear that it's either us or them." Craig stared him down for a moment, then reached into his pocket, pulling out a small gun.

Deepa gasped, but Parker gripped her hand tightly, keeping her rooted in place.

"Scott Morris," Craig said. "By the power vested in me by the government, I sentence you to death."

Scott's eyes widened as Craig raised the gun, firing off a single silver bullet that tore through his skull, blood spraying across the room.

The body went limp, hanging from the shackles as Craig put his gun away.

"Come on," Sadie said, grabbing her notes. "You guys know the drill."

Deepa and Parker rose to their feet, joining her as they entered the room.

Deepa wrinkled her nose at the scent of blood as she moved around the body.

"Any problems?" Craig asked, wiping his face with his sleeve.

"None," Parker said. "We took out two wolves and one that was just turned."

"Excellent," Craig said. "Keep it up and you might make a squad leader next month."

"Thanks, sir." Parker grinned, puffing out his chest, until Deepa elbowed him in the ribs. "Deepa also killed one," he wheezed.

Craig eyed her, looking impressed. "Very good. You're becoming quite the asset here, Deepa."

Deepa blushed, looking down at her feet.

"I'll have the body burned," Sadie said, already calling someone on her radio.

"I want you all to take the rest of the night off," Craig said. "Get some sleep, eat something, and report back in twelve hours."

"Yes, sir," they replied in unison.

"And then he was going on about how we can all live peacefully together," Parker took a sip of his beer. "Can you believe it? Like those monsters aren't the reason why we have to put people down every night."

"I know, right?" Varn mumbled through a mouth full of burger.

The bar was crowded with college students and several other Infection Control officers. It was old and smelled like stale cigarettes, but it was cheap and served food until late.

"I don't know," Sadie said while idly munching on her fries. "I read the guy's file. He didn't seem so bad. He was actually trying to help the turned by giving them medication and a place to live. I think he honestly believed what he was saying."

"Oh come on," Parker snapped. "You don't actually believe all that peace and love bullshit, do you? Those people he helped probably went mad and killed people later on."

"I'm not saying that they aren't dangerous," Sadie said. "But that doesn't mean we have to kill every single one."

"So what, you're a sympathizer now?" Parker demanded.

"Don't be ridiculous," Sadie retorted. "I'm just saying we shouldn't be so quick to pull the trigger on them."

"Hey, calm down," Deepa interjected, sensing that the situation was about to escalate. "There's no reason to fight about this."

Parker snorted, draining the rest of his beer. "Fine. Whatever. I'm getting another round."

"Wait, Parker," Deepa called after him, but he ignored her, disappearing into the crowd.

"Sorry," Sadie said. "I didn't mean to-"

"Don't worry about it," Deepa cut her off, shaking her head. "He's just.... sensitive, that's all."

Varn snorted, taking another bite of his burger.

"Hey," Sadie said while lowering her voice to a whisper. "Is it true that his parents were... you know..."

"Yeah," Deepa nodded. "Yeah, he doesn't like talking about it, but they were killed by werewolves."

"Jeeze," Sadie sighed. "I can't even imagine. No wonder he's eager to kill them all."

"Yeah, it's all he's ever talked about for as long as I've known him.

"I can imagine," Sadie grimaced.

"Well." Varn slapped his hands together to get rid of the crumbs. "I'm heading out. Early morning and all that."

"Yeah," Sadie nodded. "Same."

"Thanks for the beer," Deepa said.

"My pleasure," Varn said. "Catch you guys later."

"See you," Sadie waved, following after him.

Deepa watched them go, then glanced across the room in search of Parker.

Her gaze fell upon a cluster of blond men, quietly seated at a table towards the rear, partially obscured by shadows. Their fair faces and light complexions stood out in the subdued lighting.

A man in a white leather jacket locked eyes with her, sending a shiver down her spine.

He was handsome, in a terrifying sort of way. His short blond hair was styled to look messy, and his lips were plump and red.

But there was something wrong about him, and it wasn't just his creepy stare.

Werewolf, was Deepa's first thought, until she quickly brushed it away.

She was just being paranoid. There was no way that werewolves would dare visit a bar crawling with Infection Control officers.

"Where'd they go?" said Parker as he appeared before her, nursing two beers.

"They went home." She tore her gaze away from the strange man. "Had an early morning."

"Pussies," he grinned as he passed her a bottle.

"Thanks." Deepa took a sip. "You okay?"

He snorted. "Fine. Why wouldn't I be?"

"Well, you were a little-"

"What? Angry because some girl wants to let the monsters run around loose? Please."

"Okay, okay. Don't bite my head off." Deepa took another sip of her beer. "I wasn't the one who said it."

Parker sighed, rubbing his face. "I'm sorry. It's been a long night."

"Yeah. I get it."

They lapsed into silence, drinking their beers as Deepa tried to ignore the table of men at the back of the room.

"Come on." Parker placed his bottle down. "Let's get out of here." He laced his fingers with Deepa's, leading her out of the bar.

The car park was empty, the sky cloudy as a cool breeze blew past them.

Parker pinned her against the side of his car, his lips pressing against hers.

"Are you still pissed off?" she murmured between kisses.

"A little," he admitted.

"Want me to help with that?" she whispered seductively.

He smiled, running his hands down her hips. "I could use a distraction."

"Me too," she admitted, letting her shields fall away.

She was exhausted and sore from patrolling tunnels all night. Her shoulders ached, but all she wanted was the feel of his lips and the touch of his skin.

"What are you waiting for?" she murmured.

Parker smiled, kissing her hard as his hands roamed under her jacket, slipping underneath her shirt to grip her breasts.

"You're so beautiful," he murmured against her skin, nipping at her earlobe.

"Mmm, you're not so bad yourself," she giggled.

Everything felt better when he was beside her. The stress of their work melted away as they clung to each other, lost in their own private world.

Deepa closed her eyes and gripped his shoulders, savoring the moment.

Before it came to an abrupt end.

The sickening whack of a bat was all Deepa heard before Parker was sent sprawling across the gravel.

She instinctively reached for her gun, but it wasn't there. The one second of hesitation was enough for the assailant to land a punch to her jaw.

Deepa staggered, falling backwards as stars flashed across her vision.

The figure was blurry and distorted as they kicked Deepa to the ground, landing several blows to her ribs, knocking the air from her lungs.

"Hey!" Parker cried, jumping to his feet and rushing towards the attacker, only to be knocked back down by two blond men who began to mercilessly beat the shit out of him.

"You're all the same," rumbled a deep voice, and Deepa looked up to see the man from the bar, a sadistic smile plastered across his lips. "Infection Control. Always so confident until you take your little jackets off."

He crouched down, gripping her face and pulling her close. His breath smelled of vodka, his nails digging into her skin.

"Let's see how you fare on the other side," he grinned, fangs flashing.

Deepa tried to scream, but it was already too late. The werewolf plunged his teeth into her neck, piercing the skin.

Deepa's entire world exploded into pain, her body seizing and spasming as her nerves were lit on fire. She could feel the infection surging through her veins, her organs twitching and shifting.

She watched in horror as another muscular blond man plunged his own teeth into Parker's neck.

"No!" Deepa gasped, reaching out to him. "Parker!"

The man who bit her pulled away, wiping his mouth with the back of his hand.

"See you around," he said softly with a grin, indicating for the other men to join him.

They dashed into the darkness, leaving Deepa and Parker alone in the parking lot.

Deepa crawled towards him, her body trembling.

"Parker," she whimpered, gripping his hand. "Please."

Parker coughed, blood dripping from his lips. "Deepa," he groaned. "Did they bite you?"

"Yes," she sobbed.

"It's okay," he wheezed. "I love you."

"I love you too," she cried, clinging to him.

"You have to run," he urged, his voice weak. "Get away before anyone comes out here."

"No," she sobbed. "No, I won't leave you."

The door to the bar opened, several loud voices spilling onto the asphalt outside.

"Please," he begged, his voice a whisper. "My leg....it's...I won't be able to keep up."

"Parker-"

"Just do this for me...Please."

"Parker-"

"Promise me, Deepa. Promise me that you'll survive."

"I promise," she sobbed, tears running down her cheeks.

"Good," he smiled, wincing in pain.

"I love you," she whimpered, clutching his hand.

"Hey!" someone cried out from across the carpark. "Are you alright?"

Deepa froze, panic washing over her.

"Go," Parker urged. "Hurry."

"I love you," she whispered, planting a kiss on his lips before rising to her feet and bolting into the darkness.

Deepa darted between buildings, cutting through alleys and side streets as she tried to put as much distance between her and the Infection Control officers in the bar.

Her heart was pounding, her chest heaving with ragged breaths as her body screamed in agony. The transformation had begun, and it was a slow, torturous process.

The world blurred around her, shapes and colors blending together as the virus coursed through her system. Every muscle in her body was contracting and releasing, her bones cracking and reforming, her skin burning and crawling.

She gasped, falling to her knees as a wave of nausea washed over her.

Her stomach lurched, bile rising in her throat as she vomited. The pain was excruciating, her vision fading in and out as she fought to stay conscious.

"Please," she whimpered, tears streaming down her face. "Please, make it stop."

The moon rose above the clouds, illuminating the dark sky as the last shreds of Deepa's humanity faded into nothingness.

"Parker," she breathed, her voice hoarse.

But there was nothing but pain and darkness.

CHAPTER 2

Deepa's eyes flew open, her chest heaving as she sucked in a lungful of air.

She was lying on a hard wooden floor, a thin blanket draped over her naked body.

The room was dark, the only light coming from a small window set high up in the wall. There were scratch marks covering the floor, and a pile of small bones in the corner.

"Oh God," Deepa groaned, clutching her head. The memories were flooding back to her, the attack in the parking lot, the infection, Parker...

"Parker," she whimpered as her face went numb, tears gathering in her eyes.

If Infection Control captured him then he'd certainly be dead. They couldn't risk letting any of the infected live, even if they were one of their best officers.

He was gone.

"I'm so sorry," Deepa sobbed, her shoulders shaking with grief. She should have stayed and fought for him instead of running away like a coward.

Deepa buried her face in her hands, her body racked with sobs. This was it. It was only a matter of time before Infection Control killed her, or she was driven mad by the wolf that had been forced inside her head.

"You're finally awake," said a gentle female voice.

There was a woman peering in at Deepa through the window. She was in her mid fifties, with long dark hair and olive skin, dressed in a casual T-shirt and jeans that certainly weren't Infection Control uniform.

"Who are you?" Deepa asked warily.

"I'm Vanessa," she said with a smile. "I'm the one who found you."

"Found me?" Deepa repeated, her eyes darting around the room, searching for any way of escape, but the door was covered in locks.

"You're safe," Vanessa reassured her. "This is a safe place for people like us."

"People like us?"

"Werewolves. I've been working with them for years, trying to help them adjust. Most people think I'm crazy, but it's worth it to see the looks on their faces when they realize they're not alone."

"I... I don't understand," Deepa said, her voice shaking.

Vanessa chuckled. "There's a lot to take in, but I promise I'll explain everything."

Vanessa unbolted the door, handing Deepa a change of clothes then patiently waiting outside until Deepa had changed.

"Thank you." Deepa adjusted the large black hoodie she was wearing, it was a few sizes too big and the denim jeans were tight around her thighs.

"No problem," Vanessa smiled. "Are you hungry?"

"No," Deepa lied.

"You should eat something," Vanessa urged. "It'll make you feel better."

"I'm fine, really."

Vanessa nodded, leading Deepa down a dark hall filled with other cells. There were howls and the scratching of claws against walls.

"You don't have to worry about getting attacked," Vanessa explained. "The doors are designed to hold back the most powerful werewolves."

"So you lock them up?" Deepa frowned.

"Just until they come back to their senses, then we help them get back on their feet."

"Why?" Deepa clenched her fists. "Why would you do that?"

Vanessa stopped, turning to look at her. "Because no one else will. You've seen what Infection Control does to people like us. We have to stick together."

Deepa opened her mouth to argue, but no words came out. Before her transformation she would have readily stormed the place with a team and shot up every wolf on sight. But now...

Vanessa opened a door at the end of the hall, unveiling an old kitchen filled with people. Several were gathered around a table as a young woman tended to the stove, her blond curly hair tied back in a tight ponytail.

"Looks like we've got another one, Andrea," Vanessa called out to the woman.

Andrea glanced over her shoulder, gazing up and down Deepa's disheveled form.

"Another stray," Andrea sighed, rolling her eyes.

"Here, take a seat." Vanessa indicated to an empty spot at the table.

It was easy to tell that the other people were also freshly turned werewolves. They were dressed in a variety of mismatched clothes while anxiously glancing around them. One guy's hand kept transforming to and from its werewolf form, and another young woman was furiously scratching herself.

These were Deepa's people now.

"What's your name?" Vanessa asked, sitting down next to Deepa.

"Deepa," she replied, then cursed herself for not coming up with a fake name. What if they found out that she was part of Infection Control?

"Do you have any family?"

"Just my aunt," Deepa swallowed. "But I don't see her that often."

"Where were you turned?"

"At a park," Deepa's fingers twitched, wanting to curl into claws. "I was with my boyfriend and-"

Deepa gasped, the memory of the attack replaying itself in her mind. Parker's pained expression and his last words before she ran away.

"Are you okay?" Vanessa asked.

"Y-yeah, just..."

"It's okay." Vanessa gently placed her hand on top of Deepa's. "I've been where you are. We all have."

Deepa nodded, biting back the tears that were threatening to fall.

"Here." Andrea placed a steaming bowl of pasta in front of Deepa. "Eat up."

Deepa didn't want to eat, but she suddenly felt ravenous. She picked up the fork, shoveling the food into her mouth, savoring the rich buttery flavor.

Everything tasted a thousand times stronger than before. The spices, the salt, even the scent of the wooden table.

"You'll get used to it," Vanessa assured her. "Once you learn to live with the wolf. I remember that when Scott picked me up he-"

"Scott?" Deepa choked.

It had to be a coincidence. There was no way that-

"Sorry," said Vanessa. "I mean the guy who ran this place before I did. He never hesitated to help any one in need."

Dread settled in the pit of Deepa's stomach. Memories of Scott's blood spraying across the interrogation room flashed through her mind.

"Where is he?" Deepa asked, trying her best to keep her voice natural.

Vanessa bit her lower lip. "He was picked up by Infection Control, but he's probably okay. He's a smart guy."

Deepa tightly gripped her fork.

No, he's dead, she wanted to scream, but the words couldn't come out.

"Don't worry," said Vanessa. "You can stay here as long as you need. I'll make some space. You can bunk with Charlotte and Beth, or maybe Thea, Andrea and-"

She was interrupted by a young man across the table who let out a scream, his body violently shook as he transformed into his wolf form, shedding his clothes and frantically dashing out of the room.

"Fuck," Vanessa swore, jumping to her feet and running after him. "Not again."

Andrea rolled her eyes, continuing to stir the pot of food.

Deepa dropped her fork, her chest heaving. They were all as good as dead. If Infection Control didn't get them, then the disease would. They'd all be reduced to rabid monsters without a shred of humanity.

Deepa clenched her fist, digging her nails into her skin. She had to leave.

She got to her feet, slipping out of the room.

"Where are you going?" Andrea called out, but Deepa ignored her, heading towards the front entrance.

Deepa pushed open the heavy door, stepping out into the cool morning air.

There was nothing but rolling hills as far as she could see, long grass swaying in the wind. There were no signs of civilization other than a single dirt road.

"Deepa!" Vanessa called out, jogging to catch up. "Wait!"

Deepa spun around, glaring at her.

"Don't try and stop me," she snarled, her hands curling into claws.

"I won't." Vanessa held up her hands. "I just wanted to make sure you were okay."

"No," Deepa growled. "I'm not. I was turned into a fucking monster! My boyfriend is dead, Infection Control is going to kill me, and the only thing standing between me and an early grave is some hippy trying to save everyone!"

"I know it's hard," Vanessa's voice was calm and even. "But this isn't the end. I can teach you how to control the wolf and help you survive. Once the first month is over, you can-"

"Thanks but no thanks!" Deepa snapped. "I'm leaving."

"Just wait a sec." Vanessa's hand dove into her pocket, pulling out several notes. "It isn't much, but it should be enough for a bus to wherever you're going."

Deepa eyed the money, her anger fading.

"Fine," she grunted, snatching the notes and tucking them into her pocket.

"Be careful," Vanessa said. "One slip and people won't hesitate to report you to Infection Control. It's best to lay low until you have more control over the change."

"Yeah, thanks," Deepa muttered, turning away and jogging down the dirt road, not daring to look back.

CHAPTER 3

It felt like someone had turned the dial on her senses up to one thousand. All the sounds and smells surrounding her felt overwhelming.

There were also voices in her mind, telling her to do things that felt strangely natural.

Shift, run, hunt.

The need to transform burned like an itch. Deepa tried her best to hold it back, keeping her head down as she made her way through the city streets.

For the first time in her life, she was glad that werewolves were almost impossible to tell apart from humans. Scientists were still working on an accurate test, but unless she transformed, no one could tell.

Deepa kept her hoodie up, her heart hammering in her chest. Infection Control must have known what had happened. If any of her old co-workers spotted her, they wouldn't hesitate to put a bullet in her chest.

Deepa smashed a side window to get into her apartment. It was empty and all her and Parker's things were gone, like they had already been declared dead.

"*Fuck,*" Deepa hissed.

She paced the living room, her hands curled into claws as she fought the urge to rip into the wallpaper.

There was nothing. Nothing left to remind her of the life that they had together. Like they hadn't even existed.

Her skin crawled and itched, her body desperate to transform and destroy. The voices in her head were growing louder, urging her to hunt, kill, and maim.

It was only a matter of time before she hurt someone.

Deepa went to the bathroom, pushing on a vent and blindly feeling around the darkness until her hand landed on a familiar hunk of metal.

Deepa pulled it out, a small handgun and a round of silver bullets.

She sat down on the cold tiled floor, the weapon cradled in her lap.

She would take her own life.

But not before murdering the man who turned her into a monster.

Reconnaissance had been Deepa's job before she was assigned to patrol. She was small and unintimidating, so it had been easy for her to sniff out information on potential werewolves.

She started with the bars closest to the one where Parker was killed, silently watching from the shadows for any hint of the fuckers, eating food from dumpsters when her hunger became unbearable.

It was on her seventh night when she finally saw the group. The same blond haired assholes that attacked them in the parking lot.

They were loud and obnoxious, drinking and laughing as they exited a bar, staggering slightly.

Her attention was immediately drawn to their leader. The man who bit her, his deep voice carrying across the car park.

"We should hit up somewhere else," he slurred, running a hand through his pale hair. "This place sucks."

"Yeah," the one who had bitten Parker agreed, his large fingers rapidly texting on his phone. "The place down the road has way thirstier chicks."

Deepa strode across the asphalt towards them, gun swinging by her side. She wanted to look him in the eyes as she blew his brains out. She wanted to see the shock of recognition on his face. She wanted him to know that Karma had come to collect.

He was too wasted to even notice her until the barrel was pressed against his temple.

"Wha-" he said, the words catching in his throat.

"Time to die, monster," Deepa growled, pressing the gun harder into his skin.

Her finger was wrapped around the trigger, but it refused to move. Instead she felt swallowed by the depth of his blue eyes.

He was captivating.

The world melted away, and all Deepa could think about was the curve of his lips and the softness of his skin. His smell was intoxicating, a sweet aroma mixed with the sharpness of alcohol.

Her heart raced and her skin tingled, a thousand voices screaming in her mind.

He appeared equally perturbed, staring wide eyed at Deepa with his mouth half open.

"You..." he breathed, the words barely audible.

Deepa tried to pull the trigger again but her finger refused to move. Just the thought of his death suddenly felt excruciating. Like someone had plunged a hand into her chest and ripped out her heart.

"What the fuck, dude," the one who bit Parker snapped. "Are you just going to stand there and let her blow your brains out?"

His words snapped Deepa out of her daze.

She lowered her gun and ran, dashing in the opposite direction as fast as her feet could take her.

What the fuck was that?

She had never felt such overwhelming magnetism towards another person before. It was as if he had cast a spell over her.

Maybe there was something in werewolf saliva that caused their victims to become infatuated with them?

Deepa shuddered. She wanted to throw up. It was mortifying to think that way about the man who ruined her life.

Her feet carried her down a random street, not knowing or caring where she was going.

"What's wrong with me?" she murmured, gripping her head, her claws digging into her scalp.

It had to be the infection. It was slowly driving her mad.

Deepa brought the gun to her forehead, ready to end it all, but her hand began to shake, quickly sprouting fur.

"No," Deepa hissed as she fell to her knees, the voices in her head becoming unbearable.

Him. Him. Him. Him. Him, they chanted.

Deepa screamed, clawing at her ears, desperate to silence the voices.

The pain was blinding, her muscles contorting, her bones snapping and reforming.

She collapsed to the ground, the gun forgotten as her body writhed.

It felt like she was being torn apart and put back together again. Her skin burning, the fur covering her body doing nothing to sooth it.

She screamed, the sound coming out as a howl. Her teeth began to grow longer, sharp and jagged as they cut into her gums.

And then there was silence.

The transformation was complete.

CHAPTER 4

The wolf didn't care about Deepa's human pain. She was driven by much simpler instincts, hunger and lust.

She dashed through the dark streets until she emerged into the forest, bounding over tree roots and dodging bushes.

The air smelled of pine and earth, a refreshing change from the foul city.

The wolf inhaled deeply, her pace quickening as the scent of another wolf filled the air.

Him.

It was a call that she couldn't ignore. Making her blood quicken and her heart race.

The scent grew stronger as she drew closer, the masculine aroma making her mouth water.

She emerged into a clearing to find a large white wolf standing in the center, pale fur gleaming under the moonlight.

They locked eyes, and she could feel the electricity in the air, the tension growing between them.

His blue eyes were bright and piercing, his expression hungry.

The white wolf moved slowly towards her, his gait confident and strong.

He transformed before her very eyes, his fur retracting, his body reshaping, until the man who Deepa tried to kill was standing before her.

His muscular body shivered in the cool night air, but his cock was hard and erect between his powerful thighs.

She stared at him, unable to look away.

He was the most beautiful thing she had ever seen.

His gaze was intense, his chest rising and falling with each breath.

She slowly transformed back into her human form, her fur receding, her limbs extending.

His gaze lingered on her breasts, his cock twitching.

"It's you," he breathed, taking a step towards her.

Deepa wanted to run, but she couldn't move. Her body was frozen, her heart racing.

He took another step, his hand reaching out to caress her cheek.

His touch sent a shiver down her spine, her body trembling.

He leaned in, his lips brushing against hers, his breath hot on her skin.

Deepa's mind swirled with desire as his lips pressed more firmly against hers, his tongue tracing the outline of her mouth. She surrendered to his touch, their lips melding together in a passionate dance. Her body responded instinctively, arching into him as he deepened the kiss.

She moaned, her hands grasping his shoulders, pulling him closer.

Deepa's mind felt numb. A small part of her knew that it was wrong, that she should be choking the life from his body, but all the wolf wanted was to be closer, to feel his hard cock deep inside her.

His warm hands roamed her body, his fingers gently caressing her skin, squeezing her breasts.

She gasped, arching her back as his lips moved down to her neck, sucking and biting.

She let out a low growl, a mixture of pleasure and primal hunger. The sensation of his teeth marking her skin sent waves of ecstasy through her body, igniting the fire within her. Deepa's hands traveled down his toned chest, tracing the lines of his muscles, feeling the heat radiating from his body.

His hard cock pressed against her, hot and heavy as it searched for her heat.

He gripped her ass, massaging the soft cheeks as he ground against her, letting out a soft moan.

Her body trembled with anticipation as he pulled away from the kiss, his eyes locking with hers. Time seemed to stand still as they both drank in the sight of each other, their desires laid bare.

He lowered her down to the forest floor, caging her in with his size, his hard length rubbing against her inner thigh.

"Tell me to stop," he breathed.

She wanted to, but she couldn't. She had never wanted anything more than to become one with him.

He leaned down, his lips brushing against hers as his hand trailed down her stomach, his fingers teasing her entrance.

She gasped, her body arching.

He plunged a finger into her, curling it as he moved it in and out.

She moaned, her hips moving in time with his movements.

He added another finger, stretching her, preparing her.

She writhed beneath him, her hands clawing at the ground, her body overwhelmed with pleasure.

He removed his fingers, positioning his throbbing cock at her entrance.

Deepa shivered, her body aching with desire as she looked up into his eyes. The forest whispered around them, the moon casting a silver glow upon their entangled figures. There was an undeniable connection between them, a primal pull that defied all reason.

He pushed into her, his cock slowly filling her with several small thrusts, until his hips were flush against hers.

"Fuck," he hissed as he paused to bask in the sensation. "Fuck, fuck, fuck."

She writhed beneath him, her hands grasping his ass, encouraging him to move.

He thrust into her, his movements slow and deliberate, her body clamping around his dick.

"God," he moaned. "You feel so good."

Deepa's body trembled beneath him as he continued to move with a growing urgency. She could feel every inch of him inside her, stretching and filling her completely. She wrapped her legs around him, pulling him deeper.

His thrusts became faster and harder, his pace increasing as he lost control of himself.

Her nails dug into his skin, her body bucking against him.

It felt so natural. So right. So perfect. Like this was where she was always meant to be.

He kept his pace, thrusting into her again and again, his fingers digging into her skin.

She felt herself getting closer and closer, her body trembling.

"Fuck," he growled, his teeth sinking into her shoulder, just below the spot where he bit her, the pain mixing with the pleasure.

Deepa could feel his cock twitching inside her, his orgasm approaching.

She clung to him, her nails digging into his back, drawing blood.

His thrusts became frantic, his breathing ragged.

She felt her body tense, her muscles clamping around him, pushing her over the edge.

Deepa's entire being exploded in a kaleidoscope of colors and sensations as her climax consumed her. The ecstasy rippled through her body like a wildfire, spreading from the point where their bodies joined and igniting every nerve ending in its wake. Her vision blurred as she lost herself in a euphoric haze, surrendering to the waves of pleasure crashing over her.

"Fuck," he groaned, his movements growing erratic as he chased his own release. The intensity of her climax pushed him closer to the edge, his body trembling with desire. With one final, powerful thrust, he let out a guttural roar, his essence spilling into her, filling her with his warmth.

He collapsed onto her, his body shaking, his chest heaving as he tried to catch his breath.

Deepa lay beneath him, her chest rising and falling with each ragged breath. The air was thick with the scent of their passion, a heady mix of sweat and sex. She could feel his rapid heartbeat against her skin, the weight of his body pressing her into the soft ground.

He raised his head, looking down at her, his expression apprehensive.

Like he too had just realized how fucked they both were.

CHAPTER 5

Deepa awoke before dawn, the forest air frigid against her bare back, but her stomach was warm.

She opened her eyes in horror to find herself wrapped in the arms of the monster who turned her. His muscular chest rising and falling as he slumbered, his cock hard against her thigh.

Memories of the night before came rushing back. His fingers on her skin, his lips against hers, his cock filling her. She could feel his dried cum on her thighs.

Deepa tried to wiggle out from underneath him, but his arms tightened around her, refusing to let go.

"Mmm," he murmured, nuzzling her neck. "You smell good."

Deepa froze, her heart hammering in her chest.

This wasn't right. This wasn't real.

She had to get away and throw herself off the nearest bridge.

"Stop squirming," he groaned, his voice thick with sleep.

Deepa clenched her fists, trying to pull free from his embrace, but he only held her tighter, his arm wrapping around her waist.

"Let me go," she growled.

At the sound of her voice, his eyes shot open, staring at her with a mixture of shock and horror.

Deepa took the opportunity to slam a fist into his chest. It didn't land as hard as she intended, but he still recoiled in pain, letting her escape his grasp.

"Fuck," he hissed. "What was that for?"

"You fucking bastard," she spat, wriggling out of his grasp. "You disgusting, vile, waste of oxygen."

He stared at her, his expression blank.

"You infected me," she hissed. "I was going to shoot you, but you...you used some sort of mind control on me!"

He blinked, his brow furrowed. "Mind control?" he drawled.

"Yes," Deepa snarled, glaring at him.

"Werewolves don't have mind control," he said slowly.

"Bullshit," she snapped. "Why else would I let a piece of shit like you fuck me?"

He sighed, looking away from her. "Well...maybe I don't like you either."

Something inside Deepa snapped. She raised her fist, intending to beat the shit out of him, but he grabbed her hand, wrapping his warm fingers around hers and looking straight into her eyes.

It felt like all the energy had been sucked from her the moment that they touched. The world around them seemed to fade away as a familiar heat ignited in her core. Deepa wanted to tear him to shreds, but she also wanted to feel his hands roam her body, his lips press against hers, his thick erection rubbing against her insides.

"What the fuck are you doing?" she asked, her voice barely above a whisper.

"I don't know," he replied, his voice equally soft.

Deepa couldn't tear her gaze away from his, her mind going blank as her body reacted to his presence.

She had never felt anything like it. It was as if he had cast some sort of spell over her. She couldn't think clearly, her mind was filled with thoughts of him, her body was burning with desire.

It took every ounce of will power to wrench her hand from his grip, and even then it was difficult.

"Stop it," she breathed.

"Stop what?" he asked.

"This... whatever the fuck you're doing."

"I'm not doing anything."

"Yes, you are! I can feel it!"

"I swear, I'm not."

"Liar!"

Deepa glared at him, her eyes filled with hatred. "I don't know what the fuck your doing, but I promise that I'm going to end you. I'm going to strangle the life out of you with my bare hands, and I'm going to enjoy every second of it."

He stared at her, his expression blank.

Deepa didn't know why, but the words stung. She felt a strange sadness, as if she had lost something important.

"Fuck you," she hissed, before turning and running away as fast as she could.

Deepa was grateful for the darkness. It made it easier for her to scrounge up a worn jacket and jeans from a charity donation bin.

She tried her best to scrub the remnants of their fucking from her body in a public bathroom, but nothing could erase the disgust that she felt. It was mortifying how easily she had accepted him on top of her, inside of her.

But worse than that was the way her body seemed to crave him. His smell was intoxicating, and his touch left a searing burn that was almost unbearable. Even at that moment, her thoughts still danced with memories of him, his cock deep inside her, his teeth biting into her shoulder, his arms wrapped around her waist. It felt like there was a magnet in her chest that was pulling her back towards him.

She wanted to scream. She wanted to cry. She wanted to rip him apart with her bare hands.

But she couldn't do any of that.

Because he had done something to her. Some sort of mind control, or magic, or something. Maybe he was a special kind of werewolf who could seduce the people he had turned.

Deepa gritted her teeth, trying to ignore the ache between her legs.

"You fucking idiot," she muttered to herself. "What would Parker think?"

If Parker knew how quickly she'd gone off to fuck a werewolf, he'd be disgusted.

"Fuck, fuck, fuck," she cursed, trying to push away the images of Parker's disappointed face.

The pain was unbearable.

Deepa clenched her jaw, trying to fight back the tears.

"I have to end him," she whispered, her claws digging into her palms.

Deepa managed to hitchhike back to the city after sunrise. Her first stop was the public library. She had already long memorized the shelves after spending hours there as a teenager.

She kept her head down and made her way to a computer at the back of the room, typing in *werewolf powers* into the search engine. Infection Control had far more comprehensive archives and experts, but she wasn't going anywhere near there unless she wanted to be riddled with bullets.

Deepa scrolled down the page, clicking on several results. Most of the articles already said what she knew, or were filled with utter nonsense. One guy claimed that werewolves were mind reading aliens sent from Pluto, while another claimed that they were god's retribution for premarital sex. The existence of werewolves had become well known in the past decade, but misinformation was rife.

Deepa sighed, trying to think back on everything she'd learned about the species.

She had been trained to find and kill them, not study them.

There was a section on werewolf mating.

Deepa clicked on a link only to be bombarded with pictures of naked men and women humping in the dark. There were wolves screwing wolves, and a half transformed guy pounding into a human woman from behind.

"Fuck," she hissed, closing the tab, her cheeks burning. She should have not just found that hot.

Deepa glanced up to see a camera in the corner, fixed on her side of the room. She quickly deleted the history, and logged out, keeping her head down as she strode out of the building.

It wasn't the first time that Deepa had been homeless. She spent a month living on the streets after her aunt's shitty boyfriend kicked her out. But this time she didn't have any social services to take her in. This time the government was trying to end her.

Deepa curled up to sleep in the park under a hedge, wrapping her arms around her knees to try and ward off the evening chill. She couldn't get comfortable, the hard ground was unforgiving, and the voices in her head were relentless, urging her to *hunt, maim, and kill.*

She was exhausted and hungry. She hadn't gathered the courage to beg for money or food. Infection Control also patrolled the areas where most homeless hung out, ready to take in anyone who showed any hint of being a werewolf.

There was no one who she could trust. She was all alone in the world, with only the voices in her head and the craving for a murderer's touch.

Deepa buried her face in her hands, tears falling freely, her stomach rumbling with hunger.

Heat spread through her body as fur began to sprout from her skin, her muscles and bones contorting and snapping.

"Fuck," Deepa hissed, trying her best to fight it, but it was like someone else had taken the wheel and there was nothing she could do but watch.

Deepa's clothes tore, the cold evening air caressing her sensitive skin.

"Please," she begged, but her voice came out as a low whine.

She hated this. She hated this fucking body, she hated this infection, she hated herself, but the wolf inside her mind didn't care.

It was going to take whatever it wanted.

CHAPTER 6

The wolf dashed through the dark streets, her senses on high alert.

She could smell the faint scent of prey, growing stronger as she drew closer.

It was a group of humans, huddled together on the street corner, their faces illuminated by the light of their phones.

They looked up, their expressions turning to horror as they noticed the beast approaching.

The wolf bared her fangs, letting out a low growl.

The humans scrambled, dropping their bags and phones as they tried to run away, their feet slipping on the wet pavement.

"Shit!" one of them cried. "Someone call Infection Control!"

That name at least sparked recognition in the wolf. She turned and dashed away, disappearing down a dark street.

There was plenty of other prey that she could hunt.

The footsteps of other critters were easy to pick up on. The scurrying of rats and the squeaking of bats, the fluttering of birds.

The wolf ran towards the sounds, her paws slapping against the ground.

A small raccoon caught her attention. It was digging around in a garbage bin, searching for scraps.

The wolf pounced, her claws digging into the soft flesh.

The raccoon squeaked in terror, trying to free itself from the wolf's grasp, but it was no match for the predator's strength.

The wolf bit into the raccoon's neck, tearing out the flesh and gulping it down.

The blood was warm and fresh, the taste intoxicating.

The wolf tore into the animal, ripping it apart with her sharp teeth and strong jaws.

She had never tasted anything so good.

The wolf was satisfied, the hunger fading, but it had another craving that it needed to feed.

Him.

She bounded across the dark streets, sniffing the air, following his scent.

There was a strange pull towards him, as if his body had left a magnetic trail that the wolf could track.

The wolf slowed its pace as it neared a large two story house, surrounded by a high fence.

The wolf could sense others inside, but the only scent that mattered was his.

The wolf dug her claws into the fence, climbing to the top, her ears flat against her skull.

She could hear soft breathing, the steady thumping of a heartbeat.

The wolf jumped, landing lightly on the grass, her body blending into the darkness.

He was outside, sitting on a tree stump and smoking a vape.

His pale skin and white hair seemed to glow in the moonlight, urging her closer.

The wolf crept forward, her muscles tensing.

She had waited for this moment. She had craved it.

He raised his head, recognition drawing on his face as he let out a slow exhale of smoke.

"*You,*" he whispered, running his tongue along his lower lip.

Deepa could feel the blood rushing to her core, her pulse quickening.

It felt like someone had plunged a hand into her chest and squeezed.

Her body slowly returned to its human form, nose retracting, large teeth sinking back into her gums as her bones cracked and reshaped themselves until she had fully reverted.

He stared at her with hungry eyes, his gaze roaming her naked body, white smoke escaping from his mouth.

Deepa felt her nipples harden, her skin tingling with need, the space between her legs moistening in anticipation for what was to come.

She confidently walked towards him like a moth to a flame.

Deepa had fought hard and lost.

She was ready to surrender.

He dropped the vape, stepping forward and grabbing her face, smashing his lips into hers.

Deepa kissed him back, her hands wrapping around his waist, pulling him closer.

His fingers tangled in her hair, his teeth gently nipping her bottom lip.

"Fuck," he hissed, breaking the kiss.

Deepa could feel his erection pressing against her, his desire mirroring her own.

He looked into her eyes, his gaze filled with need. "Fuck," he cursed again before smashing his lips back against hers.

Deepa gasped, her breath catching as he pushed her down to the ground, his body on top of hers, his hips grinding against her.

"You're fucking killing me," he groaned, his lips trailing down her neck, his teeth gently scraping against her skin.

Deepa's hands were in his hair, her nails digging into his scalp. She arched her back, her body pressing against his, her skin on fire.

He moved down, his tongue circling her nipple before taking it into his mouth.

Deepa gasped, her eyes rolling back.

He continued moving down, his hands tracing the curve of her hips, his tongue leaving a wet trail on her skin.

Deepa shuddered, her toes curling as his breath tickled her thighs.

His warm tongue lapped at her entrance, his hands gripping her ass.

She moaned, her body writhing in pleasure.

He continued his ministrations, his tongue circling her clit, his teeth grazing her skin. He inserted a finger into her, moving it in and out slowly.

She gasped, her fingers tugging his hair, her body rocking against his mouth. It felt heavenly. A thousand times more intense than when she was together with Parker.

His lips roamed her wet folds, his tongue circling her entrance before plunging inside.

She cried out, her body bucking, her muscles clenching.

He continued his assault, his fingers and mouth working in unison, sending waves of pleasure through her body.

She was so close.

His tongue lapped at her clit, his fingers curling inside her.

Her body arched, her nails digging into his scalp, her toes curling.

She cried out, her muscles clamping down on his finger, her body shaking, as the pleasure washed over her.

He held her steady, his tongue continuing to work, drawing out her orgasm.

Deepa was gasping for breath, her heart pounding in her chest, her body trembling.

She stared at the night sky, the stars seeming to dance, her mind fuzzy.

He pulled away to remove his clothes, his muscles rippling, his pale skin glowing in the moonlight. He hissed in relief as his throbbing erection sprung free, already glistening with pre-cum.

He climbed on top of her, his lips finding hers, his fingers tangling in her hair.

"Fuck," he growled, his teeth biting her lip, his tongue sliding into her mouth, his leaking cock rubbing against her bare thigh.

Deepa wrapped her legs around his waist, her hands clutching his shoulders, her nails digging into his skin.

She could feel his heat radiating against her, his cock brushing against her clit, the pressure making her gasp.

"God," he moaned, his lips moving down her neck, his teeth nipping at her skin.

He was like an animal. His body moving against hers, his breath hot on her neck. He pulled back, his gaze meeting hers.

His blue eyes were intense, his pupils dilated.

"Fuck," he breathed, his hands tightening around her.

She could feel his cock twitching, his breath ragged.

"Tell me to stop," he murmured.

Deepa didn't say a word. She reached down and guided his cock into her entrance, her body aching to be filled.

He moaned, his hips bucking forward, his cock sliding into her, filling her completely.

"Shit," he gasped, his fingers digging into her skin. "You feel amazing."

Deepa was overcome with pleasure. She could feel every inch of him, his warmth spreading through her.

He began to thrust, his pace increasing, his cock hitting her in all the right places.

She cried out, her body bucking, her toes curling. This was what the wolf wanted, to be fucked senseless and bred. To be filled with his seed again and again until they created new life.

He growled, his tongue licking the spot below her ear, sending a shiver down her spine.

"Nobody," he huffed. "Nobody ever told me that it would feel like this."

Deepa couldn't speak. She could only moan, her body writhing beneath him, his cock pulsating inside her.

He gripped her hips, his thrusts becoming frantic, his breath hot against her skin.

"Shit," he growled, his cock twitching, his thrusts faltering. "Fuck, I'm close."

Deepa could feel herself reaching her limit, her muscles clamping around his length, her body trembling.

He cursed under his breath, his thrusts becoming erratic, his body tense.

Deepa bit down on his shoulder, her teeth breaking the skin, causing him to gasp as the pain mixed with pleasure.

She felt his cock twitch inside her, his warmth spilling deep within, pumping wave after wave of warm cum straight into her fertile womb.

The feeling was overwhelming. Her mind going blank, her body tingling, her muscles spasming.

They clung to each other, their bodies trembling, their hearts racing.

It felt like they had become one, their bodies perfectly in sync, their souls connected.

For the first time in Deepa's life she felt safe. She felt whole.

Even if it was in the arms of a killer.

CHAPTER 7

Deepa was awoken by the sunrise. She opened her eyes to see a pale face inches from her own.

"What the fuck?" she gasped, scrambling away.

"Hey," he said gently, still fully naked and not the least bit ashamed of himself.

"Hey?" Deepa spat. "That's all you have to say for yourself? What the fuck did you do to me last night?"

He raised an eyebrow. "I think you already know."

"No," Deepa shook her head. "No, that's not what I meant. Why the fuck did we... why did I..."

Deepa couldn't finish her sentence.

"You came to fuck me," he said bluntly. "Perhaps you tried and failed to strangle my cock to death."

"Bastard," Deepa snapped.

"Please," he huffed. "Tell me something I don't know."

"This is all your fault," Deepa said, her voice rising. "If you hadn't bit me, I'd still be normal. I'd still be human."

"And you'd still be out murdering all my friends! So don't whine to me about how you're so hard done by."

Deepa glared at him. "I had a life, asshole."

"So did I," he shot back. "A great one, full of fucking whoever I wanted until I met you. A stuck up Infection Control bitch who's decided to stick to me like a barnacle."

"What the fuck to you mean? A barnacle? You're the parasite who infected me with their fucked up werewolf germs."

"Oh, fuck off," Axel muttered.

Deepa could feel the rage building up inside her.

"This isn't fair!" she screamed. "None of this is fair. Why did you have to do this to me?"

The door to the house swung open and a thin blond man dressed in a bathrobe emerged scratching his crotch, green eyes gazing over their naked bodies.

"Well...this is new," he said. "Didn't you say that you'd never screw a turned one, Axel?"

Axel? Deepa's eyes snapped back to the man beside her.

Axel let out a low growl. "Fuck off, Luke."

"Hey, hey," Luke said, holding his hands up. "I'm not here to judge. You're welcome to screw in the bushes as much as you like."

"I wasn't-" Deepa began.

Luke cut her off. "But, please keep the screaming to a minimum, some of us are trying to sleep. And if you do end up killing him, please take the body home with you."

Deepa's face turned red. "I wasn't... I didn't mean...I didn't want to-."

Luke shrugged, glancing down at the several scratch marks lining her body. "Sure, whatever you say."

"Fuck off, Luke," Axel growled.

Luke rolled his eyes, turning to head back inside, but not before giving Deepa one last look. "You know, I heard that he likes it when girls slip a finger up his butt."

"Fuck you!" Axel shouted.

Luke laughed, the door slamming shut.

Axel's face contorted with anger, hands clenched into fists.

Shit, Deepa thought. *He's pissed.*

"Get out," he hissed under his breath.

"Excuse me?"

"Get the fuck out," Axel snarled glaring straight at her, whole body trembling.

Deepa's heart sank. She didn't know why, but his words cut her like a knife to the chest.

"But I-"

"But what?" Axel hissed, his blue eyes narrowing. "You hate me, and I don't particularly like you either. How about we call it a day and both fuck off to where ever we came from."

Deepa bit her lip, the urge to wrap her arms around him overpowering, but she squashed it down. She didn't need to kill him right now. She could regroup and come back to blow his brains out later.

"I don't have any clothes," she mumbled.

Axel rolled his eyes, turning to walk back into the house. Deepa assumed that he'd left her to freeze, until a skirt and blouse came flying out the window, landing on the grass outside.

"Here," he shouted from inside the house.

"I need shoes as well!" Deepa yelled back.

"Then get some," Axel called, before shutting the window in her face.

"Fucking bastard!" Deepa muttered as she slipped the clothes on.

Deepa had never wished so badly that she could go home to her apartment. She and Parker had started renting it once they were accepted as trainees at Infection Control. The walls were covered with cracks and the floorboards creaked, but it was theirs and they loved it.

But now it was empty. And she could never go back.

Parker was gone. Her job was gone. Her human life was gone. She had to somehow pull herself together and create a new existence on the fringes of society. Constantly running and hiding while figuring out a way to kill the arsehole she kept fucking.

Deepa was beginning to wonder if her hatred for him was so strong that it must have somehow turned into a morbid sex kink. Maybe she always had a thing for psychos and murderers.

But Parker was never like that.

They met when they were teenagers in foster care, after Deepa had nowhere else to go after her aunt's shitty boyfriend kicked her out. Parker had been kind and patient, putting her at ease with his calm and logical manner. He became the family that she always wanted, and his dream to join Infection Control gradually became her dream as well.

But now she was back to square one. Broke and homeless with nowhere to go.

Deepa regretted not robbing Axel before walking away. Her lunch was a sandwich that she unearthed from a dumpster and she drank from a drinking fountain in the park. She tried to kill time by sitting on a bench, watching as children and parents walked around her without a care in the world.

As evening approached, Deepa realized that she was going to have to spend another night outdoors, cold and hungry, and that the wolf would probably force her to shift again.

She was exhausted and angry, her mood worsening with each passing moment. She wanted to scream and punch something, or someone. She wanted to hurt and break and destroy.

It was a strange and unsettling feeling. She had never felt this enraged before.

Deepa clenched her fists, her claws digging into her palms.

It was as if something was trying to claw its way out of her. As if some dark, primal, instinct was taking over.

Axel needed to die. He and his friends needed to suffer for what they did. For the life that they took away from her.

CHAPTER 8

It was easy to track Axel down, she only needed to follow the pull in her chest and his scent in the air, backtracking to the house where she left him that morning.

She climbed up the wall and over the fence, the moon glowing bright overhead.

It was as if the wolf was guiding her, the animalistic instincts taking over, pushing her forward.

She could hear men inside, the sound of laughter and conversation.

Deepa crept closer, her steps silent, her ears picking up every word, but she couldn't hear Axel's voice.

"So," a male voice spoke. "How long are we going to wait for Axel before we eat?"

"It's already late," Luke replied. "We might as well start without him."

"I hope he's okay," another male voice spoke. "He's been locked up in his room all day."

"It's probably because he couldn't cope with fucking a turned one, probably worried that his dick will fall off."

Deepa felt her blood boil. Those fucking bastards. She was going to rip their throats out once she was done basking in Axel's blood.

She took a deep breath, her anger bubbling just below the surface, her claws sharpening, the hair on the back of her neck rising.

Deepa closed her eyes, taking another deep breath, trying to calm her nerves.

She couldn't lose control. She needed to be precise.

Deepa slowly opened her eyes, focusing her attention on the task at hand.

Axel.

His window was open, a soft light illuminating the room within. It was bare with only a bed and dresser, unwashed clothes littered the floor.

She could smell him. The scent of his skin, the warmth of his breath, the blood pumping through his veins.

The hunger grew stronger, her muscles tensing, her pulse racing.

He was lying on his bed, his blue eyes gazing at the ceiling as his phone played rock music.

The wolf inside her growled, urging her to take action.

She slipped through the window and moved towards him, her footsteps silent, her body hidden by the darkness.

He sensed her presence, sitting up, his gaze falling on her, eyes widening in surprise.

She pounced, pinning him to the bed as her hands wrapped around his throat.

He struggled, his fingers digging into her flesh, but she refused to relent.

"You killed him," she hissed, her eyes burning with rage. "You killed him."

He clawed at her hands, his legs kicking beneath her.

"You killed him," she growled, tightening her grip.

She could feel the life draining from him, his skin growing cold, his eyes rolling back. She was almost there until her grip loosened on its own accord, the heart wrenching pain in her chest becoming unbearable.

He gasped, the sound of his breathing filling the air, the warmth of his skin returning.

Deepa collapsed beside him, tears streaming down her face.

She couldn't do it.

She knew that no matter how many times she tried, she'd never be able to kill him.

Just the thought of his death was unbearable.

"Fuck," Deepa hissed, fingers clenching the sheets, turning her face away from him so that he wouldn't see her tears.

"Yeah," Axel muttered, rubbing his throat. "Fuck it is."

He remained silent as her shoulders shook, allowing her to cry it out. After half an hour, his warm arms snaked their way around her waist, pulling her flush to his body as his face pressed against her neck.

Deepa knew what was coming, but she was too tired to fight it.

He rolled his groin against her arse, letting out a hiss. "I want you."

Deepa was tempted to push him off, but she couldn't. The need to feel him was too strong to ignore.

"I hate you," she whispered.

"I know," he murmured, his lips pressing against her skin. "I hate you too."

She closed her eyes, allowing him to move his body against hers, shuddering as heat began to grow in her core. It was screwed up. The anger and hatred, the intense lust and desire.

Deepa let out a soft moan, her hips grinding against his, desperate for more.

He gripped a breast in his large palm, gently kneading it, his fingers teasing her nipple.

"Shit," he murmured, his teeth gently scraping her earlobe. "You're driving me insane."

Deepa bit her lip, her eyes squeezing shut, her body aching for him.

He continued moving his hand down her torso, his fingers brushing against her sensitive flesh, his cock twitching in his boxers.

Deepa gasped, her body tensing, her hips bucking. She could feel his desire, his need.

His lips brushed against her neck, his teeth nipping her skin.

"I can't stop thinking about you," he whispered. "Every second of the day, I'm thinking about you. Your scent, your touch, your taste. It's driving me fucking mad."

Deepa shuddered, her toes curling, her nipples hardening. She could feel the wetness between her thighs, her body begging for release.

He pulled away to slide down his pants, freeing his throbbing cock. Deepa could feel the warmth radiating off of him, his scent engulfing her senses.

He grabbed her hips, tugging her close, pulling up her skirt to unveil her naked lower half.

He ran his finger along her folds, gathering the moisture, spreading it along her skin.

"You're so wet," he breathed, shuddering with need.

Deepa moaned, her head falling back, her hands gripping his hair.

He inserted a finger into her, slowly moving it in and out, his thumb circling her clit as his cock continued to grind against her behind.

Deepa bit her lip, her body quivering, her heart pounding in her chest.

He slipped his dick between her thighs, rubbing back and forth through her soaked folds.

Deepa groaned, her hips rocking against his, his cock rubbing against her sensitive nub until it caught on her entrance, slowly pushing inside.

Deepa gasped, her hands fisting the sheets, her back arching, his warmth spreading through her body.

He pulled back, thrusting in slowly, his hips meeting hers until they built up a delicious rhythm.

He buried his face in her hair, his lips pressing against her skin, his teeth gently nipping her shoulder.

Deepa cried out, her body writhing, his cock throbbing inside her, the pressure building within.

His hands moved down, gripping her hips, pulling her against him, his thrusts becoming harder and faster.

Deepa moaned, her muscles clamping around him, her body trembling.

He cursed, his cock pulsating, his breath ragged.

She could feel her climax approaching, the pressure building, her body quivering.

"Shit," he groaned, his nails digging into her flesh, his cock pulsating.

He cried out, his muscles tensing, his warmth spilling deep inside, his body shuddering.

Deepa followed soon after, the pleasure washing over her, her mind going blank.

They clung to each other, their bodies shaking, their hearts racing as they basked in the post orgasm high.

Deepa tried to slip out of bed, but Axel's arms tightened around her. "Stay," he whispered.

She felt her heart skip a beat, her stomach fluttering.

"Okay," she whispered, allowing him to pull her closer, his warmth enveloping her.

They lay there, silent and still, his scent lulling her into a dreamless sleep.

CHAPTER 9

Axel awoke in the morning to find the girl gone.

Her scent was still fresh on the sheets, but she was nowhere in sight.

A part of him was relieved, a part of him was angry.

He shouldn't give a shit. He never gave a damn about any woman that he slept with before, especially one who wanted to kill him, but it felt like she'd taken a piece of him with her.

It confused him. She was nothing. Just another filthy Infection Control agent who'd murdered plenty of his kind. She deserved to rot in a gutter, but all he could think about was her touch and her taste.

She was like a drug. One hit and he was hooked, ever since that moment that she placed a gun to his temple.

Axel sighed and ran a hand through his hair. Perhaps all the stress from the past few months had driven him insane, maybe if he just screwed her a few more times the feeling would fade.

Axel got to his feet and pulled his clothes off the floor, slipping them on, before heading down the hall.

His cousins were in the living room, watching TV while drinking.

"Morning," Luke said, taking a sip of his beer. "Where's your girlfriend?"

"She's not my girlfriend," Axel muttered back.

"Well," Luke chuckled. "You've slept with her more than once, so she's the closest thing you've ever had to a girlfriend."

"Arsehole," Axel hissed.

"If I bite a Infection Control officer will they also fuck me?" Reese grinned while lifting weights, large muscles dripping with sweat.

"Well you did bite her boyfriend," said Bruno as his thin freckled hand dove into a bag of chips. "And he hasn't shown up to blow you yet."

Axel rolled his eyes. The three of them had been giving him shit ever since Luke walked in on him and Deepa the day before.

"So what changed your mind?" Reese asked. "Couldn't resist the sweet smell of human pussy?"

"Fuck off," Axel grumbled, taking a seat next to Luke on the sofa.

Luke smirked. "I knew it."

"Shut up!" Axel snapped.

"What are we talking about?" Bruno asked through a mouth full of chips.

"Nothing," Axel said, grabbing the remote control and turning up the volume, trying to avoid what he knew was coming.

"He's found his fated mate," Luke smirked.

Reese's hand slipped on the weight, sending it crashing to the floor.

"No way," Bruno gasped. "That shit's real?"

"We're not fated mates!" Axel snapped.

"Yes you are," Luke grinned sardonically. "How else would you explain it? Why else would that angry little woman with all the death threats keep showing up to screw you?"

Axel glared at him, but didn't deny it. He couldn't. The fact was, even though he hated her guts, and she clearly hated him, there was something between them that he couldn't explain.

"Wow," Reese said with awe. "That's just like your dad, right?"

"Don't mention that bastard's name?" Axel snapped back.

"Sorry, bro," Reese muttered.

Axel huffed and returned his attention to the television screen, trying to block out his cousins' conversation, but he couldn't help but overhear.

"I can't believe it," Bruno said. "I thought that fated mate stuff was just a fairytale."

"Me too," Reese replied.

"Do you think it'll work out?" Bruno asked. "Like, do you think they'll fall in love and live happily ever after?"

Axel snorted.

"I hope so," Luke said. "Maybe then he'll be more fun to hang out with."

Axel shot him a dirty look, which Luke ignored.

"I mean, it's pretty rare for a werewolf to find their mate," Luke continued. "You hear stories, but I never thought it was actually possible."

"Yeah," Reese agreed. "But then Axel's dad-"

"I told you to shove it!" Axel said, getting to his feet.

Any mention of his father was enough to make Axel want to drive his fist through a wall.

"Shit," Reese said, quickly apologizing, but Axel got to his feet, quickly storming out of the room.

"Fuck," Axel hissed, running his hand through his hair, his mind racing, his blood boiling.

He barely remembered his father, but the stories were enough to make him hate the man with every fiber of his being.

He was a coward, a traitor, a bastard who abandoned his family to screw his human turned werewolf side piece. All the while claiming that they were fated mates.

It was utter bullshit.

And Axel swore to himself that he'd never repeat the man's mistakes.

Not for some woman.

Spending time with women was fun. Breeding was fun.

But falling in love?

Screw that shit.

They had a war to win. Werewolves were born to rule this world, and Axel wasn't going to let anything hold him back.

CHAPTER 10

Axel survived a whole three hours before the restlessness in his chest became too uncomfortable to ignore.

It was a strange and unsettling feeling, the desperate desire to be around the woman he turned.

He didn't want her, not really.

Luke was wrong. The whole fated mates shit was just a way of explaining their animalistic nature, but the wolf inside him craved her company.

It was messed up, but Axel couldn't think about anything else.

He needed to feel her skin, to breathe in her scent, to taste her lips, to feel her shudder around his cock as she came.

"Fuck," Axel cursed. He was going mad.

He put on his jacket and slipped out of the house, hoping to make it to the forest to transform for a run, but instead he arrived at a park a few blocks from the house.

He saw her immediately, rummaging through a bin before unearthing a half eaten sandwich with a triumphant grin. She was dressed in the same shirt and skirt from the day before, smudges of dirt staining the fabric.

No fucking way, Axel thought to himself. Out of every female werewolf on the planet, fate had decided to give him this one. Perhaps it was his punishment for all the mayhem he had committed.

Axel shuddered as Deepa unwrapped the plastic around her find, and he couldn't take watching any longer. His body moved without thinking, snatching the garbage out of her hand.

"Hey!" she protested, eyes widening with shock, but then her gaze settled on him, the shock morphing into fury. "Give that back!"

"No!" Axel snapped, holding it out of her reach. "You're not eating this shit."

"Then what the fuck am I supposed to eat?"

"Anything that didn't come out of the trash."

"Give it back!" she growled.

"No," he snapped, his own anger growing. "It's disgusting."

"It's food," she shot back, reaching for the sandwich. "I'm starving."

"You want food," he hissed. "I'll get you food."

"Why the fuck would you do that?"

"Because you're not going to be fucking sick."

"Give it," she hissed, her fingers clawing at his skin, trying to pry his hand open, but Axel flung the sandwich as far away as he could, sending it flying over a nearby fence.

"Fuck you!" Deepa shouted, her face turning red with rage.

"You're more than welcome to," Axel shot back.

Deepa's expression contorted with disgust. "In your dreams."

"You were last night," Axel retorted. "No wait... pretty sure we were both awake for that."

Deepa looked ready to punch him and Axel was prepared to duck, but she surprised him by spinning on her heel and marching away.

"Where the fuck are you going?" Axel yelled after her.

"Away from you!" Deepa yelled back.

Axel cursed under his breath and raced after her, catching up and matching her pace.

"What the fuck did I do to deserve this," he grumbled.

"What did you say?" Deepa hissed, her eyes narrowing.

"Nothing," Axel snapped, increasing his speed.

"You know, I could easily murder you right now."

"But you won't," Axel retorted. "Because if you could, I'd be dead already."

Deepa's mouth opened and closed, but no sound came out.

"Look," Axel began. "I know you want to kill me, but how about I buy you something to eat first?"

Deepa glared at him. "I don't need charity from a psychopath."

"I'm not doing this because I like you," Axel spat. "I'm doing this because I..."

Axel paused, unsure of his own reasoning.

Deepa scoffed. "Like you give a damn."

"Fine," Axel snarled. "Go ahead and starve."

Axel turned on his heel, ready to leave her to fend for herself.

"Wait!" Deepa called out, causing him to pause in his step.

"What?" he hissed, glaring back at her.

"You'll really buy me food?"

Axel raised an eyebrow. "That's what I said."

Deepa sighed. "Fine."

"Fine?"

"Yes," she hissed. "Now let's go."

Axel nodded, trying to ignore the small leap of joy in his chest.

She didn't seem keen on talking as they walked to a nearby cafe, and Axel was more than happy to remain silent.

The place was almost empty when they entered, the only other customer being a man sitting alone, his eyes glued to the tablet in his hands.

Axel slid into an empty booth and she took a seat opposite him, her eyes darting around the place.

"This isn't a trap," Axel said.

She huffed. "I'm not worried about werewolves."

"Oh, that's right," Axel said with a grin. "It's your little friends that you have to worry about now."

"Shut the fuck up," Deepa hissed.

Axel raised an eyebrow. "Feisty. Looks like someone isn't enjoying the other side."

Deepa glared at him. "Don't talk about it."

"Why not?" Axel grinned. "I've spent years dodging your people, and it's a fucking blast."

"You're a monster," Deepa hissed.

"Takes one to know one," Axel retorted.

Deepa clenched her jaw, her hands fisting the table.

She looked like she wanted to say more, but then the waitress arrived to take their order.

Axel could only watch as Deepa pointed to several of the most expensive items on the menu.

"Hungry?" he asked, once the waitress left.

"Starving," Deepa muttered. "You made me waste a perfectly good lunch."

Axel rolled his eyes.

They sat in silence until her food arrived. She immediately started shoving pieces of meat into her mouth, her face lighting up with joy.

Axel couldn't understand why watching her eat brought him so much joy, but it did. It made him feel content and at ease as much as he tried to hide it.

Mental images of her swollen and round with his offspring began to surface in his mind. He imagined her breasts full of milk and her nipples dark and leaking.

It was strange and disturbing.

"What?" Deepa asked, noticing his stare.

"Nothing," Axel muttered, his cock stiffening and he shifted uncomfortably. "You take birth control?"

"Got a shot," she murmured through a mouth full of steak.

Axel felt his stomach lurch with disappointment, even though he had zero interest in being a father. The last thing he wanted was to end up forcing his childhood onto some poor brat.

"Why?" Deepa asked. "Are you trying to knock me up or something?"

"No," Axel coughed, even though his cock twitched in protest.

The bell above the door rang, and two men entered, fluorescent Infection Control jackets more than obvious.

Axel didn't even flinch. There was nothing that they could pin on him, but Deepa immediately tensed up.

"Relax," Axel muttered.

"But they-"

"You're human now," he hissed. "Act like it."

"But-"

"They won't notice if you just shut up."

"But I know them."

Axel swore under his breath. "How well?"

"I had drinks with one of them the night you attacked me."

"You're joking?"

"I'm not."

"Shit."

Axel turned his attention towards the agents. Both were tall and broad, but they had the same air of arrogance that he'd come to expect from Infection Control officers. They were usually too dumb to spot a werewolf who wasn't fully transformed.

"Just stay calm," Axel whispered, nudging her foot from under the table.

Deepa nodded, hands trembling as she tightly clenched her fork.

The two men took a seat at the counter, happily chatting away as they ordered food.

"You should finish your meal," Axel muttered. "Don't want it to go to waste."

"I'm not hungry," Deepa hissed, her face pale.

Axel frowned.

"We need to get out of here."

"We're not going anywhere."

"They'll know!"

"No, they won't."

"But-"

Axel let out a sigh. It was against his instincts to make any sudden movements, but her distress was enough to tie his stomach in knots.

"Here," he said, grabbing her hand. "Stick close to me."

He pulled her tightly to his chest as they got to their feet, tossing a handful of bills onto the table.

He kept his body between her and the agents as they slipped out the door, shielding her from view.

It felt nice, the warmth and smell of her body. The urge to wrap her up and protect her was overwhelming.

It was like she'd slipped into his veins, his lungs, his heart.

Her body trembled as they hurried down the street, her hand shaking in his grasp.

"It's okay," he said softly, pressing his lips to her forehead. "You're safe."

She nodded, her arms tightening around his waist, her scent wrapping around him.

He was intoxicated, his entire body vibrating with desire, his cock twitching in his jeans.

The urge to bend her over the closest bench was overwhelming.

"You should come back with me," he said without thinking.

"No," Deepa replied, her voice barely a whisper.

"Come on," Axel cooed, pulling her closer. "You can use my shower."

She appeared conflicted, like she was also at war with herself and whatever was going on between them.

"And a change of clothes," he continued.

Deepa's gaze met his, her lips slightly parted, her breathing ragged.

"Okay," she nodded.

CHAPTER II

Axel should have thought more thoroughly before inviting her back to Luke's house, considering that the man who bit her boyfriend was lounging around shirtless in the living room.

All he heard was a sharp intake of breath before she immediately launched herself at Reese, hands half transformed into claws.

Luke managed to hold her back just before her nails could scratch off Reese's face, and Axel pulled her off his friend, wrapping his arms around her waist, while her feet kicked out in the air, a snarl of rage leaving her lips.

"You fucking bastard!" she screamed. "I'm going to kill you!"

"Hey," Axel snapped, trying to keep her arms down. "Calm down."

"You killed him," she hissed. "You fucking murdered him!"

Axel tightened his grip, pulling her back. "That's enough."

"You're all animals!" Deepa seethed, her face red with fury as Axel dragged her towards his room. "All of you!"

"We're lucky she's so tiny," Reese huffed, rubbing his neck.

Axel shook his head, shutting the door behind him, the girl still fighting in his arms.

"Calm down," he hissed, trying to keep her pinned.

"Fuck you!" she screamed, trying to kick him, her eyes wild.

"You need to relax," he said, his voice low.

"I'm going to rip their throats out," she hissed, her nails digging into his arm. "He murdered Parker!"

"He didn't murder him!" Axel snapped. "Infection Control did, all because of something that was beyond his control."

She immediately relaxed in his grip, the truth slowly sinking in.

"If you sign up for war," Axel hissed. "Don't be surprised when the enemy fights back."

She relaxed in his grasp, tears running down her cheeks.

"I hate you," she sobbed. "I hate all of you."

"I know," he murmured, trying to suppress a pang of hurt. "The feeling's mutual."

"I should have stayed with him," she murmured. "I should have fought for him."

Axel released his grip, biting his lower lip to suppress the tirade of mixed emotions at her words.

"Suck it up," he hissed. "You're not the only one who's done things they regret."

Luckily she lost the will to rip Reese's throat out, instead locking herself away in the bathroom and sobbing under the shower spray.

Axel felt like shit. He'd done plenty of messed up things in his life, but none of them felt this... bad.

The wolf inside him howled and whimpered, demanding that he go to her, wrap his arms around her and tell her that everything was going to be okay, but that would be a lie.

Nothing was going to be alright.

Instead he was forced to listen to her cries while trying to ignore the pain in his chest.

Eventually her sobs quietened and she reemerged, hair wet and wearing only a towel.

His cock stirred in his pants, like it didn't understand that he was the source of all her angst.

Axel's hands gripped the bedsheets, trying to maintain control.

"I'll get you something to wear," he murmured, getting to his feet, but she stopped him, pressing a hand to his chest.

The look on her face was heartbreaking. The pain and desperation, but also the hunger that smoldered deep within her eyes.

"I," she whispered, her hand gently touching his skin, until she yanked him down to her level, pressing her lips against his.

The wolf inside him howled with happiness. The man himself was in shock.

Her lips were soft and warm, her fingers gripping his hair, the towel slipping away from her naked form.

He didn't even have time to process what was happening before her hand moved down his torso, reaching for the belt buckle.

Axel gasped, his brain finally catching up.

"Don't say anything," she hissed, pulling the belt off and tossing it aside, moving her hands down to the zipper of his jeans.

Axel couldn't move. It was like he'd been paralyzed.

Her small fingers reached into his pants, tugging down his boxers.

The lust was overwhelming, the scent of her arousal filling his nostrils.

His cock throbbed as her hand wrapped around it, giving him a firm stroke.

He groaned, his knees weakening, his muscles tensing.

She moved her hand back and forth, her grip firm, her palm warm and smooth.

He could barely stand, his legs threatening to give out.

"Shit," he gasped, his eyes squeezing shut, his cock pulsating in her hand.

He knew that he should tell her to stop but he didn't. He was too selfish and consumed by her. The need to plunge himself into her wet heat was overwhelming.

She was going to destroy him.

He pushed her back on the bed with a growl, kicking his clothes off.

He moved forward, his weight crushing her, his hands fisting the sheets. Their bodies melded together, a tangle of limbs and heat.

Her hips grinded against his. He could feel the warmth of her skin seeping into his, igniting a fire within him.

It felt like he would die without her.

He rolled his hips against hers, his cock rubbing against her soaked folds, his mind going blank.

"I need you," he gasped, his breath hot against her skin.

"I hate you," she whimpered.

"I know," he groaned, his teeth grazing her skin, his cock catching on her entrance.

She cried out, her hands fisting the sheets, her toes curling.

He thrust into her, his cock plunging into her tight, wet heat, his balls slapping against her skin.

She let out a loud moan, her inner muscles gripping his cock tightly as her body trembled with pleasure.

Axel's chest heaved as he inhaled deeply, trying to capture her intoxicating scent. His heart raced and his body responded with a pulsing desire. He closed his eyes, savoring the sensation of her aroma filling his senses.

He could feel her heart racing, her breathing ragged, her muscles spasming.

His head spun, his breath coming out in ragged pants, his heart pounding in his ears.

It was too much.

It was impossible to hold back his climax.

Axel let out a guttural growl as his body tensed. His hand gripped the headboard, and he thrust into her with primal force. His release was explosive, filling her womb with his warm seed.

She shuddered, reaching down to rub her swollen clit.

Axel watched her, transfixed, his cock still hard and aching.

Her moans grew louder, her hand moving faster and faster. Her eyes never left his as her cheeks flushed with desire. Her muscles tightened and she let out a breathless cry, her eyes fluttering shut as she reached the peak of pleasure.

"Fuck," he gasped, his hips rocking against hers, his cock throbbing, his balls aching.

He needed more.

He wanted more.

He wanted to feel her tight cunt around his cock forever, to watch her cum over and over again without end. He wanted her by his side for the rest of his life.

He knew in his heart that she was his.

His other half.

His mate.

PART 2

CHAPTER 1

Deepa groaned as she opened her eyes, unsurprised to find herself naked in Axel's arms once more.

Her stomach grumbled, begging for food, her head pounding.

It felt like a hangover.

The night before was a blur. She'd been a complete mess after being reminded of Parker's death, and then she was all over Axel.

The man who turned her into a werewolf and ruined her life.

Her enemy.

She was insane. The infection must have seeped into her brain.

There was something seriously wrong with her, and it was all his fault.

Deepa carefully slipped out of his grasp, hissing at the sting between her legs. They had gone twice again that evening, once on all fours as he rutted into her from behind like a dog.

Deepa pulled her clothes off the floor, quickly slipping them on and heading out the door.

Luke was sitting at the kitchen table, scrolling through his phone in front of an array of freshly cooked omelets and sausages. The enticing scent wafted through the air, causing her stomach to rumble loudly.

"Hungry?" Luke looked up from his phone with a grin. "Might as well get one last meal in before you disappear again."

Deepa glared at him.

"Or not," Luke sighed, returning his attention to his phone.

Deepa made her way to the table and grabbed a plate.

She quickly loaded it with a mountain of food that she enthusiastically shoveled into her mouth.

It was delicious, the perfect balance of egg, cheese and vegetables.

Luke glanced up, his eyes following her movements.

"So..." he said slowly. "What's he like in bed?"

Deepa choked, her eyes watering.

"Half decent at least." Luke grinned, leaning back in his chair.

Deepa shot him a glare.

"Okay." Luke raised his hands in surrender. "Barriers drawn, but can I at least have your name?"

Deepa paused, unsure of what to say.

"Come on. You're sleeping in my house and eating my food, the least you can do is tell me your name."

"Deepa," she murmured.

"Deepa," he said slowly, as if savoring the word. "I'm Axel's cousin Luke."

"Deepa?" said a deep voice from behind her. "So that's your name?"

Deepa turned to see Axel leaning in the doorway, shirtless and only wearing boxers, his pale hair in disarray.

He was gorgeous. Her first thought was running her tongue along those abs, but she was not falling for any more of his tricks.

"For fucks sake," Luke muttered. "Don't tell me that you didn't even know her name."

Axel didn't answer, instead moving across the room to take a sausage from Luke's plate.

"Don't eat that," Luke warned. "That one's mine."

"You snooze, you lose." Axel's teeth sank into the meat, grease running down his chin.

Deepa's eyes were glued to the movement, her throat going dry.

She was definitely sick.

"You have a visitor, Axel," Luke said. "Your favorite person in the whole wide world."

Axel immediately dropped his food and went to the window, letting out a curse. He stormed back to his room and emerged fully dressed moments later, disappearing out the front door.

Deepa got to her feet and followed afterwards.

"I wouldn't," Luke called out, but she ignored him.

An expensive car was parked outside, spotless windshield glaring in the morning sun.

Standing in front of it was a stunning young woman with long blond hair and blue eyes, dressed in a tight gray dress and stilettos, her gaze fixated on Axel.

"What the fuck are you doing here, Nastya?" Axel snapped.

"Nice to see you too, Axel." The woman smiled, flashing pearly white teeth.

Deepa felt a stab of jealousy, her gut twisting as she gazed over the woman's perfect make up and immaculate nails.

"Cut the crap," Axel hissed.

"You've been summoned," said Nastya. "It's time for you to stop playing around with Luke and come back to the main house."

"And if I say no?"

Nastya shrugged. "Then they'll come here and drag you back themselves." Her gaze flicked to Deepa, roaming over her unbrushed hair and stained skirt. "Who's that?"

Axel clenched his fist. "Just Luke's latest fuck."

Deepa flinched, trying not to let the pain show.

"Oh, so he fucks women now?" Nastya laughed.

"He's experimenting," Axel snapped. "You'd know all about that, wouldn't you?" He ripped open the passenger door and slipped inside the car. "Let's just go."

"Don't you want your things?"

"I'll get them later," Axel grumbled without even looking at Deepa.

Nastya shot Deepa one last glance, her lips twisted into a smirk, before getting behind the wheel and driving off.

Deepa stared after them, a lump forming in her throat.

She wouldn't cry, not now.

"Well, that was interesting," Luke muttered, coming to stand next to Deepa, placing a cup of tea in her hand.

"Who was that?" Deepa asked.

"Nastya, his older sister."

"She seems nice."

"She's a bitch," Luke snorted. "And she's going to chew him to pieces."

"Why?"

"Because he's been playing hookie with me instead of doing his job." Luke gently led Deepa back into the house and closed the door. "Our family has some very ambitious goals."

"Oh. What kind of goals?"

"Take over the world, destroy human society, make a werewolf utopia...just the usual crap."

Deepa nodded and took a seat at the table. Trying to calm the storm of emotion in her chest. She'd only known Axel a few days, but it felt the same as when she watched Parker die. Tears started to flow down her face before she could stop them.

"Shit." Luke passed her a box of tissues. "Here."

Deepa sniffed, taking the tissues and dabbing at her eyes. "I'm fine."

"Yeah, you're clearly doing great." Luke's tone was light and joking. "How long has it been since you were bitten?"

"I don't know, maybe a month, or two. I don't know how long I was a wolf the first time."

"So you're still a baby werewolf. We'll have to get you some lessons, so you don't accidentally eat someone's pet rabbit."

Deepa grimaced.

"Just kidding," Luke said. "I went to school with some guys like you, so I saw how hard adjusting can be."

"You were born a werewolf?"

"Yep, same as Axel. Our family doesn't let many turned ones in. They think that all the interbreeding keeps them pure or something."

Deepa nodded. Born werewolves didn't suffer from the same mental instability as those who were bitten. Their human and wolf minds were perfectly intertwined.

"The first thing you need to know is that it's just better to go along with whatever wolf brain wants," said Luke. "If it wants to eat steak, then just eat steak. If it wants to go frolic in the forest, then try your best to make it happen. You start running into problems if you try to push back too much. The wolf will just take over and do what it wants."

Deepa nodded. It sounded like her current situation. Her human mind wanted nothing to do with Axel, but her wolf brain was obsessed with screwing his brains out.

"There used to be a medication that would suppress the wolf brain almost entirely in humans, but it's been hard to get for a while. Neither side has any interest in human turned werewolves hiding under the radar."

"That would be nice." Deepa glanced out the window to where Axel disappeared moments earlier.

"Don't worry," Luke said with a gentle smile. "He'll be back."

"Thanks, but no thanks," Deepa muttered, trying to ignore the gaping void in her chest.

These weren't her real thoughts. It was all just the sex crazed psycho wolf in her head.

They were not a couple. She did not have feelings for him.

Not him.

Not the man who murdered Parker and destroyed her life.

Never.

CHAPTER 2

Axel tapped his fingers against his thigh as the car curved around the mountain road. He'd been gone for less than an hour, but he could already feel the familiar ache in his chest at Deepa's absence, like an impossible itch.

"Nervous much?" Nastya said without taking her eyes off the road.

"No," Axel spat.

"Liar."

"What the hell do they want?" Axel growled.

"Your presence was requested."

"By who?"

"Your adorable little brother."

Axel swore under his breath.

"Come on. It's not that bad." She pulled up to the main gate. "Why not try and play nice for once."

Axel rolled his eyes, but got out of the car, following his sister down the pathway to the mansion. They passed well-manicured gardens and expensive cars, coming to a halt in front of a large stone building.

Nastya typed the code into the door, which buzzed open with a click.

The inside hadn't changed since his dramatic exit. Still huge and overbearing, with more rooms than anyone could need. The walls were painted a sterile white, and cheap chandeliers hung overhead.

"He's waiting in his office." Nastya strode ahead of him, her high heels clacking on the tiled floor.

Axel followed behind, familiar knots of anxiety in his stomach. He hated this place. It felt like a cage.

Nastya pushed open the door to his brother's office, only to unveil a pretty blond woman bent over the wooden desk, her skirt pushed up to her waist as his brother thrust into her from behind.

The large man's face was screwed up in ecstasy as his cock plunged into the woman, over and over, his balls slapping against her thighs, her breathy moans echoing through the room.

"Fucking hell," Axel swore, quickly turning away, but Nastya didn't even flinch, looking over the scene with a grin on her face.

She fucking planned this, Axel thought to himself.

Nastya loved to think of ways to psychologically mess with him.

"Looks like fun," Nastya whispered dangerously close to Axel's ear. "Maybe I'll join in? I heard that Bethany tastes delicious."

Axel blanched. Nastya and his brother weren't related by blood, but he still found any intimacy between them disgusting, and Nastya knew it.

The screams intensified until they reached a fevered pitch, finally dying down into pants and whimpers.

Axel took the opportunity to escape, quickly slipping out the door.

"I'm done," he spat, keeping his eyes locked on the ground.

"What's wrong?" Nastya teased, poking Axel in the ribs. "Feeling left out?"

Axel clenched his fists. "Shut up."

"Aw, did you want a turn?" Nastya cooed. "Maybe she likes having both holes filled at once."

"Fuck off," Axel growled.

Nastya smiled, her eyes twinkling.

Axel was about to scream at her, when the office door opened and the blond woman emerged, reeking of his younger brother.

"Good morning, Axel," Bethany said brightly. "Have you been well?"

"Yeah, great," Axel muttered, refusing to meet her gaze.

"You're being rude," Nastya scolded, giving his ear a sharp tug.

Axel jerked away from Nastya.

"I'm so happy that he could see me." Bethany grinned. "Everyone says that his babies are the strongest in the clan."

"They're not wrong," Nastya said. "He's the only man around here with a working dick."

Axel scowled.

"I'd better be off." Bethany leaned in to kiss Nastya's cheek. "But I'll be back soon. The doctor said that it's best to do it a few times while I'm still ovulating."

"Can't wait," Nastya said.

"Bye, Axel." Bethany gave a small wave before heading down the hall.

"Bye," Axel murmured.

Nastya curiously raised an eyebrow. "Aren't you going to chase after her and beg her to let you be her personal sperm bank?"

"Just shut the fuck up," Axel hissed.

"Don't be so defensive," Nastya teased. "I'm just wondering why you don't seem as interested in Bethany as before."

"I'm not interested," Axel growled.

"Is there someone else?"

"No."

Nastya frowned, studying him carefully. It was painful when she was talking, but Axel had learned that Nastya was more dangerous when she had time to plot.

"Let's just go," Axel muttered, wanting to end the conversation before she began asking more questions.

"Fine." She stepped inside the office and Axel followed, keeping his gaze on the floor.

His brother was readjusting his belt, face emotionless, like they hadn't just walked in on him fucking Bethany. His black hair was disheveled and his pale skin flushed. He and Axel had the same deep blue eyes, something that they had inherited from their shitty father.

"Axel." His brother's voice was a low rumble. "How nice of you to finally join us again."

"What do you want?" Axel growled.

His brother sat down at the desk, gesturing for Axel to take a seat. "I was informed of your little attack. Two Infection Control agents right outside a bar full of more. Almost like you didn't give a shit about getting caught."

"You know me," Axel replied. "Always looking for a fight."

His brother's lips twisted into a thin smile. "So, since you seem so keen on turning humans, I think that it's only fitting that you lead our next attack."

Axel felt his stomach drop.

"It will be your responsibility to ensure that the targets are either terminated or turned."

"But-"

"You leave tomorrow. Don't disappoint."

Axel was about to reply when Nastya pressed a finger to her lips.

It was enough to send a clear message.

Do what you're told, or face the consequences.

CHAPTER 3

Axel's chest was tight with anxiety as he sat in the van, watching the city fly past. Usually he'd relish the opportunity to cause havoc, but his thoughts constantly strayed back to Deepa and the look on her face when he left.

He hadn't even said goodbye.

He'd been too afraid.

Too much of a coward to face what was going on between them. At least she was safe with Luke. Axel's cousin was trustworthy and simple, unlike the rest of their shitty family.

"You seem anxious," Reese muttered, breaking Axel out of his thoughts.

"I'm fine," Axel growled.

"Right," Reese sighed. "And I'm the King of the Werewolves."

"Where's your girlfriend?" Bruno kept his eyes on the road as he drove them through the dark city streets.

"I don't have a girlfriend," Axel huffed.

"Then why do you keep smelling like a girl's crotch?"

Axel rolled his eyes, turning his attention to the fourth man in the van, a silent teenager who looked ready to wet himself.

Bruno caught Axel's stare. "You can't have him. Sammy is my new lackey."

"You don't have lackeys," Axel muttered.

"That's because he's usually the one being lackeyed," Reese grinned.

Bruno flipped him off, turning his attention back to the lanky teenager.

"This is your last chance," Bruno said to Sammy. "Run back to the academy, get tons of pussy, and have a bunch of werewolf babies."

Sammy shook his head. "No. I can do this."

"If you say so." Bruno shrugged.

"That reminds me," said Axel. "Which one of you blabbed about what happened outside the bar?"

"Don't look at me," said Reese. "It was Sammy."

"Huh?" Sammy scratched his shaved head.

Axel bit his lip. As friendly as Bruno and Reese were, they were still part of his family's pack, and their loyalties lay with his brother and elders more than him.

They pulled up outside a fancy Yacht club surrounded by tall trees. Loud laughter and music spilled from inside. A couple of men staggered down the path towards the parking lot, singing at the top of their lungs.

"This is it." Bruno tapped his fingers on the steering wheel. "Whenever you're ready."

Axel scanned the grounds, taking in the few security guards and staff. There were obviously werewolves planted amongst them, but it was hard to tell without getting close. His brother hadn't been kind enough to tell him more than necessary.

"Let's move." Axel slipped out of the car, making his way towards the building.

Bruno and Reese flanked him, their movements synchronized as Sammy nervously trailed behind.

The music grew louder, the air heavy with alcohol and sweat. Inside were senators and donors, filthy rich men and women who poured money and resources into trying to eliminate all werewolves.

It was disgusting.

Axel pushed open the door, allowing himself to be engulfed by the heat, noise and smells. There were at least two hundred people seated around the dining room, gorging themselves on expensive food and wine. All living like their precious money could keep them safe from what was coming.

With a nod of his head, Bruno and Reese shed their clothes and transformed, their large wolf forms stalking into the crowd.

Axel took a deep breath and followed, pulling off his clothes and allowing the transformation to wash over him.

It was as natural as breathing.

His vision shifted, his body elongating, his nails turning into claws.

Chaos erupted instantly. Screams filled the room as everyone ran to the doors, only to find them blocked off or closed. Several of the staff and security also transformed, rushing forward to attack.

Axel lunged forward, his jaws clamping around a security guard's throat as the human tried to pull out a gun.

Blood dripped down Axel's fur, his pulse racing, basking in the thrill of battle.

The screams intensified. The humans' frantic footsteps echoed around him, the stench of their fear filling his nostrils.

It was intoxicating.

A gun fired, narrowly missing Reese.

Axel's gaze locked on the shooter, a large woman, her face streaked with tears and smudged make up. Her hands trembled as she tried to aim her gun again.

Axel didn't hesitate.

He lunged forward, his fangs sinking into her neck, tearing into the flesh. Blood spurted out, her body twitching and convulsing as it fell to the floor.

It was a bloodbath.

After ten minutes of slaughter, they got the remaining crowd under control, tying them to chairs as they wept and begged for their lives.

Axel returned to his human form, wiping the blood from his hands with a tablecloth.

The others remained in their wolf forms, circling the hostages with low growls.

"You are the lucky ones!" Axel boomed as he paced back and forth. "We've decided to give you a choice. You can either join us, or die in an Infection Control cell. It's entirely up to you."

"Please," a woman sobbed, shaking with fear. "I don't want to turn into a monster!"

"We're not monsters," Axel grinned. "We're the true rulers of this planet."

With a nod of his head, the wolves pounced, sinking their teeth into the hostages one by one.

Men and women sobbed and screamed as the infection began to take hold, consuming their minds and forcing them to change.

Their bodies contorted, bones snapping, muscles tearing, as their human forms gave way to the primal beast that now lived inside them.

Axel had seen it plenty of times before. The strong ones would learn to change back, but others wouldn't, living out the rest of their lives as savage wolves unless Infection Control tracked them down.

"This one isn't changing," said Sammy as he hovered over the body of one young man.

The guy's pants were soaked with piss, and his arm was covered with bite marks, but there were no signs of transformation.

"Shit," Axel muttered. "He's immune."

"Immune?"

"Some humans with werewolf ancestors can't be turned."

Reese returned to his human form. "What do you want to do with him?"

"Kill him." Axel turned away. "It's better if he doesn't fall into Infection Control's hands."

Axel ran off his remaining adrenaline in the woods, his white wolf form bounding over logs and bushes.

His heart hammered in his chest, his mind consumed by the thrill of the hunt, the need for violence.

He didn't feel any guilt about what happened. Humanity declared war against them centuries earlier, forcing them to live in the shadows. They were simply fighting back to take their place as the rightful rulers of the planet.

Axel soon found himself back at Luke's house.

It was stupid, and a risk, but the need to see her overwhelmed all rational thought.

He shifted back into a human and slipped through the backdoor, making his way through the dark and silent house.

Her scent filled the halls.

Axel found her asleep in his bed, dried tears staining her face as she tightly hugged a pillow.

Axel carefully climbed into bed next to Deepa, wrapping his arms around her and pulling her against his chest.

She sighed softly, her body relaxing against him.

Axel nuzzled her hair, inhaling her sweet scent, the tightness in his chest easing.

I'm so sorry, he wanted to say, but he couldn't form the words.

He pressed his lips to her throat, feeling her pulse. Her skin was warm, her heart beating strong and steady.

Deepa's eyes fluttered open, a frown forming on her lips.

"You're back," she murmured, her voice husky with sleep.

"Yeah." His hand rubbed slow circles on her hip.

She shifted slightly, her ass pressing against his rapidly growing cock.

Axel bit back a groan.

He should get up, put some distance between them before they ended up having sex again, but her scent was intoxicating, and she let out a small moan, her ass grinding against his crotch.

Axel bit his lip, his hands roaming over her hips and up her torso. He was a slave to his instincts, and there was nothing he could do to fight it.

Deepa whimpered, her eyes squeezing shut, her hands gripping his wrists.

He needed to taste her, to hear her moan his name, to feel her body quivering beneath his touch.

Axel slid his hand between her thighs, finding her already soaked.

"Did you miss me?" he whispered, his lips brushing her ear.

"Shut up," she mumbled, her hips jerking towards his fingers.

He gently stroked her, drawing circles around her clit, teasing her opening.

She squirmed, her legs spreading, her back arching.

Axel couldn't draw it out any longer, his cock was rock hard and throbbing, the need for release overwhelming.

He pulled his hand away and positioned himself between her legs, his erection pressing against her entrance.

"Fuck," he groaned, his hips jerking forward.

She gasped, her eyes flying open.

"Please." His lips trailed along her neck. "I need you."

He thrust into her, burying himself inside her warm, wet heat.

Her walls clenched around his cock, her hips rolling to meet his.

Axel shuddered, his length pulsing inside her, her scent filling his lungs.

"So good." His hands cupped her breasts, his lips sucking at her neck.

Deepa cried out, her nails digging into his skin, her muscles spasming around him.

"Fuck," he grunted, his hips bucking, his balls aching.

He couldn't stop.

It was too much.

He needed more.

More of her.

All of her.

Axel growled, his fingers digging into her skin, his body shaking with the effort to hold back his climax.

Deepa whimpered, her walls convulsing, her back arching.

Axel lost control.

His cock unleashed, his seed exploding inside her in several long spurts.

Deepa's eyes widened, her pussy spasming, her own orgasm washing over her.

Axel held her close, his forehead pressed to the back of her head, their breaths mingling.

It felt good, more than good, but he was fucked if he didn't figure out a way to separate himself from her.

Because there was no way he'd survive if something happened to her.

CHAPTER 4

Give up and they win, were the only words written on the crumbling kitchen wall.

Was it a joke? A warning? A parting motivational message?

Deepa frowned, her fingers brushing over the words. They were written in dark red lipstick, thick and freshly painted.

Vanessa's house was empty. There were no signs of a fight, so Deepa could only assume that the human turned werewolves had abandoned it and moved on.

It was a smart idea. It would be harder for Infection Control to track them down if they were constantly on the move.

They left nothing useful behind. No detailed guide on how to survive as a werewolf. Not even a single scrap of paper. They'd done a good job of erasing all traces of themselves.

Deepa sighed, taking one last look around the house, trying to imagine what her life would have been like if she'd stayed and accepted Vanessa's help. She wouldn't have tried to hunt down Axel. She wouldn't be stuck in a vicious cycle of letting him screw her.

Deepa had spent most of the previous day feeling shit about his rejection, snuggling up in his bed and inhaling his scent like a desperate creep.

She was overjoyed when he returned, responding to his touch like a well trained dog, begging him to fuck her.

But he was gone in the morning, sending her straight back to feeling shitty again.

Screw him, Deepa thought as she made her way out of the house, gazing over the outskirts of the city.

She didn't need Axel or his overly accommodating cousin. She'd leave and make it on her own, hitchhiking out of the country and hiding in the wilderness.

She would never have to set eyes on that blond arsehole again.

Deepa only managed several feet before her inner wolf began to claw to the surface, forcefully taking control of her body.

Deepa gasped, her vision going fuzzy, the familiar sensation of her limbs transforming washing over her.

Not now, she pleaded, but it refused to listen. *Please, let me go.*

The wolf brain was persistent, and Deepa soon found herself falling to all fours, shrinking and morphing, until a large brown wolf stood where a woman had been seconds before.

Deepa was unsure how much time had passed. It felt like the wolf had taken the wheel, shoving her into the trunk. There were flashes of consciousness. A glimpse of trees, a scent in the air, but no control.

It was infuriating, but everytime she attempted to fight back it would only shove her down once more, locking Deepa away deep in her unconsciousness as it chased down rabbits and pissed on trees.

Axel was there too sometimes, fully naked rutting into her like a beast, muttering gibberish about filling her up with his spawn.

The wolf relished in his attention, flipping their positions and holding him down against the cool ground, rocking back and forth on his cock as she climaxed around him.

She was fucked. Any hope of returning to a regular human existence slipped like sand through her fingers.

This was her life now, a wild animal mystically tied to the man who ruined everything.

There was no point trying to fight it. Deepa was just along for the ride.

When the wolf finally relinquished control, Deepa found herself naked in Axel's bed, her hair disheveled, her clothes nowhere to be found.

The room was different from the one in Luke's house, more sparse and lacking warmth. There was only a bed and closet with a large window overlooking a forest.

"Hey," Axel murmured, his arms sliding around her.

Deepa blinked, confused. Mind frantically trying to piece together the past few days.

"You okay?" His thumb stroked her cheek like he could sense her distress.

"How did I get here?" Her voice trembled.

"You don't remember?"

Deepa shook her head.

"Well, I'm not one to kiss and tell," he smirked.

Deepa groaned.

"It's okay." He pulled her closer. "We'll figure this out. Together."

Deepa's body relaxed, her eyelids fluttering closed, the warmth of his body lulling her back to sleep.

"It's not safe for you here." Axel shook her awake. "I'll take you back to Luke's. He's a good guy. You can stay there until I sort some things out."

"Sort what out?"

"I'll tell you later."

Axel slipped out of bed and pulled a hoodie and a pair of sweatpants from the closet, tossing them onto the bed. "Here, you can wear these."

Deepa pulled them on. They were far too large, but she found the scent comforting.

"Come on." He gently pulled her to the door. "I'll drive you before anyone else wakes up."

He led her down a silent hallway.

Deepa gazed at the perfect white walls and spotless cream carpet, feeling like she'd stepped into a showroom. There were countless windows overlooking small courtyards, each filled with colorful flowers.

"Is this your house?" Deepa asked. It didn't seem like a den of rabid werewolves.

"Just for now," he said quietly. "Come on, the cars are out back."

"Cars?"

"Yeah," Axel said with a smirk. "We have a lot of those."

Deepa followed him down more hallways, memorizing the layout out of habit. Never during her time in Infection Control did she imagine that werewolves could live so luxuriously.

They exited out the back of the house, stepping onto a massive balcony overlooking a sprawling valley.

Several cars were parked nearby, ranging from expensive sports models to large SUVs.

"Axel?" called a soft female voice.

It was Axel's sister, wearing a short blue nightdress, her long blond hair tied back into a messy braid.

"Good morning." Nastya smiled, her blue eyes sparkling.

"Shit," Axel muttered. His grip on Deepa's hand tightened.

"Who's your friend, Axel?" Nastya asked sweetly. "Didn't mother teach you that it's rude to bring a girl home and not introduce her?"

"It's none of your fucking business," Axel growled. "And she's leaving."

"So soon?" Nastya pouted. "Can't she stay for breakfast?"

"We'll pass." Axel pulled Deepa away from his sister and towards the parking lot.

"Axel!" called a deep male voice.

Deepa turned to see a large man emerge onto the balcony, thick black hair neatly combed and deep blue eyes glaring straight at them.

"Parker?" Deepa whimpered.

CHAPTER 5

"What?" Axel snapped, glaring straight at Deepa.

Deepa examined the large man before her.

He looked just like her dead boyfriend. The facial structure, eyes, hair color, and shoulders were the same, but as Deepa looked closer, she realized that certain things were different.

The man before her was clearly older. There were more wrinkles around his eyes, and he didn't have the scar on his cheek that Parker received in a fight years earlier.

"I'm...I'm sorry..." Deepa uttered as her face went red, dropping her gaze to the ground. "You just remind me of someone."

The man curiously raised an eyebrow. "Parker?"

"Just..." Deepa found it difficult to force the words from her throat. "Someone that I used to know."

"Ah, sorry to disappoint," the man replied with a smile. "I'm Ryan. I'm Axel's younger brother."

"Oh... nice to meet you." Deepa tried to ignore the way Axel's grip tightened on her arm.

"Likewise," Ryan grinned. "And you are?"

"Deepa."

"Deepa..." Ryan said softly. "That's a lovely name."

Axel's growl interrupted their conversation. "We were just leaving."

"So soon," said Ryan. "I was hoping that you could at least stay for breakfast. Axel rarely brings any friends home."

"She's not hungry!" Axel snapped.

"That's too bad," Ryan sighed. "Reese made plenty this morning."

"We're leaving!" Axel started forcefully dragging Deepa away.

Deepa yanked her arm out of his grasp. "Actually I'd like to stay for breakfast."

There was something about Ryan that intrigued her.

Axel's face dropped.

"I think that's a great idea." Nastya linked her arm through Deepa's and led her back into the house. "Reese makes the most wonderful tomato omelets."

"That sounds amazing." Deepa grinned, enjoying the sight of Axel's distress.

Nastya led Deepa down the hallway and into a spacious dining room, pulling out a seat at a long table.

Ryan and Axel followed, Ryan looking amused while Axel glared at Deepa like she'd betrayed him.

There were several other people already eating breakfast. A couple of young blond men and women chatting and laughing, while a teenage boy quietly picked at his food.

Deepa caught sight of the man who bit Parker, silently scrolling through his phone while chewing on a piece of bacon, but she quickly looked away, trying to suppress the surge of anger that rose up inside her.

She took a seat next to Ryan. Axel sat on the opposite side, glaring at her.

"Take whatever you like." Ryan gestured to the huge selection of food that lay on the table. There were sausages, omelets and fruit, along with a large pile of bacon.

"Thank you," Deepa murmured, helping herself to the bacon.

"So, how long have you and Axel been dating?" Nastya asked while daintily chewing on a piece of apple.

"We're not dating," Deepa huffed. "And I don't even know him that well."

"Is that so? Please tell me more."

"There's nothing to tell." Deepa slowly chewed, fighting the urge to gorge herself.

"Don't be shy." Ryan took a sip from a glass of orange juice. "We're all family here."

"We met at a bar," Deepa said in between bites. "He bit me, ruined my life, and now he can't keep his dick in his pants."

"So, you're not here on your own free will?" Nastya gasped.

Deepa shook her head. "Not really."

Ryan looked at Axel, his expression turning sour.

"Don't look at me like that," Axel muttered, glancing down at the table. "She showed up here on her own."

Nastya curiously raised an eyebrow while taking a sip of her coffee.

"I'm sorry," said Ryan. "My brother has always been terrible at controlling himself. He gets so excited about causing havoc, that he never stops to think about the consequences."

Axel's grip tightened around his fork.

"He's always been like this," Nastya sighed. "Always rushing in, acting without thinking, and expecting everyone else to clean up his mess."

"Cut it out," Axel hissed.

Nastya rolled her eyes, returning to her food.

"Anyway," Ryan said. "Please don't let my poor misguided older brother ruin your fun. You're welcome to stay here for as long as you like."

Deepa looked to Axel. He shook his head, mouthing the word *no*.

"Thanks." Deepa smiled up at Ryan. "That would be lovely."

"You can have my old room," said Nastya. "It has a wonderful view of the garden."

Axel slammed his fork on the table. "No fucking way."

"Oh, relax," said Nastya. "If Deepa wants to stay, she can stay."

"She can't," Axel hissed.

"Why not?"

Axel's eyes darted between his brother and sister.

"She doesn't belong here," Axel said coldly. "She's just a crazy quick fuck that I picked up for fun. She'll stink the whole place out with her vile human scent."

"Excuse me?" Deepa spat, her hands clenching.

"And we'll have to listen to her crying and groaning all night. She'll annoy everyone with her shitty attitude and sob stories about her dead boyfriend."

Deepa jumped to her feet, knocking over a jug of orange juice that spilled across the table. "Fuck you, arsehole!"

"See what I mean," Axel laughed. "Completely insane."

Deepa felt tears sting her eyes, the anger and shame mixing together. She couldn't understand why she ever let this guy into her vagina.

"Axel," Ryan said calmly. "Don't you think that's going too far?"

"Yeah, Axel." Nastya's mouth curled up into a sly smile. "Be nicer to your girlfriend."

"She's not my girlfriend!" Axel snapped.

Deepa took a step back, her chest tight as she fought the urge to cry.

"Please," Axel said, coldly glaring straight at her. "Just get out."

Deepa stared at him, her chest tightening.

She turned and ran out of the dining room, eyes burning. She didn't care where she went. She just wanted to be as far away from him as possible.

The asphalt stung Deepa's bare feet as she made her way down the rural mountain road.

Fuck Axel and his stupid family. She was going straight to Infection Control to tell them all where he lived. Maybe they'd spare her life if she brought them the biggest haul of the year.

Deepa continued onwards, the sun blazing down on her back, sweat drenching her clothes.

Several cars zoomed past, but none of them bothered stopping for her.

It was a surprise when a gleaming Lexus pulled up beside her.

Axel's brother Ryan was sitting behind the wheel.

"Need a lift?" he asked casually.

"I'm fine," Deepa growled, trying not to give him the satisfaction of seeing how flustered she was. Even his voice resembled Parker's.

"I insist." Ryan pushed open the door. "It's dangerous for a pretty girl to be walking alone in these parts."

"I'm good," Deepa muttered, continuing along the road as the car rolled forward beside her.

"Look, I'm sorry about the way Axel treated you, but we're not all dicks like him."

Deepa frowned, slowing her pace.

"I'm serious," Ryan said. "You'd be safer letting me give you a lift than wandering these roads on your own."

Deepa sighed, stopping and turning to him. "You're not going to leave me alone until I get in, are you?"

"Nope."

"Fine," Deepa groaned, opening the passenger door and sliding onto the leather seat.

Ryan hit the accelerator and steered back onto the road.

"Where to?" he asked.

Deepa bit her lip. What were her options? Her home was gone and she had no cash or job prospects. It was either a homeless shelter or the streets.

"I dunno," she shrugged. "Anywhere I suppose."

"You don't have anywhere to go?"

Deepa shook her head.

"How about you stay with us until you find somewhere. We have a ton of empty rooms that are just gathering dust."

"You're not afraid that I'll tell Infection Control about your secret werewolf compound?"

Ryan shook his head. "No. They wouldn't believe you anyway. They still think we're all rabid monsters who live in the sewers."

"I dunno," Deepa murmured. Axel had made it clear that he didn't want her there. She didn't want to run into him when she went to use the bathroom.

Ryan rested a hand on her shoulder. "If you're worried about the others, don't. I won't let anyone hurt you. I promise."

Deepa glanced out the window, at the endless woods surrounding them.

"I know that the transformation is a lot to take in," Ryan continued. "Werewolves aren't what you expected, right?"

"Not really," Deepa replied. "You're so..."

"Civilized?"

"Yeah."

Ryan shrugged. "Well, we're not all like Axel. Some of us actually learnt manners."

Deepa raised an eyebrow. "Is that so?"

"My mother was like you. She had to cope with being transformed into a werewolf. But she adjusted after a while, and I'm sure you can too."

"Your mother was human?"

Ryan nodded. "She was a lot like you. Beautiful, stubborn, and full of fight."

"I see." Deepa clasped her hands in her lap. "Axel never mentioned anything about his family."

"Axel and I are only half brothers. We have the same father but different mothers."

"Oh, that sounds...complicated."

"Yeah, it's a touchy subject for him. He blames my mother for his parents splitting up. That's just one of the many reasons why he's so bitter towards me."

"That makes sense. He was kind of a dick back there."

"That's nothing new. He's always been an angry little shit."

Deepa let out a laugh.

"I'm sorry that he bit you," said Ryan. "I saw how much my mother suffered, so I want to try and make it up to you."

Deepa nodded, feeling calmer than before. Perhaps it was his resemblance to Parker which made her feel at ease.

"I want to help you adjust," said Ryan. "And if you don't like it, you're free to leave at any time."

Deepa smiled, her chest easing. It was the first time she'd felt hopeful in days. "Thanks."

"Don't mention it." He pulled up to the gates of the compound. "Welcome home."

CHAPTER 6

Axel's claws ripped through the human security guard with ease, tearing his flesh and organs apart, blood spraying against the office desks and walls.

Several accountants were cowering behind a large steel cabinet, weeping and sobbing as chaos unfolded around them.

"Please," a skinny man whimpered. "Don't kill us!"

Axel had little pity. Their corporation was actively working on tests to determine werewolf DNA from regular humans. It was only a matter of time before they developed a test, that could expose all the werewolves hidden amongst the population.

He had no choice.

Reese and Bruno were also happily destroying the office, ripping humans to pieces and biting everyone in sight. Only Luke looked disturbed by the violence, his ears pinned back and his tail low as he stood off to the side.

Ryan had summoned Luke to the compound and assigned him to battle, no doubt eliminating any ways for Axel to hide Deepa.

Axel howled as he dug his teeth into a man trying to run, watching as the human crumbled to the ground, and spasmed as the change started to overtake him.

Violence was the only way for Axel to vent his frustration.

When they were children, Axel had been chosen as a future leader. He was doted on and adored by their elders while Ryan was shunted to the side, virtually ignored as the child of a human turned werewolf. All that changed when Ryan defeated Axel in a duel, and now, as the leader of their pack, Axel was stuck being Ryan's bitch.

Axel had to follow every stupid order or risk expulsion, and Ryan loved to use it to his full advantage.

"Shit!" cried Sammy as he came dashing towards them, naked in his human form. "Infection control vans outside!"

Axel let out a long howl, signaling to everyone to evacuate.

Dozens of wolves dashed for the exits, or shifted back to their human forms, camouflaging themselves amongst the chaos.

Axel's gaze turned to Luke. His cousin stood frozen as he stared out the window, watching several vans park around the building.

Axel snapped his teeth in Luke's direction, urging him to get a move on.

Luke turned and fled towards the stairs.

Axel followed, his eyes darting to the side as Reese and Bruno disappeared down the hallway, taking a different exit.

Gunfire erupted behind him, bullets ripping through walls and shattering glass as Infection Control officers approached, dressed in full body armor.

Axel was smart enough to know when he was outmatched.

He bolted out an open window, sailing two stories across the carpark and landing hard on the concrete, Luke following close behind. They dashed into the darkness as bullets followed, trailing them until they disappeared amongst the trees.

It had been years since Axel came so close to death, but all that he could think of was her. The taste of her, the scent, the warmth of her skin and the softness of her hair.

She was all that filled his mind.

Her lips on his, her nails scratching his skin, her thighs clenching his hips as she trembled and moaned beneath him.

He needed her.

Axel was surprised to find that Deepa hadn't gone far. He followed her scent to an annex of the compound, an isolated room with a large window overlooking the gardens.

She was lying on a double bed, fully clothed and fast asleep, the moonlight streaming through the window.

Axel gazed at her, his chest aching.

She was so beautiful, her brown skin glowing, her thick lashes and soft curls framing her face.

Axel shifted back to his human form, sliding open the window and slipping inside.

"Get out!" she hissed without opening her eyes.

"What are you still doing here? Axel growled. "I told you to go."

"I was invited to stay by your brother, who is so much nicer than you."

"You can't trust him!" Axel snapped. "He's only being nice to you to mess with me."

"Well, he's a lot better company than you!"

Axel let out a low growl. "He's only using you. Nastya too. They love to fuck around with my head."

"Well...maybe you deserve it."

Axel froze, staring down at her in disbelief.

"You don't seem to get how fucking weird they both are. They used to fuck all over the house when we were teens, right where they'd know that I'd walk in and-"

"Wait." Deepa rolled over to face him. "Aren't they brother and sister?"

"They're my brother and sister," said Axel. "But my parents were always fucking around with other people, so they're not blood related."

"So what's the problem?"

"The problem is that Nastya has started bringing in all these women for him to screw. She gets a kick out of watching him impregnate them."

"That's ridiculous," Deepa huffed. "You're just making shit up to get rid of me."

"I'm not. You have to believe me!" he pleaded. "It's not safe for you here."

"And why should I believe you? You're not even nice to me."

Axel clenched his fists. She was right, he had treated her like shit and given her no reason to trust him. Why would she believe a single word that left his mouth?

"Fine!" he huffed. "Have it your way. Stay here. But don't come running to me when they start trying to pull you into a fucked up threesome."

Axel shifted and leapt back out the window, disappearing into the night.

CHAPTER 7

Deepa fell back into an uneasy slumber after Axel left. She woke up hours later to find him naked on her bed, hovering over her body.

"I thought I told you to get out!" she hissed.

The moonlight illuminated his bare torso and well defined muscles, causing a heat to ignite within her core.

"You're so beautiful," he whispered, his gaze fixed on her, his cock already hard and ready.

Deepa pressed a foot on his chest to push him away, but Axel pulled it to his mouth, running his warm tongue along her toes.

Deepa shuddered, back arching.

"Do you still want me to go?"

Deepa shook her head.

Axel let out a sigh of relief. He took her foot into his mouth, sucking on her toes before moving to her leg, kissing and licking his way higher.

He pushed up her dress and kissed the soft flesh of her inner thighs, his hands gently pushing her legs apart and pulling off her panties.

Deepa was still groggy from sleep, but she knew exactly what he was going to do, the anticipation making her wet.

"Fuck," he grunted pressing his nose between her legs. "You smell amazing."

Deepa flushed, her body responding to the heat of his breath.

"I can't stop thinking about you," he groaned, his tongue darting out to taste her.

"Axel..." Deepa whimpered, her hand tangling in his hair.

He buried his face between her legs, his tongue sliding inside her, eating her out like a man dying of starvation.

His moans sent vibrations through her body, her back arching, her toes curling.

He licked her slowly, his tongue circling her clit and dipping into her core, lapping up her juices as Deepa trembled and groaned.

"You're so fucking wet," he moaned, his blue eyes meeting hers. "Is this what you want? Huh?"

Deepa whined, her fingers tugging his hair. "Just shut up and lick it."

Axel smirked, his tongue returning to her folds. He continued slowly, driving her crazy as he lapped her up.

She was trembling, her thighs tightening around his head. She wanted more, needed more.

"Suck it," she whimpered.

"Say it again," he growled.

"Just suck it," she moaned.

He smiled, his mouth closing around her sensitive nub.

Deepa cried out, her fingers digging into his scalp as his tongue flicked back and forth, making her tremble.

"Yes..." she gasped. "Like that."

Axel's arms looped under her thighs, holding her tightly in place as his tongue moved faster.

"More..." she panted, her toes curling.

Axel's mouth worked on her clit, sucking and flicking and lapping, driving her wild.

"Don't stop," she gasped. "Please don't stop."

She could feel the tension rising inside her, the pressure building as her orgasm grew closer.

She was so close, so very close.

"Axel," she whimpered.

His arms tightened around her thighs, his mouth devouring her as his tongue drove her closer and closer to the edge.

"Fuck," she moaned. "Right there."

The sensation crashed over her, her back arching as her whole body tensed, the pleasure surging through her, causing her to cry out.

Axel's grip tightened, holding her down as her body spasmed and shook. His tongue kept moving, his lips sucking on her clit.

Deepa shuddered, her body going limp as her orgasm subsided.

Axel planted a soft kiss on her thigh.

Deepa allowed him to climb over her body, slipping his cock inside her soaked folds.

She let out a whimper, his hard shaft stretching her wide.

Axel's hips rocked back and forth, slowly fucking her, his face buried in her hair, his hands cupping her ass.

She groaned, her legs wrapping around his waist, pulling him deeper.

He was an arsehole, but it felt wonderful when he was buried deep inside her.

His thrusts were slow and steady, his mouth trailing kisses down her neck, his lips brushing over her ear.

"You're mine," he murmured. "Just mine."

"Shut up," she hissed.

Axel's fingers gripped her hips, his movements quickening.

She bit her lip, her hips rolling to meet his, the sound of skin slapping against skin echoing around the room.

Axel groaned, his fingers digging into her flesh.

"I'm gonna cum," he gasped, his thrusts becoming more erratic.

Deepa wrapped her legs tighter around him, pulling him closer. She could feel him tense, his whole body shaking as he came, spilling his seed deep inside her.

Axel collapsed beside Deepa, pulling her into his arms.

Deepa sighed, allowing herself to sink into the warmth of his embrace.

"You're mine," he murmured against her neck.

"I'm not a fucking object," she muttered back.

Axel's hands ran up and down her spine, his lips brushing over her skin.

Deepa's eyelids grew heavy, the warmth of his body lulling her to sleep.

Axel was gone from her bed in the morning. He ignored her at breakfast, quickly wolfing down his food without saying a word, obviously still angry at her for staying.

Deepa glared at him while chewing on her toast.

Two could play at the silent game.

Most of the household disappeared after breakfast, no doubt going off to cause havoc for Deepa's old co-workers. She hoped that they didn't kill anyone that she liked.

Ryan remained, inviting her to drink tea with him in a courtyard. The white metal table and chairs were surrounded by several rose bushes.

"Nastya's creations," said Ryan when he noticed Deepa staring at the flowers. "She loves to plant seeds and watch them grow."

"They're lovely." Deepa slowly took a sip of green tea, trying not to spend too much time staring at Ryan.

Perhaps her grief for Parker was making her see him in Axel's brother's face.

Ryan elegantly poured himself another cup. "Have you ever heard of fated mates?"

Deepa shook her head.

"It's a rare thing,'" said Ryan. "Sort of like love at first sight. It's when two werewolves become overly attached to each other the first time that they meet."

"Oh."

"I've had my suspicions, but after watching both you and Axel interact, I think that this may have happened to you. You both clearly hate each other, but you can't seem to stay away."

"It's because he keeps stalking me." Deepa shrugged.

"Yes." Ryan nodded. "I think that's true. But I've noticed that you also initiate without any good reason."

Deepa frowned, taking a sip of her tea to avoid facing the confusing thoughts swirling around in her brain.

"It doesn't seem healthy for you," Ryan said. "Thanks to Axel, you were turned into a werewolf, lost your boyfriend, your job and your life. Yet you're constantly drawn to him, even though he obviously resents you as well."

"Yeah," Deepa muttered, looking back to the roses. "It doesn't make sense."

"I do have one thing that could help you."

"What?"

"My mother once separated herself from my father for years, with this." He placed a small bottle of white pills on the table.

"What are they?"

"Suppressant pills. They only work for human turned werewolves. They suppress the werewolf urges and make it possible to lead a regular human life."

"Really?" Deepa picked up the jar and unscrewed the cap, the bitter scent of medicine wafting from inside.

"Take two once a day, and you should be able to stop your inner wolf from going to Axel."

Deepa's heart skipped a beat. "That's...amazing."

"Don't get too excited. It's not a magic cure all. If you stop taking the pills your inner wolf will come back with a vengeance, but if you continue taking them for the rest of your life, it will be like you were never bitten at all."

"I see." Deepa nodded, a grin spreading across her face. "This is incredible. Thank you."

"No problem." Ryan's mouth curved up into a gentle smile. "It's the least I can do."

Deepa grabbed two pills, swallowing dry before returning to her tea.

She couldn't wait to be rid of Axel forever.

CHAPTER 8

It didn't take long for the effects to kick in. Deepa felt relaxed and calm, her thoughts no longer interrupted by a rabid animal. For the first time in weeks, she felt like the person she was before Axel attacked.

"Hey, are you okay?" Nastya asked. "You're smiling."

"Sorry," Deepa giggled, feeling a rush of endorphins. "I just feel really happy."

Nastya smiled back, holding up a cute summer dress. Several other outfits were discarded on Deepa's floor around them. "Here you should try on this one."

"Thanks." Deepa took the dress from her. "Are you sure that it's okay for me to borrow these?"

"It's fine," Nastya said with a casual wave of her hand. "I have far too many clothes, so I would just end up throwing them away."

"Thank you." Deepa smiled, slipping out of her clothes and pulling on the dress. "I really appreciate it."

"I'm glad." Nastya's smile was gentle, but her eyes watched Deepa intently.

Deepa was certain that Axel was fucking with her. Ryan and Nastya didn't seem malevolent at all. Both of them had helped her out more than Axel ever had. She could only guess that Axel didn't like anyone willing to call him out on his shit.

Deepa adjusted the blue summer dress. It only came down to her thighs and was tight across her chest, hugging her body far too snugly. "I think it's a little small."

"No, it looks great on you. It really shows off your curves."

"But isn't it a bit...revealing."

"And?" Nastya raised an eyebrow. "You shouldn't worry so much about what other people think. As long as you're comfortable wearing it, that's all that matters."

"I guess." Deepa glanced in the mirror. "It is pretty nice."

"See, I knew you'd like it." She passed Deepa a large bag full of clothes. "You can keep these ones as well."

"Seriously?" Deepa looked into the bag, her jaw hanging open.

"Of course," Nastya laughed. "I never wear them anyway. And it will make me happy to know that they're being put to good use."

"Wow." Deepa shook her head, unable to hide her awe. "You're a life-saver."

"No problem. I'm just happy to help where I can."

Deepa tried on several other outfits once Nastya was gone. They were all short dresses and revealing shirts, not what she would normally wear, but it was better than using Axel's old clothes. She slipped the blue short summer dress back on, and made her way out of her room, walking outside and across the garden to the dining room.

"Hey," greeted Axel as he walked towards her, gazing up and down at her exposed skin. "What's got you so happy?"

"Nothing." Deepa shrugged. "It's none of your business."

"Did you take that fucking dress from my sister?"

"Perhaps."

She didn't even have to fake her indifference. She didn't feel the creepy overwhelming need to be close to him like before.

"You can't wear that," Axel growled. "Not here."

"And why not?"

"Because it's what they want," he hissed.

"And why should I care about what you think?"

Axel froze, staring down at her with bewilderment. He took hold of her wrist and yanked her closer, pressing his nose to her neck.

"What the fuck have you done?" he hissed.

"What I should have done a long time ago."

Axel growled. "Who gave you those?"

"None of your business."

"It was him, wasn't it?"

"What difference does it make?"

"It makes a big fucking difference!" Axel snapped. "He's trying to split us apart and get into your pants."

"So.." Deepa said with a cock of her head. "What's wrong with that?"

"Are you serious? That fucking bastard just wants to knock you up and add the memory to his wank bank."

"You're just jealous that someone else finds me attractive."

Axel grabbed Deepa's shoulder and pushed her against a tree, pinning her in place. "You're mine."

Deepa's eyes widened. Her inner wolf was clawing at the walls of her mind, begging her to submit. She felt the urge to obey and follow his commands, but thanks to the pills, it was nothing more than an annoying buzz.

"I'm not yours," Deepa hissed.

Axel's eyes narrowed. His hand slipped between her legs, his fingers brushing against her thigh before she kneed him hard in the groin.

"Don't touch me," she growled.

"Fuck!" Axel hissed, stumbling back, his face twisting in pain.

"I'm not your fucking girlfriend."

Axel let out a pained groan, his eyes fixed on her, a flicker of anger passing through them.

"Don't you dare fucking touch me again," she hissed, her hands clenched into fists. "You don't own me. No one owns me."

"I didn't-"

"Just stay the fuck away from me, you psycho!"

Deepa turned and walked away, rage flowing through her body.

She was done with being Axel's bitch.

Nastya watched the scene from the window, grinning as Axel cupped his balls in agony. Watching Axel suffer always brought a spark of joy to her heart. It almost made up for all the years of listening to the elders rant about how wonderful he was.

"That's a new dress," said Ryan from beside Nastya. "Is that one of yours?"

"Yup."

Ryan smiled, wrapping his large arms around Nastya's waist, pulling her back against his hard body. "It looks...tight."

"I thought you would like it." Nastya turned to face him, wrapping her arms around his neck. "I picked it just for you."

"I know," he murmured, pressing his lips against hers. "You know me too well."

Nastya kissed him back, her groin tingling as his hands wandered down her body, slipping under the hem of her skirt, tugging down her panties.

Ryan nipped her lower lip. "Did you enjoy watching her reject him?"

"Yeah," Nastya moaned, her legs parting for him. "It was pretty funny."

"I'm glad," Ryan murmured, his finger slipping inside Nastya, causing her to gasp.

Nastya rocked her hips against his palm. "How much do you want to be inside her?"

"So much," Ryan groaned. "I want to feel those thighs around my waist."

"Good answer." Nastya's fingers stroked the outline of his erection.

Ryan slipped off Nastya's shirt and bra, kissing and licking her chest, his mouth trailing down her body.

Nastya leaned back, bracing herself against the windowsill. Ryan pushed her skirt up, his erect cock pressing against her soaked entrance, fully bottoming out in one long thrust.

Nastya cried out, her back arching.

"Doesn't she look soft," Nastya hissed, her insides clenching around him. "Just imagine how good she must feel on the inside."

"She will," Ryan groaned, his hips bucking into Nastya's heat, his lips trailing kisses over her throat. "Fuck, I can't wait to feel her pussy."

Ryan groaned, his fingers digging into Nastya's hips, his movements becoming more frantic.

"Just imagine her all big and round," Nastya groaned. "Maybe you can give her twins."

"Fuck," Ryan moaned. "I wanna fuck her so hard."

"I want to see her tits bouncing."

"I want to taste them."

"I want to hear her screaming your name as you cum inside her."

"I'm gonna fill her up so much."

"I want to see Axel's face when he finds out that the baby is yours."

"Fuck!" Ryan growled. "I'm going to cum."

"Do it," Nastya purred. "Fill her up with your seed. Breed her like a bitch in heat."

Ryan's hips bucked, his whole body shuddering as his orgasm tore through him, spilling his fluids deep inside Nastya.

"Good boy," Nastya murmured, affectionately running her fingers through his hair. "Just a little longer until she's all yours, okay?"

"Yeah," Ryan nodded, still buried deep inside Nastya. "Just a little longer."

CHAPTER 9

Deepa couldn't help but bask in her new found freedom. For the first time since being bitten, it finally felt like she had regained some control over her life.

She could sleep through the night, wake up in the morning, and walk around without her inner wolf howling to be close to a psycho. She didn't even feel the urge to transform. Returning to life as a regular human was finally starting to seem achievable.

Deepa scrolled through job listings on a phone that she borrowed from Ryan. It would be hard to score a decent job without any ID, but there were plenty of farm jobs that paid cash and looked willing to look the other way.

There was a knock at her door.

"Who is it?" Deepa called out.

"It's Luke," the man said softly. "Is it alright if I talk to you for a moment?"

"Is Axel with you?"

"No, it's just me."

Deepa huffed and tossed the phone on the bed, getting up to open the door.

Luke looked like he'd barely slept. There were dark circles under his eyes, his hair was a mess and his clothes were wrinkled.

"Can I help you?" Deepa asked.

"Can I come in?"

"I guess," she muttered, stepping aside.

Luke entered the room and sat down on the bed, letting out a sigh.

"What is it?" Deepa asked.

"It's Axel." He shook his head. "He hasn't been doing so well."

Deepa rolled her eyes. "And why should I care?"

"He's more unhinged than normal. If you could only talk with him-"

"He's a grown man, he can sort his own shit out."

"But you're his mate."

"No," Deepa snapped. "We're not mates. We're two entirely different people who exist outside of each other. I'm not his property."

"But it's different for him, Deepa. He was born a werewolf. He can't just turn it off with some pills."

"That's his problem. It's not my fault that he's so fucked up."

"You're right." Luke nodded. "It's not. But if you could at least try and understand..."

"I already told you, I don't care." Deepa clenched her fist. "I honestly just don't care. He's the one who brought this all on himself, he can deal with it."

Luke looked like he wanted to say more, but he closed his mouth, shoulders slumping in defeat. "Alright, I get it. I'm sorry for bothering you."

Deepa frowned as Luke got up and left her room, gently closing the door behind him.

Guilt gnawed at her stomach, but she quickly brushed it away. Axel could rot in hell as far as she cared. He was a pathetic loser who was probably just sulking because his feelings were hurt. She didn't owe him anything.

Deepa picked up the phone and returned to scrolling through jobs. She was leaving the mansion forever as soon as she got her shit sorted out.

Axel unleashed his bat on a thousand dollar microscope, sending the pieces crashing against the brick wall. He then turned his attention to an expensive computer monitor, smashing it with his bare fist.

He was furious, enraged and devastated.

His inner wolf was raging inside him, scratching and biting at his insides, demanding Deepa's attention, her focus, her love.

Bruno sat on an empty desk, enjoying a bag of potato chips as Axel unleashed his rage on the university lab. Several of the computers were reduced to small pieces and glass littered the floor. An overturned fridge had been ripped open and emptied, its contents splattered across the wall.

Axel hadn't been ordered to destroy the lab, but it seemed like a good target. The less research that humanity could do against werewolves the better.

Reese was balls deep in a curvy blond college student, rocking his hips as she clung to his shoulders and groaned.

"Make me a wolf," she huffed. "I wanna howl at the moon."

"Of course, babe," Reese grinned. "I'll bite you right when I cum."

"Promise?" she giggled, her nails digging into his back.

"Promise."

"How about you two hurry the fuck up?" Axel snapped, picking up a chair and hurling it into an expensive machine.

"Calm your tits," huffed Reese, giving the woman a wink. "Can't rush fated mates."

Axel pulled off a panel and started ripping out wires with his bare hands, snapping several of them with his teeth.

"Come on," whined the girl. "Just do it now."

"Patience, babe," Reese muttered, his hips grinding into hers. "I want to feel you turn on my dick."

Axel tried to block out their moans by picking up a keyboard and smashing it against a desk, small pieces of plastic went flying across the room.

How? How could Deepa push him away so easily?

He didn't even like her. She was rude and constantly whining about how shit he was. But she was the only thing that he could think of, the only thing that could calm the raging beast inside him.

He would do anything, anything at all, just to have her look at him the way she used to, her brown eyes glinting, her lips swollen and pink from his kisses.

But instead of wanting his dick, she took that fucking medicine and blocked him out.

It hurt.

It was a stab in the heart, a knife twisted in his chest.

Axel let out a roar, punching a hole through a whiteboard, sending dry-erase markers flying across the room.

It was all because of his fucking brother.

The fucking bastard had been after Deepa from the start, the same way he had fucked with every other woman that had ever crossed Axel's path. Ryan was a vile manipulative piece of shit who didn't deserve to breathe.

Axel should have strangled him to death back when they were kids. Ryan had been a scrawny wimp, quiet and constantly crying for his mother. It was only once Nastya became his caretaker, that he finally grew some balls.

Deepa needed to understand that Axel was the one that needed her, not his fucking brother.

"Are you gonna help?" Axel snapped at Bruno.

"Nah," his cousin shrugged. "You got this."

The college student let out a cry as Reese sank his teeth into her shoulder. He thrust in deep as her body began to shake and convulse.

"Don't pull out," she whimpered as fur sprouted from her skin. "Please don't pull out."

"Wouldn't dream of it, babe," Reese purred, his hips bucking. "Just a few more seconds."

She cried out, her legs tightening around his waist, her nails digging into his skin as she shifted into a werewolf.

"Fuck," Reese moaned as his climax hit, rapidly pumping his hips as her pussy squeezed around his cock, milking him dry. "Fucking Heavenly."

The newly turned wolf pulled away from Reese, letting out a long howl as it dashed out of the room and down the hall.

"You're lucky that didn't rip your dick off," Bruno muttered.

"Oh, come on." Reese pulled his pants back up. "It was fun."

"Not if they turn around and bite your dick off."

"Hey, you should try it sometime," Reese smirked. "It feels awesome when their body changes for the first time around you."

"You know what would be more awesome?" Bruno replied. "Never having to worry about my dick being ripped off."

Reese chuckled. "Suit yourself. But don't get jealous when she comes back as my fated mate."

"So what? You can be stuck having hate sex for the rest of your life?"

"That's the good stuff."

Axel punched a hole through the wall, causing the two men to pause and glance at him.

"You alright man?" Reese asked.

"Don't talk to me," Axel growled, kicking over a stack of chairs and sending them crashing against the wall.

"Yeah, something is definitely wrong with him," Bruno muttered, crunching on another chip.

"Shut up!" Axel hissed.

He needed to talk to Deepa. He needed her to understand that they were meant to be together, no matter how much they might hate each other.

He didn't need her to love him, just accept him, to stop taking that shitty medicine and let him back in.

He wanted to hear her say his name again, feel her touch, taste her.

Axel growled, throwing a broken chair leg at a window. It cracked but didn't shatter, so he picked up a desk and heaved it into the glass, creating a spiderweb of cracks that ran down its length.

He would get through to her. He would make her understand that they belonged together.

CHAPTER 10

It wasn't easy for Axel to see Deepa. Her room was locked up at night and Ryan kept Axel busy during the day, sending him on pointless errands to try and keep them apart as much as possible.

"Hey!" Axel called out as he knocked on Deepa's door. "It's me. Open up."

"Go away!" she yelled back.

"Just let me in, we need to talk!"

"I told you to leave me alone!"

Axel growled, pushing the door but it refused to budge.

"Come on," he whined. "I just want to talk."

"There's nothing to talk about."

"But-"

"Just leave me alone!" she yelled.

Axel groaned. He was so close to her, yet so far. He just needed to get her to listen, just for a moment.

"Let me in," he hissed. "Don't make me break the door."

"Then don't," she said coldly. "Just go away."

Axel growled. "Open the fucking door!"

"Or what? What will you do, Axel?"

Axel grabbed the handle, trying to force the lock open, but it didn't give.

"Let me in," he snarled.

"No!" she yelled.

Axel threw his shoulder against the door, but it still wouldn't move. He was running out of time. Ryan was probably on his way up, coming to save the day like the fucking hero he always pretended to be.

Axel wasn't going to lose her, not to his brother.

"If you don't open this fucking door, I'm breaking it down," Axel threatened.

"Go ahead," she said. "See if I care."

Axel stepped back, slamming his boot into the lock. The wood splintered, but the lock remained intact.

He kicked the handle, this time sending the entire lock flying through the other side.

The door swung open, revealing Deepa sitting on her bed, wearing a loose fitting t-shirt and jeans.

"You asshole," she hissed. "You're a fucking asshole."

Axel stepped inside, slamming the door shut behind him. "We need to talk."

"We have nothing to talk about."

"You're wrong. We have everything to talk about."

Deepa glared at him, her dark eyes full of anger. "Why are you acting like this? It's not my fault that you can't control your urges."

"I'm not-" Axel took a deep breath, trying to calm himself. "It's not like that."

"Then what's it like? You've done nothing but ruin my life since the moment I met you. You're a monster."

"You're the one who doesn't understand!"

"Explain it to me then. Help me understand why you think that you have the right to barge into my room, destroy the door and force yourself on me."

Axel took a step towards her, his chest tightening. "It's not like that."

"Then what's it like?" she demanded. "What could possibly make it okay for you to treat me like this?"

Axel clenched his jaw. "I'm a werewolf, Deepa. This is how it works. You can't just take suppressants and expect everything to magically fix itself."

"You're an asshole," she spat.

"Yeah, and?" Axel scoffed. "Do you think I'm just gonna sit back and watch while Ryan takes you away from me? You're my mate!"

"Mate?" she spat. "Are you saying that the way that you treated me was because you think that we're fated to be together?"

"We are," he growled.

"Fuck that," she hissed. "I would rather die than be with you."

"You're not getting rid of me." He closed the distance between them. "You're my mate, and you're not leaving me."

Deepa glared at him, her eyes burning with anger. "Get out."

"No."

"Then I'll leave."

"You're not going anywhere."

"Try and stop me," she spat.

"I will," he growled.

Deepa lunged for the door, but Axel was too fast. He grabbed her arm and pulled her back, slamming her against the wall.

"Get the fuck off me!" she snarled, her nails digging into his wrist.

Axel grabbed her other arm, pinning her in place. "You're not going anywhere."

Deepa glared at him, her eyes blazing.

"Let go of me," she hissed.

Axel's grip tightened. "I can't do that."

"What's the matter?" she sneered. "Can't get off without my help?"

"I need you."

"You don't need shit."

"I need you. You're mine."

"Fuck you," she spat.

She tried to fight him, her fists hammering against his chest, her nails clawing at his face, but Axel refused to let her go.

He held her against the wall, his hands moving to her hips, his fingers digging into her flesh.

"You're not getting rid of me," he snarled, his nose pressing against her neck. "Not ever."

"Let go of me," she cried. "Right now."

"You're mine." His teeth grazed her throat. "You belong to me."

Axel contemplated biting down, until he was ripped from her body and hurled across the room.

Axel slammed against the wall, his breath leaving his lungs in a single painful burst. He hit the ground with a grunt, his head ringing, his vision blurring.

"Fuck," he hissed, struggling to his feet.

"Stay the fuck away from her," Ryan growled, his hands clenched into fists.

Axel looked at his brother, his vision slowly coming back into focus, until the bastard slammed a foot into Axel's ribs.

"You're a disgrace," Ryan hissed.

Axel coughed, his body doubling over as pain exploded through his torso.

Ryan didn't give him a chance to recover, his fist colliding with Axel's jaw, sending Axel sprawling to the carpet.

Axel groaned, blood filling his mouth. He coughed as Ryan landed several more punches on his body, knocking the wind from Axel's lungs.

"Come on." Ryan took hold of Deepa's hand, quickly pulling her out of the room. "Let's go."

Axel watched helplessly as the two of them disappeared down the hall.

His body ached, his head throbbed, and it was a struggle to breathe.

He was angry, furious, livid, but also disappointed in himself. He had a chance to make things right with Deepa, but he only fucked himself over like always.

Axel rolled onto his back, gripping his torso.

Perhaps this was what he deserved.

CHAPTER II

Deepa tried to calm her racing nerves as Ryan's car moved through the dark city streets. It was shocking how easily Axel managed to break down the door and force himself on her. If Ryan hadn't come, there was no telling what might have happened.

"You're okay now," Ryan murmured, keeping his eyes fixed on the road. "I won't let him touch you again."

Deepa nodded, anxiously clasping her hands in her lap. "Why...why is he always like that?"

Ryan sighed. "Axel was spoiled by the elders as a child. He was always told how great and fantastic he was going to be, so it gave him a warped view of reality."

"So he's an entitled sociopath?"

"Pretty much. When things don't go the way that he wants, he soon resorts to violence. He's a bully and a coward. I'm sorry that you had to suffer through all of that."

"Thanks." Deepa leaned back in her seat, letting out a sigh. She could finally sleep in peace and not have to worry about a psycho sneaking into her room.

They pulled up in front of a cheap motel. There was a flickering neon sign out front and several cars parked haphazardly around the lot.

"The owner is one of us." Ryan climbed out of the car. "You should be safe here."

Deepa nodded, stepping outside.

Ryan took her hand and guided her into the building. They entered a small reception area that stank of wet dog. A middle aged man pulled out a key from behind the desk, giving it to Ryan without saying a word.

Ryan led Deepa into a hallway, passing several doors before stopping at one in the middle.

"Here we are." He unlocked the door and opened it for her.

Deepa walked inside, taking a moment to look around. The room was clean and well lit, with a double bed, a small TV, and a table with two chairs.

"The bathroom is through there." Ryan pointed to a closed door. "You can call the front desk if you need more towels."

"Thanks."

"Do you need anything?" he asked. "Some clothes or food?"

"No." She shook her head. "I'll be fine."

"Alright." He smiled. "I'll try and come by tomorrow night?"

"Wait." Deepa's chest constricted with panic. "You're leaving?"

"Why?" Ryan curiously cocked his head. "Is that a problem?"

"I guess not," she muttered. "But...do you have to?"

Ryan laughed. "What's wrong? Are you scared of staying by yourself?"

"No," she huffed. "It's just...it's not easy being alone."

"Don't worry. I won't let anything happen to you."

Deepa's stomach did a somersault, her heart fluttering. She needed him to stay. How could she convince him to stay?

"Please," she said softly. "Please don't go."

"I don't think that's a good idea," Ryan murmured, his finger brushing along her cheek. "If I stay..."

"I don't care." Her fingers clutched the front of his shirt. "I want you to stay."

Ryan's eyes met hers, his fingers trailing down her throat. "But I have so many thoughts....so many.... questionable thoughts when it comes to you."

Deepa bit her lip. She could feel the heat radiating from Ryan's body, and see the outline of his muscular chest. In the dim lighting, it was easy to imagine that he was Parker. That her boyfriend never died and that she wasn't a werewolf.

"Tell me," Deepa breathed. "Tell me about those thoughts."

"I imagine you.." he whispered. "Naked and laying on my bed, begging me to taste you."

Deepa swallowed. "And?"

"I press my lips to your pussy, licking you again and again until you cum hard, tugging my hair."

Deepa felt a familiar jolt of need between her legs. "Oh."

"They are such." Ryan bit his lip. "Terrible thoughts. But I know that you don't want me. Please pretend that I didn't say anything."

Deepa clenched his shirt. "What if I said that I do want you?"

Ryan's eyes darkened. His hands wrapped around her waist, pulling her closer, his mouth hovering over hers.

"Say it again," he breathed.

"I want you," she whispered, her eyes fixed on him.

Deepa knew that he wasn't Parker, but he was the closest thing to her dead boyfriend that she was ever going to get.

Ryan's mouth crushed against hers, his tongue thrusting past her lips. His hands cupped her ass, lifting her up and carrying her towards the bed.

Deepa moaned, her legs wrapping around his waist. Her heart was racing, her body burning with desire.

Ryan laid her on the bed, his hands pulling her jeans down her legs. He pushed her panties to the side, his fingers exploring her wet folds.

Deepa gasped as his thumb found her clit, his fingers pumping inside her.

"Do you like that?" Ryan breathed, his mouth trailing kisses along her jaw.

"Yes," she moaned, her hips bucking against his hand.

Ryan pushed her t-shirt up, exposing her breasts, his tongue swirling around her nipple.

"Oh, fuck," Deepa moaned, her head falling back against the pillows.

Ryan pulled her t-shirt over her head, tossing it aside, his hands trailing down her sides, his fingers gripping her hips.

Deepa whimpered as he tugged her panties off, throwing them aside. He pressed his lips to hers, his hands cupping her ass, squeezing her flesh.

"Fuck me," she breathed, her hands slipping under his shirt, tugging it over his head. She drank in the sight of his muscular torso and well defined biceps.

Ryan groaned, his lips trailing kisses down her body. He gripped her thighs, spreading her legs, his tongue swiping along her slick pussy.

She gasped, her hands tangling in his hair, her back arching off the bed. It didn't feel as good as when Axel did it, but it was good all the same. Enough to ease the ache between her legs.

Ryan's tongue swirled around her clit, his fingers pumping inside her.

"Mmm..." Deepa moaned, her hips bucking against his face. "Oh...god ..."

Ryan groaned, his mouth sucking on her clit, his fingers pumping faster.

"I'm gonna cum," she moaned. "Oh god, I'm gonna cum."

"Do it," he murmured. "Just let go."

Deepa cried out, her body shuddering, her pussy clenching around his fingers.

Ryan's mouth continued to devour her, his tongue swirling around her clit, his fingers pumping inside her until the sensation became too much and Deepa pushed him away.

"Are you alright?" he murmured.

"Yes," she said breathlessly, looking down at the tent in his pants.

Ryan grinned, removing the remains of his clothes, exposing his rock hard erection to her hungry gaze.

It was thick, glistening with pre-cum as Ryan reached down to stroke it. "I can't wait to feel you."

He pushed her knees apart, positioning himself between her legs. His cock brushed against her entrance, causing Deepa to gasp.

"Relax," he whispered, kissing her neck. "I'll be gentle."

"Okay," she breathed, her body trembling.

He slid inside her, his hips slowly rocking, his cock filling her inch by inch.

Deepa moaned, her nails digging into his back.

He bottomed out, his hips grinding against hers, his cock twitching inside her.

"Oh, fuck," she moaned.

"Are you okay?" he whispered, his hand cupping her cheek.

"Yes," she murmured, her legs wrapping around his waist.

Ryan groaned, his hips rocking against hers, his cock sliding in and out of her tight pussy.

"You feel amazing," he growled, his lips trailing kisses down her throat.

"So do you," she moaned, her fingers tangling in his hair.

Ryan thrust into her, his pace quickening, his body shuddering.

Deepa gasped, her nails digging into his back, her body arching off the bed. If she closed her eyes she could pretend that he was Parker. That it was Parker fucking her senseless instead of Axel's strange younger brother.

Ryan groaned, his hips pounding into hers, his body trembling as he tried to hold back his release.

"I'm so close," he murmured, his lips trailing kisses down her jaw. "I can't hold it."

"It's okay," she moaned, her body trembling.

Ryan growled, his hips bucking against hers, his cock slamming into her until he came with a groan, spilling his seed deep inside her.

He collapsed on top of her, his body shuddering, his breathing ragged.

"That was...incredible," he panted.

"It was," she murmured, her fingers stroking his back.

Ryan pulled out of her, laying beside her, his arm wrapping around her waist, his lips pressing to her temple.

Deepa relaxed into his embrace, trying to banish all stray thoughts of Axel from her mind.

She had a new life now, and she'd make certain that Axel would be nothing more than a distant memory.

PART 3

CHAPTER 1

Ever since she was young, Nastya was told that it was a great honor to give birth to children. It was a woman's job to have as many babies as possible to increase the werewolf population, and bring about their glorious future.

But her first pregnancy ended in disaster, leaving Nastya childless and incapable of falling pregnant again.

"How's the bleeding?" asked Nastya's great grandfather as she hobbled into his office, trying her best to avoid tearing any stitches.

The old man had sunken eyes and little remaining hair, appearing weak and frail, but Nastya knew better than to let her guard down.

"Less than before," Nastya mumbled as she carefully took a seat before his desk, wincing in pain.

If he noticed her discomfort, he didn't show it. "I've given some thought about your new role, now that you can no longer fulfill your purpose."

Nastya clutched the sides of the chair. He wasn't the first elder to say that she was useless without a womb.

Her great grandfather tapped his pen on the desk. "We brought your half breed brother here as a way to motivate Axel, but it won't be long before he starts trying to spread his seed. It would be unfortunate if his.....impurity is passed onto our next generation. Especially since we have so many fertile pure blooded men here."

Nastya raised an eyebrow. "So what do you want me to do?"

"You'll become his new guardian, and once he begins to have... urges... you'll be the one to satisfy them."

Nastya froze, blinking with shock. "But he's my brother?"

The old man let out a laugh. "Your mother is an excellent breeder who's spread her legs for half the pack men. I highly doubt that you have the same father, but we can have you both tested if it bothers you so."

Nastya bit her lip. The old man was right, the chances were very low that they were siblings, but still....

"You're a smart girl, Nastya," he continued. "Make sure that the only cunt that boy ever knows is yours."

The old man returned to his papers, a clear sign that the conversation was over.

"I'll do my best," Nastya muttered, carefully getting to her feet.

Nastya did as she was asked. She took care of Ryan and satisfied his curiosity once he began having urges.

It was strange at first, but it was better than the times when Nastya's great grandfather called her into his room, watching from the darkness as men took turns trying to impregnate her.

Once Ryan had gained enough competence in bed, Nastya found one of the most pureblooded women she knew.

Margret was everything that the elders loved, pale, fertile, submissive, and eager to reproduce.

"Ryan," Nastya said while leading Margret into Ryan's room. "This woman wants you to put a baby inside her."

Ryan blinked at Margret and the woman giggled.

"She's very pretty isn't she?" Nastya encouraged, wrapping her arms around Margret's waist. "Would you like to play with her?"

Ryan looked between the two women, then nodded, getting to his feet.

Nastya's heart raced with excitement, imagining her grandfather's face when Margret gave birth to a child that resembled his half-breed great grandson.

It was the perfect way to fuck over the elders who ruined her body.

CHAPTER 2

"Fuck... just stop," Deepa muttered as she tugged on her hair, trying to fight the werewolf urges that were floating to the surface of her mind.

She wanted to throw up, she wanted to scream, she wanted to lock herself in the bathroom and never come out.

It had been two days since the last dose of anti-werewolf suppressors and the effects were starting to wear off.

Her inner wolf was restless, desperate to come out and play.

Desperate to go to *him.*

Deepa tried to focus on anything but the growing urge to run to her psycho werewolf lover.

It wasn't easy.

All she could think about was Axel's touch, his lips, the way his cock felt as it moved inside her. She wanted to feel his fingers on her skin, his tongue exploring her body, his teeth sinking into her flesh.

She wanted him.

She needed him.

"Deepa!" called out Ryan as he knocked on her door. "Deepa are you in there?"

"Ryan!" she cried hopefully as she pulled herself to her feet, making her way through the one room apartment, almost tripping over her backpack and shoes.

Deepa threw open the door, collapsing into his arms.

He was dressed in an expensive suit jacket and denim jeans, black hair neatly combed.

"Are you alright?" He scanned her sweaty face.

"I need it," she panted, hands shaking as they threatened to transform into claws. "I need it now."

"The medicine?"

"Yes," she pleaded.

"It's alright," he said softly, pulling a small container from his pocket. "I got you."

Deepa snatched it out of his hand, ripping the cap off and downing two pills.

"Thank you," she breathed, letting her forehead fall against his chest.

Ryan gently stroked her hair. "You can always count on me."

Deepa shuddered, her hands clinging to his shoulders. Without Ryan she was screwed. He was the only one who could provide her with the pills that she needed.

"What's the matter?" he asked.

"I can feel it," she whispered, her eyes squeezing shut.

"The wolf?"

"Yes," she whimpered, her body trembling. "It wants him."

"Shhh," Ryan soothed, his hands rubbing her back. "It's alright. The meds will help."

Deepa nodded, burying her face in his neck. He wasn't Axel but he still smelt good, like leather and trees. She could feel her pulse slowing, the ache in her joints easing.

"Come on," Ryan murmured. "Let's get you inside."

He guided her into the room, shutting the door behind him. Her apartment was basic with only a small kitchen, bathroom, and a bed. Ryan helped pay the rent so that she could live within driving distance of him.

Deepa leaned against him, her breathing steady, her skin no longer hot.

"I'm sorry," she said softly. "I shouldn't be like this."

"Don't worry about it." Ryan sat her on the bed. "I understand. My mother was the same way."

"Really?"

"Yes." He sat beside Deepa on the bed. "She was often on and off the medication, so her health was all over the place."

"I'm sorry," Deepa whispered.

"It's fine." He took her hand. "You just need to stick with the medication and everything will be alright."

Deepa nodded.

"Do you have work today?" he asked.

"Yes," she sighed. "But I'm gonna get fired at this rate."

"You could quit. I can provide for you so that you don't have to worry about anything."

"No." Deepa shook her head. He had made the offer several times already, but she didn't feel comfortable taking more of his money. "It's okay, I want to work."

"Picking cherries?"

"Next will be apples, I heard that they need more permanent workers, so hopefully the next job will last longer."

"Alright," he sighed. "Just let me know if you need anything."

Deepa squirmed under his intense stare. There was so much about him that reminded her of Parker, but she could also see traces of Axel in his features.

"Are you sure you're alright?" His thumb stroked her cheek.

"Yeah," she said. "Just tired."

"Maybe you should take a shower."

"That's probably a good idea," she chuckled, pushing her hair back from her face.

"I can come with you, if you want." His hand rested on her thigh. "Help with those hard to reach places."

"Uh, sure." Deepa's pulse quickened.

She knew that look. She had seen it enough times on Ryan's face. She could feel the heat rising in her body, the need to be touched.

Ryan leaned closer, his hand trailing up her leg, his lips pressing to her neck.

Deepa moaned, her eyes fluttering shut, her heart racing.

"I can't stop thinking about you," he whispered, his tongue tracing her earlobe. "What you feel like when you tremble around my cock."

"Mmm," she murmured, her fingers tangling in his hair.

"Do you want me to touch you?" His hands slipped under her shirt.

"Yes," she whispered, her lips parting.

"Where?"

"Everywhere."

Ryan smirked, his hands squeezing her breasts, his thumbs circling her nipples.

"I'll start here," he murmured, his lips trailing kisses down her jaw, his teeth nipping her throat.

"Oh god," she breathed, her back arching.

Ryan pulled her shirt over her head, tossing it aside, his mouth capturing her nipple.

"Oh," she moaned, her fingers tugging at his hair. "What about the shower?"

"Later," he huffed. "Right now I want to taste you."

"Okay," she breathed, her hips bucking as his hands trailed down her stomach, slipping beneath her shorts.

"Does your birth control still work?" His fingers grazed her pussy, lightly brushing over her clit.

"I dunno." Her legs parted, allowing him better access. "Probably."

Ryan kissed her, his tongue swirling around hers, his fingers massaging her wet folds.

"Oh fuck," she moaned, her toes curling, her hips thrusting. "Parker." Deepa cringed as she realized her mistake. "I'm sorry... I didn't mean..."

"It's okay," Ryan hummed. "I don't mind. You can call me that if it feels good for you."

Deepa bit her lip, her eyes squeezing shut. She could feel him moving inside her, his fingers stroking her inner walls. She remembered Parker and her, making love after a night of drinking, his lips tasting like whiskey and beer, his fingers tracing patterns on her skin, whispering sweet nothings into her ear.

"Parker," she murmured, her hips bucking against Ryan's hand.

"Good," Ryan purred. "Does that feel better?"

"Yes," she moaned, her body arching, her skin burning.

Ryan chuckled, his thumb circling her clit, his fingers pressing inside her wet pussy.

"Parker," she whimpered, her nails clawing at his back.

"That's it," Ryan murmured, his teeth scraping her nipple. "Cum for me."

Deepa moaned, her toes curling, her legs shaking, her body shuddering as her climax washed over her, sending her spiraling into the abyss.

Ryan pulled his hand away, sucking her juices from his fingers. "Delicious."

Deepa's chest rose and fell as she struggled to catch her breath, the post orgasm high washing over her body.

Ryan pulled away to remove his clothes. Deepa watched, biting her lip, her eyes roaming his muscular torso.

His cock was hard and thick, bobbing between his legs as he positioned himself between her thighs.

"You're so beautiful," he murmured, his erection pressing against her entrance. "You'll make a wonderful mother one day."

He pushed inside her, filling her with one smooth thrust.

"Oh," Deepa moaned, her back arching.

"Say it again," he growled, his arms holding her tightly against him, his hips rolling against hers. "Call me Parker."

"Parker," she whispered, her fingers tangling in his hair.

He groaned, his tongue swirling around her nipple, his fingers massaging her other breast.

"Does that feel good?"

"Yes," she moaned, her pussy clenching around his length.

His hands gripped her ass, his cock thrusting deeper.

It was like this every time that Ryan visited. He'd give her medication and then screw her senseless, cumming inside her every time.

Ryan would go along with any fantasy that Deepa wanted. As long as she didn't slip out Axel's name.

"Parker," she murmured, her legs wrapping around his waist, her hips grinding against his, her pussy squeezing his cock. "Give me a baby, Parker."

Ryan grunted, his fingers digging into her arse, his hips rolling against hers, his cock pumping her dripping pussy.

"You want a baby?" he growled, his teeth nipping her shoulder, his lips trailing kisses down her throat.

"Yes," she whimpered, her body tensing, her toes curling. "I want it."

"Then let me give it to you," he purred, his tongue swiping along her pulse.

"Please," she begged, her body shuddering.

He groaned, his cock slamming into her, his teeth sinking into her neck.

She cried out, her body trembling as she came hard around his cock, her pussy milking his length as she shuddered and sucked him deeper.

He moaned, his hips frantically thrusting against hers as his climax approached.

"Fuck," he gasped, his cock twitching, his balls clenching as his release swept through him, his seed pouring into her womb.

Deepa gasped, her hands gripping his shoulders, her body still twitching.

Ryan's dick continued to throb as he gently thrust his hips, working out the remains of his release.

"Did you mean it?" he groaned.

"Mean what?"

"You want a baby. Is that true?"

"No." Deepa averted her gaze to the wall as her face flushed red. "Maybe I did once...with Parker... but not anymore."

Ryan laughed, his hands moving to her hips, slowly pulling out of her. "It's alright."

"I'm sorry," she choked. "I didn't mean to make it sound like I actually wanted a baby. I guess I got caught up in the moment."

"It's alright," he said. "You don't need to apologize. But you know that I can help you... If you change your mind."

Deepa bit her lip. It was a nice fantasy, to have a baby with Ryan. But she couldn't shake the feeling that Axel could walk back into her life at any moment.

"Thank you," she said. "But I'm not ready for that. I can barely keep my own shit together."

"I understand." He pressed a kiss to her temple. "Now how about that shower?"

CHAPTER 3

"How long is he going to be like that?" Bruno asked as he gazed at Axel's motionless form.

Axel's head rested on the table as he lifelessly stared at his untouched lunch. The only evidence that he was still alive was the faint rise and fall of his chest.

"Dunno," Reese muttered through a mouthful of sandwich. Loose blonde curls tumbled haphazardly across his furrowed brow

Bruno eyed Axel's plate. "Is he gonna eat that?"

"Doubt it." Reese reached across the table to snag a slice of cheese.

"Hey, wake up!" yelled Bruno, giving Axel's shoulder a shake. "It's time to eat!"

"Leave him alone," muttered Luke. "Can't you see that he's suffering?"

"Man, I think I'll give the fated mates shit a pass if it's gonna turn me into that," said Reese.

"I don't get it," said Sammy, eyeing Axel nervously. "Why does he let Ryan treat him like this?"

"Because he lost a duel," said Luke.

"A duel?"

Reese chomped down the rest his sandwich. "Axel was supposed to be the next leader of the pack, but Ryan challenged him and Axel accepted."

"Ryan won," said Luke.

"The loser had to fall into line," said Bruno. "Or be exiled from the pack."

"So now he's stuck being Ryan's bitch," said Reese.

"Damn," Sammy said.

"I mean Ryan's the leader, so we're all kinda his bitches once you think about it," said Reese.

"Can you all shut up," Axel moaned. The last thing he needed was to be reminded of his shitty life choices.

"He lives!" Bruno sarcastically gasped.

"Can't he just challenge Ryan again?" Sammy asked.

"No," Bruno answered. "Just look at him. Axel clearly doesn't have the balls."

"And Ryan would just win again," said Reese. "Especially after he beat Axel up and stole his girlfriend."

"She's not my fucking girlfriend," Axel hissed, even though his heart ached at the mere mention of Deepa.

He was past the point of anger, instead choosing to wallow in self loathing and regret.

"Don't worry, man," Reese said with a pat on Axel's back. "I'm sure you'll get her back."

"Maybe Ryan will lose interest after he knocks her up," Bruno added.

"Nah, that just turns him on more," said Reese. "My old girlfriend said that Nastya likes watching him screw the pregnant ones too."

Axel groaned, burying his face in his hands. "Stop. Talking."

"I'm just saying." Reese shrugged.

"What's worse?" Bruno asked. "Him stealing your girlfriend, or the time that he screwed your mom?"

Axel let in a sharp intake of breath. It had been his twenty-first birthday party, and Ryan deliberately shat on it by having sex with Axel's mother in the bathroom.

"Stop it," Luke snapped. "You're making him miserable."

"Sorry." Bruno shrugged. "I was just asking."

Axel banged his head against the table, trying to use the pain to distract himself. He needed to forget about Deepa and move on.

Even though every fiber of his being screamed out in protest.

Bruno straightened as Ryan approached, quickly shoving down his food.

"Hey, boss." Reese gave Ryan a casual salute.

Ryan stopped at the table, looking down at Axel's pathetic state. Ryan's shirt was wrinkled, and his hair was a mess. His scent still contained traces of Deepa, like he didn't want Axel to forget that they were fucking.

"Axel." Ryan crossed his arms. "I've given you enough time to mope. Time to get back to work."

Axel groaned, letting his head drop onto the table.

Ryan huffed. "You have a job tonight."

"Don't care," Axel muttered.

"Don't care? Infection Control has been scouting the southern mountains. I need you to go in and fuck up the hotel they're staying in so that they'll focus more of their resources over there instead of here."

"Go yourself."

"I have a meeting with the elders," Ryan hissed. "You're the only one who can do it. Now get up and do your fucking job."

Axel lifted his head, glaring at Ryan. He hated his brother, but they were stuck together. He didn't have any outside friends or family to fall back on. It was either suck up his current situation or live out the rest of his life alone in the woods.

"Fine." Axel slammed his hand on the table, standing up and trudging away down the hall. Perhaps ripping a few humans to pieces would help work out some frustration.

Luke got up from the table and followed afterwards.

"Where are you going?" Axel demanded.

"With you," Luke said.

"Don't you have some kind of pacifist bullshit to do?"

"I can do that anywhere."

Axel groaned, continuing on. He didn't understand Luke. His cousin was far too calm and willing to give a shit about other people.

"I tracked Ryan's car," Luke whispered. "I put one of those GPS things under the seat."

Axel stopped dead in his tracks. "You did what?"

"I tracked Ryan's car."

"I know," Axel angrily whispered. "Why the fuck did you do that?"

"For you."

Axel's eyes narrowed. "Why would you do that for me?"

"Look..." Luke nervously glanced over his shoulder. "I know that Deepa deserves better, but you're no good to us like this. I don't want someone to end up dead because you're too miserable to put up a good fight. So... just go throw yourself at her feet until she gives you a pity fuck or something."

Axel's nostrils flared. "I'm not that pathetic."

A wry smile tugged at Luke's lips. "Well, you could have fooled me." He fished into his pocket and retrieved a crumpled scrap of paper, holding it out. "Here, take this."

"What's that?"

"The address where Ryan goes every time that he comes back smelling of your girlfriend."

"What about the mission?"

"The others and I will handle it."

Axel's eyes narrowed, his hands twitching. He knew that he should tell Luke *no* and let her go, but the spark of hope in his chest was too difficult to ignore.

"Just...don't do anything to make her hate you more." Luke gently placed his hand on Axel's shoulder. "

Axel snatched the paper from Luke's hand. "I won't."

"Good." Luke nodded. "Now go."

CHAPTER 4

Deepa found the fruit picking job online. The farm was desperate for workers, so they were willing to pay in cash without asking any questions. Most of the other workers were all immigrants and young teenagers.

The sun beat down on her as she picked cherries from the trees, filling her plastic bucket. Her hair stuck to her neck with sweat and her back throbbed, but she was making enough money to support herself.

Deepa picked up the bucket and turned to go to the packing shed, only to find Axel standing right behind her.

"Fuck!" she swore, knocking over the bucket and sending cherries rolling across the grass.

Axel wasn't even wearing clothes. White fur shimmered along his arm as he completed his transformation.

"What are you doing here?" Deepa angrily hissed, quickly glancing around to make sure that no one could see him. "How did you even find me?"

"Your scent," Axel said softly, his voice lacking its usual bite. "I followed it from your apartment."

Deepa felt the familiar urge to reach out and touch him, to run her fingers through his soft hair, but she quickly shoved it aside.

"Get out of here," Deepa snapped, her eyes darting around. "Someone's gonna see you."

Axel wet his lips. "Can we talk?"

"About what? There's nothing to talk about."

"I miss you," he said softly.

"No." Deepa's heart hammered in her chest. "You don't get to say shit like that."

Axel's gaze fell to the ground. "But I just want to talk... that's all."

Deepa let out a sigh. She knew that she should smash her bucket into his face, but he looked sad and pathetic, like a kicked puppy,

"Fine," she muttered. "Just go hide in the bushes until I can bring you some clothes."

Deepa pulled a plain shirt and shorts from a co-worker's locker.

Axel emerged from the bushes when she returned, bare muscular torso glistening with sweat.

"Put these on," Deepa muttered while trying not to look at him, tossing the clothes at Axel's feet.

"Thanks." Axel picked up the shirt and slipped it over his head. The size was too small, causing his biceps to strain against the fabric.

Deepa's breath hitched as she tried her best to pretend that it didn't turn her on.

"How have you been?" Axel asked.

"Great," Deepa huffed. "I actually have a life now."

"Good," he said like he wasn't the one who fucked it up in the first place.

"Why are you here?"

"I wanted to see you."

"Right...I don't know what you're expecting, but you're not getting any sympathy from me."

"I'm not expecting sympathy." Axel slipped on the shorts. "I just want to talk."

"Talk about what?"

"Stuff."

"Stuff?"

"Yes."

"No apologies, no self reflection? Just stuff?"

"That's what I said."

"God, I can't believe you," Deepa groaned, rubbing her temples.

"And to tell you to stop fucking my brother."

Deepa crossed her arms. "Oh yeah?"

"Yeah. He's just playing with you. Giving you an apartment and dangling medication in your face. He's just keeping you on the side as a convenient weekend fuck."

"And how would you know?"

"I've seen him do it before. He likes the control, the thrill of having power over women until he knocks them up."

"Right, and what do you want? For me to just come running back to you instead?"

Axel shrugged. "Well...yeah."

"Fuck you."

"I'm just saying."

"You're just saying? I don't owe you a damn thing! You don't get to tell me who I can and can't have sex with."

"Well don't come crying to me when he starts inviting Nastya over to watch."

"You're disgusting."

"I'm disgusting? You're the one sleeping with him!"

"Wow, that's intense," muttered a voice behind them, and Deepa turned to see several farm workers watching them.

"Shut up!" one woman hissed, elbowing the guy who spoke in the ribs. "It was just getting good."

"Yeah," nodded another woman. "Keep fighting."

Deepa's face flushed red. She wanted to sink into the grass. How could her day get any worse?

Axel crossed his arms. "This is a private conversation."

"No, it's not," said the guy. "The whole field can hear you."

"And we want more," said the woman. "So keep going."

"I'm not doing this," Deepa muttered, turning and stomping away. She needed to get a new job and apartment where Axel would never find her.

"Deepa!" Axel called out. "Wait!"

Deepa ignored him, her fists clenched, her jaw set.

"Hey." His fingers brushed her arm when he caught up to her.

Deepa flinched away from his grip as though it was a live flame. "Go away!"

"Not until we talk."

"We already talked."

"No, we fought."

"Well, you can go fight yourself."

Deepa marched into the packing shed, past several buckets of fruit and into the locker room, trying to ignore the sound of Axel's footsteps behind her.

"Deepa!" he called out.

Deepa threw open her locker, shoveling her belongings into a backpack. "Leave me alone."

"Please," he called from outside the door. "I want to fix things between us."

"There's nothing to fix. We're not even a couple. We're just two people who used to hate fuck each other."

"Yeah, we could go back to that."

Deepa groaned. He was impossible. Were all werewolves this insensitive and self centered?

She slammed the locker door shut and stormed outside, Axel hot on her heels.

"What do you want me to say?" he demanded.

"You can start by apologizing."

"Apologize for what?"

"I dunno...how about biting me and killing my boyfriend?"

"But you were Infection Control. You were both screaming to be bitten and murdered."

Deepa spun on her heels, her hands flying up. "Fuck you!"

"What?"

"Fuck. You. You always have an excuse for everything, don't you? Like it would kill you just to admit that you were wrong. God forbid you show an ounce of empathy for anyone!"

Axel let out a laugh. "Oh, so that's what you're mad about? The fact that I won't cry and whine and beg you to forgive me?"

"I just want an apology, a little bit of sympathy for all the shit that you've put me through."

"Okay." He raised his hands defensively. "Fine, I'll apologize if it will make you feel better."

"Really?"

"Yeah." Axel stepped closer, his voice low. "I'm sorry."

Deepa's shoulders relaxed, but her anger did not subside. She still wanted him to hurt, to feel the same pain and confusion that she felt.

"Now can we have sex?" Axel asked.

"Are you fucking serious? No."

"But you said that if I apologized, we could have sex again."

"No, I never said anything about us having sex again."

"Come on."

"No."

"You can't leave me like this," he grumbled. "Half hard."

Deepa's nostrils flared. "I'm not touching your cock."

"Why not?"

"Because I'm done. I'm so fucking done."

Deepa was ready to make a dash for the exit, until several farm workers walked into the shed.

She took hold of Axel's arm and pulled him behind a pile of boxes. She assumed that the workers would dump their buckets and leave, but several more workers entered, along with the farm owner and his wife.

"Listen up guys," the owner nervously called out, clapping his weathered palms together. "There's been some reports of wolves in the area, so Infection Control would just like to ask you some questions... Hopefully nothing about your visa status... or age." He let out a strained laugh.

Deepa glared at Axel

"Don't look at me." Axel shrugged.

A middle aged Infection Control officer entered the room, wearing black tactical gear under a fluorescent jacket, his graying hair cropped short.

He was accompanied by a petite woman, with thick brown hair pulled back into a tight bun. Dark eyes scrutinized them from behind black-rimmed glasses.

"Do you know them?" Axel hissed.

"A little," Deepa whispered back. "The woman gave a speech at training, but I doubt she'd remember me."

"It's okay," Axel placed a hand on Deepa's shoulder. "Just stay calm and pretend that you don't speak English."

"I've been here for weeks. They all know that I can speak English."

"Shit."

"Thank you for your time." The woman announced, her voice crisp and authoritative. She slowly paced in front of the workers, hand resting casually on the gun at her hip. "I'm Officer Diaz, and this is Officer Jones. We have reason to believe that there are werewolves in the area. So for everyone's health and safety, we'd like to ask you all a few questions."

"Let's keep this friendly, shall we?" Jones said, his voice smooth and relaxed. "No reason we can't have a simple chat while maintaining everyone's civil liberties."

Deepa felt her body tense, her pulse quickening.

Axel took hold of her hand, squeezing it tightly.

"We appreciate your cooperation," Officer Diaz continued. "We promise that this won't take long. We just want to look over your IDs and take your names."

I'm so fucked, Deepa thought. *So utterly fucked.*

Deepa's mental breakdown was interrupted by a sudden scream. One of the farm workers shuddered and transformed, his body bulging and morphing into a giant black wolf, shredding his clothes as he let out a deep howl.

The wolf knocked over several boxes as it lunged for the open door.

Officer Jones immediately raised his gun, firing multiple bullets into the wolf's head and body, sending it tumbling to the ground in a sea of blood.

"Shit!" Deepa gasped, her hand flying to her mouth.

Chaos unleashed. The other workers started screaming and running for the door, desperate to escape, but officer Diaz blocked their way, raising her gun and pointing it straight at them.

"Hold on!" she yelled. "Don't move!"

The workers froze, their hands held up, their eyes wide with fear.

"Everyone remain calm!" yelled Officer Jones.

The wolf stirred, its legs kicking weakly.

"It's still alive!" someone screamed.

Officer Jones fired another round into the wolf.

"Is anyone else a werewolf?" Officer Diaz demanded, sharp eyes examining each of them one by one.

"No," several workers chanted, shaking their heads.

"No?"

"No, no," the farm owner nervously stammered. "No way that I'd hire any of those."

"Fuck," Officer Diaz hissed and reached for her radio. "We need to put these people into lockdown."

CHAPTER 5

Officer Diaz kept her gun firmly locked on the workers, narrowed eyes trained on their faces, searching for the slightest hint of suspicion.

The farm workers crowded together, their eyes wide and terrified.

"What's gonna happen?" a young woman whispered.

"We're gonna die," muttered a man. "I heard that they fuck up and accidently shoot people all the time."

"I need to pick my kid up from school," another woman cried, but Officer Diaz didn't respond, face stone cold.

To Deepa it was nothing new. Infection Control was trained to put people under pressure and wait for them to crack.

Axel wasn't the least bit affected by the tense standoff, instead providing Deepa with progressively worse ways of talking their way out.

"You can say that you're my sister," he hushed under his breath.

"Half the people here now know that we've had sex."

"And?"

Deepa blanched. "Maybe that's fine where you're from but not here."

"Okay, well how about a cousin?"

"That's not any better."

Axel rolled his eyes. "Or I could just fight our way out?"

"No," she whispered, horrified at the very suggestion. "There's only one of you."

"So? I've taken on more than these two."

"But what about everyone else? What if the bullets hit them during the fight?"

"Well, if they die it's their fault."

Deepa groaned, looking over her shoulder for a window to slip out of. "No. There has to be a better solution."

"Hey, you!" Officer Diaz cried out, pointing her gun in their direction. "Come out!"

Deepa froze, her heart thundering in her chest. She glanced at Axel who shrugged.

"Now!" Officer Diaz ordered.

Axel sighed and stepped out, pulling Deepa along behind him.

Diaz's grip tightened around her gun. "What the hell were you doing back there?"

Deepa's mind raced to come up with an excuse. "We were just-"

"Having sex," Axel smirked, pulling Deepa close. "It was just getting good until you guys showed up."

Deepa's face heated up. She elbowed Axel hard in the ribs, but he just let out a laugh.

Officer Diaz rolled her eyes, pointing her gun towards the other farm workers. "Over here, with everyone else."

Deepa and Axel silently obeyed, moving across the room and taking a seat on the floor.

Deepa wrapped her arms around her knees, trying to appear as small as possible. She was fucked. It was only a matter of time before she was discovered and shoved in a cage.

"Relax," Axel whispered, his hand reaching down to give her ass a squeeze.

Deepa smacked his hand away and glared at him.

"I've missed this." He grinned. "You screaming at me, me getting beaten up. It's just like old times."

"I miss your brother boning me," Deepa muttered back.

"Hey, shut up," a woman beside Deepa hissed. "I don't want to get shot because you two freaked them out."

The wailing of sirens filled the air, steadily getting closer.

"Thank fuck," Officer Jones muttered, slumping his shoulders.

The sirens grew louder as several vans pulled up outside.

The doors flew open and heavily armed guards spilled into the shed, quickly moving to surround them, dressed in black tactical gear. Several figures in bright yellow hazmat suits followed close behind, clutching cases of medical equipment.

A tense silence fell over the farm workers as Infection Control took up positions around them, assault rifles held at the ready.

Escape seemed impossible now.

The hazmat team carefully stepped around the pools of blood left by the fallen werewolf.

One figure knelt down beside it, examining the corpse. The others began setting up tables and medical stations. The sound of latex gloves snapping on and equipment being prepped filled the space.

"We'll be conducting individual interviews," one of the hazmat men explained. "If you're not infected, you won't have anything to worry about."

"Do you know any of these ones?" Axel whispered.

Deepa nervously scanned every face. "There's one guy that I worked with a year ago, but he probably doesn't remember me. He was always bragging about how many kills he'd made."

"Just relax," Axel whispered. "Just tell them some bullshit sob story, then they'll have to let us go. They can't legally detain us without evidence, right?"

"They're not the police, Axel," Deepa hissed. "Having a crappy backstory is enough for them to throw you in a cell for days."

"And you'd know all about that, wouldn't you?"

Deepa bit her lip. It was true. As an Infection Control officer she had helped round up countless homeless and innocent people. Denying them food and water for days to test if they would snap and transform.

All for the sake of protecting humanity.

"Hey," Axel murmured, gently clasping her hand. "I won't let anything happen to you."

Deepa took a shaky breath, squeezing his hand like a lifeline. It was fine. She'd just relax and stick to her story, giving them no reason to detain her.

One of the hazmat men removed his helmet. His black hair brushed the tops of his ears and his familiar blue eyes were sharp and calculating.

Deepa's heart clenched. "Parker?"

CHAPTER 6

There was no denying that it was Parker. He had the same face, the same scar on his cheek, the same cold expression that Parker used when trying to suss out potential turned ones.

How? How had Parker survived and returned to Infection Control? Did Axel's minion fuck-up? Or had Parker also been turned into a werewolf?

"Fuck," Axel hissed when his gaze landed on Parker. "He's immune."

"Immune?" Deepa gasped.

It sparked a memory. A small mention during training that those with werewolf ancestors could be immune to werewolf bites.

Axel clenched his fist. "We need to get the hell out of here."

"How?" Deepa squeaked, her heart hammering.

Axel's gaze darted to the exit. "We could start a distraction... use it to escape."

"We'd never make it," Deepa hissed. "They'll shoot us before we reach the door."

"Not if I bite someone."

"Don't you dare."

Deepa looked to Parker. They were once each other's family. He begged for her to run and live on. There was no way that he would sell her out.

"It's okay," said Deepa. "I've got this."

Deepa kept her head down until Parker left the room. Most of the armed officers remained, guns firmly fixed on them as they waited for someone to snap.

All the farm workers were forced to sit in silence for hours. Deepa's stomach growled and Axel hungrily gazed at the man beside him.

It was a common Infection Control technique. Deprive people of food and water and wait to see if their inner wolf came out.

Deepa was thankful for the suppressant pills. If she hadn't taken a dose that morning, she would have easily lost control.

They were then forced into a single line, and made to sit and wait while they were taken one by one to be interviewed in a tent outside.

Deepa shoved herself in front of several people in the line, leaving Axel to fend for himself.

When she reached the front of the line, she was escorted by two armed men in hazmat suits outside into a large tent.

Two Infection Control officers were sitting at a desk with computers, while Parker sat on a metal chair, holding a clipboard and pen.

His face immediately went pale the moment that Deepa stepped into the tent, pen dropping to the ground.

"Are you okay?" asked a woman sitting behind a computer.

"I'm fine," Parker mumbled, quickly picking up the pen. "Let's start."

Please, Deepa prayed while her heart thundered in her chest. *Please help me Parker.*

"Can you state your name?" Parker coughed, clearing his throat, expression schooled and purposely devoid of emotion.

"Bethany," Deepa answered, voice steady and calm. "Bethany Miller."

"Do you have any identification?"

"Yeah." Deepa rummaged through her pocket, pulling out her wallet and handing it to him.

There was nothing inside except a few receipts and loose change, but Parker flipped through it, pausing to glance at a plastic bus pass before handing the wallet back to her.

"It's legit," he called to the officers over his shoulder.

The officer behind the computer gave a curt nod, her fingers tapping against the keys. "What's her date of-"

"We'll get that later," Parker quickly interrupted, looking at his clipboard. "I want to ask some questions first."

"Go ahead." Deepa tried to keep her body language as relaxed as possible.

"Any known or suspected werewolf contacts?"

"No."

"Any past encounters or exposure to werewolves?"

"None that I can remember."

"Alright." Parker nodded, quickly writing on his clipboard. "Do you feel sick or have any physical symptoms that you feel are noteworthy?"

"No."

"When was the last time you ate?"

"Yesterday evening."

"Have you had any unusual experiences recently, such as nightmares, anxiety, or hearing voices?"

"No."

"Okay." Parker tilted his clipboard towards her. *Wait for me outside,* was scrawled in small letters on the page.

Deepa nodded.

Parker turned his clipboard back towards him, scribbling over what he just wrote. "We'd like to check the rest of your belongings as well. Please gather what you have and wait outside for assessment."

"Thanks." Deepa nodded, getting to her feet and stepping out of the tent.

The two men in hazmat suits had disappeared inside. No one spared Deepa a second glance as she slipped into the car park, camouflaging herself amongst the other farm workers who were waiting for a bus.

She sat down on a bench and idly scrolled on her phone, using the camera to check over her shoulder for any sign of Parker.

A bus pulled up as Parker came outside, slipping past several men as he walked towards the parked vans.

Deepa turned and made eye contact, getting to her feet and walking into one of the fields, disappearing amongst the trees but keeping her pace steady so that Parker could easily follow behind.

"Deepa?" Parker said softly, pushing his way through the foliage.

"How are you still alive?" Deepa gasped, throwing her arms around him.

He was warm and smelt just like she remembered. Like better times and home.

"I should be the one asking you that," Parker murmured, tightly hugging Deepa back. "Where have you been? I've been looking for you."

"I...I...I've been hiding. Trying to avoid Infection Control."

"So you're a werewolf now?"

"Yeah."

"Fuck," Parker hissed.

"What about you? I saw you get bitten."

Parker pulled away and tugged down his collar, showing off an obvious scar. "He bit me but nothing happened, turns out that I'm immune."

"Really?"

"Yeah."

"Wow. That's amazing."

"Yeah, I guess that my grandma or someone must have screwed a were-wolf," he said bitterly. "As disgusting as that sounds."

Deepa's gut twisted as she remembered Parker's hatred towards all were-wolves.

"So where have you been living?" he asked.

"In a shitty apartment in the next town."

"Are you okay? Are you safe?"

"Yeah, I'm fine. I even managed to get a job here."

Parker took hold of her hand, and affectionately ran his thumb along her palm. "I can't believe that we've found each other. After everything that's happened..."

Deepa forced a smile. She couldn't tell him about Axel or Ryan. He'd be disgusted to know how easily she had jumped into bed with the enemy.

"We should run away," said Parker. "Over the border where nobody knows us. We can have a fresh start."

"Aren't you worried about me biting you?"

"No. I'm immune, so you can chew on me as much as you like."

Deepa let out a laugh, taking a moment to bask in Parker's presence. It brought back memories of when they were younger, when Parker would joke around with their friends at high school. Before he got into Infection Control and became so consumed by vengeance.

"Deepa!" Axel's voice called from amongst the trees.

Deepa's blood ran cold.

Axel emerged before them, letting out a low growl as he spotted Parker.

Parker looked taken aback, until his face morphed into an equally angry scowl. "It's you," he hissed. "You're the werewolf from the bar."

He pulled out his gun, pointing it directly at Axel's face.

"Wait!" Deepa cried, dashing between them.

"Step aside!" Parker spat.

"Please don't shoot," Deepa begged. As much as she resented Axel, the idea of his death still felt excruciating.

"Deepa, move," Parker hissed.

"Parker, please."

"He's a monster. He needs to die."

"Please," Deepa begged.

"Deepa, I can't let him live. He's one of them!"

"No," she cried. "Don't shoot!"

Parker let out a curse, his finger curling around the trigger.

"Please!" Deepa cried, grabbing Parker's hand and attempting to wrestle the gun from his fingers. "Don't do it."

"Stop!" Parker growled, trying to push her off, but Deepa wouldn't let go. "Stop it! He needs to die!"

Axel lunged at Parker, tackling him to the ground. They crashed to the grass in a tangle of limbs, the gun skittering across the field. Grunts and curses erupted as they grappled, Parker's face contorting in agony as Axel's knuckles collided with his jaw in a sickening crunch.

"No!" Deepa cried, her voice shrill with panic as she lunged forward, desperately trying to pry them apart.

Axel swatted her away with a brutal shove, sending her stumbling back.

"Get off him!" she pleaded, tears welling in her eyes.

"You want to kill me?" Axel roared in Parker's face. "Then do it with your bare hands!"

Parker coughed, blood flying from his mouth. "You fucking monster!"

"Axel, stop it!" Deepa yelled. "Let him go."

"No," Axel hissed, his tone dripping with venom. "This asshole is going to die."

"No!"

"It's either me or him." Axel landed a punch to Parker's stomach. "Pick a side."

"Stop!" Tears pricked Deepa's eyes. "Please, just stop."

As much as she wanted Axel to back off, Deepa knew that he was right. There was no way that Parker would ever let Axel live. He'd rather fight him to the death than allow Axel to walk away.

"Fuck," Deepa gasped, tears flowing down her cheeks. She rose her boot, stamping down hard on Parker's leg as he let out a cry of pain. "I'm sorry," Deepa sobbed, her entire body quivering. "I'm so sorry."

Axel took hold of Parker's shirt, pulling him off the ground and throwing him at the nearest tree, his head colliding with a dull thud, sending him slumping to the ground.

"No," Deepa gasped, rushing to Parker's side. There was blood dripping from his nose and mouth and one of his eyes was swollen.

"Deepa," Parker groaned weakly.

"Come on." Axel tugged Deepa away by the arm. "We're leaving."

"Wait," she sobbed, resisting his pull. "He's hurt."

"Yeah, so?" Axel's voice was devoid of empathy. "It's either us or him."

"But he's my boyfriend!"

"No, he's an enemy! If he wasn't half unconscious, I'd fucking kill him. Now come on!"

"I can't," Deepa sobbed. "I just can't."

"Do you want to die here?"

Deepa shook her head.

"Then come with me."

Deepa allowed Axel to drag her away. Every step away from Parker's battered body felt like agony, but no matter how much she wanted to stay, she knew that following Axel was her only hope of survival.

CHAPTER 7

The gravel mountain road twisted and turned dangerously close to the edge of steep cliffs.

Axel held the steering wheel firmly as he drove past towering mountain peaks and deep valleys.

He looked over at Deepa, who was staring silently out the window with tears streaming down her face.

Axel rubbed his jaw, trying to suppress his growing frustration. What was so great about that Parker bastard anyway? The first time that Axel saw him in the bar, loudly bragging about how all werewolves needed to die, with a face that so closely resembled his brother, Axel couldn't resist the urge to fuck him up.

If he'd known that biting the girlfriend would have led to an eternal fuck buddy, Axel would have passed.

"You could have killed him," Deepa croaked.

Axel let out a groan. "We can go back there if you like, waltz right up to Infection Control and ask how he's doing."

"Dick," she snapped back.

Axel's grip tightened on the steering wheel. Deepa's devotion to her ex-boyfriend was getting on his nerves. Axel should have just ripped Parker to pieces so that he'd never have to see that stupid face again.

"Stop the car," Deepa hissed.

"Why?"

"Just stop the fucking car!"

Axel pulled over, the tires kicking up dust.

Deepa flung open the door, stomping across the road and disappearing into the bushes.

"Deepa!" Axel called after her, parking the car and following afterwards.

The sun was slowly sinking below the horizon, the sky tinged a light orange.

The trees rustled as Axel pushed through the thick foliage, leaves crunching beneath his feet.

"Deepa!" he called out, his voice echoing through the trees.

"Go away!" she yelled back.

"Where are you?"

"Just fuck off!"

Axel took a deep breath, following the sound of her voice.

Deepa was leaning against a tree, breathing heavily. Her fingers were tightly clenched into fists. Tear stains striped her red cheeks, but her eyes were wild and angry.

"Are you okay?" Axel cautiously stepped towards her.

"Do I look okay!" she snarled with a furious glare.

Axel sighed, running a hand through his hair. "What's wrong?"

"What do you think is wrong? I just helped a werewolf beat up my boyfriend!"

"He's not your boyfriend," Axel grumbled.

"And you are?" She arched a brow, daring him to answer.

Axel bit his tongue, trying to suppress the urge to say *yes*.

"Just stay away from me," she spat. "I never want to see you again."

"Fine." Axel swept his arm out, gesturing to the sprawling wilderness surrounding them. "Go live your perfect little life."

"You fucking bet I will!"

"You can go back to that Infection Control loser, you can go back to my brother, but either way we both know who you'll come crawling back to the moment that you transform."

"Don't act like you own me," Deepa spat.

"Yeah, tell that to your wolf. She knows exactly what she wants, and it happens to be my dick."

"You're disgusting!"

"Yeah, but you like it." Axel smirked, taking a step towards her. "You're probably thinking about how much you want me to rip your clothes off and fuck you against that tree."

Deepa inhaled sharply. "Get over yourself."

"Admit it," Axel hissed. "You missed me."

"No." Deepa shook her head. "Never."

"Liar!"

"I fucking hate you!" she yelled, stomping through the undergrowth.

Axel let her go, a smile spreading across his face. She was miles from humanity with no medication. It was only a matter of time before her wolf came out to play.

And he'd be ready.

Deepa wiped her face with her sleeve as she tried to pull her shit together. This was what she got for taking pity on Axel. She let him in for a moment and he ripped her life to shreds yet again.

She pulled her phone from her pocket, cursing at the lack of reception. There was no way that she could call up Ryan to rescue her. She'd have to find her own way back to civilization and soon. She could already feel the withdrawal symptoms starting to kick in.

A tree branch snapped behind her.

"I know that you're there!" Deepa called out over her shoulder.

Axel emerged from behind a tree, looking far too cool and composed for Deepa's liking.

"Stop following me," she hissed.

"I'm not following you." Axel shrugged. "I just happen to be going this way too."

"Go in the other direction."

"Nah." He smirked. "I like it here. I think I'll just chill for a while until you decide to be friendlier."

Dread settled in the pit of her stomach. If she didn't get back soon, there was nothing she could do to stop the animal in her brain from jumping his dick.

"You got a phone?" Deepa snapped.

"Yep." He pulled a smartphone from his pocket, tossing it in her direction.

Deepa caught it and took one look at the screen, letting out a groan. It didn't have reception either.

"Hey, are you feeling okay?" Axel asked. "You look a little flushed."

"I'm fine," she muttered, trying to keep her breathing steady.

"Your pupils are really dilated."

"I'm fine." Deepa tossed Axel's phone to the ground by his feet.

"I could help you out." He smirked "If you need a little release."

Deepa shuddered. His personality was foul but his body was starting to look appealing. She could always sit on his face and use that stupid mouth to get off.

Deepa bit her lip, trying to force all sinful thoughts of Axel's lips out of her mind.

"I'd rather screw your brother," she muttered.

She expected those words to cut him, but Axel let out a laugh.

"Deepa, no matter how many other men you screw, we both know where your true loyalties lie."

"Shut up," she hissed, turning and marching into the trees.

The world around her became hazy. The colors of the trees blurring together. Her heart hammered as the rush of blood pounded in her ears.

Deepa stumbled, catching herself on a tree.

Axel stepped towards her. "Woah, are you sure that you're okay?"

"Leave me alone," Deepa whispered, her legs shaking.

"Hey, seriously. I think you might be going into withdrawal or something."

"No."

Axel reached for Deepa, placing his hand on her forehead. "Yeah, you're burning up."

Deepa slapped his hand away. "Stop it."

"Deepa."

"Stop touching me!"

"Fine." Axel threw his hands up in defeat.

Deepa pushed herself away from the tree, her legs stumbling beneath her.

Axel took hold of her arm, but Deepa shoved him away. "Stop that."

"Come on... just let me help you."

Deepa tried to hit him again, but Axel caught her fist in his palm.

"Just stop fighting it," he said softly.

Deepa growled and shoved him, making him stumble backwards.

A cold chill ran over her body as fur began to sprout from her arm, her nails morphing into claws.

"It's okay," Axel said calmly. "Just relax and let it happen."

"No, no, no, no, no," Deepa whimpered, her teeth sharpening into fangs.

"Just let it happen," Axel soothed, stripping his shirt and pants as his body began to transform along with hers.

Deepa screamed as her bones cracked and her body morphed. Her clothes tore to pieces and fell away from her body, replaced by fur.

She landed on all fours, her claws digging into the earth as she let out a pained howl.

Axel finished his transformation, towering over her with his powerful wolf body and piercing blue eyes. He nuzzled her cheek with his muzzle, letting out a soft rumble.

Mate, the bond between them hummed, and the wolf inside Deepa readily embraced it.

CHAPTER 8

Things were always easier as a wolf. Axel didn't have to worry about stupid human shit, like clothes, and pleasing stuck up elders who'd constantly pit him and his younger brother against each other. He could just relax and allow his wolf instincts to take over.

Deepa was easier to deal with too. Instead of constantly pushing him away and bitching about her ex-boyfriend, wolf Deepa was far more receptive to his affection, eagerly rubbing her body against his, and letting him bury his face in her fur.

He watched Deepa wander around the forest, happily following behind her as she chased down squirrels and howled at the moon.

After hours of playing and wading through streams, Deepa's eyelids grew heavy, and they found a place to nest in a small cave.

She curled up on the ground, resting her head on her paws, her dark eyes following his every movement.

Axel circled the area, carefully examining the space, checking for any potential threats. Once he was satisfied, he returned to Deepa's side, nudging her gently with his muzzle.

Her body morphed and changed, returning to her human form, but there was something vacant about her stare. She had the same spaced out look that all turned ones had when their wolf selves were in control.

Deepa crawled onto his body, her skin soft and warm against his fur.

Axel shifted back to his human form.

Deepa lay her head on his shoulder. She pressed her lips to his neck, leaving a trail of kisses along his throat, her body sliding up and down his.

Axel let out a groan.

"Shit," he hissed, his arms wrapping around her waist. "You want it, don't you?"

She moaned, sucking his neck.

"I want it too," he groaned, his fingers digging into her flesh

She hummed, grinding her hips into his, rubbing her warm wet core against his rapidly swelling cock.

"Fuck." Axel's body trembled with need. He had dreamed of this moment for weeks.

Axel pulled her into a kiss, her lips hungry and eager. His hands slid down her body, grabbing hold of her ass and squeezing.

She cried out, her nails digging into his shoulders.

"Yeah," he moaned, rolling them over and pushing her down into the dirt.

Her thighs were already spread wide and eager, her eyes half-lidded and her skin flushed.

"Do you want me to breed you?" he whispered, rubbing the tip of his cock against her swollen clit. "Do you want me to fill you up with pups?"

Deepa's fingers tugged on his hair as she squirmed beneath him, her teeth biting his earlobe.

"Fuck," Axel groaned, slowly pushing his way inside her dripping hole, savoring every inch.

Her inner walls tightened around him, squeezing his length and sucking him in deeper.

"So wet," he murmured, rolling his hips into hers.

Deepa's head fell back, her breath coming out in quick gasps, her breasts rising and falling.

"How's that feel?" he growled, giving her a rough thrust, but she didn't answer.

It was hard to tell if human Deepa could see what was happening, or if her consciousness was buried too far beneath the wolf's instincts and desires.

Axel didn't care either way. He needed her badly, and she was happily spread out on the forest floor for him.

He moved at a fast and furious pace, pounding her into the dirt, her tits bouncing and her head lolling from side to side.

"So fucking hot," he growled, taking hold of her breasts and pinching her nipples, making her gasp.

She writhed and moaned, her legs wrapping around his waist, pulling him in deeper.

"That's right," he moaned, his cock sliding in and out of her slick channel. "You like that?"

It comforted him to know that no matter how much Deepa despised him, her wolf self would always be on his side, always happy to open her legs and let him fill her with cum.

Deepa cried out, her pussy walls clenching around him.

Axel fucked her relentlessly, her body trembling, her pussy sucking him in, until finally she came, her cries of pleasure echoing through the trees.

He fucked her right through her orgasm, his balls slapping against her ass.

He felt himself reaching his own climax, and he slammed his cock into her, burying himself as deep as he could.

"Shit," Axel moaned, his cock pulsing, spurting wave after wave of hot cum inside her.

Deepa let out a contented hum, hugging him close.

Axel had never felt so happy.

She was his. Truly and completely. Deepa could go off and fuck a million other men, but she would always come back to him.

Axel collapsed onto Deepa, his chest heaving, basking in the post orgasm high and the warmth of her body.

"We've still got a long way to go." He rolled onto his back and pulled her on top of him, burying his face in her neck to inhale her delicious scent.

She purred, snuggling up to him, her breasts pressed against his chest, her soft cunt still wrapped around his dick.

Axel ran his hands up and down her back, her soft hair tickling his face.

This was the way that things were supposed to be. Him and her, together.

It was easy for Axel to lose himself to his wolf instincts, his mind blissfully blank and free from all the bullshit that had plagued him for years, consumed only with thoughts of her.

They hunted together. They nested together. And at night, they fucked together. Deepa on her hands and knees like a dog as Axel pounded into her from behind.

Her human self failed to surface after a week, but Axel didn't care. Deepa was no longer consumed by anger and spite. She enjoyed the nature around them and her body readily responded to their bond.

Axel told himself that Deepa was happier like this.

She'd pin him down and take what she wanted under the light of the moon, her cunt soaking wet and eager for his cock.

"You're so perfect," he gasped as his pleasure spiked, their bodies moving in unison.

She gasped, her fingernails digging into his shoulders as she took what she wanted.

Axel groaned, relishing in the sensation of his climax building.

"I love you," he murmured, pulling her in for a kiss. He knew that she wouldn't remember, but it made saying the words easier. "I'm going to breed you. I'm gonna knock you up so many times."

Deepa cried out, her hips slamming into his, her thighs shaking, her inner walls milking his cock, trying to suck his cum out.

"You want that, don't you?" he growled. "You want to have babies, don't you?"

Deepa threw her head back, her fingers clawing his shoulders.

Axel groaned, his hips thrusting up to meet hers, his balls tightening, his seed threatening to spray forth.

"You're mine," he moaned, his fingers grasping her thighs, pulling her closer. "You'll always be mine."

Deepa cried out, her thighs shaking as she reached the point of no return. Her fingers grabbed hold of his hair, her hips grinding into his.

"That's right," he groaned, his own orgasm threatening to take him. "Cum on my dick."

She threw her head back, letting out a howl as she came, her cunt gushing around his cock.

Axel let out a cry of ecstasy as he reached his peak, his balls emptying inside her, filling her up with his fluid.

He knew that she was still on birth control, but the idea of her being round and swollen with his child filled Axel with joy.

She collapsed onto his chest, their bodies slick with sweat and cum.

"I love you," Axel whispered, affectionately running a hand through her long hair.

Deepa hummed happily, nuzzling his chest.

Axel knew that they needed to go back, but he couldn't bring himself to do it, not when they were so fully immersed in their own little world.

He didn't need a pack, not when they had each other.

"Hey," he murmured softly, nuzzling the top of her head and inhaling her sweet familiar scent. "How about we go away somewhere, just the two of us?" His fingers lightly traced patterns along her back. "We could live somewhere where no one will find us. You'd like that wouldn't you?"

Deepa let out a soft sigh, slowly shifting back to her wolf form.

"Okay," Axel whispered, understanding her unspoken answer. With a gentle smile, he allowed his own transformation to take place, his human form melting seamlessly into that of a powerful wolf.

CHAPTER 9

Deepa felt lost in a dream. Her days passed in a blur, scattered with bread-crumbs of consciousness. There was the singing of birds, the smell of moss, and the metallic taste of blood in her mouth.

Throughout it all there was always Axel. Axel, with his soft fur, his piercing blue eyes, and the comforting scent of pine and musk.

Sometimes she woke to the sound of him snoring, or the feel of his lips on her neck, but mostly her days and nights passed in a haze, the wolf's instincts and desires overwhelming her own.

She'd wake, her limbs tangled with Axel's, and for a moment the world would seem normal, but then her body ached, her teeth sharpened, and the urge to mate and breed consumed her. She'd pin Axel down and wrap her warm lips around his cock, bobbing her head up and down until he was hard and ready for her.

The rest was a blur. Her body moving on its own, her mind sinking back into darkness, the only thing that existed was his body, and the burning desire to have him deep inside her, to fill her womb with new life.

"That's it," he'd affectionately hum in her ear. "Take what you need."

He'd push her onto her hands and knees, mounting her from behind, his teeth gently nibbling her shoulder, his fingers rubbing her swollen clit.

"You're doing so good," Axel's deep voice would purr. "My perfect little mate."

Mate.

The word made her heart beat faster. The bond between them buzzed with excitement.

"I'll never let you go," he growled, his nails digging into her waist.

Deepa's breath hitched as he drilled her from behind, his thick cock rubbing her inner walls, her breasts swaying.

"Cum for me," he begged, his voice husky. "I can't hold out much longer."

She was already reaching her peak, the sensation overwhelming. Her inner walls clenched and her body shuddered.

Axel grunted, his length throbbing inside her, his hips frantically pumping.

"You're mine," he whimpered, his voice cracking.

The wolf in her let out a purr. She felt her pussy tightening, gripping the massive dick in her folds. Her eyes rolled back as she was hit by her climax, rocking back and forth as she lost control of her body.

Axel rumbled and wrapped his arms around her, nuzzling her neck and licking the delicate shell of her ear. He nipped and kissed her pulse, his thrusting growing erratic, his breathing ragged.

With one final thrust, he plunged deep inside her and filled her quivering body with hot seed.

Deepa let out a low moan, her back arching. Her muscles relaxed and the bliss was enough to make her fall asleep.

"That's it," Axel cooed, still filling her womb. His hands gently traced her body, cupping and squeezing her full breasts, then running over the curve of her belly. "I love you," he murmured, nuzzling her neck. "So much."

"What did you say?" Deepa murmured, the words slipping out of her mouth without any thought.

Axel pulled away, eyes open in awe. "You're back."

Deepa groaned, her brain pounding against her skull as she slowly regained control of her limbs. "How long was I gone?"

"A while." Axel brushed a strand of hair from her face. "The withdrawal must have forced your body into a heat."

"Heat?"

"It's just something that happens to female wolves when they need to mate."

Deepa nodded. Just more weird werewolf shit that she needed to get used to.

They sat on the floor of a badly built wooden cabin. There were holes in the ceiling and a draft flowed through the cracks in the walls. The furniture was sparse with only an old couch, a bed frame, and a small table with two chairs. It didn't look like anyone had lived there in years.

"Where are we?" Deepa groaned.

"Our new home," Axel purred, pulling her closer.

"Are you serious?"

"I found it a few days ago. Do you like it?"

"Fuck no." Deepa pulled away. She took pity on him, let her guard down for a moment, and now he'd dragged her to some sort of murder hut.

"Oh come on. It's got lots of potential. Just give it a chance."

"I'm not living here. There's probably bodies under the floor."

"Well, yeah. It's not exactly a five star hotel, but once it's fixed up it'll be great."

"Fuck that. I'm not living in this cabin with you. I hate you."

Axel fell silent and pulled away.

Deepa could tell that she'd hurt him, but she was too mad to care. She got up and threw open the door, only to be greeted by thick forest with no signs of civilization.

"Fuck," Deepa hissed.

"I'm not living here," Deepa told Axel for the eleventh time that day. "There's no electricity, plumbing, or any clothes."

"You don't need clothes when you have fur," Axel mumbled through a mouth full of dead possum. The carcass was laid out on the table as he happily munched on the insides.

"What about winter?"

"We'll make a fire and curl up to keep each other warm."

"And food?"

"There's plenty of food. Last night I caught three of these."

Deepa crossed her arms. "I'm not eating that. I'm going back to a place that has supermarkets."

"What's the point?" Axel grumbled. "None of those humans will ever accept you. At least out here we don't have to hide what we are."

"I can't live like this," Deepa whined, pacing the room. "I'll go insane."

"You were fine a few days ago. You even ate a whole family of ducklings."

"That's because I was a wolf!"

"Well...You can always change back."

Deepa groaned, collapsing in the chair opposite his. It was impossible to get through to Axel. He was completely caught up in his morbid happy family fantasy.

"Look," Axel sighed. "There's no reception, and no roads leading out here, which means that Infection Control will never find us."

"What about your family?"

Axel shrugged. "They won't miss me."

"So what.. we're just going to live out here alone forever?"

"No. Eventually we'll have children."

Deepa let out a curse. She couldn't deal with the idea of spending the rest of her life trapped with him and a dozen poor infants, who'd be forced to hunt down their own food.

She got to her feet and walked out the door, deciding to take her chances in the wilderness. She assumed that Axel would stop her, but he didn't even budge.

"Fucking werewolves," Deepa muttered under her breath, branches cracking beneath her bare feet as she made her way into the forest.

She could have sworn that Axel had even professed his love for her, but that must have been a hallucination. There was no way that a monster like him could even understand what love was.

The only thing he cared about was getting his dick wet.

The further Deepa walked, the more apparent their isolation became.

The landscape surrounding her was breathtaking, rolling mountains blanketed in lush greenery, but there wasn't a single power line or man-made structure in sight, only the pristine beauty of untamed nature.

Deepa's inner wolf clawed its way to the surface, itching to frolic amongst the bushes and hunt down prey, but Deepa ignored it.

She was the one in control of her own body, not some rabid dog.

"Get back," she snarled through gritted teeth, her voice laced with strain. "This is my body, not yours."

A tremor suddenly gripped her legs, and Deepa crumpled to her knees, fingers digging into the soft earth. A low, guttural growl rumbled from the depths of her throat, a warning sign of the impending transformation.

"Stop it," she commanded, though it sounded more like a desperate plea. "You don't get to come out whenever you like. I'm in charge here."

An unbearable itching sensation spread across her skin, as if her flesh was trying to crawl away from her bones.

"I hate you," Deepa whimpered.

It was impossible to resist the animal fighting to the surface. Her nails grew into claws, her bones cracking and snapping,

"No!" she screamed, but the word came out as a pained, agonizing howl as her humanity slipped away, consumed by the ravenous wolf that now claimed her body as its own.

When Deepa came to, she was back inside the cabin, riding Axel's dick as he groaned beneath her.

"Fuck." He gripped her arse and thrust upwards. "You're so wild."

Deepa didn't respond. She kept her eyes locked on his. Her body moved of its own accord, her hips rocking back and forth as she chased her own pleasure.

Axel's breath hitched, eyes screwing shut with bliss.

Deepa dug her nails into his shoulders, grinding her swollen clit against the base of his cock.

As shit as Axel was, he did feel delicious, the sensations were far more intense than when she slept with Parker or Ryan.

Axel let out a moan, his grip on her hips tightening as he struggled not to climax.

Deepa leaned down, pressing her lips against his neck, scraping her teeth against his jaw.

Axel moaned, his hips bucking as his cock unleashed, spraying his cum into her womb.

Deepa soon followed, rocking back and forth until she came on his dick.

The wolf inside her felt satisfied and happy, and that made Deepa feel content.

CHAPTER 10

Days passed in a familiar pattern. Axel continued his caveman lifestyle, while Deepa searched for any hint of civilization. At nightfall, her body turned back into a wolf, and she'd return to screw Axel's brains out.

"We can't live like this forever," Deepa snapped one morning while attempting to scrape the mold from the walls.

Axel shrugged. "Why not?"

"Because it's fucking insane! You expect me to just happily live out your deranged little fantasy after all the shit you've put me through?"

"Hey, what have I done to you?"

"Let's think..." Her voice dripped with biting sarcasm. "Attacking and beating up my boyfriend, kidnapping me-"

"I didn't kidnap you."

"Yes, you did."

"No I didn't. I'm not keeping you here. I'm not holding you hostage. You can leave whenever you like."

"And walk back into civilization naked? With no medication, and a wolf trying to bust out of my skin every five seconds."

"Then don't go back," he said with a casual shrug of his muscular shoulders. "You've got nothing to go back to anyway, just admit it."

Deepa felt pure rage ignite in the pit of her stomach, her nails morphing into claws.

"And as for your ex," Axel continued, seemingly oblivious to her building outrage. "He would have killed me if I didn't get the first punch in. So that was just self-defense. And besides..." He flashed her a wolfish grin. "You're better off with me than that dickhead."

Deepa let out a growl of frustration, picking up a chair and hurling it at the wall.

Axel didn't even flinch as several splinters flew in his direction. "Feel better?"

"No," she growled.

Axel sighed, running a hand through his tousled hair. "Look, I know you hate me, but trust me when I say you're better off here. You don't want to be around when all the shit goes down."

"When what shit goes down?"

He waved a dismissive hand. "Just...stuff."

"Like what?"

"Don't worry about it," Axel shrugged.

"Axel, what are you talking about?"

Axel bit his lower lip. "The elders have been planning it for decades. When the time comes, humanity will fall, and we'll rise to take our rightful place as the dominant species."

"What the hell is that supposed to mean?"

"I don't know all the details, but us werewolves will be the ones to rule the planet."

Deepa let out a laugh.

"What?" Axel grumbled.

"You seriously expect me to believe that you and the rest of your weirdo family are going to overthrow humanity?"

"Not just us, there are plenty of others, hidden amongst you, just waiting for the right signal."

"And what's the signal?"

"I don't know."

"Oh really?"

"It's just something that will happen."

"What, like the zombie apocalypse?"

"Something like that."

Deepa scoffed. "This is fucking stupid."

"It's not stupid."

"How could a bunch of werewolves take over the world? It's the most ridiculous thing that I've ever heard."

"Just wait and see."

A shiver ran down Deepa's spine at the conviction in his voice. It was obvious he wasn't joking. He truly believed the madness spilling from his lips.

"I need some fresh air," she muttered, disappearing outside.

Deepa had started a small vegetable garden in front of the cabin. It was a good way to distract herself from Axel's insanity.

The seeds had just started to sprout, poking their little heads through the soil.

Deepa squatted down to poke one.

Axel's story didn't make any sense. The werewolf population wasn't large enough to take down governments, and the turned ones were too unstable to make an army.

Deepa sighed heavily, pulling her knees up to her chest as she settled on the soft earth.

Axel had to be delusional. His elders had obviously fed him lies of werewolf grandeur.

The door behind her opened.

"I know that you don't believe me." Axel sat down beside her. "But you'll see soon enough. When the time comes, I'll protect you...you and our babies."

Deepa flinched at his words, an involuntary shudder rippling through her. "Don't say that," she bit out, harsher than intended.

"Why not? It's true."

Deepa pinched the bridge of her nose, struggling against the fresh wave of rage building inside. "I don't want to talk about this insane shit anymore."

"Okay." His voice was little more than a whisper as he reached out, enveloping her small hand with his calloused grip.

Deepa allowed her fingers to entwine with his, her stomach flipping.

Axel had no right to make her feel like this. None at all.

"We don't have to talk at all," he whispered, the words ghosting warmly against her skin.

Deepa could feel the weight of his intense gaze boring into her, both scorching and unreadable. She knew she should simply pull away, put a decisive end to this unsettling moment. But some deeper, baser part of her was drawn to the heat of his touch, the predatory wolf inside her practically purring at his unrelenting attention. It would throw another fit if she tried to reject him.

"Fine," she grumbled, feigning nonchalance.

Axel's responding smile was brilliant, vivid in the waning evening light.

Deepa found herself quickly averting her gaze, flustered warmth blooming across her cheeks

With a tug, he drew her slender frame against his solid warmth, his muscular arm draping comfortably around her shoulders.

"See?" His deep voice rumbled with a purr of satisfaction. "You do love me, deep down."

"No, I don't," Deepa protested weakly, the words ringing hollow even to her own ears, as her body subconsciously molded itself against his hard planes.

"You just need to give it a chance," Axel murmured. "Things will work out."

"Yeah," Deepa scoffed. "And in a year you'll be a deadbeat dad who'll try and feed a newborn dead possum."

"It's good meat," he said defensively. "And I won't be a deadbeat. I'll take good care of you and our children."

Deepa's face felt numb and she tried to stop the tears forming in her eyes. His words of being a father shouldn't affect her, but they did.

"You okay?" he asked softly.

"I'm fine," Deepa sniffed, rubbing her eyes.

"It's okay," he whispered, stroking her hair. "Everything will be okay."

Deepa's resolve began to melt, tears falling down her cheeks.

She should hate him, she should run away, but he felt so nice, his scent comforting.

"You're my mate," he murmured, nuzzling her neck. "I'm always going to be here for you." He pulled her closer, his hands resting on her hips.

Deepa sniffled, her heart beating faster, the wolf inside her content and happy.

She leaned in, pressing her lips against his.

He deepened the kiss. His touches were gentle and unhurried, his mouth tender.

A pleasant sigh escaped Deepa's lips and she lost herself in the feeling, her hands running up his chest, sliding along the dips of his muscles.

Deepa gently rocked against him as his manhood hardened beneath her. Her thighs parted, allowing her warm center to rub against his pulsing length.

She began to feel light headed, her pulse and his breathing drowning out the world around them, until there was nothing else.

"Deepa," he breathed, as his lips trailed down the graceful slope of her throat.

"Axel," she moaned, rocking back against his hips, whimpering as his erection throbbed. The need growing within her was undeniable, begging him to take her, to quench her desperation. "I want you inside me."

With a pleased growl, Axel wasted no time, flipping her over so that her chest was flat against the grass, and her plump backside was positioned deliciously in the air before him. He thrust his rock hard erection into her pussy without any warning, filling her in one fluid stroke and setting a rough pace.

She writhed beneath him, moaning pleas for more as her folds engulfed him, contracting hot snug against his cock, coating him with her wetness as he pistoned into her.

"Do you like being claimed by me?" he demanded, digging his fingers into her hip and drawing her tighter against him.

His teeth gently grazed the skin of her neck. He groaned in approval when she whined at his actions, submitting completely.

She panted, unable to muster enough composure to come up with a snappy response. Her cheeks flushed a darker red and her walls tightened deliciously.

"I asked you a question," he growled into her ear, giving her a harder thrust that pushed a lewd keen from her lungs.

"That's such a shitty-" She was cut off by another well-angled thrust. "Oh, God-"

His chest rumbled with a chuckle. "Do I make you feel good?"

He pounded harder, drawing out another cry of pleasure. Deepa's fingernails clawed against the grass.

"That wasn't an answer," Axel muttered. He nipped and sucked his way across her bare flesh, his hand wandering down her quivering stomach. His finger came into contact with her sensitive clit and she groaned, her pussy clenching at the sensation.

Her reactions fueled his lust. Axel pressed two digits against the swollen flesh, drawing rapid circles, as he maintained a punishing pace between her legs.

"Tell me, Miss Infection Control," he commanded, breath warm against the shell of her ear. "Do you like being fucked stupid by a werewolf?"

She didn't respond verbally but rather quaked harder beneath him. Her toes curled and she arched, a string of high pitched cries escaping her throat. Deepa's insides began to tighten and tingle in warning, signaling her imminent climax. She grinded desperately against his hand, whimpering loudly.

"You know what's fucking hot?" he snarled into her ear. "The thought that if we continue on like this, you're gonna be knocked up by spring."

He punctuated each word with a snap of his hips, grinding the tip of his cock against her sweet spot. He grunted and sucked in a shallow breath as she clamped harder, almost painfully snug against him. "Shit."

A vulgar wail came from between her lips as her climax ripped through her. Pleasure washed through every cell and her inner walls quivered around him.

Axel continued to stroke her clit, keeping his pace steady as she quaked through her orgasm.

Her release triggered his.

He tensed and snarled, spilling his cum, hot and heavy into her eager womb.

Deepa collapsed onto the ground, her chest rising and falling, her thighs coated in their shared fluids.

Axel rested his weight against her back, letting out a contented hum.

"You'll see," he murmured against her flushed skin. "We can create a good life out here."

Deepa was too fucked out to answer.

The snap of a tree branch drew her attention.

She looked up to see Ryan, standing naked before the cabin, gazing nonchalantly over their entwined bodies.

"Axel," he said calmly. "It's time to stop fucking around and get back to work."

CHAPTER II

Deepa nervously clasped her hands in her lap, glancing at Axel who was seated beside her. She was freshly washed and showered, wearing another of Nastya's short dresses, but all she could think of was what was awaiting her inside Ryan's office.

"Are you nervous?" she whispered to Axel.

Axel let out a grunt and crossed his muscular arms over his broad chest. "No. It's just the same old shit. *Pull yourself together Axel, just do your fucking job Axel. If you wanted to be leader then you should have put more effort in Axel.*"

"And me?"

Axel reached out, lacing his fingers through hers, his touch reassuring. "Just sit there and look pretty."

"Axel!" Ryan called out from inside the office.

Axel sighed and got to his feet, deliberately making his way inside as slowly as possible, shutting the door behind him.

Deepa silently waited, her leg bouncing with nervous energy, until Axel emerged moments later, his face grim and jaw clenched as he walked out the door and down the dimly lit hallway, without sparing her a second glance.

"Deepa!" Ryan called out.

Deepa nervously rose to her feet, smoothing her hands over the fabric of her dress. She entered Ryan's office, taking in the spartan decor. The room was bare, with only a sleek modern computer and an outdated fax machine resting on a large mahogany desk. The walls were adorned with a few framed paintings, but otherwise devoid of personal touches.

"Please, sit down." Ryan gestured towards the chair in front of his desk, his expression unreadable.

Deepa did so, her hands trembling. She didn't know why she was nervous. She'd allowed him between her legs plenty of times, but there was something about his cold stare that unnerved her, like she was speaking to a different person.

"So," he drawled, tapping a pen against the desk. "Enjoy your little holiday with Axel?"

"I wouldn't call it a holiday," Deepa muttered.

"Funny," Ryan hummed. "Seemed like the two of you were having a great time to me."

"That's only because I didn't have the medication.... the wolf made me do it."

Ryan arched a brow. "Made you?"

Deepa nodded, her hands clenching.

Ryan curiously raised an eyebrow. "Is that what you think, or are you just using it as an excuse?"

Deepa bit her lower lip, looking away. "I need more."

"More what?"

"Of the pills, I can't control it without them."

Ryan let out a sigh. "Infection Control has done their best to eliminate all suppliers, so they don't come cheap, but perhaps we can work out some kind of deal."

"Deal?"

"If you work for me, then perhaps I can get you some in return."

Deepa's eyes narrowed. "What kind of work?"

"Oh, just the same thing that you used to do, but just in reverse."

Deepa bit her lip as the meaning of those words slowly sank in. "You want me to kill people?"

"You can leave all the biting and killing to the others if it disgusts you so much. I just need you to shoot anything that gets in our way."

"How is that any better?"

"I suppose it's not, is it?" Ryan chuckled. "But we all need to make sacrifices to get what we want. Make yourself useful, and I'll get you enough pills to last you a lifetime. Then you'll never have to see Axel's stupid face again."

"And if I refuse?"

"Then you can spend the rest of your life as Axel's little cum dumpster. I do hope you like children Deepa, because that birth control of yours won't last forever, and I doubt that Axel will give you much rest between births."

Deepa glared at him, her nails digging into the leather of the chair.

"So," Ryan continued. "What do you say, Deepa? Want to go back to human life, or be that arsehole's baby machine?"

Deepa's teeth dug into her lower lip. She wanted control over her werewolf urges, but the idea of turning her gun on innocent humans made her feel sick.

"I have conditions," said Deepa, her voice firm despite the nervous fluttering in her stomach. "I won't attack innocent civilians, and I need you to promise that you won't kill one particular Infection Control officer."

Ryan leaned back in his chair, studying her carefully. "Your ex-boyfriend?"

Deepa nodded.

"You still love him?" There was an undercurrent of amusement in Ryan's tone.

Deepa bit her lip. Her love for Parker felt different than when she was with Axel. More familiar and safe, like a close friend or brother.

"Parker and I only had each other for so long," said Deepa. "We promised to keep each other safe, no matter what."

Ryan gave her a pitying look. "Do you really think he'll keep that promise if he knows that you're fucking a werewolf?"

Deepa flinched as if struck, her carefully maintained composure cracking. She took a steadying breath, stamping down the flare of hurt and anger. "It doesn't matter. Just promise not to kill him, and I'll work the rest out later."

"Fine," Ryan said with a casual shrug. "I'll try and keep him alive, but that could change at any time if you don't uphold your end of the bargain."

"Understood."

A sly smile curved Ryan's lips, sending a shiver down Deepa's spine. "Why so grim, Deepa? I thought the two of us were friends."

She scoffed, pulling herself to her feet with as much dignity as she could muster. "We're not friends. We're just two people who use each other to get what we want." Unlike Parker, there was no warmth or sincerity behind Ryan's smooth façade, only cold calculation and lies.

"And how do you know what I want, Deepa?" Ryan stood to his feet and moved towards her. "Perhaps I want you bent over this desk every morning until you're too pregnant to walk."

"Is that how you get it up?" Deepa scoffed. "By imagining all your partners knocked up?"

Ryan didn't even blink. "And what's wrong with that?"

"It's fucked up."

"Is it? You seemed to like it when I came inside you as you begged for a baby."

"That was different," Deepa spat. That was before she learned that Parker was alive. She didn't need Ryan to fill that void in her heart any longer.

"Is that because you'd rather have Axel fuck you now instead?"

Deepa glared at him, searching for a biting reply.

"You don't have to answer," Ryan laughed. "I can tell from your face that it's true."

Deepa's cheeks went red, her chest hot. She didn't know why Ryan's words affected her so much. She'd made no promises to Axel. They had no future. She'd be gone once she got more medication.

Ryan leaned closer, his lips pressed against her ear.

"Tell me the truth, Deepa. Do you get wet just thinking about him?"

She couldn't answer, the words caught in her throat.

"You can tell me." His fingers traced the line of her jaw. "It's better if he thinks that you actually love him, it'll make the pain so much greater when you leave."

"Fuck you," Deepa whispered.

Ryan chuckled, his breath hot against her skin. "You can fuck me anytime. My door is always open."

"You're a fucking creep."

"I am," he purred. "But you seem to like that."

Deepa jerked away as though burned. Her hands clenched into fists, reading to strike.

Ryan smirked, returning to his chair with casual nonchalance. "Go on, hit me. See what happens."

Deepa stared at him, nostrils flaring as she wrestled with the urge to wipe that smug look off his face.

"Hit me," Ryan insisted, leaning back in his chair. "Might as well get some practice in before killing your old coworkers."

Deepa's jaw clenched. She knew that she should leave, but there was one last burning question that she needed to ask. "Why... why do you hate Axel so much?"

Ryan let out a pained sigh. "Axel was always the golden child, the heir apparent. But he was arrogant, lazy. The elders thought pitting me against him as a rival would motivate him."

"Did it?"

Ryan shrugged. "In a way... he couldn't stand being upstaged by his half bred younger brother. Especially after our father abandoned the pack for my mother."

"So that's why you hate him?"

Ryan shook his head. "There was a duel between us, to see who would become the next leader of the pack. I thought that if I won it would break him, but once it was over..." Ryan broke off with a frustrated growl.

"What happened?"

"When he pulled himself off the ground, there was no anger or disappointment." Ryan's lip curled in a sneer. "Just fucking relief, and I soon realized why."

Deepa raised an eyebrow.

"He lost the duel on purpose," Ryan snarled. "So that he could pass off all his responsibilities onto me."

"But why would he do that?"

"Because he's a lazy arsehole, that's why. And he'd rather leave me to deal with all the elder's shit than handle it himself."

Deepa didn't know what to say, her heart twisting in her chest, resisting the urge to sympathize with Ryan.

"So you better be prepared on those missions with Axel," Ryan's voice was low and dangerous. "Because I won't be rushing in to save him."

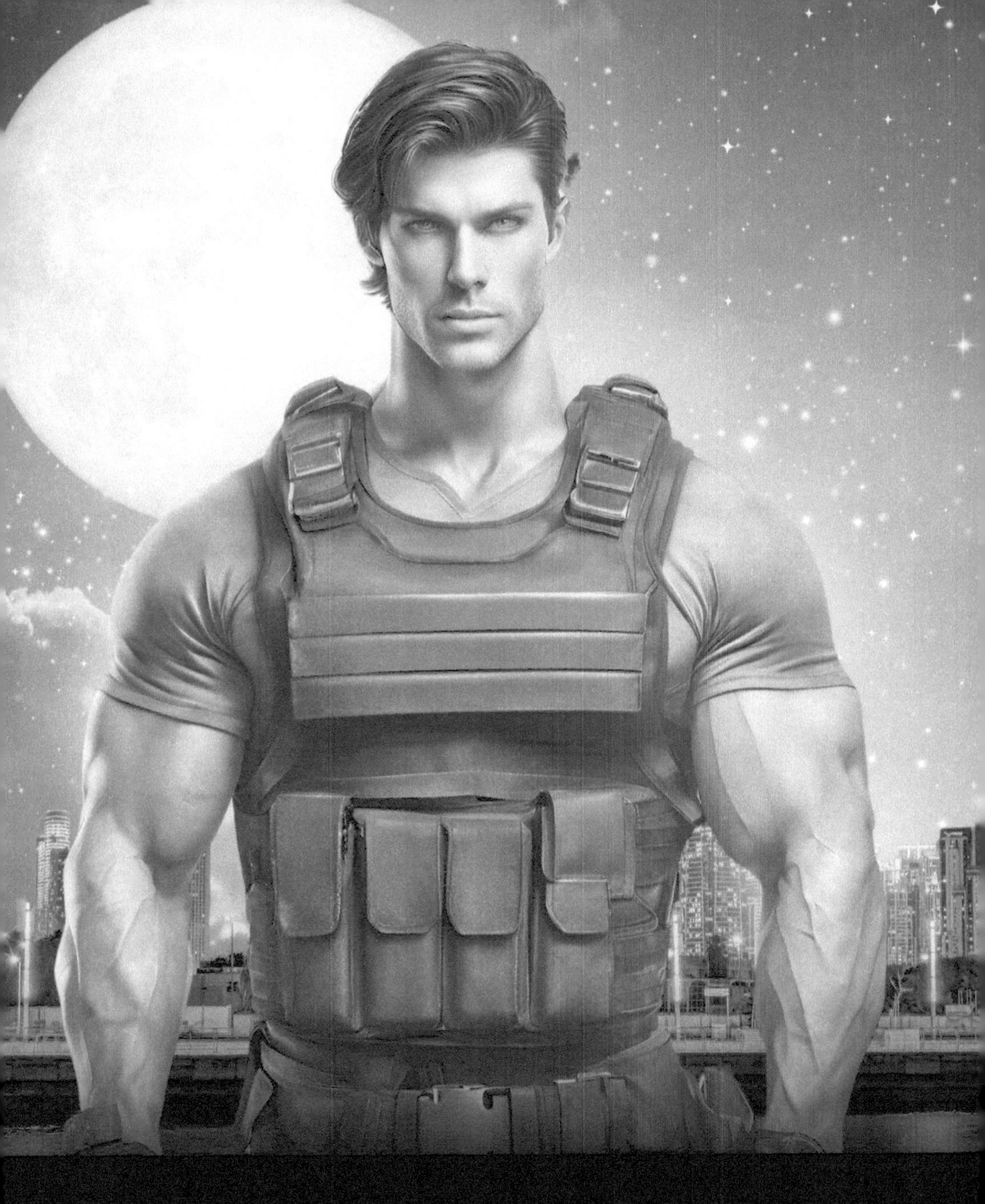

PART 4

CHAPTER 1

"But you promised!" Parker cried, stomping his foot on the ground.

His mother knelt down, placing a gentle hand on his shoulder. "I know, sweetie. I'm so sorry, but I'm not feeling very well today. How about we go next Saturday instead?"

Parker's face crumpled. "That's what you said last week. And the week before that!"

Parker's mother sighed and looked at his father who gave a small shake of his head.

"Darling, why don't you go play outside for a bit and let me and Daddy have a chat."

"No! I don't want to. I want to go see the movie like you promised."

"Please.." Her voice held a warning edge.

Parker huffed. He knew better than to argue with his mother when she used that tone.

He trudged towards the front door, slamming it behind him harder than necessary. Tears of frustration stung at his eyes. It wasn't fair. His mother was always making promises that she didn't follow through on, and his father did nothing to back him up.

Parker stomped across the porch, the worn wooden boards creaking beneath his feet. The garden was overgrown and the grass came up to his knees. His parents had stopped taking care of it ever since his mother started feeling ill.

The curtains were pulled shut, but he could hear his parents talking inside.

"You shouldn't go out," his father said sternly.

"I'm fine," Parker's mother insisted.

"No, you're not."

"It feels better today. I'll be okay as long as you come too."

"I don't think that's a good idea."

"Please. I have been promising him for months."

There was silence as his father mulled it over. "Fine," he finally muttered.

"Thank you."

"But you have to promise me that if it gets worse, we'll come straight home."

"Of course."

Parker triumphantly pumped his fist in the air.

His father poked his head outside, blue eyes narrowed. "What are you doing?"

"Nothing," Parker said innocently, shoving his hands back in his pockets.

"Then get inside. We're leaving soon."

The movie was as great as Parker expected, a barrage of special effects and intense action scenes flashed across the huge screen. He barely blinked as each epic moment played out.

Parker's father sat beside him, munching on popcorn as he stroked Parker's mother's dark hair. She'd fallen asleep a few minutes after the movie began. Her head rested against his shoulder.

"Mom, you're missing all the good parts!" Parker whispered loudly, giving her arm a shove.

"Shhh, let her rest," his dad scolded, pulling her closer.

"But the movie..."

"Just let her rest," Parker's father snapped.

Parker huffed and turned his attention back to the screen, trying to block out the sounds of his mother's raspy breathing.

But just as the action reached a fever pitch, a blood curdling scream sliced through the theater like a knife, causing Parker's heart to freeze in his chest.

"Get down now!" his father shouted.

He seized Parker by the shoulders of his sweater and shoved him down forcefully, until the boy's face smashed against the sticky theater floor.

All hell broke loose in an instant. Terrified screams erupted from every direction as people frantically stampeded over each other, desperately scrambling for the exits.

The stench of fresh blood filled the air.

Parker struggled to control his terrified breathing as he flattened himself against the floor, trying his best to hide under the row of seats.

A woman seated one row in front, convulsed unnaturally, her body contorting as coarse black fur erupted from her skin. Sickening cracks of snapping bones preceded her transformation into a snarling beast.

It wasn't real.

It couldn't be.

"D-Dad?" Parker whimpered, frantically scanning for his parents in the carnage.

But they were nowhere.

More horrifying howls filled the air, followed by the sickening sounds of human flesh and muscle being shredded by feral jaws and razor-sharp claws.

"Mommy?" Parker whimpered, but there was no reply. "Dad?"

He curled up into a ball and covered his ears. The screaming continued, his whole body shaking as his world came tumbling down around him.

After what felt like an eternity, an Infection Control team burst through the doors. Their hazmat suits shimmered under the emergency lights as they quickly fanned out, rifles raised.

They showed no mercy, unleashing a torrent of gunfire. Crimson sprays erupted from the chests of each snarling wolf as bullets tore through their bodies.

Parker remained frozen under the seat, quivering violently as he watched the gruesome scene unfold before his eyes. Mutilated corpses and piles of tattered flesh surrounded him.

"You okay, kid?" A gentle voice finally reached his ringing ears.

A firm hand wrapped around his arm, coaxing him out from his hiding spot.

Parker looked up to meet the concerned gaze of a younger Craig, his features obscured behind a protective mask.

"I...I..." Parker's lips trembled, unable to form any words.

"It's over now," Craig said in a low reassuring tone. He placed his hands on Parker's shoulders. "You're safe."

"M-My dad...Mom..." Parker whimpered through uncontrollable sobs, frantically scanning the grotesque scene.

The room was littered with the bodies of people and wolves, their blood seeping out into the carpet and seats. The movie credits rolled across the screen.

"C'mon, let's get you out of here," Craig said.

He guided Parker through the debris, careful to shield him from the worst of the carnage. "There's a team waiting outside. They'll get you some-place safe, okay?"

"What about my mom and dad?" Parker mumbled.

"I'm not sure where they are right now," Craig replied hesitantly.

"Can't I just wait here for them?"

Craig sighed heavily. "Sorry kiddo, but the whole building is on com-plete lockdown after an incident like this."

Craig ushered Parker out into the harsh daylight. Several ambulances were parked outside, paramedics tending to a dozen other dazed and shocked moviegoers who had escaped.

"You see your parents over there?" Craig asked, scanning the small crowd.

Parker slowly shook his head, eyes searching each bloody frightened face.

Craig exhaled deeply, lowering himself to Parker's eye level. "Look...there's no easy way to tell you this, but..." He paused, carefully weighing his next words. "Your mom and dad were attacked and turned into werewolves back in that theater."

It felt like all the air had been sucked from his lungs, his stomach bottoming out.

This couldn't be real.

"Once someone gets infected with this disease, there's nothing more we can do," Craig continued solemnly. "It takes over their minds completely. They're not...people anymore. Just rabid animals focused on one thing, biting and spreading the infection."

Parker's throat tightened until he could barely breathe. Tears welled up in his eyes as the weight of Craig's words hit him all at once.

"Is there any other family we can call for you?" Craig asked cautiously after a moment.

Parker couldn't hear him through the rushing in his ears, mind racing.

If only he hadn't begged his mom to take them to this stupid movie...

"Hey, kiddo? You okay?" Craig's voice finally reached him.

"They're gone..." Parker whispered, hot tears streaming down his cheeks as his hands clenched into tight fists.

"I'm so sorry." Craig lowered his head.

"No, it's your fault!" Parker shouted through gritted teeth. "You could have saved them!"

Craig's eyes widened, raising his hands. "We did everything we co-"

"You murdered them!" Parker's whole body shook with rage.

"When people turn, they become monsters. It's just like a rabies outbreak. Putting them down quickly is the only way to stop the disease from spreading out of control. They're not-"

Parker turned on his heel and dashed away, feet pounding against the pavement as he disappeared down the street. He stopped to catch his breath in an alley, slumping against the wall.

Infection Control was wrong, they had to be. There was no way his mother and father were just...gone like that. They'd be found soon, Parker was sure of it. Then they could all just go back home together like nothing had happened.

A dull throbbing pain radiated up from Parker's right ankle.

He reached down and lifted the cuff of his jeans, revealing a large oozing bite mark.

Parker should have known from that moment that he was immune, but his mind was too broken from his parents' deaths to connect the dots.

He told himself that the wolf wasn't turned enough to infect him, or perhaps it didn't bite hard enough.

He was too consumed by his new hatred for werewolf kind to think much about himself. Craig was right, Infection Control did the right thing and all werewolves needed to die.

"Looking good," Sadie said with an approving nod as she gently turned Parker's face from side to side, examining the faded marks. "Those wounds have healed up nicely."

"Still can't believe that you let a bunch of wolves get the jump on you," Varn laughed from his seat in the corner.

"Shut up," Parker muttered.

Varn had been giving him shit about the attack ever since Parker woke up in the Infection Control infirmary, the image of Deepa and the blond werewolf beating the shit out of him fully burned into his mind.

What was Deepa thinking? Why had she aligned herself with that monster? Was he holding her captive?

The lab around them was a flurry of constant motion and noise. Scientists in white coats rushed back and forth, carefully transporting vials and test tubes filled with various samples. They had been working around the clock, pushing themselves to the brink of exhaustion to create a vaccine that could finally halt the spread of the werewolf virus.

"Well, looks like you're back in fighting shape," Craig said as he strode into the room, eyeing Parker up and down. "Ready to get back in the field?"

"Yes sir." Parker saluted. "I can't wait to get back out there."

To try and find Deepa, Parker didn't dare say out loud.

"How are the samples going?" Craig asked Sadie.

"Just about to draw some fresh ones now, actually." She signaled to a nurse who immediately retrieved a large syringe from a tray and moved over to Parker.

Parker sucked in a sharp breath and averted his gaze, as the nurse swabbed his arm and slid the needle into his vein to draw several vials of his blood.

"Do you really think this could help?" he asked.

"If we can isolate what makes you immune," said Sadie. "Then hopefully we can use it to manufacture a vaccine."

"How many other immunes have you found?"

Sadie exchanged a glance with Craig.

"Well, you're the first," she admitted.

"The first?" Parker gawked. "And you've been working on this for how many years?"

"It's...complicated," the nurse said with an apologetic shrug. "We can't identify who is immune and who isn't, until each subject is directly exposed to the virus strains."

"Yeah, and that last vaccine trial was a total shitshow," Varn interjected with a chuckle, pushing himself up from his chair. "Turned all the test volunteers into werewolves."

Parker shuddered. "That sounds horrifying."

"We've made significant strides since then, I assure you," Craig stated firmly, shooting Varn a warning glance. "And your blood could be the breakthrough that we need."

Parker nodded. He'd do anything if it meant wiping all werewolves out for good.

CHAPTER 2

Just do your fucking job, echoed Ryan's words in Axel's head. *And I'll let you go live happy families with your girlfriend once everything's over.*

Axel kept his eyes on Deepa as the van moved through the dark city streets. She'd barely taken her gaze off the gun in her hands.

"She better not choke," said Bruno from the driver's seat. "I don't wanna get turned into cheese just because your girlfriend doesn't have the balls to shoot her friends."

Axel ground his teeth. "If you idiots don't waste time screwing around, we'll be in and out before anyone shows up."

It was stupid of his brother to force Deepa to go on missions. What if her precious Parker showed up to save the day? Axel didn't want to spend the rest of his life listening to her moan about how he slit the stupid human's throat.

"We should have left her behind," Bruno muttered.

"Yeah, she's dead weight," Reese agreed. "Newbies always puke."

"Fuck off," Axel growled. "This wasn't my idea."

Only Luke seemed to share Deepa's unease, quietly looking out the window while tapping his fingers on his knees.

"Who are we fucking up this time?" Bruno's lacky Sammy asked, anxiously bouncing his knee.

"Some mayor or shit," Bruno said. "The elders want him out of the way."

"I didn't realize that wolves are big into politics," said Deepa.

"They're not," said Luke. "They just like to take out anyone who gets in their way."

"Lot easier to take over if only idiots are in power," Reese nodded.

Deepa shuddered.

This was a fucking bad idea, Axel thought to himself.

The van pulled into a dark side street, parking beside a tall fence.

"All out." Bruno turned off the engine. "And take all your shit because I'm going to torch this once we're done."

"You all know the plan," said Axel. "Let's make this quick."

"Not gonna draw it out today, Axel?" Bruno drawled. "Don't want your girlfriend to see you rip any organs out?"

"Shut the fuck up and just do the job," Axel snarled.

Bruno had been a pain ever since Axel returned, obviously bitter that he'd tried to ditch them all and disappear into the wilderness for a girl.

Bruno snickered as he got out of the car, slamming the door shut behind him.

Axel helped Deepa out of the van. "You okay?" he asked softly.

"Yeah," Deepa nodded, her hands clammy in his grasp.

"Don't worry. Just stay back with Luke. I'll take care of everything."

"Right," she nodded, her expression grim.

"Axel!" Bruno shouted.

"Coming," Axel growled, scaling the fence after his cousins.

Axel jumped down onto the lawn, silently moving into shadows to survey the estate. The house was a modern mansion with several cameras surrounding the grounds, but there was only one security guard making his rounds.

It wasn't anything that they couldn't handle.

Axel stripped his clothes and tossed them over the fence, shifting into his wolf form. His muscles tensed and contorted, realigning with pops and cracks. White fur sprouted across his body as his mouth morphed into a muzzle.

The guard gasped, his whole body frozen as he saw Axel approach, his mouth hanging open in horror until he pulled himself together and reached for his gun.

Axel leaped forward, knocking him to the ground and tearing out his throat.

Blood splattered onto his muzzle, his claws sinking into flesh.

It was easy to forget how nice it was to just tear shit up, to allow the monster inside him to roam free.

His cousins dashed past him towards the house, entering through an open window on the second floor. The sounds of screams spilled outside as Axel followed behind.

He jumped through the window and landed in what appeared to be a teenager's room. A fifteen year old girl vomited onto the floor as her body began to shift and change, gray fur sprouting from her skin as she let out a deep howl.

Axel found her brother in the hallway, his blood spilling onto the carpet, his neck torn open, his eyes lifeless.

Axel shifted back to his human form. "Where's the mayor!" he shouted.

"Found him!" called Reese from down the hall.

Axel walked into the master bedroom to find Bruno and Sammy tearing two people apart, their limbs strewn across the room, the walls and sheets covered in blood.

"Is that him?" Axel asked.

"I suppose," Reese shrugged. "Didn't get a good look at his face before Bruno ripped it off."

Axel swore under his breath.

There was a small whimper from behind him. He turned to see Deepa in the doorway, her face drained of color, her hands shaking violently.

"Shit," Axel hissed. He didn't want her to see this.

Deepa staggered backwards, dropping the gun to the floor as her hands covered her mouth.

"Deepa," Axel said softly as he moved towards her.

"Get away from me!" she hissed, her whole body shaking.

"It's okay," he murmured.

"No, it's not. Nothing about this is okay. I...I can't..." She turned and dashed down the hall.

"See," Bruno muttered as he returned to his human form. "Told you that she can't take it."

CHAPTER 3

Deepa's feet pounded against the pavement as she tried to put as much distance between herself and Axel as possible. She could hardly believe that she'd begun to care about that monster, thinking that he was nothing more than a deluded idiot, until she was reminded of what he was capable of.

Axel ripped the security guard's throat out with ease, then walked straight into a gruesome murder scene like it was nothing new.

He didn't even look the slightest bit remorseful.

Deepa's stomach churned, her breath came out in short gasps as she fought the urge to throw up.

How could she be so stupid, letting his words and gentle caresses trick her into thinking that he was more than just a mindless beast.

The echo of footsteps behind her made Deepa's heart lurch.

"Go away Axel!" Deepa cried, but she spun around to find Luke instead.

"Hey," Luke said gently.

"What do you want?" Deepa snapped.

Luke held out her gun. "You dropped this."

Deepa eyed the weapon warily. "Keep it. I don't want it anymore."

Luke gazed at her, his eyes sympathetic as he slipped the gun into his back pocket.

"How can you stand it?" Deepa asked.

"Stand what?"

"Seeing the things they do. The killing."

Luke's jaw tightened, and he looked away. "I don't like it, but I don't have a choice. Not anymore."

"Everyone has a choice!" Deepa insisted.

Luke shook his head slowly. "Not when you're a werewolf. It's nearly impossible to go against the pack."

"Why?"

"We're not like humans. The pack is our entire world, our family, our purpose. We don't have lives outside of it."

Revulsion twisted Deepa's features. "So you just murder whoever Ryan tells you to?"

A haunted look flickered across Luke's face. "Only when there's no other way to survive," he said heavily. "Sometimes, the only choice is to kill or be killed, whether you want to or not."

Deepa frowned.

"We weren't always like this. We weren't supposed to do anything till the end, but then Axel lost favor with the elders and we were all assigned to this grunt work."

"Lost favor?"

"Axel became too arrogant, too sure of himself. When Ryan challenged him for future leadership of the pack, Axel accepted, but he lost."

"I know about that. Ryan told me."

Luke nodded. "Except that the elders never liked Ryan because his mother was human. They delegate the most gruesome jobs to him, which he then passes onto us."

"So? That doesn't mean that you have to do it."

"You don't understand, Deepa. You're human. We're werewolves. When our leader gives an order, we must obey. I was told to blend in as a regular person. I had a normal job and boyfriend, but when Ryan called me back, I couldn't refuse."

"There's always a choice," Deepa mumbled stubbornly.

"It's like with you and Axel. You must have noticed by now how overwhelming the urges are, how hard they are to resist."

Deepa flinched at the comparison. "I'm never going back to him."

"Okay," Luke said softly, but his tone made it clear he didn't believe her.

"I mean it," Deepa insisted, jaw clenched. "I can't just pretend I didn't see what he did."

"But you don't have a choice. You know that by now."

Deepa's fingers curled into fists as she shook her head.

No, there was no way she could face Axel again, not after witnessing that security guard's brutal death. The thought of Axel touching her made her stomach churn.

"You'll get used to it over time," Luke said gently. "We all do."

"No, I won't," Deepa said firmly. "I can't."

Luke looked at her with pity in his eyes. "Just don't stay out too late." He turned and walked away. "Axel will worry."

Deepa's heart pounded as her hands clenched tighter. She wouldn't become like them, no matter what Ryan ordered. There had to be a way out.

Deepa circled familiar places, trying to kill time before the wolf in her brain went running back to Axel.

She passed the foster home where she met Parker, remembering how he always acted like an older brother, even though he was younger than her.

She passed the diner where they used to sneak off to at night, talking about their dreams and how they'd both join Infection Control.

Her fingers trembled as she remembered their first kiss, all awkward and nervous because it was the first time for them both.

He promised to never leave her, because Deepa couldn't stomach the idea of losing her family again.

It wasn't fair. Why had things changed so much?

She wanted her old life back. She wanted the Parker who wasn't obsessed with killing werewolves. She wanted her innocent self who didn't know the feeling of Axel's body against her own.

A familiar scent wafted towards her. Her stomach twisted into knots.

"Parker," Deepa murmured.

He had been there recently and his smell remained, a mixture of sweat and his shampoo.

It was an easy trail for her to follow.

Her legs carried her forward, her mind focused on the need to see him again, to know that he was okay.

Deepa walked until she arrived at an old apartment building. She climbed the stairs to the second floor, examining each door until she found one saturated with Parker's scent.

Deepa nervously knocked.

There was a sound of movement from inside, then the door slowly creaked open to reveal Parker, dressed in a worn t-shirt and sweatpants, his hair still wet from a shower.

"Deepa?" Parker's eyes widened in surprise as he took her in.

"Hey," she whispered, her voice trembling.

In an instant, Parker's arms were around her, pulling her into a tight embrace. "Are you okay?" he murmured against her hair.

"No." The single word came out choked as she buried her face into his shirt, fingers clutching the fabric desperately.

"It's alright, I'm here now," Parker soothed, one hand stroking her hair.

But Deepa could only shake her head, sobs wracking her body. "I'm so sorry, Parker."

"Shh, it's okay."

"I'm so sorry."

"You don't have to apologize."

"Yes I do," she cried. "I shouldn't have let him hurt you."

"It wasn't your fault."

"Yes it was. It was all my fault."

Parker sighed, gently pushing her away. "Look, it's late. Please come inside."

Deepa wiped her eyes and stepped through the doorway into Parker's apartment. It was small, consisting of a narrow kitchen area, a table with a single chair, and a bed tucked against the wall. But what struck her were the little mementos from their life together, scattered around the space. The shirt she had given him for his birthday, the framed photo from their high school graduation day, the stuffed bear he had won for her at an arcade years ago.

It all felt like a lifetime ago.

"I'm sorry that it's so small." Parker closed the door behind her. "Infection Control was constantly monitoring me to check that I was really immune, so I thought it was best to move in case you tried to come home. I put most of your things into storage. We can go together if you need anything."

Deepa sat on the edge of the bed, watching as Parker moved to the small refrigerator.

"Want something to drink?" he asked over his shoulder.

"Sure."

"I only have orange juice. Is that okay?"

She nodded. "That's fine."

Parker poured two glasses and brought them over, settling beside her on the bed. "How did you find me here?"

Deepa stared down at her hands, clutching the glass tightly. "Your scent," she admitted in a small voice. "I followed it."

Parker was silent for a beat. "Oh. So you can...do that now?"

Deepa slowly nodded.

"Any other things that you can do now?"

"Just turn into a wolf," Deepa murmured.

Silence fell between them, the only sound being the buzz of the fridge.

"Did he hurt you?" Parker finally asked.

"Who?"

"That guy who bit you?"

Deepa chewed her lip, finding it impossible to think of a way to explain her relationship with Axel that wouldn't enrage Parker.

"It's okay." Parker took hold of her hand. "You don't have to talk about it until you're ready. I just want you to know that I'm here for you, no matter what."

Tears pricked Deepa's eyes. How could Parker be so kind to her after everything that happened?

"Is it still true what you said?" she asked. "About running away together?"

Parker's gaze met hers. "Of course," he said firmly. "I can find somewhere for you to hide, but there are things that I need to do here first."

"Things? What sort of things?"

"They're working on a vaccine. They think that my blood might help, so they need me to provide samples."

"Samples?"

"Just blood, so far."

Deepa's hands trembled. On one hand it would be fantastic if no one else had to suffer the way that she had, but there was no telling what would happen to Parker if the werewolves found out. The scene from the mayor's bedroom flashed through her mind.

They'd tear Parker to pieces if they found out that his body could ruin their plans.

"Once we finish a vaccine." Parker smiled. "We can finally stop this fucking infection for good."

"Yeah," Deepa whispered, her stomach twisting into a knot. "Sounds great."

Parker frowned, his expression sympathetic. "Hey, I'm sorry. I know you're probably scared. You can stay here with me until things settle down."

"What?"

"We can keep the curtains closed and lock the door. Infection Control stopped coming by weeks ago, so you should be good until I can find somewhere better."

Deepa wanted to lock herself away with Parker and pretend that the past few hours never happened, but it was only a matter of time before her wolf took over. She didn't know if she could stop it from clawing Parker's face off.

"I can't," Deepa muttered. "It's not safe for you."

"What do you mean?"

"I..I..can't control it." Deepa's voice cracked. "If I stay in here... I'll only hurt you."

"I won't let you," Parker said firmly.

Deepa shook her head. "You don't understand. It's too strong. It's like this wild animal that lives in my head. Without medication I can't stop it from taking over and doing whatever it wants."

"Medication?" Parker's eyes widened as the understanding dawned on him. "But Infection Control destroyed all the suppliers."

"I found someone who can give it to me. But he wants some things in return. After that, I can be with you."

"Is that the guy who bit you?"

Deepa shook her head. "No, somebody else."

Parker's eyes narrowed. "What sort of things does he want you to do, Deepa?"

Deepa's heart raced in her chest. "If I told you you'd only hate me."

"I'd never hate you, Deepa. Tell me what's going on. What do you have to do for this guy?"

Deepa shook her head. "Please don't ask."

"What are you doing, Deepa? Are you sleeping with him?"

"No," she whispered, her gaze drifting to the floor, but it wasn't enough to fool Parker.

"Fuck." Parker ran a hand through his hair. "Deepa...I.."

Deepa didn't want to stay to see his reaction, to hear his inevitable pity.

"I'm sorry." Deepa scrambled to her feet and raced towards the door.

"Deepa, wait!" Parker cried, reaching out to grab her arm, but Deepa wrenched herself free and bolted for the door.

She flung it open and raced into the hallway, not daring to look back, ignoring the cries of Parker from behind her.

Deepa ran until her lungs burned.

She needed to put as much distance between Parker as possible.

She needed to run away from herself.

Her hands morphed into claws, fur sprouting along her body as her bones shifted and cracked into place.

Her mind went numb, allowing the wolf to fully take over.

CHAPTER 4

"Staying up for your little girlfriend?" Nastya smiled, leaning up against the dark window.

"Don't you have some cunt to lick?" Axel growled, eyes firmly fixed on the world outside the mansion.

Nastya didn't even flinch. "Such the doting boyfriend you've become, you must love her so very much."

Axel's jaw clenched. He didn't have the patience for Nastya's games. It was a mistake to allow Luke to go after Deepa. He should have dragged her back himself.

"You're so lucky that she's bound to you," Nastya continued. "No other woman would have endured you for this long."

Axel's hands balled into fists, his nails digging into his palms.

"What will you do if she finds another way to leave you?" Nastya taunted. "Better get reacquainted with your hand."

"Just go suck a dick!" Axel snapped.

Nastya looked taken aback for a moment, but quickly recovered her composure. "Gladly." She smiled and turned on her heel, hips swaying as she strutted down the hallway.

Axel watched her go, hating her yet disturbed by how much her words preyed on his own insecurities. He knew he didn't deserve Deepa, not after all the hurt he'd caused her. Every attempt to make amends only made things worse.

A blur of movement outside caught his attention.

Axel's eyes darted towards the fence, searching for the source.

The wolf within him began to stir, his senses heightened and body tense.

He pushed open the front door and stepped out into the cold night air. "Deepa?"

She emerged from the shadows, completely bare with dirt caked under her nails and matting her hair. Streaks of blood, likely from her latest kill, were smeared across her face.

The vacant look in her eyes told him that it was the wolf in control.

"Hey," he said softly, taking hold of her hand.

She lunged forward, wrapping her arms around his body, resting her face against his neck.

Axel hugged her back, feeling her body press against his, the heat radiating off her.

"Come on," Axel whispered, struggling to let go. "Let's go inside."

Axel stripped off his clothes and guided Deepa into the shower, gently lathering shampoo through her hair. She leaned into his touch, a stark contrast to how she had reacted to him just hours before.

Her hands roamed over his bare arms and chest as she gazed up at him with smoldering desire. Leaning in, she flicked her tongue against his nipple, sending a jolt through his body.

Axel's pulse quickened as he sensed her arousal, feeling himself stir in response. His hands drifted down to cup her breasts, thumbs circling her hardened peaks.

Deepa's fingers threaded through his hair, pulling him into a searing kiss, her tongue stroking against his.

He pulled her flush against him, his growing erection pressing between them as his hands kneaded the soft curves of her ass.

Backing her against the shower wall, his mouth trailed down the column of her throat, her mewls of pleasure only stoking his want.

The warm spray cascaded over their entangled bodies.

Deepa let out a low, needy growl against Axel's ear, her lips brushing the sensitive skin as her teeth grazed his earlobe teasingly.

His hands roamed down her sleek curves, caressing along her thighs before his fingers delicately traced the warm folds of her arousal, feeling how slick she had become for him.

Slowly, he slid one finger into her entrance, his thumb finding her aching bud to stroke in maddening circles. Deepa's grip on him tightened, soft whimpers escaping her lips as he gradually worked another digit inside.

Axel curled his fingers upwards, massaging the sensitive flesh while his thumb swirled faster against her throbbing clit.

Deepa's eyes fluttered shut, her trembling body threatening to buckle under the exquisite stimulation.

His mouth blazed a trail of kisses down the column of her throat, teeth scraping lightly against her flushed skin. His free hand palmed the generous swell of her breast, rolling and tugging at her peaked nipple.

Deepa's cries grew more urgent, her breathing ragged as the coiling tension built higher.

"Yes...just like that..." Axel rasped against the curve of her neck, determined to make her utterly undone before taking his own pleasure.

She whimpered, her nails digging into his shoulders.

He sucked and kissed her neck, his cock grinding against her thigh.

She bucked her hips, her back arching, her whole body shuddering as her climax washed over her.

Axel couldn't take it any longer.

He pressed his cock inside, basking in the sensation of her pussy hugging him tight.

"Fuck," Axel moaned, thrusting in and out, his hand grabbing onto her leg, hooking it over his hip.

She kissed him back, her hands moving up his chest, her fingernails leaving red lines across his skin.

Axel picked up the pace, his breathing labored, her scent overwhelming his senses.

He moved faster, harder, slamming his body into hers.

It felt too good, and Axel struggled to hold himself back.

"Fuck," he hissed. "Why are you so fucking hot."

She growled, biting his shoulder hard enough to draw blood.

"Ow," he muttered, but the pain only fueled his need.

Axel gripped her tighter, pounding into her, her body shaking with every thrust.

"Fuck," he hissed. "Fuck. Fuck. Fuck."

Axel's mind went blank, his orgasm ripping through him, his warm cum spurting inside her.

He kept going, riding the high, until he collapsed onto her shoulder.

The two of them slid down the shower wall, until they were sitting on the floor, a mess of tangled limbs and soap bubbles.

Axel held her close, stroking her hair, his heart still beating wildly in his chest. "I don't know if you're listening, but I want you to know that I had to do it. It's the only way that we can win against them."

Deepa snuggled closer.

Axel sighed, his hand running over her shoulder, his fingers grazing the bite mark that he inflicted on her. "Once we destroy humanity we'll finally be free."

CHAPTER 5

"Dude, how long is she gonna be like that?" Bruno said as he examined Deepa's vacant expression.

Deepa let out a growl, pressing herself closer to Axel, her fingers curling into the fabric of his shirt.

Axel wrapped his arm around her waist, keeping her close. "For as long as she wants to be."

"Do you seriously fuck her like this?"

Axel shot Bruno a look.

"What?" Bruno raised his hands. "I'm not judging. I might give screwing one of the turned ones a shot if they're all this quiet."

"It's awesome man," Reese grinned while texting on his phone. "This one chick who I met online was totally nuts, used to ride my dick till morning while howling like a dog. If she hadn't kept biting the neighbors, Infection Control would have never put her down. "

"Fuck," Bruno hissed. "Maybe I can find a hot one inside."

Thumping music spilled out from the club's doors. A long line snaked around the block, with people dressed in an array of fake fur coats, ripped jeans, and fluffy scarves.

"Are you sure this is the place?" Axel asked.

"Should be," Reese muttered while scrolling through his phone. "The chick I screwed last week told me that it would be here tonight."

The club didn't look any different from the others on the street, an unassuming black building with large tinted windows and neon signs, except for the two large werewolf bouncers who were guarding a side door. They reeked of forest and dead animals, leaning forward to sniff every person that tried to get through.

"This is it." Axel tugged Deepa forward.

The bouncers gave them a nod as they approached, pushing open the door to unveil a narrow set of dark stairs, the walls covered with neon graffiti.

Deepa growled and buried her face in Axel's shoulder.

"It's okay," he murmured, leading Deepa down the stairs beside him.

A second set of bouncers awaited them on the basement floor, inhaling deeply before pushing open a heavy set of iron doors.

Inside, the vast hall was filled with people and wolves, their bodies bathed in multi-colored lights. They shamelessly grinded against each other on the dance floor, kissing or openly fucking in plain view, flaunting their naked bodies without a care in the world.

A naked woman was on her hands and knees on a podium, being pounded from behind by a half transformed man. The werewolf let out a howl before biting into her shoulder, causing the crowd to let out a row of applause as her transformation began.

"What the fuck," Deepa hissed, watching in horror.

"And so she's back," Bruno drawled, slipping into the crowd. "I'm gonna go get laid."

"Peace out." Reese saluted, eyeing the stage where several human women had lined up to be transformed. "I'll see you guys tomorrow."

Deepa tugged her hand out of Axel's grasp, glancing at the guarded door.

"Hey," Axel said gently, grabbing hold of her elbow. "Don't be like that."

"Be like what?" Deepa glared.

"Just come with me for a bit," Axel said softly, dragging her into the crowd.

Deepa allowed him to lead her, telling herself that it was to learn more about the layout and how an Infection Control team could infiltrate the building, but she was quickly distracted by the writhing bodies.

The smell of sweat and sex mixed together, sending a thrill of arousal down her spine.

A naked man openly thrust into a curvy woman in time with the music, a second man had his lips wrapped around one of her exposed breasts. His large fingers played with her clit as the woman arched her back, a cry spilling from her lips.

What the fuck was this place?

Axel pulled Deepa against him, his hands sliding over her waist, his hips grinding against her ass.

"You're not gonna run away again, are you?" he asked.

"What do you think," Deepa said flatly, trying to keep her cool.

Axel leaned down and brushed her hair aside, kissing the bite mark that he left on her neck. "We're wolves now, and this is our world. If you want to survive you're going to have to get used to it."

Deepa clenched her fists, her breath coming out in short gasps, her pulse racing.

"Look at them," he murmured, glancing at the humans on the stage. "They all want to be here. They all want to join us. They know that our side is the right one."

"They just don't know any better," Deepa hissed.

"Oh, but they do," he insisted, hands traveling down her waist as he pressed against her from behind. "They're tired of being weak. Tired of humanity's constraints holding them back."

"Is that what they teach you in werewolf school? That everyone secretly wants to be a werewolf?"

"Among other things," Axel hummed, swaying in time to the music. "Like how it's impossible to create a new society without any casualties."

"Is that what you call killing people? Casualties?"

"Like humanity has treated us any better. You of all people should know that."

Deepa stiffened, the words stabbing into her. She'd personally shot and killed countless werewolves without a second thought. One hint of a transformation was enough for her to legally end their life.

"I didn't have a choice," she said. "It was my job."

"And this is mine," Axel growled, his grip on her waist tightening.

Deepa shook her head, the truth sinking into her stomach like a stone. "I'm not like you.....I didn't kill defenseless people..."

"Oh." Axel's breath brushed her ear. "Is that what you tell yourself?"

Deepa swallowed, her heart pounding.

"Tell me, Deepa," Axel whispered. "Were none of them defenseless?"

Deepa's stomach churned, memories flashing before her eyes. The teenage boy who she shot in the sewer. Captured people in cages that she watched die. Scott who was chained to the table as Craig put a bullet through his skull.

"They were all infected," Deepa muttered. "They had to die."

"Because your boss said that they were monsters?"

"Yes."

"Is that truly what you believe?" Axel asked. "Or just the lies Infection Control has fed you?"

"It's not a lie," Deepa said, her voice wavering.

"You know, you're quite skilled at pretending to still be human."

"I am human."

"If that's what you wish to believe," Axel murmured, lips grazing her ear. "But I think you stopped being human long before I turned you."

"Shut up," Deepa hissed, spinning around and shoving him away. She wasn't like him. She was only trying to help people by stopping the infection from spreading.

Axel laughed, a cruel and cold sound that echoed in her ears. "Perhaps there's a reason we became bound. Perhaps you're more like me than you realize." His blue eyes blazed. "Once you stop lying to yourself, you'll understand."

"Never," Deepa growled, baring her teeth as she pushed him again.

Axel stumbled back, but his expression remained amused.

Deepa spun on her heel, her gaze drifting across the room, searching for a way out. She spotted a bathroom sign near the back and hurried towards it, not daring to glance at Axel.

She locked herself in a grimy stall, slumping onto the toilet seat and burying her face in her hands.

How could she let him get under her skin so easily?

She should have expected him to say something like that. He had no concept of right and wrong, fully believing in whatever werewolf shit he'd been taught.

Deepa squeezed her eyes shut, forcing his hurtful words away.

She was human. She wasn't a monster like him. All she needed to do was put up with him until she got the medication. Then she could leave and be free.

The wolf in her mind clawed to the surface, obviously pissed that Deepa turned down an easy lay.

Deepa's first instinct was to fight it, to ignore the horny bitch until she ripped back control, but Deepa knew that she couldn't continue on like this forever.

If she wanted to gain some control back over her body, she needed to learn how to live with the wolf.

Even if it meant screwing Axel's brains out in a room full of strangers.

"Fine, bitch," Deepa muttered, pulling herself to her feet. "I'll give you what you fucking want."

Axel nervously eyed the bathroom, waiting for Deepa to return. Reese was already on the stage, eagerly stripping off his clothes and showing his dick to the crowd.

"Come on humans!" he yelled out. "Who wants a bite?"

The crowd cheered. A thin man with red hair and freckles crawled up onto the stage and presented his arm.

Reese smiled, grabbing the guy's wrist and pulling him close. He sank his fangs into the man's flesh as the human screamed in pain.

Bruno was trying to seduce a turned woman who was having none of it, swinging her glittery handbag at his head and growling like a feral dog.

Axel knew that he'd upset Deepa, but he only said what she needed to hear. He couldn't stop the attacks, even if he wanted to. It was the only way for their species to survive. It was impossible to go back to quietly living in the shadows after their existence was exposed.

Deepa emerged from the bathroom, a scowl on her face, furiously glaring in Axel's direction.

Axel's heart sped up, his stomach fluttering.

She was hot when she was angry.

Deepa marched towards him, her eyes blazing, her expression murderous.

Axel smirked, meeting her halfway, ready for a fight.

But Deepa didn't say a word, her hands grabbing his collar, roughly pushing him back into a nearby wall.

Her lips slammed into his, her tongue pushing past his teeth.

Axel's eyes widened, his mind going blank.

"Don't say anything," Deepa snarled against his lips.

Axel let out a strangled laugh, his cock stirring to life.

"And what's so funny," Deepa hissed.

"Just you," Axel hummed, grabbing her hips and pulling her flush against him.

He could feel her breasts through the fabric of her shirt, her hard nipples grazing his chest.

Deepa's nails dug into his shoulders, her teeth biting into his lip.

"I just told you not to talk," she hissed.

"Make me," Axel whispered, his lips moving down her throat.

Her eyes flashed, her hand drifting down his body, squeezing his cock through the fabric of his pants.

Axel moaned, his hips bucking, his grip tightening. "Fuck. You're really hot when you're mad."

Deepa's teeth grazed Axel's earlobe as her warm breath danced across his skin.

His hands roamed the toned planes of her stomach, feeling the muscles tense beneath his touch.

Her fingers dipped beneath his waistband, finding his rigid length and giving it a squeeze.

"Shit..." Axel hissed out a sharp breath.

Rather than reply, Deepa simply stroked him with increasing speed and pressure.

Axel groaned deeply, pressing his forehead to hers as his hips canted forward, chasing the delicious friction.

His fingers found the clasp of her bra, flicking it open and sliding the straps down her shoulders until the fabric fell away completely.

"Fuck..." he breathed, cupping the full weight of her breasts, thumbs brushing over the taut peaks.

Deepa let out a guttural moan of need, her grip tightening around his arousal.

Axel's hand drifted lower, fingertips trailing along the damp line of her panties, feeling the warmth and slickness that had seeped through the fabric.

Axel hooked his fingers in the fabric, tugging them down.

"Not here," Deepa gasped, eyeing the people around them.

Axel paused, letting out a slow exhale. He flipped their positions so that Deepa was against the wall with his body shielding her from any onlookers. "Better?"

"Yeah," she nodded, her cheeks flushed.

"Good," Axel purred, his palm gliding higher along Deepa's inner thigh until his fingers delved into her slick heat.

"Ah, fuck..." she whimpered, nails raking through his hair as he set a steady rhythm.

His lips blazed a path along the sensitive column of her throat, teeth grazing and tongue soothing in mesmerizing waves.

Deepa's breathing grew ragged, whimpering cries spilling freely from her lips as the pleasure mounted.

The heady scent of her arousal hung thick in the air, stirring Axel's own burning need. The pulsing rhythm of the music echoed through his body in time with his heartbeat.

Hastily, he unfastened his jeans, freeing his rigid length to glide through her slick folds.

"Oh god, yes..." she rasped, fingernails scoring his back as she arched shamelessly against him.

"You want this, don't you?" he taunted, the swollen head of his cock circling over her aching bud. "Tell me how badly you need it."

"I hate you," she forced out through gritted teeth, even as her body writhed wantonly.

"Do you now?" he purred, his tip tracing the outline of her pussy, feeling the heat radiating off her body.

"Fuck, I can't stand you," she moaned.

"Then why do you always come crawling back to me?"

"Fuck you," she spat.

Axel laughed.

Axel eased himself slowly into Deepa's entrance, savoring the velvet heat enveloping his rigid length inch by aching inch.

"Shit..." she whimpered, head thrown back and lips parted as he gradually hilted himself fully within her.

Rather than pounding away, Axel kept his strokes slow yet purposeful, determined to etch every heated second into her memory. This joining was about more than just carnal release, it staked his claim, branded her as his in a way she could never forget nor escape.

"Look at me," he rasped, fingers grasping her chin to tilt her face towards his piercing gaze.

Deepa's eyes fluttered open, dark pools of desire locked onto his.

"Say my name." His words were soft yet laced with undeniable command.

"Axel..." she gasped out, inner walls fluttering around his thick length.

"Again." He traced the plump curve of her lip with the tip of his tongue.

"Axel!" This time it was a breathless moan, torn from her very depths as he angled his hips for deeper penetration.

Only then did he allow his control to unravel. Hips snapping, he drove into her with harsh, claiming strokes, her cries echoing off the walls as her body surrendered utterly to his possession.

Axel couldn't help but admire her, the way her dark hair framed her face, her eyes glistening with lust, her cheeks flushed, her mouth open and gasping, her whole body trembling.

"Fuck," Deepa whimpered, her legs quivering. "Just a little more."

Axel leaned down and kissed her, his tongue pushing past her lips.

Her body tensed, her walls clenching around him.

Axel groaned, his hips thrusting forward.

Deepa's orgasm rippled through her, her nails digging into his shoulder, her whole body shaking.

Axel continued to thrust, riding the wave, his balls tightening, his orgasm building.

He moaned, his cum spurting inside her, filling her up until it dripped out from where their bodies were joined.

He slowly pulled out, his softening cock slipping from her as cum spilled down her thighs.

Deepa collapsed onto his chest, her breathing ragged.

"You okay?" Axel asked, brushing the sweat from her forehead.

"Yeah," she breathed, her eyes closing, her head resting against his shoulder.

"Want to go home?"

"Yeah," she murmured, her hand slipping into his.

"Alright." He smiled, holding her close as he led her back through the crowd and into the night.

CHAPTER 6

Deepa wove between bushes and trees, pushing her wolf body to the limits as she chased after rabbits and birds.

She was trying her best to co-exist with the wolf, discovering that if she let it out for walks at least once a day, it was more likely to leave her in peace.

It also made it easier to avoid Axel.

He still came to her at night, rutting into her dripping pussy while the wolf moaned in delight, but there was little talking. No more lectures about right or wrong, no more shitty excuses to justify his actions. Every time he tried to initiate a conversation, she'd silence him by slanting her mouth against his.

She didn't need any more reminders of her past actions.

Deepa slowly shifted back to her human form, reaching for her clothes that lay discarded on a log.

"You're getting good at that," said a gentle female voice.

Nastya stood with her arms crossed over her chest, her pink lips curled up into a smile. She was wearing another barely there summer dress that went down to mid thigh.

"Thanks," Deepa replied, pulling a shirt over her head. "Can I help you with something?"

Axel's sister had always been kind towards her, but she couldn't shake Axel's warning from her mind. He still insisted that Nastya was a self-centered bitch with morbid kinks.

"Ryan would like a word." Nastya gestured towards the house. "He sent me to fetch you."

Deepa internally swore. She wasn't keen to watch another fucked up murder spree.

"Don't look so worried," Nastya chuckled. "We're only going over some plans. You'll be back to pissing on trees in less than an hour."

Deepa pulled on her shorts. "Lead the way."

Nastya smirked, spinning on her heel to strut back towards the house. "So...what's it actually like being intimate with Axel?" she called over her shoulder.

Deepa sputtered. "Excuse me?"

"Oh come now, it can't be that thrilling," Nastya said with a casual wave of her hand. "He was always more of a quick fuck type of guy. No other woman stuck around for this long."

Deepa blinked, unable to come up with a response.

Nastya's eyes glinted mischievously as she ran a teasing hand along Deepa's arm. "You know...if you ever want to experience a real man, I'd be happy to introduce you to some of my cousins."

Deepa instinctively recoiled, brushing off the unwanted touch. "That's really not necessary, thanks."

Nastya wasn't phased. "They're all exceptionally skilled lovers, and quite...gifted in size. Sparticus in particular has an impressive track record, his partners rarely fail to conceive within months."

"How...fortunate for him."

"He's a master at hitting all the right spots," Nastya purred. "Whereas if you prefer things a bit...rougher, dear Klaus would be delighted to take you for a ride. Discreet too, he'd have you screaming his name over breakfast before Axel even realized you were gone."

Deepa cringed. "And I suppose that you'd want to watch that?"

"Oh, don't be silly," Nastya giggled. "Unless you invite me of course. Klaus loves having an audience. I bet he could make you cum ten times in one sitting. Wouldn't that be far more exciting than enduring Axel's little pencil dick?"

Deepa bit her tongue, glancing over her shoulder as she contemplated transforming back into a wolf and disappearing into the forest.

"Oh come on." Nastya wrapped an arm around Deepa's waist. "It's just a little joke. I didn't mean to make you mad."

"Whatever," Deepa mumbled.

"I just find the moment of conception so fascinating," Nastya hummed. "Perhaps because I can't have children myself."

"Oh," Deepa responded quietly, unsure how to react.

"I became pregnant once, but it didn't go well. They had to remove the baby and my uterus."

"I'm sorry," Deepa said, her eyes drifting over the smaller woman.

"Don't be." Nastya pushed open the door to the house. "Perhaps it was for the best. I doubt that I would make a good mother. My own is a cold frigid bitch, so I never had any good role models."

Deepa shuddered, following Nastya through the hallway towards Ryan's office.

"Finally," Ryan sighed as they entered. He was hunched over his desk. "I need you to look at this. Our informant made this map, but I need you to double check it to make sure that he's not fucking with us."

Deepa leaned over and gazed at the sketch on the table. "This is Infection Control."

"So it's correct?"

"Yes," Deepa said. It was almost perfect, eerily so. "How did you get this?"

"Doesn't matter," Ryan grunted. "What's their defense plan?"

A knot formed in Deepa's stomach, dread coiling within her. "What? You're not seriously thinking of attacking Infection Control, right?"

Ryan raised an eyebrow.

"This building is full of agents who spent years training to take down werewolves," Deepa spat. "You can't just walk through the front door."

"And that is why we have you." Ryan pointed a finger at her chest.

"I'm not gonna help you kill my friends," Deepa hissed.

"Really? Because they all seem so keen on keeping you alive," Ryan retorted, his words landing like a punch to the gut.

Deepa stiffened, her hands clenched into fists at her sides, her stomach churning with a mix of anger, fear, and betrayal.

"Infection Control is working on a vaccine," Ryan continued. "They want to try and make as many people immune as possible."

"And how is that a bad thing?"

"Because it will give them an advantage," Nastya said. "And that's something that we can't allow."

"The ability to be turned is also the one thing keeping people like you alive," Ryan said. "Werewolves don't care about sparing the immune."

Deepa swallowed. She knew that what he was saying was true. There was no way that werewolves would bother keeping people who couldn't be infected alive.

"That's why we need your help," Nastya said. "If you tell us how we can infiltrate the building, then everyone gets what they want."

"No," Deepa hissed. "I won't do it."

"Axel will be going," Nastya said with a coy smile. "Don't you want to make sure that he comes back alive?"

Deepa's breath caught in her throat, Nastya's words striking a nerve. "Why... why are you doing this? Can't you just ask for a truce and call it a day? Why do you want to kill everyone?"

Nastya chuckled softly, her eyes gleaming with mischief. "Because that's what the universe has chosen for us."

"It's too late to stop," Ryan sighed. "Infection Control will never let us live. It's either kill or be killed."

"But there must be another way." Deepa said.

"We're long past that point." Ryan slammed a hand down on the map. "Are you going to help or not?"

Deepa took a deep breath, her shoulders slumping. "Fine, but promise me that no one has to get hurt."

"We'll do our best," Ryan said, his attention shifting back to the map. "But I make no promises."

CHAPTER 7

"Here," Axel said softly as he pressed an Infection Control uniform into Deepa's arms.

Deepa's heart skipped a beat as she looked down at the black and yellow jacket, her eyes drifting over the ID tag still attached to the front. There was a photo of a young woman with dark brown hair and olive skin, but the face was unfamiliar.

"Where did you get this?" she asked.

"Doesn't matter," Axel shrugged. "It's yours now."

Deepa angrily shoved it back at him. "You can have it. I won't do it. I'm not coming on another stupid mission with you."

Axel let out a sigh. "It wasn't my idea."

"Then talk to him, make him change his mind."

"It won't make a difference. These orders come from above him and they're not up for discussion."

"And you're okay with that?" Deepa hissed, her fingers twitching as they threatened to turn into claws.

Axel placed a comforting hand on her shoulder, his thumb brushing the nape of her neck. "It's the way things are. If it was up to me, I'd keep you safe and locked away from all this shit."

Deepa shivered, his touch sending a wave of heat through her.

"Put on the uniform, Deepa," he murmured, his lips grazing the shell of her ear. "Please."

"Fine!" Deepa ripped the uniform out of his hands and stormed off towards the bathroom.

"Don't forget to put the helmet on too," Axel called after her.

Deepa swore under her breath, slamming the bathroom door behind her.

She quickly changed into the uniform, zipping the jacket up and securing the helmet over her head. She checked her reflection in the mirror, the image staring back at her making her stomach twist.

Her role was simple. To just talk the guards at the gate into letting them inside so that they could destroy the lab, but she couldn't shake the feeling that it was all wrong.

"Are you finished yet?" Axel called from outside.

Deepa let out a slow exhale, pulling the door open.

Axel's gaze roamed over her, lips curving up into a smirk. "Very cute."

"Fuck off," Deepa spat, crossing her arms over her chest.

Axel let out a soft laugh, reaching for her hand and pulling her towards him. "My big bad Infection Control girl."

He wrapped his arms around her waist, pulling Deepa closer.

She could feel an unmistakable bulge pressing against her stomach, rapidly growing larger.

"Fuck no," Deepa hissed. "This shit can't seriously turn you on?"

Axel smirked, his hand gripping her ass to press her closer against his groin. "Maybe I just like a woman in uniform."

Deepa groaned, burying her face in his shoulder, her hands resting on his chest. She wanted to push him away, but her body was reacting differently, hungry for every ounce of affection that he was willing to give.

Axel's fingers worked her helmet off, letting it fall to the floor. He ran his fingers through her hair, tugging her face upwards to meet his lips.

She opened her mouth, her tongue gliding against his, allowing him to take all that he wanted and more.

Axel groaned, his teeth sinking into her bottom lip, his cock hardening against her stomach.

Deepa let out a whimper, her hips bucking, her body pressing against his, her own arousal growing. At least a nice orgasm or two would help calm her nerves.

Axel pulled away. "Suck me."

"What?" Deepa gasped.

"I want to see an Infection Control Officer down on her knees sucking my big werewolf dick."

Deepa groaned. "That's so fucking weird."

Axel chuckled, his hand cupping her chin, running a finger along her lower lip. "Don't tell me that you haven't thought about it."

Deepa's cheeks burned.

"Come on, baby," Axel cooed, his other hand drifting down to her crotch, palming her pussy.

Deepa moaned, her body melting into his.

"I want to feel your tight little mouth," he whispered, his lips brushing her ear. "Please."

"Fine," Deepa grumbled, her hands drifting down his chest and resting on his belt.

"Good girl," Axel grinned, unzipping his pants and pulling out his erection, affectionately running a finger over the head. "Open wide."

Deepa rolled her eyes, lowering herself to her knees, her gaze drifting up his body.

Axel pulled his shirt up, revealing his toned stomach, his jeans were hanging low on his hips, his cock swelling larger as it jutted out from his body.

Deepa's lips parted, her tongue flicking out, teasing his tip.

"That's it," Axel whispered, his fingers weaving into her hair, his eyes glued to her.

Deepa took him into her mouth, her tongue gliding along the underside, her lips wrapping tightly around him.

"Oh, fuck," Axel groaned, his fingers digging into her scalp, his hips jerking forward.

Deepa's pussy clenched as she felt his dick throbbing against her tongue, the musky scent of his arousal filling her nostrils. She didn't expect it to feel good for her too.

"You like that, don't you?" Axel purred, his hips bucking, his dick pressing against the back of her throat.

Deepa hummed, bobbing her head, her eyes closing, her tongue swirling around his cock, sucking and licking, tasting every inch.

Axel's hands gripped her hair, his cock sliding down her throat, taking his fill.

Deepa swallowed, her throat squeezing his shaft, her fingers curling into the fabric of his jeans.

"Oh fuck, that's good," Axel groaned, his head tilting back, his cock throbbing.

Deepa slipped a hand into her pants to ease her own need, unsurprised to find that she was getting wet. Deepa let out a groan, her pussy clenching around her fingers, her hips grinding against her palm.

"Fuck," Axel hissed, pulling her off him.

He pushed her to the floor and tugged at her pants, pulling them down to expose her dripping core.

"What are you doing?" Deepa gasped.

"Fucking your brains out," he growled, spreading her thighs apart, his cock grinding against her wet folds.

Deepa gasped, her face pressed against the carpet as Axel rubbed his tip against her, teasing her entrance.

"Wanna cum inside you," he groaned, pushing himself inside with several small thrusts.

Deepa's nails dug into the carpet as she felt him filling her, stretching her, her pussy pulsating around him.

"That's it," he panted, grasping her hips tightly as he rocked back and forth, pounding against her cervix. "Always taking me so well."

Deepa whimpered, her face flushed, her heart pounding, her pussy clenching. She felt herself growing wetter with every powerful shove of his hips.

"Oh fuck, yes," he groaned, his pace quickening.

Deepa moaned, her pussy spasming, her toes curling as intoxicating pressure grew in her core.

Axel continued to pump, his balls slapping against her clit, his cock sliding against her slick walls.

"That's it," he rasped, his breath hot on her skin, his fingers slipping between her legs to rub her drenched clit. "Cum around my cock like a good bitch in heat."

Deepa whimpered, her body shuddering, her eyes fluttering closed as she surrendered to the pleasure, the blissful release of her orgasm.

"That's it," he growled, his lips brushing her neck, his teeth nipping her skin. "Cum for me."

Deepa's vision blurred as her walls clamped down on him, milking him for all he was worth.

Axel grunted, his cock pulsing inside her, his balls drawing up tight as his seed shot deep into her womb.

"Oh fuck," Axel groaned, his chest pressed against her back, his weight resting on her, his face buried in her hair as he continued to pump his hips.

Deepa panted, her chest heaving, her breath coming out in short quick gasps as her climaxed faded. Her body went limp, her legs shaking, her arms folded under her head as she struggled to keep herself upright.

Axel collapsed against her back, his hands still gripping her hips, his dick still speared inside her, the warmth of his load pouring into her depths.

Deepa closed her eyes. She could hear Axel's heartbeat hammering in her ears, the sound filling the room as their breathing slowed, the tingling in her limbs fading, replaced by a warm, comforting glow, washing away all her anxiety and fears.

The wolf sighed and sunk back down under her skin, satisfied with being filled with his seed.

Axel nuzzled her neck, his lips brushing her flushed skin. "I should have cum on the uniform. Spilled my whole load on it, and made you walk up to your old friends like that."

"Gross," Deepa murmured.

Axel laughed, kissing her neck.

"Axel!" called a voice from down the hall and Bruno appeared in the doorway, dressed in an Infection Control uniform with a bulky helmet covering his face. "Put your dick away. We've gotta go."

Axel hummed, nuzzling Deepa's neck. "Do we really?"

"Yes!" Bruno snapped, disappearing back down the hall. "We're already behind schedule because you can't keep it in your pants."

Axel reluctantly pulled out, tucking himself away. He snatched the helmet off the floor, pulling it over Deepa's face. "Next time we'll do it with the helmet on."

Deepa shoved him away, pulling a sheet from the bed to clean up the cum between her legs. She quickly adjusted her clothing and stood to her feet.

CHAPTER 8

There was a large Infection Control van parked outside. The door was heavily scratched and splattered with blood. Deepa didn't want to know how they got it.

"Why don't you have to do any of this shit?" Bruno snapped at Nastya.

Axel's sister was attempting to clean the blood off the van with a sponge. "Because...Someone needs to guard the house."

"Bullshit," Bruno snapped. "It's because you're a fucking coward."

"Bruno," Ryan growled, coming out of the house. "Stop arguing and get in the van."

"Fine." Bruno rolled his eyes, stomping over to the vehicle and getting behind the wheel.

"You ready?" Ryan asked, placing a hand on Deepa's shoulder but Axel tugged Deepa away.

"We'll be fine," Axel snapped, leading Deepa to the passenger seat.

"Don't fuck around!" Ryan called after them. "Get in, get the job done and then get out."

Axel ignored him, pushing Deepa into the seat and fastening her seatbelt.

He pressed his face close to hers. "I'll be in the back," he said softly. "No matter what happens, just stay out of danger."

Deepa blinked, her eyes drifting over his face, feeling overwhelmed by his concern. "Okay."

Axel leaned forward and kissed her, his lips warm and soft, lingering far longer than Deepa expected.

She blinked when he pulled away, a knot forming in her stomach.

"See you soon." Axel brushed her lips one last time before he hurried off, diving into the back of the Infection Control van as it roared to life.

"Just remember, if you do anything stupid it won't end well for anyone!" Ryan yelled, his gaze locked with Deepa's.

Deepa scowled and turned away.

Bruno revved the engine, slowly rolling out of the driveway.

"What about the others?" Deepa asked.

"Luke and Reese have a different mission," said Bruno. "Everyone else is in the back."

Deepa pulled back the curtain behind her, peering through the glass to see several large cages crammed in the back.

They were all filled with werewolves. Deepa easily recognized Axel's white fur. He was curled up with his head resting on his paws.

"Don't worry," Bruno chuckled. "They'll get a chance to run free once we get there."

"That's what I'm worried about," Deepa muttered.

"Oh come on," Bruno grinned widely. "You used to hunt werewolves for a living. How are humans any different?"

Deepa didn't reply, her nails digging into her thighs.

Bruno snickered. "Thought so."

"Shut up and drive," Deepa snarled, her fingers trembling.

"Yeah, yeah." Bruno waved his hand, speeding up the truck.

"We're almost there," Bruno muttered, his fingers tightening on the steering wheel as they approached the gate to Infection Control.

"Yeah," Deepa mumbled, eyes fixed on the road ahead as her heart anxiously pounded in her chest.

"Don't get cold feet now." Bruno shot her a warning glare. "Axel might think you're the shit, but I won't hesitate to slit your throat if you sell us out."

Deepa clenched her jaw.

"Just stick to the plan," he said. "Get us in, and then we'll handle the rest."

"Right," Deepa mumbled, trying her best to keep her cool.

Bruno slowed the car as they approached the gates. Security cameras surveyed the area, and signs warned of the consequences of trespassing.

"State your business," said a guard through a speaker.

Deepa leaned over Bruno to get closer to the speaker. "Transfer. We have a truck full of pure ones for analytics."

"Hold," the guard said.

Deepa held her breath, her eyes focused on the road ahead, trying her best to pretend that she belonged there.

The speaker crackled. "All three of you?"

Deepa glanced at the side mirror to see two trucks waiting behind them.

"Just say yes," Bruno hissed.

"Yes," Deepa replied into the speaker.

"Proceed," the guard said.

Deepa slumped back into her seat as the gates slowly opened, a wave of relief washing over her.

Bruno drove forward, his fingers gripping the steering wheel, his knuckles white.

"Keep calm," Deepa whispered. "You look suspicious."

"Fuck off," Bruno hissed. "You're one to talk."

There were several armed guards awaiting them outside the research department, clad in hazmat suits with thick layers of protective material covering them from head to toe. Their faces were obscured by helmets with tinted visors, and large rifles were gripped tightly in their gloved hands.

"Shit," Bruno swore.

"Just play it cool," Deepa whispered, keeping her voice low as she rolled down the window.

"We don't usually get three at once," one man said, glancing between them and the trucks.

"They're for the analysis lab," Deepa said. "It was a real battle to get all these fuckers inside the cages, so I can't wait to get rid of them."

"Understandable," the guard replied, looking back at the trucks. "But we don't usually get transfers so late in the day."

"That's what I told them." Deepa gave an awkward laugh. "But Craig wanted them today."

Deepa hoped that name-dropping her old boss would make the questioning end faster.

"Yeah," the guard muttered, his attention shifting back to them. "Let's get this over with. You can park in bay eight."

"Got it." Deepa forced a smile.

The guard turned and signaled for the others to open the doors to a large warehouse.

"See," Bruno hit the accelerator. "Not so hard."

"We haven't made it inside yet," Deepa snapped back.

"Just remember what I said," Bruno warned. "One wrong move and it will be your head."

"Yeah, yeah," Deepa hissed, her teeth grinding.

Bruno drove over the painted lines, parking the van in a marked space.

The two trucks stopped beside them. Several men in Infection Control hazmat suits slipped out, opening the back doors to wheel out trollies full of wolves in cages.

"What are they doing?" Deepa asked.

"It doesn't concern you," Bruno snapped, anxiously tapping his fingers on the steering wheel.

The men in hazmat suits wheeled the cages down the hall and out of sight.

"Where are they taking them?" Deepa's stomach churned with anxiety. "What's going on here?"

"Just stick to the fucking plan," Bruno snarled.

"This isn't the plan," Deepa shot back.

Loud screams echoed from down the hall, followed by gunfire.

"Finally," Bruno huffed, pulling a large gun out from behind the seat.

"Let's burn this whole motherfucking place to the ground."

Deepa's stomach dropped. She wanted to slap herself. She was a fool for believing that they'd ever bother to minimize the death toll.

She was just another tool in their bloody crusade to take down humanity.

"Guard the truck." Bruno slammed the door and hurried after the others, enthusiastically brandishing his gun.

Deepa took a deep breath, slipping her hand under the seat and grabbing the gun that lay hidden beneath.

It was a heavy but familiar weight in her hands.

Move, she told her trembling body.

The halls were engulfed in chaos. The air was thick with fear, and blood stained the floor. Infection Control workers screamed and shook as the werewolf infection took control of their bodies, forcing them to mutate and shift, until they were riddled with bullets from their own side.

Axel could smell the terror in the air, his body shivering with anticipation. His teeth ripped into a young woman's throat, tearing the flesh away, her blood spraying over his face.

He'd already killed several humans, his claws and fangs dripping with their blood.

They all deserved it.

Infection Control was going to burn.

They had spent weeks coordinating this attack, sneaking in as many captured werewolves as possible, before their spies released them all at once, creating absolute chaos throughout the building.

Axel rushed towards his next victim until he was suddenly tackled to the ground.

"Stop it!" Deepa shouted, attempting to hold him down.

Axel shifted back to his human form, prying her off him. "What are you doing?"

"You have to stop this," she begged, her eyes red and swollen. "Ryan promised me."

"Ryan is a manipulative little fucker," Axel snapped. "I can't believe that it's taken you this long to figure it out."

"Please," Deepa cried. "If you don't stop they'll kill everyone."

"That's the point Deepa! Why else do you think we're here."

Deepa froze as his words slowly sank in.

"Infection Control has to go down," Axel spat. "They've been a threat to us since the very beginning. And now that they're close to a cure, it's even more important that we stop them. We can't afford to let anyone live today."

Axel felt like an arsehole for lying to her, but he didn't have any choice. If she knew the truth from the start she would have never agreed to help.

Deepa's lip trembled, tears streaking her cheeks.

"Just stay in the van and we'll be back soon," he said softly.

He wanted to kiss her, to pull her into his arms and whisper promises that he didn't believe, but he was running out of time, they needed to take down as many people as possible before reinforcements arrived.

"No," she choked, grip tightening on the gun in her hands.

"What are you gonna do?" Axel laughed. "Shoot me? Just go back to the van like a good girl."

"Don't call me a good girl," she snarled, raising the gun, the barrel aimed at his head, but he knew that she didn't have the guts to shoot him.

Pain ripped through Axel's torso. Gunfire echoed through the hall as another two shots rang out, tearing through his arm and chest.

Axel thought that Deepa had finally mustered up the courage to end him, until his gaze drifted to a young woman at the end of the hall, long red hair tied back into a tight braid.

"Sadie," Deepa gasped, eyes wide in horror.

"Deepa?" The red haired woman faltered for a moment before her expression hardened. "You're one of them now, aren't you?"

Deepa's grip on the gun faltered, her shoulders slumping, her face contorting into a painful grimace.

"What's going on here?" Sadie yelled. "Why are they attacking us?"

"I- I don't know," Deepa stuttered.

Axel groaned and fell to his knees, clutching his stomach in a poor attempt to stop the blood flow. This wasn't the time for Deepa to catch up with old friends.

"Drop the gun, Deepa," Sadie cried.

"Don't," Axel grunted, his voice weak, blood leaking from his mouth. "Shoot her."

Deepa froze, glancing between Axel and Sadie with her eyes wide in terror. The one time that he needed her to do something, and she choked.

Sadie raised the gun, aiming it directly at Deepa's chest. "I'm sorry," her voice shook. "But I don't have a choice."

Deepa stiffened, her hands trembling, the gun falling to the ground.

Axel struggled to stand, but his body refused to respond, pain burning through his limbs.

Deepa slowly raised her hands above her head. "S-Sadie, I'm not-"

Sadie's head exploded, her brains splattering over the wall, her body crumpling to the ground.

A large blond man in an Infection Control uniform walked towards them, gazing over Sadie's corpse with a cold sneer.

"Varn?" Deepa whimpered.

CHAPTER 9

It was most definitely Varn who just blew Sadie's brains out, the man who always joked in the breakroom and invited them out for drinks, but Deepa had never seen him look so cold, so detached. It was like a switch had flipped and the man she used to work with had been replaced with a stranger.

"Long time no see, Axel," Varn said, his tone mocking. "How's the stomach?"

Axel hissed, his face pale, his skin drenched with sweat. "Who the fuck are you?"

Varn chuckled, pulled a cartridge from his jacket and reloaded his gun. "Guess that the family golden boy has no time to remember us peasants."

"You're a werewolf," Deepa gasped.

"Bingo." Varn smirked. "At least your girlfriend has half a brain, Axel."

Axel let out a groan as he fell to the floor, collapsing face first into a puddle of his own blood.

"Axel!" Deepa cried, dropping to her knees, her hands trembling as she tried to turn him over.

Varn rolled his eyes. He picked up Axel, throwing him over his shoulder like a sack of potatoes, and started down the hallway.

"What are you doing?" Deepa shouted, scrambling after him.

"Infirmary," Varn grunted. "Unless you'd rather watch him bleed out?"

Deepa shook her head, rushing after Varn, stomach churning with fear. Several Infection Control officers hurried past them in the hall, but didn't stop.

Varn shoved open the door to the lab, pointing his gun straight at a terrified nurse.

"You," he growled, dropping Axel onto an empty bed. "Fix him."

"I-I'm not sure I can," the nurse stuttered, his gaze flickering to Axel's bloody stomach.

"Yes, you can," Varn snapped. "Or you can join your colleagues on the other side."

The nurse swallowed, his eyes wide in terror. He rushed to grab the tools, his hands trembling as he began tending to Axel's wounds.

Deepa collapsed in a chair beside the bed, watching as the nurse began cleaning a bullet hole. "Will...Will he be okay?"

"The...the bullets went right through." The nurse's voice trembled. "I'll stitch them...but he lost a lot of blood."

Deepa felt sick. She wanted to reach out and grab Axel's hand, but the sight of his bloodied stomach made her dizzy.

Varn closed and locked the door, but it didn't block out the sounds of explosions and gunfire from outside.

Deepa clenched her hands into fists. This was all her fault. If only she hadn't been so stupid. Just the thought of Axel's death was enough to make her whole body freeze with panic.

How could she continue to live if he died?

Varn sat down in a chair beside her, his fingers brushing the blood from his face. "He'll be fine. His family is full of stubborn bastards who refuse to kick the bucket."

"How do you know that?" Deepa asked.

Varn shrugged. "We lived in the same settlement for a while back when we were kids. But Axel was so far up his arse that I'm not surprised he doesn't remember me. The Brants don't give a shit about anyone outside their group."

"But you killed werewolves," Deepa stammered. "Tons of them. How could you do that if you're a werewolf yourself?"

Varn shrugged. "They were all turned ones. They were going to die sooner or later."

A chill ran down Deepa's spine as she pressed further. "But didn't it make you sad? Taking their lives?"

A deep, rich laugh rumbled from Varn's chest. "Sad? Not a chance. They were nothing but weaklings who wouldn't have lasted a minute against a pure-blooded one like myself. They would have been culled eventually, spared from their pitiful existence."

Deepa shuddered, her skin crawling. Axel and his family were monsters, but Varn was on a whole new level of depravity.

Swallowing hard, she mustered the courage to ask. "How many are there? How many werewolves are there inside Infection Control?"

"Not a clue. The secret to being a good plant is not knowing who's a plant too. We simply follow orders and fight when the time comes."

Deepa's mouth went dry, her stomach twisting into knots. How could they have been so naive, so utterly blind to the truth unfolding around them?

"It's not just Infection Control," Varn continued. "The elders have spent decades infiltrating the human military and politics. They have plants everywhere. Sooner or later, we'll take control of everything."

"So you're just gonna kill everyone?"

Varn shrugged. "Maybe. Depends on what the elders decide."

Deepa swallowed hard, her throat constricting with fear.

"Don't look so worried." Varn smiled. "There will always be immune ones. Plenty of them will make great slaves to serve our new order."

The implications of his words left Deepa too shocked to speak. They sat in tense silence as the nurse diligently stitched up Axel's wounds, cleaning away the blood and applying fresh bandages.

Axel's face was pale and clammy, but the steady rise and fall of his chest provided a small reassurance that he still clung to life.

"There," said the nurse. "That's all I can do."

"Good," Varn grunted, standing and shooting the nurse in the head. Blood splattered across the wall as the body crumpled to the floor.

"What did you do that for?" Deepa screamed.

"Another rule about being a plant," said Varn. "Destroy all evidence."

Deepa couldn't breathe, her chest tight, her whole body trembling.

Varn kicked the corpse aside and made his way to the door. "I'll leave the rest up to you. If he dies on your way out then that's on you."

"Where are you going?"

"To finish my job." Varn slipped outside.

Deepa slipped the nurses' bloodied outfit onto Axel and wheeled him out of the room. The halls were littered with the bodies of humans and werewolves, the smell of smoke thick in the air as the lights flickered.

Deepa searched the faces of every corpse she passed, looking for anyone familiar. There were people that she trained with, people that she ate lunch with, but now they were just a pile of bodies, covered in scratches or bullet holes.

"Parker," Deepa whispered. She'd been too consumed by Axel to think of him until that moment.

She prayed that he'd escaped the slaughter, that maybe he was still alive and safe, but she knew that was probably too much to hope for.

"Fuck," Deepa hissed as a bullet whirled past her. She backtracked to the nearest corner, hiding behind it as the gunfire continued.

"Fuck, fuck, fuck," Deepa muttered, her eyes burning.

A shrill alarm pierced the air, red lights flashing as the fire sprinklers activated, soaking both her and Axel in seconds.

She glanced around the corner, watching two Infection Control officers get riddled by bullets.

"I know that you're there!" called Bruno. He emerged from around the corner, soaked from head to toe with a white wolf trailing behind him. "Hurry up so that we can get the fuck out of here."

"Fine." Deepa pushed the cart towards him.

"Axel?" Bruno hissed. "The fuck did you do to him?"

"He got shot," Deepa snapped back.

"By who?"

"Some girl that I used to work with."

"Probably because he was too busy staring at your tits to dodge."

"Just shut up and help me," Deepa growled, pushing the cart as hard as she could.

Bruno sighed, grabbing the front and pulling. "This is the last fucking time that I ever go anywhere with you."

Deepa pushed as Bruno cleared the way, shooting any humans who crossed their path, until they eventually reached the parked van and trucks.

"In the back!" Bruno snapped, pulling a pair of truck doors open and helping Deepa to get Axel inside.

Deepa climbed in and Bruno slammed the doors behind her, dashing to the driver's seat.

The truck roared to life and quickly sped down the road, causing Deepa to tightly grip Axel's bed just to remain standing.

She glanced out the back window to see thick black smoke rising from the building as sirens raged in the distance.

Deepa's throat felt tight, her hands shaking as the image of Sadie's dead eyes burned into her memory.

She had done this. She had helped them to destroy humanity's only chance of beating the werewolf infection.

CHAPTER 10

Deepa didn't even wait for the truck to stop before jumping out of the back, storming across the manicured lawn towards Ryan.

"How could you?" she snarled, rage boiling up inside her. "You said that you were going to minimize the damage and then you go and pull that?"

"Ah, Deepa," Ryan smirked. "Good job on completing your mission."

"Good job?" Deepa sneered, her fingers twitching, every instinct in her body telling her to beat him to a bloody pulp. "Axel got shot and Infection Control is on fire!"

"Excellent job then." Ryan grinned.

"We had a deal!" Deepa screamed, tears burning her eyes.

"That I tried my best to follow, but I can't turn down orders from above. You're a sweet girl, Deepa, and an excellent fuck, but at the end of the day, all you are is just another pawn like the rest of us."

Deepa's jaw dropped. She put her hand into a fist and slammed it into his face.

Ryan didn't even try to dodge, rolling into the force with an amused expression on his face. "Feel better?"

Deepa growled, her body shaking with rage.

"Hey!" Bruno cried out, sliding himself between them. "Just calm the fuck down."

"If Axel dies it's on you!" Deepa spat.

Ryan wiped the blood from his mouth, rolling his eyes. "I highly doubt we'll get that lucky."

"You," Deepa seethed, shaking with rage.

She wanted to punch him until his teeth were nothing but dust and all his bones were broken, but her murderous thoughts were interrupted by a red sports car racing up the driveway.

It parked next to the truck.

Reese and Luke clambered out, both looking exhausted. Reese's clothes were torn and there was a large gash across Luke's cheek. Dirt and grime caked their skin.

"How did it go?" Ryan called out.

"Shit," Reese muttered. "The merry little fucker led us on a chase through the suburbs."

"But you caught him?"

"Not before he popped Sammy. The poor guy's brains exploded all over a teenager's BBQ."

"Shit." Bruno clenched his teeth as his gaze fell to the ground.

"Shit indeed," Reese huffed. "Now you're gonna have to find a new lackey."

"But you caught him?" Ryan asked.

Luke sighed and pulled a man from the back of the car, wrists hand-cuffed together with a black bag over his head.

The man shoved his shoulder into Luke, trying to escape his grasp.

"Just calm down," Luke said.

"Where the fuck have you taken me?" the man growled in a familiar voice.

"Parker?" Deepa gasped.

Parker froze. "Deepa?" he called back.

"See," Ryan grinned. "I at least fulfill some of my promises."

Deepa rushed towards Parker and gripped his shoulders. "Oh my god, are you alright?"

Parker slumped to his knees, wincing. "I'm okay. They jumped me outside my place."

With trembling hands, Deepa removed the bag over his head, revealing Parker's battered face and disheveled hair matted with blood.

Her chest constricted painfully as tears blurred her vision. She fell into his embrace, nestling her head into the crook of his neck as his arms enveloped her.

"I'm so relieved you're alive," Parker murmured.

Deepa shuddered, clinging to him tighter. After fearing the worst, having him there, warm and solid, was almost surreal.

"Same here," she choked out between ragged breaths.

Parker pulled away, but his expression instantly hardened when his gaze landed on Ryan. "You," he growled.

Deepa's brow furrowed in confusion. "Parker?"

Ryan let out a laugh. "Parker? I can't believe that you still use that stupid nickname."

"Do.. do you know each other?" Deepa stuttered.

"Know each other?" Ryan snickered. "This idiot is my younger brother."

CHAPTER II

Ryan was fifteen when he finally met his mother again. The last time he saw her was when he was five, watching her from a distance before he was spirited off to live with the other half breed children.

His father Elijah would make short appearances in his life, coming to check and make sure that Ryan was still breathing, but Ryan cared little about him. The man was virtually a stranger.

Elijah finally spilled the location of Ryan's mother after years of Ryan begging, handing Ryan a piece of paper before disappearing again.

The address led Ryan to a single story white brick house in the suburbs, sheltered from the hot summer sun by several overgrown trees.

His mother was outside pulling weeds from the lawn, black hair tied back into a tight bun. She was still beautiful, but older and more gaunt than he remembered.

Ryan approached her hesitantly, his heart heavy.

What could he possibly say to the woman who had abandoned him for ten years? Who left him to rot in a place where love was a distant fantasy, and weakness would only lead to more pain.

His mother slowly stood to her feet. She wiped her brow and turned to him, her dark eyes wide, her mouth hanging open in surprise. "Ryan?"

Ryan froze, his mind going blank.

She crossed the distance between them and buried her face in his chest, body shaking. "I never thought... I never thought that I'd see you again."

She held him tight, weeping softly, and all the anger and resentment he had against her disappeared into thin air.

Her touch was painful and bitter-sweet, her words muffled by her wailing. She wept into his chest, apologizing for not being there to stop them from taking him away.

"I'm sorry," she sobbed. "I thought that you were safe with the elders. I didn't know that they'd take you away like that...I looked so much... but I..."

He rested his hand on her head and awkwardly stroked her hair. His eyes were painfully dry, but everything that his mother wanted to say was exactly what he had yearned to hear for so long.

"Come on," she said softly, mouth curving into a gentle smile. "Come inside and meet your brother."

Ryan swallowed, gazing down at her with wide eyes. "My brother?"

She nodded, taking his hand to lead him inside.

Riley put her hands on Ryan's shoulders. "Austin," she said. "This is your older brother Ryan."

Ten-year-old Austin Park stared at Ryan in shock. Milk and cereal dripped off his spoon onto the table.

Austin looked just like a younger version of himself, with the same blue eyes and black hair. But there were differences too. Austin's nose was more prominent and there were freckles scattered across his cheeks.

"But everyone said that he was dead," Austin gasped.

"No," said their mother, taking the spoon from Austin and placing it back in the bowl. "Just... missing that's all, but now he's here."

Austin looked back at his mother like she was mad, nervously glancing at Ryan like he was a random kid that their mother had abducted off the street.

Ryan's mind raced, unsure of what to say next.

Their mother had warned him repeatedly, Austin was just a normal kid.

He didn't know anything about his family being werewolves. She wanted to shield Austin from the truth for as long as possible, to give him an ordinary childhood.

Ryan had to be careful not to let anything slip, not to shatter the life his little brother knew.

The life that she had failed to give Ryan.

Ryan's earliest memories of his mother were the two of them living away from human society, in an isolated house full of other human turned werewolves.

His mother seemed constantly frustrated. Upset that Ryan couldn't control his shifting and blend in with human children.

"What am I going to do?" he overheard her sobbing with another woman. "How can I ever leave here if he's always running around naked and turning into a wolf?"

But with Austin she seemed to have found her dream child, a perfect human boy that would never turn into a wolf.

Ryan watched his brother from a distance. Always outside playing with the neighborhood kids who'd smile and call him Parker. He always looked happy, always free, always doted on by both their parents without having to worry about stupid werewolf shit.

"Parker?" Nastya hummed while kissing Ryan in his new room. He'd agreed to stay with his family, but Nastya still snuck in to visit him. "Why do they call him that?"

"I dunno?" Ryan shrugged. "I guess because his last name is Park."

Nastya nodded, continuing to lather Ryan in attention. "Margret had her baby. It looks just like you."

Ryan groaned and buried his face in her neck, mind filled with memories of making that baby.

"You'll have to give her a little brother or sister next time you come back," said Nastya.

Ryan shuddered at the thought, but they were interrupted by the door swinging open.

"Ryan?" Riley said hesitantly, gasping when she spotted Nastya on the bed, and the positions they were in. "Get out," she said darkly, pointing at the door.

Nastya sighed and pulled herself to her feet, slipping on her jacket and shoes, then confidently strolled out the door.

Ryan let out a huff of frustration. He'd been looking forward to letting off some steam.

His mother crossed her arms over her chest. "Who was that?"

"Nastya."

"Nastya? As in your older sister Nastya?"

"She's not my sister," Ryan huffed. "She's not really dad's daughter."

His mother angrily pulsed her lips together as she tried to contain her rage. "Really? And how do you know that?"

Ryan rolled his eyes. "They did a DNA test and everything to make sure that it would be okay for us to have sex."

"Sex?" his mother spat. "Ryan, you're only fifteen. You shouldn't be having sex with some twenty year old woman."

"She's only eighteen. And why not?" he shrugged. "Everyone does it."

Riley's face was turning red, and he could smell the distress rolling of her body. "Who's everyone?"

"All the guys back at the settlement. Most of the guys my age sleep with women older than Nastya all the time."

Riley's face paled. "Ryan, this isn't right. Those elders are using you, forcing you to have children for their twisted beliefs. You're still just a teenager. You should be out having fun, not being made to grow up too fast."

Ryan shrugged. "But I don't mind it. I've made plenty of babies and it felt natural to me."

"Because they brainwashed you!" Riley's voice rose in anguish. "I knew sending you there was a mistake. I knew they'd try to change you, manipulate you into serving their sick agenda."

"They didn't change me," Ryan retorted. "I'm a werewolf. This is just how we are raised. I can have kids whenever I want, with whoever I want."

Riley trembled, fists clenched at her sides as she fought for composure. "Ryan, you don't have to live like this. You can leave, you can..."

"Pretend that I'm not a werewolf. Become a little obedient human child like Austin? Lie to everyone like Dad does?"

"But-"

"How the hell can you live with yourself?" Ryan scoffed, rolling his eyes. "Keeping Austin in the dark, pretending this werewolf stuff doesn't even matter while he lives his lame human life. It's all bullshit."

Riley's jaw tightened. "Maybe that's all I can give him." Her voice strained with hurt. "He's not...he'll never be like you."

Ryan rolled his eyes and got to his feet. "I'm out. Enjoy your perfect little human life."

"Where are you going?" she called after him.

"Nastya's probably waiting for me. We're going to go have lots of hot werewolf sex in the forest."

"Fine! Just go. Run back to that horrible place and just... just fuck whatever you want like you're nothing more than a wild animal!"

"Fine," Ryan said roughly.

He turned and stomped out of the house, slamming the door behind him. He bit his lip hard to hold back the painful tightness in his chest.

His father Elijah, was sitting on the front porch steps. He sighed heavily and rubbed his beard, like he wasn't surprised this was how things turned out.

Ryan didn't say a word. He walked down the street in silence, disappearing into the darkness without looking back.

The next time that Ryan saw his brother was at the funeral. It was a complete sham. Their parents weren't dead. They'd merrily caused havoc, then fucked off and left everyone else to clean up the pieces.

Austin was a mess. Sobbing his little heart out while being comforted by an elderly woman, probably their grandmother.

Ryan was too disgusted to bother hanging around for long.

If his mother wanted Austin to have a human life then Ryan obviously couldn't be part of it. He was born a werewolf and despised the human world, so why the fuck would he have anything in common with a human boy who was raised to be ignorant of their world.

Six years passed before Ryan caught a faint familiar scent drifting on the breeze. He followed the trail to a cheap fast food joint and found Austin hunched over a battered table, textbooks and papers strewn about.

Austin glanced up, his eyes going wide when they landed on Ryan. A soft curse slipped from his lips.

Ryan steeled himself and entered the restaurant, stopping before Austin's table. Up close, the familiarity of those blue eyes was almost painful.

Austin's brow furrowed into a glare. "What do you want?" he asked flatly.

Ryan's lips curved up into a smile. "Is that how you greet your older brother after so many years?"

"Brother?" Austin huffed. "You showed up once for a week and then disappeared again."

"It's nice to know that you haven't forgotten me."

"I try to forget everything about that week," he sneered back. "Mom was miserable for months after you left."

Ryan rolled his eyes and slumped into the seat in front of Austin, gazing at the papers laid out on the table. "What is all this shit?"

"School work. I have an exam tomorrow and it's too loud to study at home."

Ryan picked up one of the papers and frowned at the page full of unfamiliar names and numbers. "It looks dull as shit."

"Of course it is," Austin muttered. "But I need decent grades if I want to get into Infection Control."

Ryan's heart froze. "Infection Control?"

"Yeah. I want to make sure that no more werewolves can kill people the way that Mom and Dad were murdered."

Ryan was too stunned to speak, shocked that Austin still believed all the bullshit that he'd been fed.

"Don't give me that look," Austin grumbled. "I know that you never gave a shit about Mom or Dad."

"How the fuck can you say that?" Ryan snapped.

"You never visited. Never wrote. Never even showed up at their funeral or when Grandma died. You clearly never gave a shit about any of us."

Ryan bared his teeth and threw the paper back on the table. "Don't you dare talk to me like you know what my life is like. People like you disgust me."

"People like me?" Austin huffed.

Ryan growled in a way that wasn't entirely human, drawing several curious glances from the surrounding tables. "How can you be so stupid? Why don't you grow the fuck up and learn something for yourself instead of sitting around believing every word you're told!"

"Fuck you," Austin hissed. "You have no right to talk to me like that."

"Then grow a fucking spine."

"Whatever," Austin rolled his eyes. "Now can you please leave. I have a fucking exam tomorrow."

Ryan snarled and snatched a textbook off the table, ripping the cover off in one savage move.

Austin's eyes widened, panic setting in. "Shit.. that's from the library. Fuck. Fuck you."

Ryan slammed the book back on the table and stomped out of the restaurant, rage churning in his stomach.

Austin was on his own. If he chose to be oblivious, let his family leave him behind, then there was nothing more that Ryan could do to help him.

CHAPTER 12

"Brother?" Deepa's eyes went wide with shock. "But that would mean..."

"That dear little Austin is from a family of werewolves," Ryan finished for her.

Parker clenched his teeth. "What's that supposed to mean?"

"Well, what do you think it means?" Ryan smiled, stepping closer and ruffling Parker's hair. "It means that our shitty parents never bothered telling you that they were werewolves."

"What the hell are you talking about?" Parker hissed. "Mom and Dad weren't like that."

"Of course they were, idiot." Ryan laughed. "Why else do you think you're immune? Where do you think all those werewolf genes came from?"

Parker stilled, staring at Ryan in shocked silence.

"It's okay," Ryan said. "They fucked me over as well."

"But the attack... I saw them killed."

Ryan shook his head. "That was all because Mom lost control of her wolf and transformed, biting everyone around her in the theater, or at least that's what our shitty father told me."

"You're lying!" Parker snapped, his face red. "Our parents are dead."

"You'll wish they were dead," Ryan sneered. "Once you find out that they abandoned you and fucked off to their little sex cabin in the woods to pump out more kids."

"Stop saying stupid shit!"

"Maybe you just can't see the truth because you're an idealistic idiot like our mother. More interested in living in a fantasy world than accepting the reality around you."

Parker lunged himself at Ryan, his forehead colliding with Ryan's mouth, splitting his lip.

"Idiot," Ryan groaned, spitting blood onto the grass. "If you don't believe me, I'll show you."

The rough gravel road came to an end halfway up the mountain. Ryan and Parker had no choice but to continue on foot, hiking through thick vegetation and tall grass.

Ryan was going to kill him.

That was the only explanation Parker could think of to explain why his estranged older brother was taking him to meet two people that Parker had witnessed die years ago.

But had he really seen them die?

So much time had passed that Parker couldn't fully trust his own memories. He hadn't actually seen their bodies, only trusting what Craig had told him, but there was no other reason for them to disappear from his life.

His parents loved him. There's no way they would have abandoned him.

Unless they were hiding something.

Parker felt sick, his heart racing and stomach churning.

"Relax," Ryan smirked, clearly enjoying Parker's distress.

"How much further?" Parker snapped.

"Perhaps an hour or two," Ryan sighed. "It would be a lot faster if you could shift."

Parker glared at him, clenching his jaw. He had no doubt his brother was a werewolf, carrying the same arrogant confidence as the other natural-born ones.

Parker wished that he had his gun.

They hiked the rest of the way in silence. The overgrown trees eventually opened up to a clearing, revealing a small cabin hidden within the tall weeds.

A group of small children played outside, shifting between human and wolf forms as they chased each other through the weeds.

The resemblance was unmistakable. Parker could see traces of his own features scattered across their faces.

"Ryan!" A small girl cried, rushing up to meet Parker's brother. "I missed you!"

Ryan grinned and ruffled her hair. "I'm sorry that I haven't had time to visit. Is Mother home?"

Yep," the little girl said cheerfully. "She's sewing inside." She glanced at Parker, her large eyes full of curiosity. "Who's he?"

Ryan's lips curved into a bitter smile. "That's Austin."

"Austin?" The small girl tilted her head inquisitively. "What's an Austin?"

Parker clenched his jaw and brushed past them, storming into the log cabin.

The interior was cluttered with worn mats and animal skins. A wooden stove burned at the center of the room, and a woman with shoulder-length graying hair sat at a table beside it, sewing patches onto a tattered shirt.

She glanced up as he entered. "Ryan?"

Parker froze. He'd spent years longing to speak to his mother again, but now that she was there, he couldn't find the words.

She cocked her head. "Ryan, what brings you here?" Her expression was warm and genuine, as if nothing was amiss.

As if she hadn't abandoned him.

"Mom?" Parker's voice cracked. His eyes burned, vision blurring as the walls seemed to close in, making it hard to breathe.

Her gaze met his. "Austin," she gasped, dropping the shirt. "It can't be." She pushed herself up and rushed over, throwing her arms around him.

Enveloped in her tight embrace, he felt like he was home. His body relaxed against her warmth as he shook uncontrollably, mouth salty with tears.

A million questions buzzed in his mind, but the only word he could form was, "why?"

"I'm so sorry," she sobbed, her face buried in his hair.

"Why did you leave me?"

She squeezed him tightly, her warm hands rubbing his back. "I'm sorry... So sorry..."

"I watched them all die." Parker's voice trembled. "I thought you were dead."

"I'm so sorry," she murmured, gripping him tightly.

"Explain it to me!" Parker cried. "Why would you lie to me?"

His mother sniffled, loosening her grip on him and pulling back. "I thought that you'd have a better life without us. I thought... that it would be better for you to live as a human."

"So it is true," Parker hissed. "You and Dad are werewolves."

"I..I.. was bitten when I was about your age, but all I ever wanted was to be human again, for us all to be a normal family who did normal things... But I lost control and ruined everything." Her hands shook. "I thought that without us you could still have a normal childhood and-"

"Grandma died," Parker spat. "Two years after you did. I spent years in foster care. How the fuck is that normal?"

Her gaze fell to the floor. "I'm so sorry." Her voice trembled.

They were interrupted by the door swinging open and in walked Parker's father, naked with a dead deer swung over his shoulder.

He deposited it on a table inside without giving either of them a second glance, trailed by a small dark haired boy who transformed and chased after him.

Parker's mother swallowed. "It's better for your father out here. He's... too much wolf to coexist well with humans. I'll call him back, I don't think he realized that it's you...I.."

"Don't bother," Parker snarled. "He seems to have plenty of new sons to replace me."

"It... wasn't planned. Once we came out here. They all just happened.

There was one who was kinda like you. I gave her away to a human family, so that she could-"

Riley paused when she realized Parker was silently storming away.

"Wait!" she called out, following him to the front door. "Please, I'm so grateful you're here and-"

Parker grabbed the door and flung it open. "I'm not a werewolf and you've made it more than obvious that I have no place in this fucked up family."

He stomped outside, wiping his face with his sleeve. He preferred his life when he thought his parents were dead, when he could pretend they were decent people who would never abandon him.

His whole life had been built on lies and he'd been too stupid to question any of them.

"That was fast." Ryan jogged to catch up with him. "You didn't even stay long enough to hear their lame excuses before they go off to screw in the forest."

"Why?" Parker hissed. "Why are they like that?"

Ryan shrugged. "Mom could never hack losing her human life, and Dad can only follow her around like a lost puppy because he thinks that they're fated mates."

"Fated mates?"

"It's a screwed up form of werewolf imprinting. They're obsessed with each other, and everything else comes second."

"Including their own children?"

"Oh yes," Ryan laughed. "They fucked up with us, so they just went off and made more. Mom's probably pregnant again. They don't even bother with birth control anymore."

Parker stared at his brother's smirk, an angry fire burning in his chest.

"Your little girlfriend isn't going to end up any different, you know," Ryan said. "Axel is gonna turn her into his devoted little breeding bitch just like Mom, and you won't even exist to her anymore."

Parker lunged out, grasping Ryan by the shoulders and slamming him against the nearest tree. "Shut the hell up. What the fuck does that bastard have to do with anything?"

"Don't tell me that you didn't notice how devoted that crazy freak is to Deepa," Ryan chuckled, his lips curling in amusement. "Any werewolf can smell his seed dripping from her cunt."

Parker's head spun. His grip tightened on Ryan's shoulders. "You're fucking with me," he hissed.

"Maybe." Ryan smirked. "Maybe not. Maybe you should go back and see for yourself."

Parker's heart pounded in his ears, his mind a mess, unable to think straight.

No. It couldn't be true. The Deepa he knew would never sleep with a man like that. There was no way that she'd fuck the man who beat him and turned her into a werewolf.

Ryan let out a laugh like he could see the seeds of doubt begin to sprout in Parker's mind.

Gritting his teeth into a snarl, Parker pulled his fist back and slammed it hard into Ryan's smug face.

His brother didn't fight back, allowing Parker's fists to connect with his cheek, knocking him back a few steps

"You can throw as many tantrums as you like," Ryan laughed. "But it won't change the truth. Your little girlfriend is probably over there riding out shitty older brother's dick right now."

Parker's fist shook as he resisted the urge to beat his older brother again.

"You're sick," Parker spat. "All of you!"

He stormed off into the woods, dead branches and leaves cracking under his feet.

His brother had always been self centered and deranged. There was no way that Deepa would ever betray him and sleep with the enemy.

CHAPTER 13

"Ouch," Axel groaned. "Can you be any rougher?"

"I'm trying," Deepa huffed as she ran a wet cloth over his bruised stomach. "But Luke said that we need to clean all these scratches with soap to make sure they don't get infected."

"What would he know?" Axel moaned.

"Wasn't he a nurse?"

"In training, I bet he didn't even show up for class half the time."

Deepa let out a huff, making sure to give the next scratch a rough scrub.

"Ouch!" Axel whined.

Luke had patched Axel up the best that he could. There was nothing that they could do but confine Axel to his bed and wait for him to heal, as much as the werewolf wined and bitched about how bored he was.

Deepa had become his default nurse, changing his dressings and helping him bathe. It helped ease some of the guilt over him being shot.

Deepa's heart clenched whenever she remembered how close Axel came to dying. How it felt like someone had shoved a hand into her chest, and she had no desire to experience the feeling once more.

"Does this hurt?" Deepa asked, gently cleaning along his side, making sure not to disturb any of the bandages.

"A little," Axel grumbled. "But do you know what would really make this sponge bath better?"

"What?"

"If you were naked."

Deepa let out a huff, tossing the wet cloth on his stomach. "You're supposed to be healing."

"Come on," Axel moaned. "It's so boring here. The least you can do is give me a sexy sponge bath instead of this sadist nurse shit."

"You could pull a stitch," Deepa crossed her arms over her chest. "Luke said that you're not allowed to have sex until you're better."

"Come on," Axel huffed. "Just...take off your clothes and show me your tits for a while. Please just bring back some joy into my shitty existence."

Deepa rolled her eyes. "You won't die if you don't fuck for a week."

"How do you know? This dick detox could be enough to send me over the edge. Having something nice to look at would give me more of an incentive to live."

"Don't be dramatic," Deepa muttered. "You'll be fine."

"But is my dick going to be fine? What if having it so deprived stresses it out and makes it smaller?"

"That's not how dicks work, Axel. Didn't they ever teach you that at school?"

"No," Axel huffed. "The elders said that I was way too important for school."

"Explains so fucking much," Deepa muttered under her breath.

Axel quirked an eyebrow. "What was that?"

"Nothing." Deepa reached behind her back to undo the clip to her bra. "Look, I'll take off my clothes for a bit if you just promise to shut up."

"Fine," Axel grinned. "I won't say another word."

"Good." Deepa unhooked her bra and pulled it off, tossing it onto the floor along with her t-shirt. Her jeans and underwear came next until she was fully naked before him.

Axel's icy blue eyes drank in her naked form. "Yeah, that's good. Now bathe me."

Deepa let out a huff and dabbed her cloth in the water basin. She ran it along his leg, fully aware of Axel's gaze.

"Nice and slow," said Axel. "And more sensual. Turn more so that I can get a better view of your butt."

"I thought that you said that you weren't going to talk."

"I wouldn't have to if you weren't so terrible at this?"

"Then what am I supposed to do, pretend to be your maid? Call you Master?"

Axel's eyes went wide with excitement. "You'd do that for me?"

Deepa let out an exasperated sigh. "Fine." She washed him more gently, mouth curving up into a fake smile. "It's time for me to wash you with my breasts, Master."

"Fuck yeah," Axel hissed, relaxing back on the pillows.

His attitude was annoying, but it was nice to see Axel so lively for the first time in days, so Deepa tried her best to softly wash his legs and feet.

"Just remember" Axel said. "It's not a sexy sponge bath without a happy ending."

"Sorry Master," Deepa groaned. "But you don't pay me enough for that."

"Hey, who's the master here and who's the slave?"

"Maid," Deepa corrected.

"Yeah, same difference."

Deepa rolled her eyes, running the cloth over his thighs. When she looked up, Axel had one hand in his boxes, slowly stroking himself while watching her bathe him.

Just the sigh was enough to make Deepa's cheeks flush red. "Serious?"

"What?" Axel pulled down his boxers to free his erection. "Luke never said that I couldn't get myself off."

Deepa bit her lip, switching to washing his arms. "Touch yourself all you want, but I'm not helping."

"Yeah, whatever," Axel muttered, stroking faster. "Just knowing you're naked and wet while touching me is enough."

Deepa's hands faltered as Axel's breath quickened, his eyes fully focused on her as if there were nothing else that mattered.

She rinsed the rag out and restarted washing his arm, biting the corner of her mouth as he shamelessly pleasured himself.

"Can you spread your legs a bit?" he huffed. "I want to see your pussy."

The words sent a shock straight to her crotch, a slight dampness forming between her thighs.

Deepa adjusted herself on the bed, planting her knees firmly against the mattress and spreading her legs.

She continued running her hands along his skin as Axel traced her curves, a deep flush spreading across her body.

She glanced up to see him staring straight at her, mouth parted, breathing heavy.

His lust was just as much a part of him as his wolf. It was in his needy expression, the tight grip he had on his erection, the rapid pulse of the bulging veins.

"Fuck," he groaned, his eyes fully fixed on her crotch. "Wanna be inside there so much."

That was when Deepa knew that she was done. Something about watching him jerk off as if it were the most important thing in the world had driven her over the edge, desire tearing at her like an angry predator.

"Here?" she said softly, slitting her hand down to insert a finger into her dripping entrance.

"Yes," he groaned, pumping his length harder. "Just like that. Wanna taste you."

"You'll have to wait for that," Deepa teased, moving her hand upwards to brush against her swollen clit.

"Tease," he mumbled. "Wanna feel that mouth... on my cock."

"Soon," she whispered, grabbing his hand and replacing it with hers. "But you haven't earned it yet."

Axel moaned as her hand began to move over his swollen head. "You're the fuckin worst...."

Deepa smiled, carefully stroking the velvety flesh, running her thumb along the tip.

Axel closed his eyes, his hands fisted in his sheets, breath hitching with every soft touch of her hand, a sheen of sweat forming over his forehead.

His cock throbbed in her hand, and she wanted to see him cum, wanted to feel his warm seed flow over her fingers as he shuddered with euphoria.

"Deepa?" called a voice from outside the door.

Deepa barely had time to remove her hand from Axel's groin before the door swung open.

Parker stood frozen, eyes wide as he glanced between Axel and Deepa's bare form. "I...uh..."

"Parker," Deepa gasped, sliding off the bed to grab her shirt. "It's not...it's not what it looks like."

Parker's mouth opened and closed, struggling to find words until he finally turned and stormed out, slamming the door behind him.

Cursing under her breath, Deepa scrambled into her jeans and pulled her hair into a messy ponytail.

"Where are you going?" Axel asked.

"After him," Deepa said. "I need to explain."

"Explain what?"

Deepa ignored him, rushing out the door, her heart racing.

She had no idea what Parker would do or say, but she couldn't let him leave like this.

Deepa rushed to the front door and flung it open, catching a glimpse of Parker's black hair disappearing down the driveway.

"Parker!" she called out, but he didn't stop. "Please, wait!"

He kept walking, not pausing or even glancing back, vanishing into the darkness as if she wasn't there.

"I can explain," Deepa pleaded, running to catch up.

Parker spun around. "Explain what? What is there to explain?"

"What you saw back there, it wasn't what it looked like."

"It's exactly what it looked like. You were screwing that piece of shit."

"No, I was just giving him a sponge bath," Deepa muttered.

"Naked? I don't know how they do things in werewolf land, but where I come from that's a sex act."

Deepa felt herself flush. "It's not like that."

Parker frowned. "Do you think that I'm stupid. I know what I saw. You've completely lost your fucking mind and been brainwashed by that freak!"

"Parker," Deepa cried. "Calm down. Just let me explain-"

"There's nothing to explain! You're fucking the monster who turned you into a werewolf."

Deepa flinched back, eyes wide.

"I thought that you were better than this, Deepa," Parker hissed. "I thought that you loved..." he stopped, turning away from her and letting out a bitter laugh. "But it looks like I was wrong."

"I didn't mean for it to happen," Deepa croaked, her face going numb. "I tried to fight it, but-"

"But you fucked him anyway," Parker snapped. "You like being one one of them, don't you? You like all this fucked up wolf shit."

Deepa froze. She couldn't move, couldn't speak.

Parker glared at her like she was something horrible that he'd found on the bottom of his shoe.

"I... I," she stuttered, her head spinning.

He didn't understand. He could never understand the bond that tied her to Axel.

"I'm done with this bullshit," Parker hissed. "Go screw that monster if that's what you want."

Parker spun around and stormed off into the darkness.

Deepa reached out to stop him, but her feet felt heavy. She couldn't bring herself to follow him, just standing frozen as he disappeared down the road.

Her chest tightened, her mouth dry, her hands shaking.

What had she done?

Deepa stumbled back inside, her body weak from the shock. Reese, Bruno, Luke, and Nastya had gathered around the T.V, watching a news report intently.

"Deepa, come here," Nastya called out with an enthusiastic grin. "You should see this."

Deepa didn't have the energy to respond, collapsing onto the sofa beside them.

The newscaster's face was grim. "After attacks on several Infection Control headquarters around the country, the werewolf group responsible has released the following message."

The screen cut to shaky footage of a large half transformed werewolf man standing before a burning building. "Dear all humankind," his deep voice began, "turn to our side or die."

A chill ran down Deepa's spine. This couldn't be happening.

"They're giving all humans a week to willingly undergo the transformation into werewolves," the newscaster continued solemnly. "After that time period, any remaining humans will be forcibly turned or killed."

Nastya laughed, a harsh, manic sound. "Can you believe this? It's really happening!"

Deepa swallowed hard, her mouth dry. Just days ago, the idea of werewolves taking over seemed ludicrous.

Now it had become a terrifying reality.

PART 5

CHAPTER 1

"And where do you think you're going, human?"

Parker bristled at those words, coldly glaring back at the recently turned werewolf blocking his way. The try-hard wore nothing but an oversized fur coat and a pair of tight leather pants.

His three minions looked equally outrageous, covered in fake fur and chains like it would somehow make them more intimidating.

Parker pulled down his collar to show the scar from Axel's bite. "Get out of my way."

"Wow, sorry bro," the new werewolf said and stepped aside, allowing Parker to pass through.

He attempted to give Parker a fist bump, but Parker didn't respond, remaining silent until he was halfway down the street.

Gunfire echoed in the distance, and a nearby explosion caused the ground to vibrate under his feet.

The city had descended into chaos. Werewolves and humanity were at war with each other, and the streets were overrun by the newly turned, desperate to bite any human in sight and convert them all to their cause.

The police, government, and military were barely holding on, and it was up to Infection Control to try and wrestle back control of the city.

Parker crouched in a narrow alley, pulling out his radio.

"This area's mostly clear," he reported quietly. "There are seven werewolves blocking the main road, but they don't have any firearms."

He waited, listening to the static on the radio until a response came through.

"Understood," Craig's deep voice replied. "We'll move forward."

Tucking the radio away, Parker carefully looked out from the alley to check his surroundings. As someone immune to werewolf bites, he was the ideal scout, able to move freely through werewolf-controlled areas without fear of transformation.

But his arm throbbed, a painful reminder of his last brutal encounter. The newly turned werewolf had attacked with savage ferocity, lunging at him like a creature possessed. Its jaws had snapped inches from his face, forcing Parker to empty his gun into the beast's body.

In those final moments, Parker had seen the creature's eyes, feral and devoid of any remaining humanity. It had been completely overtaken by its animalistic urges and was unlikely to shift back to a human form again.

The quiet of the alley was shattered by the sound of claws scraping against concrete.

Parker drew his weapon with practiced speed, heart racing in his chest. He aimed into the inky blackness of the alley, straining his eyes to pierce the gloom.

From the depths of the shadows, a massive black wolf materialized. Its eyes locked onto Parker's with unnerving intensity.

There was something hauntingly familiar about its gaze.

A cold dread settled in Parker's gut as recognition dawned, but before he could squeeze the trigger, the wolf's form began to shift.

Fur receded, bones cracked and realigned, and within moments, a man stood where the wolf had been.

"*You,*" Parker hissed as he came face to face with his older brother Ryan.

The months had changed Ryan. He was broader, more muscular, as if the war against humanity had sculpted him into a living weapon. His dark hair hung long and unkempt, framing a face rough with stubble.

"Hello, little brother," Ryan's deep voice rumbled with a hint of amusement.

Parker's gun remained trained on Ryan. "What the fuck are you doing here?"

A smirk played across Ryan's lips. "Really? Is this how you greet family?"

"I've never once thought of you as family, now tell me what the fuck you're doing here before I blow your brains out."

"Deepa misses you," said Ryan. "She's worried that you're going to get yourself killed out here."

Parker's hand twitched, but his face remained passive. "So, why would I give a shit about what that werewolf bitch thinks?"

"Come on now. Didn't mother ever tell you that it's not good to tell lies?"

Parker's grip tightened around his gun. "Fuck off."

"No, can do." Ryan shrugged. "I made your girl a promise, and I intend to keep it. You're much safer back with us than running around as Infection Control's little errand boy."

Parker pulled the trigger, blowing a chunk out of the concrete beside Ryan's head.

"Don't come near me again," Parker hissed.

Ryan didn't flinch. Instead, he let out a low whistle, his eyes gleaming with dark amusement. "You seem to have misunderstood. This isn't a request. You're coming back with me whether you like it or not."

Several white wolves emerged from the darkness behind Ryan, teeth bared as they circled Parker.

Parker's knuckles went white around the gun. His eyes darted from one wolf to another, counting, calculating.

"Come on now, little brother," Ryan chuckled. "Even you can't take them all out before they chew your arm off."

Parker took a step back, several possible plans running through his mind before he let out a curse, lowering his weapon.

"There's a good boy," Ryan cooed. Several wolves shimmered and shifted, taking on human form. "Time to come back to your real family."

CHAPTER 2

Deepa groaned as Axel pounded into her from behind, gripping her naked hips hard enough to leave marks. Her nails dug into the dirt as he slammed into her dripping pussy, fucking her like the animal that he was.

The air was cool and her nipples hard. Leaves crunched under her knees, and a twig bit into her shin.

But it felt good, the sensation of him inside her, the warmth spreading throughout her body, his scent, and the noises he made when he was fucking.

Like he was desperate to make sure that she never forgot that they belonged together.

Their daily fuck in the forest had become routine ever since Axel healed. The house was full of people coming and going, all talking of the war, so Deepa was eager to escape it all, to surround herself in nature and pretend that the world wasn't crashing down around them.

Axel's body shimmered and transformed, taking on more of his wolf form. His teeth sharpened and his skin sprouted fur, but his hands and limbs remained human.

Deepa moaned, feeling him grow bigger inside her, feeling his cock swell as his knot took shape.

Axel started to grind, pushing in deeper, desperate to have his big thick werewolf knot lodged deep inside her eager pussy.

Deepa squirmed, the intense pressure from his knot was almost unbearable, filling her in a way that was both exciting and frightening. Her nails dug into the leaves as her eyes clenched shut.

"Fuck," Axel growled, voice deep and rough. "You like that don't you?"

Deepa reacted to his words. Warmth washed over her body, flowing down all the way to her toes.

She shuddered and nodded, unable to speak as wave after wave of pleasure assaulted her senses.

It became too much. Her brain went foggy and her legs shaky. Deepa trembled and moaned, her pussy convulsing around his pulsating knot.

Deepa screamed as her orgasm hit like a bolt of lightning, surging through her body in one explosive climax after another.

Axel continued to slam his cock into her hole, her moans spurring him on.

Deepa could only submit to his forceful rhythm.

His breathing became erratic and his pace frenzied, the warm swelling of his cock deep inside her pulsing in time with her own orgasm.

A roar erupted from Axel's throat as he filled her with a flood of cum.

Axel kept thrusting and thrusting, filling her pussy as his knot locked them together, a rope of semen spurting with each motion.

Deepa would have found it fucked up when she was human, but as a werewolf, she basked in the sensation of his cock wedged deep inside her.

Axel let out a deep satisfied groan as he rolled onto his side, pulling Deepa close. They lay together in the secluded clearing, their bodies intertwined and still tingling.

Deepa nestled against Axel's chest, savoring the warmth of his skin and the soft bristle of his fur against her cheek. She breathed in his musky scent, a mix of pine and earth that always made her feel at home.

The air was crisp and sweet, a gentle breeze running along her naked skin. The sky above was a deep blue, and the sun hung low in the sky.

Deepa glanced at Axel. He gazed up at the foliage above them, his chest rising and falling rapidly, a satisfied smile plastered on his face as he shifted back to his human form.

Deepa could feel her inner wolf beam with joy, delighted that her body had pleased him.

They washed themselves off in a nearby stream, splashing the cool water onto their bare bodies.

Smoke rose up into the sky from a battle in the distance.

"Just a bit longer," Axel said.

Deepa's stomach twisted. "Until what?"

"Until we no longer have to hide. Until we can finally come out of the shadows and live as we are, free from human oppression."

Deepa remained silent. She'd learned that nothing she said would ever get through to him. He refused to accept that humans could win this war.

Axel laced his fingers through Deepa's as they made their way back to the house.

"Don't fucking touch me!" yelled a voice from the front lawn.

Deepa's eyes widened when she saw a struggling Parker flanked by a group of blond men. Ryan stood triumphantly beside him.

"I can walk myself," Parker growled, ripping his arm out of Ryan's grip.

Ryan laughed. "Don't get pissy now. I'm only doing what's best for you."

"Don't act like you give a shit," Parker hissed. "I know you just want me back to show me how you've turned Deepa into your bitch."

"What can I say?" Ryan shrugged. "Your girlfriend just can't resist my charms."

"You're disgusting!"

"Parker," Deepa gasped, her grip slipping from Axel's as she rushed towards Parker.

Parker froze when he caught sight of her.

"Deepa." His eyes widened with surprise, then quickly switched to a look of cold indifference. "Are you happy now? Is this what you wanted?"

"It's not like that." Deepa reached out for him. "Let me explain."

Parker recoiled from her fingertips. "There's nothing to explain. It's perfectly clear whose side you're on."

Axel threw an arm over Deepa's shoulder, pulling her close. "If you've got a problem, why don't you take it up with me?"

"You," Parker hissed, teeth clenching as he balled his hands into fists.

Ryan watched on with amusement. "Go ahead." He smirked, placing a hand on Parker's shoulder. "You're more than welcome to use Axel as your personal punching bag."

"Please," Deepa begged, grabbing Parker's arm. "Can we please talk?"

"About what!" Parker snapped, ripping his arm out of Deepa's grip. "I'm done listening to your shit!"

Deepa froze, heart clenching in her chest. "I'm sorry," she whispered, gaze falling to the ground.

Axel let out a growl. "Why don't you just get the fuck out of here, you werewolf murdering piece of shit."

"Axel," Deepa whispered. "Stop, please."

"What?" Axel pulled Deepa close. "We both know that you don't need him anymore."

Parker's jaw tightened, his eyes narrowing. "Give me a gun and I'll-"

"Parker," Ryan said with a smirk. "Is this really the right way to talk to our dear older brother?"

Parker's body tensed, his eyes going wide. "Brother? Oh fuck no."

"Oh yeah," Ryan chuckled. "It's a funny story actually. Our darling father was fucking his mom, which makes us half brothers."

The color drained from Parker's face as he stared at Axel, his breathing ragged.

"Well, if you're done chatting, let's go." Ryan grabbed Parker's shoulders, steering him towards the house. "I need to show you to your room."

Parker stumbled forward into the house, followed by the rest of the pack.

"You didn't have to be so harsh," Deepa said to Axel.

"What?" Axel shrugged. "It's better to make him realize how pointless fighting against us is. He needs to learn his place as a human, otherwise it's just going to be harder for him later."

"He's still my friend, and I want him to stay."

"As a friend? Are you sure that you're not hoping to have a little threesome on the side?"

"What-" Deepa froze, her cheeks heating.

"I wouldn't mind," Axel muttered. "Just as long as I'm the one fucking you and he's only allowed to watch."

"Don't make stupid jokes like that," Deepa hissed.

"I wasn't joking."

Deepa glared at a tree, trying to get the sinful image of both Axel and Parker screwing her at once out of her mind.

"He's your brother," she murmured. "You should be kinder to him."

Axel rolled his eyes. "I already have plenty of brothers. I don't need a defunct one who can't even shift. Plus I'm pretty sure that he's just going to stab me the first chance that he gets."

Deepa wasn't sure how to reply. She knew that keeping Parker there wasn't a good idea, but it was the only way to stop him from getting ripped apart on the battlefield. She just needed to keep him safe until the war was over.

"Come on." Axel took hold of Deepa's elbow to pull her inside. "Dinner should be ready soon."

CHAPTER 3

Parker collapsed onto the mattress, staring blankly up at the ceiling.

Ryan and his group had taken Parker to the basement, locking him inside a small windowless room. The only light came from the bulb overhead, casting the bare walls in an eerie orange glow.

If his so-called family were trying to make him feel at home, they were doing a shitty job.

He still felt disgusted at the way that his parents had lied to him for years, covering up their werewolf selves and parading around as humans. All for his so-called benefit. They were all pieces of shit and he didn't need any of them. The moment that he got out of that room he was going back to Infection Control to sell them all out.

A click came from the lock, and Parker bolted upright as the door opened.

Nastya stepped inside, dressed in a short skirt and tight top, a tray of food in her hands as two men closed the door behind her.

"Here you go," she said, placing the tray down on the mattress.

"I don't want your shitty food," Parker muttered, turning his back to her.

Nastya sat beside him. "Oh come on. Don't be like that. We're all one big happy family here, and once you stop being so grumpy, you're more than welcome to join us for meals upstairs."

Parker rolled his eyes. "Fuck you."

"Hey." Nastya frowned, her hand brushing against his thigh. "That's not very nice. I was hoping that you could come to think of me as a sister."

"You're not my sister."

"Of course not by blood," Nastya said softly. "But I helped raise Ryan, so I'm looking forward to getting to know you as well."

Parker stiffened as her hand rested on his leg. "What are you doing?"

"Just trying to make you feel welcome," Nastya purred, leaning in to lick the shell of his ear.

"Stop that." Parker swatted her hand away.

"Oh, come on," Nastya huffed. "I'm just trying to help you relax. You've had a rough day, so why not let off some steam?"

"Not interested." Parker moved away to the other side of the bed.

Nastya frowned. "Well you're no fun. And here I was hoping to find out which brother has the bigger dick."

Parker glared at her. "Seriously?"

"Hey, can you blame a girl for being curious?" Nastya leaned back on the bed, giving Parker a perfect view of her cleavage. "Deepa's probably screwing our brother upstairs right now, so don't you deserve some fun too?"

"Not interested," Parker growled, pointing to the door. "Get out."

"Fine, fine." Nastya sighed and got to her feet. "I'll leave for now, but the offer's always open."

She flashed him one last sultry smile before slipping out the door, leaving Parker alone once again.

CHAPTER 4

Axel woke up alone the next morning. He wandered the house searching for Deepa, only to walk into the dining room to find a grumpy Parker chained to the table.

Ryan sat beside him, lips pulsed and face blank as an untouched plate of eggs sat before them.

Their father Elijah sat on the other side of the table, happily munching on a piece of bacon while two of his sons glared daggers at the older man.

It was the first time that Axel had seen his father in years. He left when Axel was small and was too busy screwing Ryan's mother to ever drop by to visit.

The older man still looked good for his age, upper body muscular with strands of blond remaining amongst his gray hair.

"What the fuck are you doing here?" Axel spat.

Elijah took a moment to swallow his food. "Do I need a reason to visit my own children?"

"Yes, you do," Axel growled, glaring at him. "Especially since you haven't bothered showing up until now."

"Their mother wanted me to check on Austin. She's worried about how he's been coping."

Parker let out a huff. "There's no amount of therapy in this world that will ever help with what you guys did to me."

"That was your mother's decision, not mine," said Elijah. "If it were up to me, you would have been born and raised amongst our kind."

"As their personal punching bag," Ryan scoffed. "The elders don't give a shit about werewolves who can't shift."

"We could have made it work." Elijah took another bite of his food.

Ryan rolled his eyes.

"There is one more reason why I came," Elijah continued. "I've heard that the three of you haven't been getting along."

"I hate them." Parker tugged at his chain. "And I'll kill them the first chance I get."

"Well...I don't want you alive either," Axel snapped.

His life would be far easier without Deepa's ex-boyfriend hovering around, stealing her attention.

"Now boys," Elijah said, his voice gentle. "You're all adults, and I expect you to treat each other as such."

"I'm not being friends with that fucker," Parker snapped, glaring at Axel. "He murders people."

"Only so that people like you won't murder us first," Axel growled back.

Ryan's mouth curved into a smile as he watched with amusement.

"Austin, Alex," Elijah said calmly. "I-"

"Alex?" Axel spat. "You still can't remember my fucking name?"

Ryan burst out into a laugh.

"I wanted to name you Alex," Elijah said, his fork hovering mid-air. "But your mother, as always, had her own ideas, just like with your sister Nastya."

Axel's jaw tightened. "Funny how you remember *her* name perfectly when the two of you aren't even related."

Elijah's chewing slowed to a halt. "Not related? She's my daughter."

"But she's always going on about some DNA test the elders forced her to take."

"DNA test?" Elijah's brow furrowed. "They never asked me. Your mother was only with me when she got pregnant with Nastya."

Ryan stopped laughing.

The silence that followed was deafening.

A slow triumphant smile spread across Axel's face.

"Oh." He was unable to mask the satisfaction in his voice. "So maybe she is my full sister after all."

Sister fucker, he mouthed at Ryan from across the room, laughing as the other man's face turned pale.

"This family is so fucked up," Parker muttered to himself.

"Regardless of whatever your name is," said Elijah. "The three of you need to learn to get along, so I've devised a little challenge for you all."

"No, thanks," said Axel, eyeing the food on the table. He'd had enough of his father for one day, but he wanted to stay and watch Ryan mentally suffer.

Ryan sat motionless, his eyes unfocused, as if his entire history with Nastya was flashing before him in a cruel montage.

"Don't you want to know where Deepa is?" said Elijah.

"Where is she?" Parker's head snapped up, but then he quickly looked back at the floor. "Not that I care," he muttered.

"She's tied up in a cabin at the top of the mountain," said Elijah. "The three of you should get moving if you want to make it back before nightfall."

"You did what!" Axel snarled, his fingers elongating into razor-sharp claws as he fought the urge to lunge at his father.

"What's the problem?" Elijah cocked his head. "This is the perfect opportunity for the three of you to work out your differences."

"You sick mother fucker," Axel snarled. "What are you planning to do with Deepa?"

"Nothing." Elijah shrugged. "All you need to do is bring her back safely, or you can fight each other to the death and the winner gets to mate her, it's all up to you."

"Well, I'm not going," Parker huffed. "She can rot there for all I care."

Ryan remained frozen, still trapped inside his own head.

Axel's chair clattered to the floor as he bolted upright. He sprinted to the door, his body quickly shifting. Bones cracked and reformed, fur sprouted from his skin, and by the time he burst into the open air, he was fully wolf.

A primal howl tore from his throat as he bounded up the mountain.

In that moment, only one thought consumed him, he would rescue his mate, or die trying.

CHAPTER 5

Axel was almost at the top when a shot ran out, the bullet bouncing off a rock by his head.

He looked up to see Parker waiting for him on the narrow mountain trail, a gun clutched in his hands.

"What the fuck," Axel growled shifting into his human form. "How did you get here before me?"

"It's called a car, idiot," Parker drawled. "You could have used one instead of dashing out the house like a dog."

Axel's lip curled. "What the fuck do you want?"

"I'm here to save Deepa from you," said Parker. "I don't know what you did to her, but I know that she's better off with you dead."

"So you're gonna fight me to the death?" Axel growled. "Fine then, bring it. I've been itching to tear you to shreds as well."

Axel knew that Deepa wouldn't be happy when she discovered Parker's organs splattered over the mountainside, but he was certain that she'd get over it eventually.

A feral grin split Axel's face before his features contorted, bones cracking and reforming as he seamlessly transformed into a massive snarling wolf.

He lunged at Parker, all fangs and fury.

Parker dove and rolled, coming up in a crouch. In one fluid motion, he drew his gun and fired.

The shots cracked through the air, so close that Axel felt the heat of the bullets as they whizzed past his fur.

Axel snarled and leapt at him, knocking Parker down and pinning him against the ground.

"Fuck," Parker hissed, his knee digging into Axel's stomach, but his brother refused to budge.

Axel bared his teeth, ready to tear into Parker's throat, until a dark blur slammed into Axel's side.

The impact sent him tumbling, yelping in surprise.

Axel rolled several feet down the mountain trail until he regained his footing, returning to his human form.

"What the fuck are you doing?" he snarled at Ryan.

Ryan shifted back, his dark hair tousled. "Just standing up for my younger brother, but you wouldn't know anything about that, would you?"

Axel's chest heaved. "As if you actually give a fuck about him."

"I know what it's like to have a shitty older brother," said Ryan. "So unlike you, I love and cherish all my younger siblings."

"Just like how you cherish your sister?" Axel yelled back. "Guess that incest is just another one of Nastya's fucked up kinks."

Ryan's expression darkened. "We're not related."

"Yeah, keep telling yourself that if it helps you get hard."

"Go," Ryan hissed at Parker.

"But-"

"Go rescue Deepa," said Ryan. "I'll keep Axel busy here."

Parker froze for a moment, glaring at Axel like he wanted nothing more than to fill him with bullets, but then he nodded, dashing up the mountain trail.

"You're dead," Axel spat, his fists clenched.

"Are you proposing a duel, Axel?" Ryan stretched his arm. "Remember how well that turned out for you last time?"

Axel's jaw tightened. He went into that duel intent on winning, but the moment that his body hit the floor, he lost the will to get back up.

The idea of escaping all his responsibilities by passing them onto Ryan was just too tempting.

"I'm up for a rematch," said Ryan. "Winner gets to impregnate Deepa."

"Go fuck yourself!"

"Just once is enough." Ryan grinned. "I want to give her back to you when she's big and round with my child. I want you to feel it moving inside her, a constant reminder of how I'm more man than you."

Axel growled, charging at Ryan. He shifted and pounced, aiming for the other man's throat.

Ryan transformed and dodged, kicking out with his hind leg and sending Axel flying backwards.

"She was so enthusiastic when we had sex," Ryan growled, shifting halfway back to human so that he could talk. "I still remember what it felt like when she came on my cock, screaming *Parker Parker* as she imagined his face instead of yours."

"Shut the fuck up."

"Don't believe me?" Ryan taunted. "She was always talking about her little human lover, and how he was her one true love."

Axel charged again, slamming into Ryan's body and pinning him to the ground.

Ryan transformed back to his full wolf form, his jaws clamping down on Axel's neck as he flipped their positions.

Axel growled, struggling under Ryan's weight.

He thought of giving up, allowing his brother to win because it was less effort than fighting back, but the mental image of Ryan keeping his mate locked away until she fell pregnant was too much.

He and Deepa were fated mates.

He refused to allow her to be used by his deranged brother again.

Axel's hind legs shot out, catching Ryan square in the chest.

The impact sent Ryan flying backward, his paws scrabbling for purchase on the rocky ground.

Ryan regained his footing, his dark fur bristling like needles along his spine.

With a snarl, Axel launched himself at Ryan, jaws wide and aiming for the throat, but Ryan ducked and sidestepped, Axel's teeth snapping shut on empty air.

Undeterred, Axel spun and pounced again.

Ryan met the attack head-on.

The two massive wolves collided in midair, a tangle of claws and fangs.

Their momentum sent them tumbling down the mountainside, locked in a vicious struggle.

They rolled over rocks and roots, each fighting for dominance. Claws raked through fur and flesh. Teeth found purchase in whatever they could grab.

The sound of their battle echoed through the trees, growls, yelps, and the thud of bodies against earth.

They crashed onto a flat stretch of the trail, sides heaving as they gasped for air.

Blood matted their fur, dripping onto the dirt and leaves beneath them.

Ryan shifted back to his human form, wiping the blood from his mouth. "I used to think that you lost to me on purpose, but now I can see that you're just weak and pathetic."

Axel charged at Ryan before he could shift back, sending his younger brother colliding with a tree.

Ryan cried out in pain as the wind was knocked from his lungs, giving Axel the opportunity to dash past him and make his way up the mountain.

Axel's front leg throbbed with pain and his back was bruised from his fall, but all he could think of was Deepa. Deepa tied up alone in the cabin, Deepa desperately waiting to be saved, Deepa showering Parker with gratitude if the human bastard arrived there first.

Axel followed Deepa's scent until he spotted the cabin in the distance, covered with vines and weeds.

"Deepa!" He cried out halfway through his transformation.

Axel burst into the cabin, his eyes adjusting to the dim interior. Dust swirled in the air.

In the corner, Parker sat alone, clutching one of Deepa's shirts.

"What did you do to her?" Axel snarled, grabbing Parker's collar and slamming him against the wall.

Parker grunted in pain. "Nothing! She's not here!"

"Then where is she?" Axel demanded, his grip tightening.

"I don't know," Parker choked out. "The place was empty when I arrived."

"Liar," Axel growled, his knuckles turning white.

A weak laugh came from behind them.

Ryan stumbled into the doorway, blood trickling down his face from a gash on his forehead.

"How long will it take you two to realize that Father is fucking with us?" Ryan collapsed against the doorframe, gasping for breath.

"Shit," Axel hissed, loosening his grip on Parker's collar.

"You knew?" Parker snapped, shoving Axel away.

"No." Ryan shrugged. "But I'm not surprised. This is exactly the kind of dumb bullshit that our father loves."

"Fuck." Parker punched the wall, leaving a dent in the weathered wood.

Axel clenched his teeth, fury and embarrassment washing over him. How could he have been so stupid to fall for his father's lame tricks? "Then where the hell is Deepa?"

"We should creep up on him," said Parker. "Surround him from all sides and then attack when I give the signal."

"No," said Axel. "He'll hear us coming. I say that we dash in and overwhelm him."

"But what if he out runs us?" said Ryan, shutting the car door behind him. "Someone needs to block the exit."

"Fine," Parker muttered, heading towards the entrance of the mansion. "I'll aim for his legs if he tries to get away."

The three of them had agreed to a truce instead of murdering each other on the mountain. They needed to combine forces if they wanted to take down their father.

Axel's stomach churned with anxiety. He needed to know where that bastard had taken Deepa. Was she tied up in the basement, or had he shipped her off to live with the elders?

Laughter echoed from inside the house.

"Deepa?" Parker cried, rushing ahead of them.

"Hey!" Axel ran after him.

They crashed through the front door and into the dining room, only to find Deepa and Nastya sitting at the table with Elijah.

"Parker?" said Deepa, eyes widening in surprise as she gazed over their bruised and bloody bodies. "What happened to you guys?"

"Where the fuck were you!" Axel snapped.

"I went shopping with Nastya."

"All morning?" Axel growled.

"The fucking city is blown to pieces," Deepa snapped back. "We had to drive over an hour just to buy food."

Axel angrily pointed a finger at Nastya. "You helped him, didn't you?"

"Helped him do what?" Nastya shrugged.

"Fuck with our minds."

Nastya took a sip of her tea. "He called yesterday, said he wanted alone time with you three. I just helped make that happen."

"Bullshit!" Axel slammed his fist on the table, making the dishes rattle.

Elijah calmly took a sip of his tea. "I take it that the three of you had fun together."

Parker's face hardened. "You're dead to me," he spat, turning on his heel and storming out of the room.

Ryan slid into a seat next to Nastya, his hands trembling. "Father, about Nastya... she's not really your daughter, is she?"

"Of course she is," Elijah replied smoothly, giving Nastya a fond smile.

Ryan looked like he might be sick.

Nastya let out a sharp laugh. "Actually, no. Mother told me my real father is Patrick."

"Ah, Patrick." Elijah nodded, unfazed. "Your mother was always close with him."

He did a DNA test," Nastya added. "He's definitely my father."

Relief washed over Ryan's face, his tense shoulders relaxing.

Axel glared at his father. "What the hell? Doesn't this bother you at all?"

Elijah shrugged. "No. Your mother is free to be with whomever she chooses."

"That's not a normal reaction!" Axel shouted.

Elijah sighed. "You're always so uptight, Alex. Your mother had needs, and I wasn't always around to fulfill them."

"Why? Because you were too busy banging your new girlfriend?"

"Maybe you should talk to your mother if you want all the details about who fathered each of her children."

"Fuck this." Axel took hold of Deepa's arm and dragged her away from the table.

"Where are we going?" Deepa said as he led her down the hallway.

"My room," Axel spat. "We're staying inside until that bastard is gone."

CHAPTER 6

They ate dinner in tense silence, the only sound was the clink of cutlery against plates.

Deepa could feel Axel's anger simmering, even though she'd had no knowledge of his father's plan.

"Do you want me to apologize?" Deepa stabbed a meatball with more force than necessary. "Because I will if it'll stop your sulking."

Axel let out a grunt.

"Well I think it's nice that he came to visit you," said Deepa. "He seemed like he wanted to try and fix things between you."

"You mean fix things with his other sons to keep their mother happy," Axel grumbled, pushing food around his plate.

Deepa sighed, placing her plate on the bedside table. "Look, I know that you hate him, and you have every right to, but I think he genuinely does care about you."

"He can't even be bothered remembering my name."

"I'm sure that he was just joking."

"He's not. He's been calling me Alex since I was born."

Deepa couldn't help but let out a small laugh, quickly stifling it at Axel's glare.

"It's not funny," he growled. "He can't keep track of half his kids."

"Maybe you should sit down and have a proper talk with him."

"I'm not talking to that man," Axel spat. "He's a monster and a coward."

"But-"

"No," Axel growled, attacking his pasta with his fork. "He can rot for all I care."

Deepa sighed, her shoulders sagging. "Okay, I get it. My father was a dick too."

Axel cocked an eyebrow. "Worse than mine?"

"He was married when he met my mom. Stuck around for a bit after I was born, but as soon as his visa expired, he went back home to his other family. Cut off all contact."

"Wow," Axel muttered. "That is fucked up."

"Yep." Deepa popped one of his meatballs into her mouth, chewing slowly.

"And your mom?" Axel asked, his tone softening.

Deepa's eyes dropped to his plate. "Cancer."

"Shit," Axel breathed. "That's... I'm sorry."

"I lived with my aunt for a while," Deepa continued. "Until she got a new boyfriend. He... he convinced her to kick me out."

Axel's fork clattered to his plate, his eyes wide with shock. "What the fuck..."

Deepa nodded slowly. "I slept in the park and a library for a few weeks... then I moved in with Parker's foster family until I aged out of the system."

"Damn," Axel muttered, running a hand through his hair. "That's... I can't even imagine."

"It wasn't all bad," Deepa said, attempting a smile. "Parker's foster family was really kind."

"That still sucks."

Deepa shrugged. "Yeah, it was pretty shit. My mom... " Deepa paused to compose herself. "She wasn't really around much even when she was alive. She was always working or studying. Talking about how she was gonna get some great life for us both, but she never stopped to look after herself so..."

Deepa's face went numb as memories came rushing back, of her mother passed out on the couch, the countless medicine bottles, and her mother refusing to take a day off work, even though she was clearly falling apart.

Axel took hold of Deepa's hand, giving her fingers a squeeze.

Deepa swallowed, a lump forming in her throat. She had to be careful not to cry. If she started crying, she'd never be able to stop.

"Anyway." Deepa cleared her throat. "That's enough about me."

Axel shook his head. "I'm sorry."

"It's fine."

"It's not fine." Axel wrapped his arms around her, pulling her in for a hug. "You deserved better than that."

Deepa let out a deep sigh, burying her face in his chest.

She hadn't told anyone that story before, except for Parker. Her past was something that she kept locked away, and yet she had just spilled it all to Axel.

Axel's body was warm, and his heart beat against her ear, soothing her.

She closed her eyes and let herself sink into him, embracing the strange bond between them.

Axel shifted and Deepa looked up at him, his blue eyes watching her intently.

She licked her lips, his mouth hovering over hers, his breath ghosting over her skin.

He pulled her closer, crushing their lips together, and she melted against him, her hands running up his chest.

They toppled, hitting the mattress, but their mouths remained joined. He slipped his tongue inside, a low rumble of approval echoing in her throat.

He stripped her clothes in seconds, his rough palms sliding along her breasts, cupping the heavy curves.

"Fuck," Axel growled, flicking her nipples with his thumb. "I need you naked."

Her back arched and she gasped into his mouth, sparks of heat coursing through her.

He roughly groped and teased her breasts, making her nipples harden. His mouth moved down her throat, biting and sucking.

She hooked her legs around his body and bucked her hips, rubbing herself against his thick erection, whimpering for more.

His body rolled, grinding into her as his lips traveled across her shoulder, licking the scar tissue left from his bite mark.

A rumble of pleasure rolled through her core, and he mouthed her neck hungrily, teasing the delicate skin with his teeth.

Her wolf stirred, watching but not taking control, relishing in the sensations pulsing through Deepa's body.

Axel tore his head away with a groan. "Are you sure you're okay doing this now?"

Deepa lifted her head. "Yes," she hissed. "I need to." She arched her body, desperate to be skin to skin. "Please."

His eyes widened, a thrill running down his spine at her words. He leaned forward and crashed their lips together.

His tongue plunged inside her mouth, swallowing her moans as he worked at his own clothes, fumbling with the button on his pants.

Her hands rubbed over his torso, reveling in the planes of smooth muscles.

She licked her lips as she yanked down his pants and boxers, his erection bobbing free, a dribble of precome oozing from the tip.

Deepa climbed on top of Axel and straddled his hips, his hands sliding to her waist.

She rose onto her knees and guided him inside her. The blunt head spread her wide, and she cried out, dropping her hips and sinking all the way to the base.

"Fuck," Axel moaned.

Deepa whimpered in agreement, her inner walls adjusting to his size. The fullness stretched her pleasantly, a sense of belonging flowing through her.

She rocked against him, her breath coming out in short pants.

His lips captured hers in a heated kiss, one hand tangling into her hair, keeping her lips prisoner, while the other clutched her ass.

Deepa groaned in pleasure, his taste flooding her mouth, and her hips picking up their rhythm, sliding him deeper inside her.

Deepa broke the kiss, throwing her head back and moaning his name, "Axel, Axel, Axel!"

Her thighs shook, a tremor rolling through her body.

Axel flipped her under him, hooking her leg over his arm and burying his face between her thighs.

Axel licked her long and slow, from hole to hole, a growl in his throat as her taste exploded on his tongue.

Deepa shivered, a moan on her lips and her hips bucking up towards him, demanding more.

Axel's hot breath flowed over her as he chuckled at her desperation. He trailed the tip of his tongue to her throbbing clit, tracing circles over her tight bundle of nerves.

"Fuck," Deepa moaned, her fingers curling in Axel's blond strands, holding him tight against her aching body. "Don't stop."

He slid two of his fingers inside her slick entrance and crooked them upwards, working a rapid rhythm.

The pleasure coiling inside Deepa came loose and she writhed, gasping and mewling beneath him.

He drew away to lap at her clit, his fingers never halting as he teased her, keeping her riding the waves of pleasure.

"Axel." Deepa tossed her head, a ragged breath escaping her mouth. She rolled her hips into his ministrations.

Axel surged upwards, kissing her hard, the musky flavor of her pussy on his lips. His cock prodded her opening, the wide head spreading her slick folds.

Deepa tangled her arms around his neck and pulled him closer, crushing her lips to his and making him let out a groan.

He rubbed against her entrance, teasing her, his erection pulsing with need.

Deepa whimpered and squirmed under him, spreading her legs wide, inviting him in.

He pushed into her, groaning at the feel of her snug warmth around him, clenching as she adjusted.

He rocked into her gently, taking his time until she let out a shaky exhale, his name a soft moan, and he started driving into her with passion.

Their moans merged, cries and curses echoed through the room, sweat dampening their skin.

Deepa kissed him fiercely, his stubble grazing her cheeks, his hips colliding with hers in an uneven beat.

Deepa tangled her hands in his hair and yanked his mouth down to her neck, exposing her flesh to him.

Her skin throbbed in time to her racing heart, aching for his sharp fangs.

"Axel." The growl echoed from her chest, and her mate responded instantly, sinking his teeth into her tender throat.

A high pitched whimper escaped her at the wave of blissful ecstasy.

Her channel gripped him tight and he followed suit, filling her with his hot essence, grunting against her neck, his fangs lodged deep within her skin.

Deepa trembled under him as aftershocks flowed through her body, her face flushed and lips parted.

Axel slumped, his weight on top of her, his face nestled between her neck and her shoulder.

Deepa nuzzled into his cheek. They stayed like that, her warm arms circling around his shoulders, as she ran her fingers through his soft hair.

"I'll never leave you," Axel murmured.

"I know," Deepa whispered, basking in the warm glow of their love making.

She knew that things would never be simple, or if they'd even live to see the end of the war, but in that moment, she was happy.

CHAPTER 7

The rumbling of his stomach was the only thing that could extract Axel from Deepa the next morning. He locked the door behind him, just to make sure that none of his relatives could snatch her away while he was gone.

The memories of his father's visit still haunted his mind, but he emerged into the kitchen only to be confronted by an equally horrifying sight.

"Fuck, no," Axel muttered. "First Dad and now you?"

His mother, Latavia, sat at the table, a glass of orange juice cradled in her manicured hands. Her long platinum blond hair cascaded over her shoulders in carefully styled waves, framing a face covered in several layers of makeup.

Axel wasn't surprised to see that she was at least seven months pregnant, round stomach straining against the fabric of her tight summer dress.

Just like his father, Latavia was barely around when he was growing up, always too busy fucking around and pumping out babies to help increase the werewolf population.

"Axel," she said wearily, which wasn't anything new. She always acted like his mere presence was exhausting. "They want you to come back."

"Who?" he asked.

"You know who," she sighed.

Axel's eyes drifted to the window, catching sight of Nastya ripping out weeds in the garden, no doubt trying her best to avoid their mother.

"Why?" The word came out strained. "Why now?"

Latavia rose to her feet with visible effort, one hand supporting her swollen abdomen. "Come with me and ask them yourself."

Axel hadn't set foot in the main settlement since his humiliating defeat to Ryan. He was struck by how much had changed. New mansions dotted the landscape, each more opulent than the last, a testament to the pack's growing wealth and influence.

"What is this place?" Deepa asked, her voice hushed with awe as they passed a sprawling mansion crafted entirely from gleaming white marble.

"Home," Axel grumbled, his jaw clenching as they approached the security checkpoint. The air grew thick with the mingled scents of pack members, a cocktail of familiar and new that set him on edge.

"Don't be like that," said Nastya from the backseat. "You could have come back any time you wanted."

"And you could have gotten a lift with Mom!" Axel snapped back.

Nastya frowned, crossing her arms.

"Who are these people that you have to meet?" Deepa asked.

"The elders," said Nastya. "A group of people who basically run our werewolf community."

"So... A government?"

"No," said Axel. "Just a bunch of old geezers who think that they're the shit."

"Don't let them hear you say that," Nastya hissed.

"It's true," Axel shrugged. "Half of them can't shift anymore, but they expect us to bend over and do whatever they say."

"And you'd know all about that wouldn't you?" said Nastya. "How many of them did you take up the arse in order to make them love you so much?"

"Well... maybe if you weren't such a conniving bitch, they would have made you Father's replacement instead."

"You fuc-"

"Just stop it!" Deepa snapped. "Can the two of you just try and get along for once?"

Axel clenched his jaw, hating how easily his sister could provoke him. He took a deep breath, trying to center himself as they pulled up to an imposing stone mansion.

The building loomed before them. Intricate carvings adorned the entrance, depicting scenes of wolf packs and ancient battles.

Axel's mother was already waiting for them outside. Ryan, Parker, Reese and Bruno emerged from the car parked beside hers.

"Why have you brought me here?" Parker hissed, tugging at the ropes that held his hands behind his back.

"Why not?" said Ryan. "It's the perfect opportunity for you to meet more of our wonderful relatives."

"I don't care." Parker struggled to free himself.

"You might have fun." Reese grinned. "It's gonna be a blast. Sometimes Bruno's grandfather starts turning blue when it's time to replace his oxygen tank."

Parker didn't look amused.

"Come," Axel's mother gestured to the mansion. "They're waiting for you."

Axel's chest tightened, his pulse pounding in his ears. He could already feel the weight of the elders' expectations pressing down on him, but he took a deep breath and tried his best to ignore it.

That was his old life. All that shit had been passed onto Ryan along with his dignity.

"Maybe you'll get lucky this time," Axel said to his mother. "And have a boy that you can use to replace me."

"Oh Axel," she huffed, glancing at Deepa. "Maybe you should have found yourself a pure blood girlfriend if you wanted to dump all your responsibilities on a baby like your father."

"Well maybe Dad wouldn't have left if you weren't so frigid."

"Frigid?" she scoffed. "You of all people should know that it doesn't work like that, especially if the rumors about you and this girl are true."

"What rumors?" asked Deepa.

Latavia gave her a pitying look. "That Axel may have inherited a certain undesirable trait from his father."

"What do you mean?"

"Let's just get this over with." Axel took hold of Deepa's wrist and tugged her ahead, anxiety churning in his stomach.

If the elders all knew about his bond with Deepa, then there was no telling what they had planned for him.

CHAPTER 8

They walked into a sprawling ballroom that buzzed with activity. Elderly werewolves congregated in small clusters. They sipped expensive champagne from delicate flutes, their wrinkled faces animated as they discussed the ongoing war with enthusiasm, congratulating themselves as their grandchildren died on the battlefield.

"The rest of you can wait here," Latavia pointed to a table filled with finger food. "Axel, follow me."

"But Deepa-"

"Clearly has four chaperones." Her gaze flickered dismissively to Parker. "And... whatever that is."

"Go ahead, brother." Ryan placed his hands on Deepa's shoulders. "She'll be nice and safe for you here."

Axel bit his lip, wanting nothing more than to tear his brother's throat out and drag Deepa out the door, but he forced himself to follow his mother down the hall and into his great grandfather's office.

The elderly man was waiting for him behind his desk, dressed in a spotless white suit and red tie. He'd become more gaunt since their last meeting, but his eyes were as sharp and calculating as Axel remembered.

"Welcome back, Axel," he said, his voice a low, rasping whisper that seemed to suck the warmth from the room. "Take a seat."

Axel lowered himself into the chair opposite, acutely aware of his mother closing the door with a soft click. The scent of old paper and leather filled his nostrils.

"You're probably wondering why I called you here," his great grandfather began. "After the humiliation you subjected me to after your little stunt with your brother."

Axel remained silent, his throat constricting as he fought to keep his expression neutral.

"But I'm a forgiving man," his great grandfather continued. "And I'm prepared to give you another chance."

"Another chance?" Axel croaked. "For what?"

"To take your father's place."

Axel's heart thundered in his chest, a cold sweat breaking out across his skin.

"Your mutt brother may be a decent strategist and a good fighter." Disgust colored the elderly man's tone. "But he doesn't have the same breeding as you. The rest of the pack won't accept him as our future leader, not while you're still breathing."

Axel's fists clenched involuntarily, nails biting into his palms. "But he won against me in a duel."

"Which is why you must challenge him, and take back your rightful place."

Axel's blood ran cold. He often imagined what would have happened if he won that day, but continuing to live as the elders' favorite puppet always made him feel sick.

"I won't win," Axel mumbled, the words tumbling out of his mouth. "He's... Stronger than me."

His great grandfather's glare intensified, causing Axel to flinch.

"What are you saying, Axel?" The old man's tone was dangerously low.

"I'm saying..." Axel swallowed, forcing the words out. "That even if I challenge him... I won't win."

"So you won't even try? You'll leave the pack's future in the hands of a half breed bastard?"

Axel's shoulders drooped. The room seemed to grow smaller, and the air felt thick and hard to breathe.

"Do you have no pride at all?" the old man spat.

Axel couldn't find the words to respond.

The following slap stung, sending Axel toppling out of his chair.

"I gave you everything!" his great-grandfather shouted, looming over Axel. "Everything. And this is how you repay me?"

"I.. I.." Axel felt like he was seven again, desperately trying to please the man in front of him.

"Look at me, boy."

Axel lifted his head.

"This is your last chance for you to fulfill your potential," the old man hissed. "You will not get another."

CHAPTER 9

Deepa watched the party from her spot against the wall. It was obvious that the people before her were loaded, flashing thousand dollar handbags and watches like they were nothing.

Beside her, Nastya picked at a plate of salad, her expression sour.

"They're all assholes," she muttered. "Using their children and grand-children like tools. Half of them could be out on the battlefield instead of getting wasted here."

Deepa nodded, sipping her water. The contrast between the party's extravagance and the grim reality of the ongoing war was jarring.

"And don't get me started on their obsession with bloodlines," Nastya continued, rolling her eyes. "All this talk about keeping the pack pure. Guess how many of them married their cousins?"

"That's disgusting," Deepa grimaced.

"Welcome to my world," Nastya replied dryly, stabbing a piece of lettuce with her fork.

Deepa watched as Reese and Bruno navigated the room with ease, being greeted and praised by several elderly women.

A couple stumbled towards Ryan, their faces flushed from too much champagne.

"Congratulations on the latest victory, Ryan dear," the woman slurred. Her bleary gaze shifted to Parker, confusion clouding her features. "And... congratulations to you too... other Ryan?"

Ryan forced a smile. "This is my younger brother, Austin."

"Ah, yes..." The woman nodded, comprehension dawning slowly. "An-other one of Elijah's... Well, you know..." She trailed off, waving her hand vaguely.

Her husband let out an undignified snort, swaying on his feet.

Parker rolled his eyes, hand clenching against his thigh like he longed to draw out his gun.

Most of guests didn't bother to greet them, glancing at their group and whispering amongst each other.

"I don't think we're popular," Deepa said to Parker.

"Really?" Parker replied sarcastically. "I never noticed."

Deepa settled into the chair beside him, their shoulders almost touching. "Can I get you something to eat? You must be hungry."

Parker shook his head, his eyes never leaving the crowd of werewolves. "If Infection Control knew about this place, we could have ended this war before it even began."

"Yeah," said Deepa. "But it's too late for that now."

Parker exhaled heavily. "Why are you talking to me, Deepa?"

"W-what do you mean?" she stammered, caught off guard.

"You know what I mean," he huffed. "After sleeping with that guy and everything."

Deepa felt her throat constrict, words failing her.

"Look," Parker continued, his tone softening slightly. "I still care about you. I'm relieved you're safe. But I'm also angry, and hurt. Being around you... it's not easy."

"I'm sorry," Deepa managed, her voice barely above a whisper. "It's complicated. Axel, he-"

"You don't need to explain," Parker cut her off, turning away. "Just... give me some space. Please."

Deepa swallowed hard, feeling a lump form in her throat and a burning sensation behind her eyes.

She stood up, her legs feeling unsteady, and made her way to a dessert table across the room.

A waiter approached, offering her a glass of red wine.

Deepa grabbed it from the tray, then piled her plate with cake, stuffing it into her mouth while fighting the urge to look at Parker.

"Trouble in paradise?" a deep voice rumbled beside her.

Deepa turned to find Ryan, casually swirling a glass of white wine. His lips curled into a knowing smirk.

"No," Deepa muttered, stabbing at her cake. "Everything is fucking wonderful."

"And here I was thinking that we'd all work out our differences, and happily live out our lives as a foursome."

Deepa choked on her drink, face going red. "You wish."

Ryan let out a laugh, his eyes sparkling. "No, but seriously Deepa, I want things to be better between us. All this hostility is making it hard for me to sleep at night."

"Can't Nastya help you with that?"

"Not when she has.. A new hobby." He tilted his head towards Nastya.

Deepa followed his gaze. Nastya sat close to Parker. She was attempting to spoon feed him a piece of salad as Parker scowled and turned away from her.

A complex mix of emotions churned in Deepa's stomach, jealousy, confusion, and a twinge of hurt she didn't want to acknowledge.

"So what?" Deepa forced the words from her mouth. "Why should I care?"

"You shouldn't, but don't you want to make him a tiny bit jealous?"

"No." Deepa's voice wavered. "Why would I want to do that?"

"Dance with me." Ryan extended his hand with unexpected grace.

Deepa hesitated. "I don't think-"

"Just one dance," he insisted, his voice softer than usual. "Then I'll leave you to your cake and wine."

Deepa glanced at the dance floor. Several couples moved to a gentle waltz. Against her better judgment, she found herself nodding.

"Fine," she relented, placing her hand in his.

Ryan guided her onto the floor. His hand was warm and steady as it settled on her waist, effortlessly leading her into the rhythm of the music.

Deepa squeezed his hand. "You're... actually good at this."

Ryan's lips quirked in a wry smile. "This is what happens when you're raised by these people. I was forced to learn a variety of old people skills."

"Such as?"

"Knitting, cross stitching, and tea making."

Deepa chuckled. "Sounds thrilling."

"It was awful. We didn't have T.V so I think watching children dance like monkeys was their only entertainment."

"Oh, that's horrible."

"Well," Ryan murmured, his grip tightening, drawing her closer. "At least it's useful now."

Deepa felt her breath catch.

The warmth of his hand on her waist, the faint scent of his cologne, the intensity in his eyes as he looked down at her, it was all disarming.

Deepa didn't pull back, basking in the familiar intimacy. This was the Ryan who she allowed into her pants. The Ryan who made her feel like the center of the universe and went out of his way to make her happy.

"You know that you're always welcome in my bed," he said softly. "Axel doesn't have to know."

Deepa stiffened. The man was intolerable. He couldn't even last a whole conversation without talking about sex.

"No thanks," she said. "I think I'm good. One man is enough for now, thanks."

"Are you sure," he said softly. "Your birth control should have run out by now, but you still aren't pregnant. Maybe you need some extra help."

"Extra help?"

"Axel and I are brothers, so it would be easy to pass the baby off as his."

Deepa let out a laugh. "And you don't think that he'd ever notice?"

"No, Axel is far too full of himself to ever admit it."

Deepa rolled her eyes. "So you're saying that every time that Axel and I want a kid, I should just come to you?"

"Yes." Ryan's eyes glazed over like he'd entered his own morbid fantasy. "Wouldn't that be wonderful?"

Deepa groaned and tried to extract herself from his grip, but Ryan pulled her closer.

"Don't go now," he whispered in Deepa's ear. "Your ex is watching."

Deepa's heart fluttered in her chest. "Is he?"

"Yeah, and he's shit at being subtle about it. He looks like he's ready to rip my head off."

Deepa risked a glance behind her, meeting Parker's eyes. He immediately turned his head away, scowling.

"See?" Ryan whispered, his warm breath sending an involuntary shiver down her spine.

"You're a piece of work, you know that?"

"You say that like you don't enjoy it."

Deepa sighed, letting her head drop onto Ryan's shoulder. "What's he doing now?"

"Looking away. Pretending that he doesn't care."

Deepa's stomach churned with guilt. It was her fault that Parker was so miserable, her and the stupid bond with Axel.

"And now he's looking again," said Ryan.

Deepa sighed.

"You two must have been cute together," said Ryan.

"We were." Deepa remembered their first dates in the middle of the park, the sun shining down on them as they walked home, hands interlocked.

"Maybe he'll take you back once the war is over," said Ryan.

"I wouldn't count on it," Deepa murmured into Ryan's shirt.

"Don't say that," said Ryan. "Maybe he'll forgive you if you present him with Axel's dead body."

"You're horrible."

"You know I'm right. No man can resist a woman who has killed their greatest enemy. It's like a law of nature or something."

Deepa rolled her eyes, wishing that the song would end so that she could go back to the food table, when a powerful grip suddenly wrenched her away from Ryan.

She stumbled, disoriented, before finding herself staring into Axel's furious face.

His icy gaze bore into Ryan with murderous intensity.

"What do you think you're doing?" Axel's voice was low, dangerous, each word dripping with barely contained rage.

Ryan didn't flinch. He met Axel's glare with infuriating nonchalance, one eyebrow quirked.

"What's it look like?" Ryan shrugged. "I was just dancing with Deepa."

"Just dancing?" Axel spat. "With your hand so close to her arse?"

"Oh, that." Ryan smirked. "It was an accident. We just got carried away in the moment."

"Sure you did." Axel growled.

"Don't get so upset. Deepa's a big girl who can choose her own friends."

"Don't treat me like a fucking idiot. I know what you're up to, all the lies that you and Nastya whisper in her ear when I'm not around."

"Well someone needs to be honest with her. Tell her that she still has options, that she doesn't need to be your little sex slave for the rest of her life."

Axel's hands clenched into tight fists, his knuckles turning white.

"I challenge you," Axel declared, his voice low and dangerous as he pointed at Ryan.

Ryan's eyebrows shot up. "Challenge?" he chuckled. "Are you serious?"

"Deadly," Axel hissed. "I challenge you to a duel."

The room fell silent around them.

"Why?" said Ryan. "Because I danced with your girlfriend?"

"You know exactly why," Axel snarled.

"Fine." Ryan shrugged off his jacket. "Let's get this over with."

Axel tore off his shirt, tossing it to the floor. He was seconds from shifting and launching himself at Ryan, before his mother Latavia stepped in between them.

"As wonderful as seeing my son grow a backbone is," said his mother. "There's a proper time and place for these things."

"Then name a time and place." Ryan rolled up his sleeves. "I'm sure that the elders all want to come see their little golden boy get beaten to a pulp."

"You're dead," Axel snarled.

"Enough." Latavia said sharply. "Grandfather will decide the date of your duel."

"But-"

"But nothing. Go home and wait for me to call you."

"Fine," Axel growled, grabbing hold of Deepa's wrist and dragging her out the door.

"What the fuck was that?" Deepa said once they were out of the building. "Challenging him to a duel."

"He's gonna pay," Axel growled.

"For what? Dancing with me?"

"For everything. The lies, the manipulation. All the shit that he's put us through."

"You're being ridiculous."

"No, I'm not. You know what he's capable of. Do you really want that guy being in charge of us for the rest of our lives?"

"Well, no," Deepa mumbled. "But that doesn't mean that you have to beat him up. Can't you just have a vote or something?"

"Werewolf society doesn't work that way."

"So what? You're gonna fight to the death?"

"If I have to."

Deepa let out a sigh of exasperation. "You're all fucking insane."

Axel tugged at his belt, pulling it from the loops.

"What are you doing now?" said Deepa.

"Come run with me."

"Here?" Deepa looked around the mansion's courtyard. She had no desire to be seen naked by Axel's relatives.

"I need to work off some steam." Axel pulled his pants down.

"Can't we just take a walk around the block?"

"I'm a wolf." Axel shifted, his fur standing on end. "This is how we deal with things."

Deepa took a deep breath, then quickly undressed and transformed into her wolf form.

Axel darted forward, racing across the lawn. Deepa sprang after him, her paws pounding the earth.

CHAPTER 10

Axel's sleek body moved like a shadow through the trees, his bushy tail swinging back and forth.

They passed other wolves along the way, some in pairs, others alone, their playful barks echoing through the forest.

Axel kept up his relentless pace, leaping gracefully over fallen logs and jagged rocks.

Deepa pushed herself to keep up, her lungs burning with the effort.

He stopped beneath a massive oak tree, its leaves whispering in the breeze above them.

Axel shifted back to his human form and leaned against the tree trunk, catching his breath.

Deepa followed suit, her chest heaving as she gulped down air.

"What happened to your face?" she asked, noticing a dark bruise on his cheek.

"It's nothing," Axel said, touching the mark gently. "Just ran into a branch."

Deepa nodded, her gaze sweeping over the vast expanse of forest surrounding them.

"I used to come out here a lot when I lived here," Axel said softly. "It always made me feel... peaceful."

"It's nice," said Deepa.

"It's easier to disconnect from everything here, to just embrace the wolf part of myself."

"Are you really going to fight him?"

Axel's smile faded. "I don't have a choice," he muttered, his jaw clenching. "They were going to force me to do it sooner or later."

"They?" Deepa pressed, her brow furrowing in confusion.

Axel swallowed hard, averting his gaze. He could feel the weight of his troubles pressing down on him, threatening to shatter this moment of peace.

He didn't want to burden Deepa with all his problems. He just wanted to disconnect from his life for a little while, to lose himself in the simplicity of the forest and the company of someone who didn't demand anything from him.

"Don't worry about them." Axel took hold of Deepa's wrist and pulled her towards him. "Just let me lick your tits."

"Axel-"

He silenced her by wrapping his lips around one pert nipple, sucking eagerly at her chest, savoring the taste and feeling of the little bud hardening under his tongue.

"Axel," she gasped, hands grasping his hair.

He moaned as his teeth closed over her sensitive flesh.

He wanted to disconnect from his shitty human life, he wanted to be fully wedged deep inside her.

"Wanna knot you so bad," Axel murmured.

Deepa hesitated, as she did whenever he suggested doing anything in his transformed state.

He knew that she loved it, that she always orgasmed harder and longer when his body was part wolf, but she was still self conscious about her enjoyment of the animal aspect, about being fucked by something other than a human man.

He reached down and caressed her labia with his thumbs, trying to gauge whether he should insist on switching or not.

Her fingers twisted in his hair. A tiny gasp of pleasure escaped her lips. "Do it."

Axel's dick stirred. "Are you sure?" he murmured.

"I said yes," Deepa answered, biting her lip. "Stop asking."

Axel grinned, wasting no time shifting into his half wolf form.

It was a challenge to maintain, the urge to transform all the way was overwhelming, but he liked having both his human limbs and animal strength.

Not to mention a fully formed knot, which felt far more sensitive than his human dick.

Deepa's breath hitched at the sight, hungry gaze drifting over his pulsing erection and fur covered torso.

His stomach dropped, nerves tingling with anticipation as his instincts howled, the urge to take, rut and claim clouded his mind.

"What is it with you guys and going full monster on girls," Deepa muttered.

"I'm not full monster," he grumbled, a hint of a growl in his voice. "Only half."

"But your fangs..." Her eyes settled on his canines, each point glinting sharply.

Axel frowned. "Are you scared of them?"

"No," she replied, and to his surprise, it sounded genuine. "It's... hot."

Hot? The word did things to Axel. Made his cock twitch with want, his pulse pounding loudly in his ears.

"Really?" he rasped.

Her cheeks flushed. "Yeah."

Heat churned low and deep in his stomach, every primal fiber in his body desperate to take her.

His claws raked along her scalp as he fisted her hair and smashed his lips against hers, devouring the soft warmth of her mouth.

The animal part of him howled with victory when she returned the kiss eagerly, moaning low and loud against his lips.

His cock hurt as it throbbed against her thigh, a flood of precum escaping the head to smear against her naked skin.

He needed relief. Needed to sink his knot into her, pump her full of his cum until her belly bulged with it.

"Axel..."

Axel kissed a wet trail from her lips, down her neck. He savored the sweet, earthy taste of her skin, mumbling unintelligible words against her. His blood thundered through his veins, a feral energy humming under his skin.

Her hand found his aching member. He stiffened at first, worried that she might be too frightened or repulsed by his half form, but his fears vanished when her delicate fingers wrapped around his shaft.

"It's so thick," she said. "And warm."

His response died in his throat when she began to stroke him, the pressure of her palm rubbing the sensitive tip.

He could only moan, rutting shamelessly into her grip.

Things got even better when Deepa lowered herself to her knees, face close enough for her breath to fan over his leaking member. Her beautiful hazel eyes peered up at him as she dragged her pink, wet tongue across his engorged knot.

Axel's entire being lit up, electric shocks of pleasure spreading through every nerve ending in his body.

His fingers fisted the hair on the back of her head, holding her in place as he thrusted shallowly into the warmth of her open mouth.

She pulled away for a split second. He tensed, fearing rejection, but Deepa just stuck her tongue out, licking eagerly along the underside of his length.

Her free hand moved up to squeeze his swollen balls, kneading gently as she lapped at his dick.

"Good girl," he growled, voice rough with lust and affection, fighting the urge to shamelessly fuck her throat.

He wanted her to take him all the way in, gag on his shaft until tears filled her pretty eyes, but this was enough.

Every muscle in his body strained as her velvety, wet tongue swirled and danced across every ridge, vein and bump of his knot, shooting bolts of bliss straight up his spine.

He bit down on his tongue as his eyes fluttered shut, drowning in the ecstasy her lips and tongue brought.

Eventually the sweet torture became too much. His eyes snapped open, glaring into hers.

"Get on all fours," he ordered.

She paused for a brief second before complying, facing away from him and bending over, her curvy hips high in the air.

He didn't bother easing in, simply kneeling behind her and spearing his thick cock into her wet waiting entrance. Her pussy swallowed him to the root, his knot bumping against her labia.

Her whimper spurred him into action. Without a second thought, he thrust hard, using his werewolf strength and stamina.

In mere moments, the only sounds leaving her lips were guttural moans and broken cries of his name, her head drooping low between her shoulders and hands fisting the earthy ground.

Every hard piston of his hips dragged her forward, and Axel had to fight to keep her in position as he took her hard.

The animalistic side of him howled in triumph and pleasure, watching his thick dick slide in and out of her pussy, the pink ring stretching obscenely over the dark skin of his knot. He leaned down and buried his nose in her hair, inhaling the earthy scent that filled him with raw possessiveness.

This was what he was supposed to be. Not human, but a wild predator, dominating and claiming the woman meant for him.

The thought filled Axel with heady power and adrenaline. He drew his hips back, and slammed them forward, driving his member all the way in.

Deepa threw back her head and screamed as he repeated the movement, each brutal plunge tearing the scream a bit louder from her throat.

"That's right," he growled, his voice feral and distorted. "Howl."

He moved closer and planted both hands over hers, the fingers now tipped by lethal claws. He buried his face in her neck, sharp teeth grazing her sensitive skin.

He could feel his knot expanding as his release drew close, and he pushed the rest of it past the resistance of her tight entrance, her pussy locking his cock snugly in place.

"Mine," he snarled into her ear, feeling the first tinglings of orgasm beginning at the base of his spine.

He pushed and ground his hips as best he could, fighting to get the knot as deep into her core as possible as his release claimed him.

Pleasure pulsed through his entire being as he spilled inside her, his warm seed coating her walls and womb.

Deepa cried and shook under him as her own orgasm overtook her, but Axel couldn't make out her words over his howl of euphoria.

This wasn't like any other orgasm he had had in his life. This one obliterated him, each jet of thick white essence making his whole body convulse.

He panted for several seconds as the last waves of ecstacy and sensation died down, every single cell buzzing in the aftermath.

He collapsed on top of Deepa, who squirmed in discomfort.

"Hey, get off," she huffed. "You're a lot heavier than you look."

"But you feel good." He mumbled into her hair.

"Axel," she huffed and squirmed more vigorously.

Axel lifted himself on trembling arms and rolled off her. His heart stuttered as the wolf features on him began to fade, the fur disappearing back into his skin as his dick returned to normal and slipped from her body.

He studied his hand and clenched his jaw. Axel never enjoyed the transformation back into a human. He hated losing his connection to his wolf side and the primal energy that flowed in his blood.

Axel moved his hand to rest on her abdomen. He stroked the skin lovingly, his throat constricting with an intense surge of emotions.

He'd think about the duel when he got back. All he wanted to do at that moment was quietly rest beside her.

CHAPTER II

Parker made his way through the darkness, using the light of the moon to guide his way as he quietly followed the road down the mountain.

His relatives were horrible jailers, spending most of their time on their phones or disappearing to meet girls. They didn't even bother locking the door after they returned from the mansion, allowing Parker to slip outside once everyone had gone to bed.

The air was cool and damp, a faint breeze causing goosebumps to rise on his skin, but Parker forced himself to keep walking until he finally reached a white car parked outside a burnt out house.

Varn stepped out of the vehicle, his blond hair glowing in the moonlight.

"Took you long enough." Varn smiled. "I thought that one of those wolf freaks had finally popped you."

Parker huffed. "Where's Craig?"

"Inside." Varn pointed to the remains of the house. "The war's got him smoking like a chimney again."

Parker ducked through the gaping hole where the door once stood, carefully navigating the debris-strewn floor. The ceiling was gone, leaving the room open to the sky, but the remaining walls cast long shadows across the rubble.

Craig stood near a partially collapsed wall, a cigarette dangling from his lips.

He took a long drag as Parker approached, then exhaled slowly. "About time you showed up. What did you find out?"

Parker straightened. "Their leadership structure is more organized than we thought. They call themselves the Elders. They're spread out in settlements across the country, but there's a gathering planned in a week's time."

Craig's eyebrows raised. "A gathering? What for?"

"A duel."

"A duel?"

"Some kinda pissing contest to decide their future leader."

Craig dropped his cigarette, pulling a new one from his pack. "Interesting. Can you pinpoint the location on a map?"

"Yes, sir. I've got the coordinates."

"And in your opinion, is this our best shot at taking out their leadership?"

Parker nodded firmly. "Absolutely, sir. We'll never get another chance like this."

Craig nodded and pulled out a smartphone from his pocket. He handed it to Parker. "Mark the location. We need to be precise."

Parker quickly input the coordinates and returned the phone.

Craig studied the map, a grim smile spreading across his face.

"Alright, good work." Craig pocketed his phone, pulling out a lighter and igniting his cigarette. "I want you to go back and gather any additional intel you can. This could be the key to ending this war once and for all."

"Understood, sir."

"If you find anything useful, contact either me or Varn via radio."

"Yes, Sir."

Craig let out a long exhale of smoke. "And be careful."

"Sir."

"You're my best operative. I can't afford to lose you now. Try not to get yourself killed."

"Yes, sir." Parker saluted, trying to suppress his unease.

He didn't have the guts to tell Craig that the werewolves who kidnapped him were his estranged family. He had no idea if the older man would still trust him if he knew.

"Dismissed," Craig said gruffly, dropping the cigarette from his fingers and pulling another from his pack with practiced ease.

Parker nodded and walked back outside, taking a deep breath.

"Need a lift?" Varn smiled, patting the bonnet of his car.

"No thanks, I don't want to put you in danger."

"Aw, come on, man. It's no problem. If any werewolf scum gets in our way, I'll just flatten them with this baby."

"That thing's barely holding together," Parker countered, eyeing several holes that had been covered with tape. "They'll hear us coming from miles away."

"You wound me, Parker," Varn clutched his chest in mock offense. "She runs like a dream. Come on, you're not seriously considering hiking all the way back in the dark?"

Parker's feet ached and the offer was tempting, but he didn't want Varn to risk his life for him.

"I'd rather take my chances," Parker said.

"Suit yourself," Varn sighed. "But radio me if anything comes up."

Parker gave Varn a final nod before setting off, his muscles already protesting as he began the climb back up the mountain.

Halfway up, the forest suddenly erupted with movement. A large wolf burst from the undergrowth, powerful muscles rippling beneath its sleek coat as it bounded towards him.

Parker's heart hammered in his chest as he instinctively recoiled, throwing up an arm to shield his face.

The wolf's form blurred and shifted, transforming into a naked woman.

"Parker," Deepa panted, her chest heaving. "What are you doing out here?"

"I just..." Parker strained his mind to come up with an excuse. "Needed some air."

"Everyone thinks that you tried to escape. They're all out looking for you."

"Well you caught me." Parker shrugged. "Guess that you've gotta drag me back to the basement now."

"I'm sorry. I know that it sucks in there but-"

"Come on, Deepa. Stop pretending that you give a shit. If you really cared about anything you'd be out there fighting them instead of sucking werewolf cock."

Deepa went silent and looked down at the ground.

"Yeah, that's what I thought," he muttered.

"I..I wish that I was like you." Deepa's voice trembled. "I.. wish that I was immune but... I can't ever go back to being human. This is just the way that I am now."

Parker swallowed. He hated seeing her like this, but he didn't know what else to say. Why couldn't she see reason instead of following along with his psycho family like a trained puppy?

"I know that you hate me," Deepa sniffed. "And I don't blame you, but I still care about you. You're the closest thing that I have left to family."

"Don't say that," Parker groaned. "You're not that pathetic."

"What?"

"The Deepa that I knew would have never reduced herself to...this. The Deepa that I loved would have given her life to protect people from these monsters."

"These monsters are your family, Parker."

"This so-called family locked me away in the basement."

Deepa clenched her hands into fists. "All you ever talked about was how much you missed your parents, but now that they're here you don't even talk to them. You have everything that you wanted, but all you care about is throwing your life away for this stupid war."

"You swore an oath! You promised to give your life to Infection Control."

"I only joined Infection Control because of you!"

Parker stood silent, stunned.

"I never really gave a shit about killing werewolves or protecting society," Deepa continued. "I only joined because I thought that it would make you happy. That it would make you never want to leave me."

"Deepa-"

"But I'm done doing whatever will make you happy. I'm not going to stand here and let you throw your life away when you have a whole family full of people who are willing to protect you."

A white wolf emerged from the bush behind her, shifting into a tall blond man.

"Come on, Deepa." Luke placed a hand on her shoulder. "Let's take him back."

"Fine." Deepa wiped the tears from her eyes as Bruno and Reese emerged from the darkness, taking hold of Parker's arms.

CHAPTER 12

"Don't try anything funny," Bruno huffed as he shoved Parker back into the basement room. "You already owe me a lacky."

"If you didn't want him to die, you shouldn't have made him attack me."

Bruno's face twisted into a scowl. "You go around acting like some big bad human, but in our world you're nothing more than a werewolf dud. A weak, puny little half breed that's only good as a slave."

Parker gritted his teeth.

"You're lucky that you have the same blood as our leader," said Bruno. "Or we would have torn you limb from limb the second you stepped through the door."

"Lucky me," Parker spat.

"Yeah," said Bruno, slamming the door in Parker's face.

Parker sighed, moving towards his bed, only to find it occupied by Nastya.

She was laying on top of the covers. Dressed only in a pair of black lace underwear that barely covered her crotch.

"What are you doing?" Parker growled.

"Waiting for you," Nastya smiled, bearing her neck.

"Get off my bed," Parker growled.

"Why don't you make me?"

Parker's jaw clenched, his fists curling into a ball. "I don't know what kind of game you're playing, but it's not funny."

Nastya rolled her eyes. "It's not a game."

"Then why are you dressing like that?"

"Because your brother thinks that you need a little motivation to stop you from running away again," she purred, running a finger down her cleavage.

Parker bit his lip, forcing his eyes away.

"Stop it," he muttered.

"Why?" Nastya pouted, stretching her arms above her head. "Don't you want a taste?"

"No."

"Haven't your balls gone blue from lack of use? Or do you spend all your alone time down here jerking yourself off?"

"Shut up," Parker muttered.

"Do you picture your ex's face as you rub one out? Is that the only way that you can cum nowadays?"

"Shut the fuck up."

"Oh, I've hit a nerve. What's the matter? Sad that she's too busy sucking my brother off to give you any attention?"

Parker lunged forward and grabbed hold of Nastya's shoulders, pinning her to the bed.

"Shut the fuck up," he spat, shaking her. "Don't you dare talk about her."

Nastya laughed, a cruel smile twisting her lips. "I think about fucking her too sometimes, about how soft she must feel on the inside, and how she must sound when she cums. She's a screamer isn't she? I can't wait to find out."

"Shut up."

"Do you think she'd moan like a slut if I ate her pussy?"

"Stop it."

"She looks like the kind of girl who could take a big dick. Do you think she's ever had a threesome?"

"Stop talking."

"You two must have been such an odd couple. Did you really expect a hot girl like her to be happy with a pathetic little human like you?"

Parker's fists clenched around Nastya's bra strap, causing the material to tear.

Nastya giggled, her pale breasts spilling free.

"Go on," she purred. "Take a taste. I won't tell."

"I..." Parker swallowed, his gaze transfixed on her chest as his cock stiffened.

"That's it," Nastya cooed, guiding his hand to her chest. "Touch them. Feel how real they are."

Parker's palm brushed her breast, his heart racing as the warmth of her skin radiated through him.

Nastya giggled and pressed herself against him, the sound sending a shiver down Parker's spine.

"That's it," she cooed, placing her hand on top of his.

Parker swallowed. His head was swimming with the sensation, and it had been so long since he had last had sex.

Nastya guided his hand down, her fingers curling around his, as she guided him beneath the hem of her panties, the soft curls of her pubic hair tickling his skin.

"Come on," she breathed.

Parker's finger slid into her heat, her wetness coating him, as her hips began to move.

"Fuck," Nastya breathed, her nails digging into his arm.

"That's it," she purred, pressing her hips against him. "Punish me with your cock."

Parker groaned as he felt his pants being unzipped.

"Oh," Nastya gasped, her eyes widening. "You're fucking huge."

Parker swallowed, his cheeks flushing, as Nastya took hold of his member, running her soft fingers up and down his shaft.

"Fuck," Parker moaned, his cock throbbing.

"Yes," Nastya cooed, rubbing the tip, smearing the precum along his length.

"God, I'm so horny," she purred, slipping off her panties, revealing her moist pink slit. "I need your cock so bad."

"But, you're with-"

"Shh." Nastya silenced him by pressing her lips to his, her tongue delving into his mouth, exploring his warmth, as she ground herself against him.

"Please," she gasped, pulling back and looking at him with desperate eyes. "Please, fuck me. I need it so bad."

"I-" Parker swallowed.

He knew that this was a terrible idea, but he couldn't bring himself to pull away. Not when her soft breasts were rubbing against him, and her tight pussy was sliding along his cock.

"Please," she begged. "Just give it to me. It doesn't mean anything."

Parker hesitated for a moment, then let out a groan, allowing his cock to slip into her, her tight wet heat swallowing him.

"Yes," Nastya gasped, her breath tickling his ear. "Yes, yes, yes."

Parker grasped her hips, his cock twitching, as his fingers sank into her soft skin, the sensation overwhelming his senses.

"You're so big," Nastya moaned, grinding her pelvis against his.

"Don't you want me to wear a condom?" Parker huffed.

"Nah," Nasya hissed. "I won't get pregnant."

Parker knew that it was wrong, that whatever she was doing was just part of some fucked up plan to control him, but he didn't care. He just wanted to forget about his shitty situation and feel good for a moment.

He gripped her tighter, his muscles bulging, and began to thrust, his hips moving of their own accord.

"That's it," she gasped, her nails digging into his shoulders. "Fuck me, Parker. Fuck me with your big fat cock."

Parker groaned, the pressure in his stomach building as his pace increased, his cock sliding in and out of her, her warm juices coating him, until he came with a groan, his cum spurting deep inside her.

"Yes," Nastya breathed.

She leaned forward, pressing her forehead against his, her hot breath tickling his face.

"Did you like that?" she cooed.

"Yeah," Parker gasped, his breath still ragged.

"Good," Nastya smiled, her lips brushing his.

She moved away from him, the sensation making him feel cold, as she slid her underwear back on and fixed her torn bra.

"That was nice," she smiled. "Perhaps we can do it again later."

"Okay." Parker swallowed, his cock still pulsing.

"Bye, now." She turned her back to him, swaying her hips as she walked towards the door.

She knocked on it twice and Bruno opened it for her, mouth curving up into a sly grin as he took in Parker's flushed appearance.

"That was fast," he chuckled. "Werewolf pussy too much for you human?"

"Oh shush." Nastya placed a hand on Bruno's chest and pushed him back out into the hallway. "Don't be so mean."

She closed the door behind her, leaving Parker alone, his mind swimming with shame.

He looked down at his softening cock, and the glistening mess that they had made on the sheets.

"Fuck."

She was the enemy, but all that he could think of was her soft wet pussy wrapped around his dick.

"It's okay," he told himself, taking several slow breaths. "Soon she'll be dead."

PART 6

CHAPTER 1

"So how was he?" Ryan asked with a roll of his hips, thrusting deep into Nastya's wet heat.

Nastya hummed, grip tightening around Ryan's biceps. "Angry...and unrefined. Like the first time he'd tasted pussy since Axel stole his girlfriend."

Ryan huffed, his breath hot against Nastya's cheek. "He still looks miserable. Maybe he needs a few more pity fucks to cheer him up."

"That could be fun." Nastya wrapped her legs around his waist, urging him to go deeper.

Ryan groaned, his hands sliding down her curves. "Did you enjoy fucking my brother?"

Nastya smiled. "It would be more fun if I could have you both at once."

Ryan growled, the sound rumbling deep in his chest. He nipped at Nastya's collarbone.

Nastya's hands found Ryan's broad shoulders, her nails digging into his skin, the sharp sensation making him moan.

"Do you like that?" she cooed. "Imagining what it would be like to fuck me together?"

Ryan's hips picked up speed. His grip on her thighs tightened.

"I bet that it would feel good," she continued. "To have me sandwiched between you as you fuck my arse and pussy."

Ryan quickly ripped his dick out of Nastya, burying it deep inside the naked woman lying on the bed next to them.

Lydia was the closest thing to Deepa that Nastya could find, a dark haired beauty with tanned skin and full curves.

Lydia's gasped as Ryan's dick entered her, his thick manhood stretching her walls as he relentlessly fucked her.

Nastya watched on with a twisted smile.

Ryan relentlessly pounded into Lydia, his abs rippling with the effort, his teeth digging into his bottom lip as he held back his release, determined to prolong his pleasure.

"Tell me how it feels," Nastya breathed, eyes hungrily raking over his form, enjoying the view of his tight rear and bulging thighs. "Does she feel good? Do you like the way her tight cunt clenches around you?"

"Not as good as the real Deepa," Ryan grunted, the sweat on his body gleaming. "Want...to put...so many...babies inside her."

Lydia gripped Ryan's shoulders, her brown eyes clenched shut, her features twisted in bliss as Ryan slammed into her again and again.

"Can you see how much she wants it?" Nastya smiled. "How much she wants you to fill her up?"

Ryan let out a soft moan as he gave into his desires, his balls slapping against Lydia's flesh, her cries growing louder and louder with each stroke.

He knew that it wasn't Deepa, but he could pretend, pretend that she was willing and eager to let him breed her.

Maybe the real Deepa would let him if he ripped Axel to pieces.

"That's it," Nastya cooed. "Fill her up."

Ryan threw his head back and let out a groan, his cock exploding as it shot his seed deep inside Lydia's body, filling her womb. His heart fluttered as his muscles clenched, his limbs shaking with pleasure.

Lydia's body trembled, her mouth falling open, her legs shaking, and she clung to him as if her life depended on it, her eyes rolling back in her head.

"How did that feel?" Nastya licked her lips.

"Fucking incredible," Ryan huffed.

Lydia groaned, her legs trembling as Ryan slipped out of her, his essence oozing out of her warm wet sex.

Nastya knelt down, her pink tongue slipping out and trailing along Lydia's soaked slit. Her fingers slipped inside the woman's pussy, pushing the cum back inside her.

Lydia arched her back and whined, her hands grasping Nastya's blond hair.

"Good girl," Nastya praised. "Such a good girl."

Lydia keened, her face flushed.

Ryan got up from the bed, leaving Nastya to play with her latest toy.

He pulled on a pair of sweatpants and left the room, walking into the kitchen.

He came face to face with Axel's angry glare.

"What are you doing?" Axel spat.

"Nothing much." Ryan shrugged, taking a glass from the cupboard and filling it with water. "Just having a little fun."

"Aren't you supposed to be training?"

"I was training."

"Training what? Your dick?"

"Why do you even give a shit?" Ryan rolled his eyes. "This is the perfect opportunity for you to bulk up and beat me."

Axel growled, his eyes burning with fury.

Ryan's mouth curved into a smile. "Or are you worried that I'll just throw myself to the ground and let you win?"

Axel's fists clenched, the muscles of his jaw tightening as a low rumbling sound reverberated from his throat.

Ryan leisurely took a sip from his glass. "I'm just practicing for all the fucking I'll be doing once I don't have to do your job anymore. I'm gonna be balls deep in one of your sisters every night."

Axel's lip twitched, and before Ryan could react, the other werewolf was upon him, grabbing hold of his neck and slamming him against the wall.

"You're disgusting," Axel growled. "Don't you have any fucking pride?"

Ryan laughed, his throat vibrating under Axel's grip. "Pride? That sort of shit doesn't run in this family."

Axel's teeth clenched, and Ryan could feel the tension in the other werewolf's arm.

"I might consider trying to win." Ryan smirked. "If there's something good in it for me."

"Like what?" Axel spat.

"A nice fertile cunt that's already tasted my dick plenty of times."

"No," Axel growled. "I'm not giving you Deepa."

"Come on, Axel. I already promised her a lifetime supply of medication. Once she's drugged up enough to tear herself away from you, we both know that she'll come running back to my bed."

"No."

Ryan sighed. "Then what else do you have to offer me? The chance to micromanage a bunch of assholes who hate me?"

"I'll kill you," Axel growled. "I'll rip your fucking arms off if you lose on purpose."

Ryan let out a laugh. "Don't be so dramatic."

"I'm serious. If I catch even the slightest hint that you're trying to throw the fight, I'll kill you."

"Fine," Ryan huffed. "Whatever."

"And I won't let you near Deepa."

"Whatever," Ryan repeated.

"I'm not kidding. I'll kill you."

"Yeah, yeah," Ryan muttered, shoving Axel's hands away and moving past him.

"Hey!" Axel barked.

"I heard you the first time," Ryan sighed. "You'll kill me if I lose on purpose. Got it."

"I mean it," Axel insisted. "If you so much as think about faking it, I'll end your miserable existence."

Ryan shut the door in Axel's face, ignoring the muffled insults from his brother on the other side.

Ryan returned to the bedroom, pleased to find Nastya still naked on the bed with her new friend.

He dropped his sweatpants, his cock growing stiff as the women eyed him hungrily.

"What are you waiting for?" He smirked, crawling onto the bed and pulling Lydia's head to his crotch.

She obediently took his manhood into her mouth, the warm wetness making him groan.

"Good girl," he praised, guiding her head up and down.

Lydia hummed around his member, her brown eyes looking up at him with reverence. Her fluids dripped onto the sheets as Nastya played with her from behind.

"Come on," he encouraged. "Take it deeper."

She did, the head of his cock sliding down her throat, the sensation making his balls tighten.

He grasped her hair, pushing her head down, forcing his cock deep into her throat, as he ground his hips against her face, her nose pressed into the coarse hairs at the base of his shaft.

Maybe beating the shit out of Axel wouldn't be a bad idea, if it meant that Deepa would be free to suck his cock again.

CHAPTER 2

"Are you going to be like this all week?" Deepa sighed.

"No," Axel huffed, slamming his fist into a punching bag. Sweat dripped down his naked chest as he continued his assault.

Deepa took a sip from her can of soda, watching the muscles of Axel's back ripple as he struck the bag. He'd been moody and irritable all day. She was starting to miss his cocky attitude and attempts to get into her pants.

Watching him work out half naked seemed like the closest she was going to get to seeing his cock.

Deepa took a seat on a bench press. "Do you think you can win?"

Axel didn't answer, giving the bag a final blow, then moving onto a set of weights.

Reese was on a treadmill in the corner, broken arm in a sling after an intense battle on the front lines. The war against humanity was heating up, and numbers were beginning to thin on both sides.

"Ryan hasn't lost a fight in years," said Reese. "Not since we were kids."

Axel grit his teeth and lifted a set of barbells.

"And he's bigger than Axel," Reese added. "Probably stronger too."

Axel ignored Reese, continuing his workout.

"Not that size is everything," said Reese. "Maybe they'll find Axel's loss so mortifying that they'll try and end the fight early like last time."

"Shut up," Axel growled.

Deepa sighed, sipping her soda. She wasn't sure of how much more of Axel's man period that she could take.

"Maybe you'll get lucky," said Reese. "Ryan's always talking about how he hates being leader, so everyone thinks that he'll just throw the fight and let you win."

Axel's jaw clenched.

"Or he might just kill you so that he can steal your girlfriend again," said Reese.

Axel dropped the weight in his hand, the metal clanging against the floor.

"What?" Reese scoffed. "Just saying."

"Leave him alone," said Deepa. "He's under a lot of stress."

"So are we," said Reese. "I spent all of last week dodging tanks."

"Go." Deepa pointed to the door.

"Fine." Reese got off the treadmill and headed towards the exit. "Maybe a blow job or two will cheer him up."

Deepa sighed and got up from her seat, moving to sit next to Axel on the weight bench.

"Just ignore him," said Deepa. "I saw him snorting painkillers for breakfast."

Axel took a long drink from his water bottle, his expression tense.

"Want to talk about it?" Deepa asked softly.

He shook his head. "What's there to say?"

"Anything," she urged. "Help me understand what's going on in your head."

"You wouldn't understand," he muttered.

"Maybe not," she shrugged. "But maybe I can help."

Axel swallowed, his gaze falling to the floor. "I don't know what's better. Winning or losing."

"Isn't winning better?"

"No, because then I'll get saddled with all the Elder's crap."

"Oh." Deepa frowned. "Why?"

"Because if I win I'll be stuck being their favorite bitch again."

"I see." Deepa clasped her hands in her lap. "That sucks."

"It does," Axel muttered.

"So..what's gonna happen if you lose?"

"I don't know." Axel rubbed his jaw. "Probably get sent to the front lines like everyone else."

Deepa's stomach tightened, the blood draining from her face.

"Don't worry." He smiled. "I'm not going down without a fight."

"You can't go out there," said Deepa. "I'll think of something...I'll..."

Axel gave a sly smile. "But I thought that you wanted me dead."

"I don't," said Deepa. "Not anymore."

"Oh really?"

"Yes."

"Why not?"

Deepa looked down at her feet, her cheeks growing red. "Because..."

"Yes?" Axel leaned in, his blue eyes piercing hers.

"Because...you're growing on me."

Axel chuckled. "Are you falling for me, Deepa?"

"No," she huffed. "Of course not."

"Oh, I think that you are," he teased.

"No," she protested.

"Then why else would you want to keep me alive?"

"Because.." Deepa swallowed. "I don't want to see you die."

"Aw," Axel cooed, moving closer to wrap an arm around Deepa's waist. "That's sweet."

Deepa's cheeks flushed, her heart racing. "I mean...you're still kind of a dick."

"But you don't want me to die." Axel grinned.

"No." Deepa swallowed, the scent of his sweat tickling her nose.

"Come on," he purred. "Admit that you like me."

Deepa's cheeks burned. "Okay."

Axel's hand moved up her skirt, cupping her sex.

"Say it," he purred, his fingers slipping into her panties, sliding along her lips.

Deepa gasped, her legs spreading open, her body trembling as he played with her pussy.

"I like you," she breathed, her hands gripping his broad shoulders.

"Yeah?" He smirked, his fingers parting her slick folds, the sensation sending sparks of pleasure through her body.

"I..I like the way you touch me," she whimpered, her inner walls fluttering around his digits.

"That's it," Axel purred, his palm pressing against her clit, his fingers curling inside her. "You're doing good."

"Ah." Deepa's back arched, her thighs trembling.

"Keep talking," Axel coaxed. "Tell me how great I am."

"You..." Deepa's voice trembled. "Are so full of yourself," she whimpered as he thrust his fingers inside her. "And..."

"And..?" Axel grinned, the cocky bastard. "I'm what?"

Deepa swallowed, the pressure in her belly rising, her breaths growing shorter and more desperate.

"And.." Her gaze fell on his bare torso. "You're talking too much instead of getting naked."

Axel pulled his hand from her pants and Deepa moaned with disappointment at the loss of sensation, until Axel shoved down her shirt and bra, taking one of her breasts in his mouth, the wetness of his lips searing her sensitive flesh, the warmth of his body enveloping hers.

Deepa moaned, the pleasure overwhelming, her insides fluttering and clenching as her muscles quivered.

She could feel the press of his manhood against her thigh, the firm bulge close to her own burning heat.

Her whole body seemed to come alive, the room spinning as her senses were flooded.

Axel continued to worship her breasts with his tongue and lips, making her mind spin.

Her pulse quickened, her breaths shallow and uneven as her heart beat faster, her muscles spasming around his fingers as her orgasm erupted, the force of her release sending waves of pleasure through her body, her insides clamping down hard.

"Fuck," Axel's breath was hot against her collarbone, making her shiver.

He growled and pulled away to claim her lips, their teeth crashing together in a desperate need to taste the other.

She didn't know how she had existed without him. Without his skin flush against hers.

His scent filled her nose, the intoxicating fragrance driving her mad with need.

Axel fumbled with his sweatpants, pulling them down to free his hard leaking dick.

Deepa slipped off her panties, spreading her legs wide to expose her flushed naked groin.

Axel lined himself up with her wet waiting entrance, teasing his head across her soft lips.

Deepa whined, her pussy burning with heat, her aching breasts pressing against his naked chest.

With a low growl, he slid the head of his cock between her folds, his throbbing shaft piercing her heat, stretching her open and sliding in deep.

Deepa groaned, her head swimming with desire as her muscles tensed around him.

"Fuck," he groaned, his arms wrapping around her shoulders, pulling her closer to him.

His heady scent washed over her, the warmth of his body radiating from his bare skin as their hips began to roll together in slow fluid motions.

It was enough to make Deepa tremble, the sensation of being filled and stretched, coupled with the weight of his strong muscular form draping over her.

His breath was hot and damp against her throat, his hips grinding against hers, his length thrusting deep inside her, filling her up again and again.

Deepa's nails sank deeper into his shoulders as her moans grew louder and her heart rate increased. Her mind barely registered his hand coming up behind her to press the base of her skull, holding her close to his shoulder.

She clung to him, her nails leaving long trails of red marks on his back as he rocked her slowly, his strong hands massaging her shoulders as he buried his face in her neck and sucked at the tender flesh, his rhythmic pace rocking her into a blissful state.

"You're so gorgeous," he panted, his grip on her waist tightening as his cock stroked her insides, making her quiver. "You feel so fucking good," he breathed into the soft skin beneath her ear. "So perfect. Like you were made for this."

His fingers twined in her hair and she held onto his arms, her own head rolling as she bucked her hips back, her pussy milking his throbbing member.

"Tell me you love me," he whispered as he pressed into her soft body, their legs intertwined as their movements gained a frantic speed. "Tell me you'll never leave me."

Her heart pounded in her chest, and she clung to his broad muscular frame as she rolled her pelvis, pressing herself against him, relishing the sensation of him deep inside her, the pressure building and coiling in her womb.

"I..I..ahh," she sobbed, the pleasure overwhelming her senses.

"Say it." Axel groaned with a roll of his hips.

"I.." she whimpered, her hips jerking. "Love you."

Axel grinned and pressed his forehead against hers. "Again."

"I.." she panted, the heat of his body enveloping her. "I love you."

Axel ground his teeth, his grip on her hips tightening. His movements grew desperate as her insides fluttered around him.

A jolt of electricity ran through her body, her toes curling and legs going numb as her orgasm overtook her.

Her inner muscles pulsed and squeezed around him and he groaned, his balls tightening and her sex clinging to his length as his manhood pumped his hot cum into her womb.

She held him tightly and did not let go. Not until their breath had evened and the afterglow of pleasure began to ebb.

"So..." Deepa rubbed comforting circles against Axel's skin. "Are you feeling better now?"

Axel sighed and nuzzled the hollow of her throat. "A little."

Deepa stroked his hair. "Well...I think that you can win."

He gripped her tightly. "There is no winning. Only two different ways of losing."

Deepa swallowed, her stomach twisting. There were multiple doubts and fears swirling around in her mind, but she buried them deep down and held Axel, choosing to immerse herself in that moment rather than think about their future.

CHAPTER 3

"There should be minimal security," Parker said quietly into his radio, nervously eyeing the basement door. "They seem to prioritize sending the younger ones to the front lines. Over."

"Copy that," crackled Craig's static filled voice after a moment. "And how are their preparations progressing? Over."

"No change, still fighting with each other and fucking around. The event should take place as scheduled. Over."

"Good. Stay alert and play along. See what other information you can get out of them."

The basement stairs creaked.

Parker quickly switched off his radio and shoved it under the mattress as footsteps echoed down the hall.

He stood up and stretched his arms, trying to look like he was in the middle of working out.

The door swung open and Nastya strolled inside, dressed in a low cut tank top and short skirt.

"Hey, sexy," she hummed, gaze raking over Parker's muscular form. "Did you miss me?"

"No," Parker muttered, memories of how he'd shamelessly stuck his dick in her floated to the surface of his mind.

Nastya hummed, and took a seat on the desk, spreading her legs wide, revealing her bare sex.

Parker immediately turned to look at the wall.

"Don't be like that." She pouted. "Don't you want to play?"

Parker gritted his teeth, attempting to bury his mortification and shame.

He wanted to tell her that their last encounter was a mistake, that he would never fuck her again, but Craig's words of playing along echoed in his mind.

What could he find out if he got closer to Nastya?

What if she knew something that could help them win the war?

Nastya licked her lips and pulled her top over her head, revealing her perky breasts.

Parker's mouth watered at the sight of her pale nipples, his cock stirring to life despite his mortification.

This wasn't for him, he told himself as he walked towards her. *He was only doing it to help Infection Control.*

Nastya smiled and wrapped her legs around his waist, pulling him into an embrace and claiming his mouth.

Parker couldn't help but moan against her soft warm lips, his hands gripping the swell of her hips.

Nastya smirked, running her hand down to cup the bulge forming in his pants.

"Did you get lonely without me?" she teased, a wicked grin flashing across her face as he shivered.

"Yeah," he lied, cringing at how stupid he sounded. "Where were you?"

"Just busy," she purred, squeezing his thick erection. "Tending to some plants."

"Plants?" he panted.

"You'll understand soon enough." She smiled, pulling down Parker's zipper to free his erect cock.

He groaned as she rubbed the slick slit of her pussy against his shaft, his length stiffening and swelling beneath her.

"Put it in," she hummed, nails gently scratching the skin of his lower back. "I want to feel you inside me."

"Okay," Parker moaned, holding his breath as he pressed his manhood inside the warmth of her pussy, her inner walls tightly clasping around him.

"That's it," she hummed, leaning her head back. "That's a good boy."

He took a shaky breath, holding her hips and slowly thrusting his shaft deep into her pussy, basking in the damp warmth that surrounded him.

"How long do you plan on keeping me down here?" Parker huffed.

"Until you learn to behave," she cooed.

"I can be good." Parker gave a low exaggerated whine.

Nastya rolled her hips, making Parker moan, his face scrunching up. He rested his head on her shoulder, letting out a ragged breath.

Nastya was clearly deranged, but her pussy felt like paradise.

"We'll see," she hummed, burying her fingers in his hair. "You can start by finishing inside me."

Parker nodded, rutting into her faster, allowing the needs of his dick to take him higher and higher. He focused solely on the sensation, the heat that pooled inside him as Nastya's smooth legs hugged his hips.

Nastya's breaths became short and rapid, her eyelids heavy as she pushed her hips up.

Parker grunted as his balls tightened, his cock throbbing as he reached his limit.

He moaned into her shoulder, shuddering as he unloaded his seed deep into Nastya's warm body, a traitorous part of his mind wondering if it would be okay to let her live.

Nastya sighed, wrapping her arms around Parker's shoulders, and pulling him into a hug as he came down from his high.

"There, there," she hummed. "Was that good? Feel nice to empty your balls?"

Parker nodded, basking in her warmth. "Can you tell me about the elders? I want to learn more about my family."

"Let me think..." Nastya pulled Parker's mouth down to her breast. "Let's see how good you are at sucking my tits first."

CHAPTER 4

"That's the leader of the southern pack," Luke said gently as he pointed to a car rolling up towards the mansion. "Our families were bitter enemies until they decided to join forces to take on the humans. Now they send us gift hampers every year."

Deepa gripped her seatbelt as she watched an elderly woman hobble out of the vehicle, accompanied by several other men in suits.

"And that's the leader of the east pack," Luke added, pointing to a graying man accompanied by a young blond woman who was heavily pregnant. "With one of Axel's sisters."

Axel blanched, his head falling forward to rest against the steering wheel.

"How many sisters do you have?" Deepa asked.

"Too many," Axel groaned. "My mother would usually pump one out every year to keep the elders happy."

"Why so many?"

"So that my family would have plenty of brides to offer up in return for the loyalty of all these fuckers."

Deepa swallowed. Just when she thought that she was becoming accustomed to Axel's fucked up family, they'd throw something new in her face.

They'd been sitting in the parked car in front of the mansion for at least half an hour, but no one seemed eager to move.

Axel froze up the moment that he turned off the engine, staring into space as various guests rolled up the driveway and parked beside them.

Deepa could feel the apprehension radiating off him in waves, but every time she tried to reach out and touch him, he'd shake her off.

"Oh fuck no," Parker hissed, glaring at Bruno in disgust as the other man produced a bag of dog treats from the back seat.

"What." Bruno shrugged with fake ignorance, pulling the packet open. "I don't have anything else."

Deepa cringed. She hated the way that Bruno had restrained Parker in the backseat.

Her ex-boyfriend's hands were tied behind his back, and there was a leather dog collar wrapped around his neck, tying him to the seat. She would have rather left him in the basement, but Nastya had been insistent about bringing him to the mansion.

"Open up wide." Bruno grinned while trying to shove a dog treat into Parker's mouth.

"No." Parker twisted away.

Bruno caught Parker's jaw and pried his mouth open to shove the treat in.

Parker choked and spat it straight out.

Bruno laughed.

"Let's just go." Deepa undid her seatbelt and shoved open her door, snapping Axel out of his unresponsive state.

"Right," Axel muttered, opening his own door. "Let's go."

Bruno attempted to shove another treat into Parker's mouth, but Luke tugged him away, snapping, "seriously," as he pulled his cousin out of the car.

"Hey!" Deepa glanced back at Parker. "We can't just leave him there."

"This event is werewolves only." Bruno smirked, giving Parker the middle finger. "Humans need to stay in the car."

"Axel," Deepa begged, but Axel didn't respond.

"Some of the people inside aren't very friendly to humans," Luke said gently, placing a hand on Deepa's shoulder. "Let's just leave him here for now."

"Fine." Deepa gritted her teeth and reluctantly walked towards the entrance, praying that Parker would not be mauled by distant relatives while they were away.

"Almost forgot." Bruno grinned, tossing a rubber dog toy through a crack in the car window. "In case you get bored."

"Fuck you!" Parker spat, focusing all his anger through his eyes as he glared back at Bruno.

Deepa shuddered and gripped Axel's arm, telling herself that she'd help Parker once the duel was over.

The ballroom had been rearranged for the duel. Several stands had been set up against the walls, and the furniture had been cleared to create a large circle in the center.

The seats were crowded with elders from various groups, all eager to see who would become their future leader.

Axel's great grandfather sat at the front and center, dressed in a spotless red suit that hung off his frail form, his eyes burning with a feverish intensity.

Axel's mother Latavia sat beside him, her face a stoic mask as she rested one hand on her swollen stomach.

"No matter what happens," Deepa whispered as she and Axel descended the stairs, fingers intertwined. "I'm here for you."

Axel swallowed and gripped her hand tighter.

Ryan was already waiting for him in the ring, dressed in a pair of dark pants and nothing else.

Nastya stood behind him, along with Reese, because no matter how well Axel got along with Reese, Ryan was still officially their leader.

"Took you long enough." Ryan smirked as Axel approached the ring. "Too busy with your goodbye blowie?"

Axel ignored him, his jaw clenching. All he had to do was get through this and then he'd either be Ryan's leader or sent to the battlefield.

Axel's great grandfather got to his feet. "Dearest friends," he said to the room with his arms extended. "You all know why you are here today. Because the future of our race rests entirely on our leaders, and no leader deserves respect without first proving their worth."

Axel fought the urge to roll his eyes. His father had been handed the position on a platter before he fucked off.

"Today, my great grandson Ryan will battle with my great grandson Axel," the old man continued. "Once more for the right to succeed me. As custom dictates, there will be no interference and no outside aid. Whoever keeps their opponent down for more than a minute will be declared winner."

Axel stripped off his shirt, the eyes of his elders boring into him, their expectations almost overwhelming.

This was how he spent his childhood. Fighting tooth and nail to gain the approval of old geezers, always losing out to Ryan, always feeling like he was never good enough.

No matter how hard he tried, he could never escape these people who called themselves family.

"May the fight begin!" his great grandfather declared, raising his hand into the air.

There was a moment of tense silence, then Ryan transformed and launched himself at Axel, tackling Axel to the ground.

Axel's snarl cut through the room as his body convulsed, muscles rippling beneath his skin as his own transformation took hold.

His vision sharpened, locking onto Ryan's form with predatory precision, his canines elongating into lethal points.

Axel sprang forward, his jaws closing around the side of Ryan's neck.

Ryan let out a guttural growl. He twisted, muscles coiling as he retaliated, snapping his powerful jaws toward Axel's leg.

Axel rolled away, his sleek form slipping out of reach as they began to circle each other.

Low rumbling growls filled the air.

Ryan lunged, his eyes wild as he aimed for Axel's throat, but Axel was ready. With a fluid motion, he ducked under Ryan's attack, his own jaws closing around Ryan's foreleg in a vicious counter.

Ryan yelped, the wound slowing his movements.

Axel didn't hesitate.

He pounced onto Ryan's back, his claws digging deep into the thick fur and flesh, anchoring him as he drove Ryan to the ground.

Ryan bucked violently, his body thrashing in a desperate attempt to throw Axel off, but Axel held firm, his own growl resonating through the room as they clashed in a whirlwind of fur and fangs.

Blood stained the floor beneath them, the scent of it thick in the air, but neither wolf was willing to surrender.

Deepa watched with clenched fists, her heart pounding as she silently urged Axel on, every fiber of her being willing him to win.

Ryan threw Axel off, using his superior size to gain the upper hand. He pinned Axel to the ground, his massive jaws snapping dangerously close to Axel's throat.

Axel's muscles strained against the crushing weight, his breath coming in ragged gasps as Ryan's hot breath seared the back of his neck.

It was just like the last time they fought. When Axel decided that it was better to just lie back and let Ryan win.

Maybe it was better to just lose and allow Ryan to kill him. At least then he wouldn't have to face the elders or suffer a brutal death on the battlefield.

But his gaze locked onto Deepa. Her expression was etched with concern, yet her eyes held an unwavering faith in him.

Something primal and ferocious stirred deep within Axel.

A raw, unbridled rage ignited, burning through his veins like wildfire.

With a guttural roar, Axel's body began to transform.

His muscles bulged and rippled as his form rapidly expanded, fur bursting forth and coarse hair thickening across his body until he had become a monstrous half-human, half-wolf creature.

Ryan's grip loosened.

Axel seized the opening, unleashing his newfound strength to violently throw Ryan off, sending his younger brother crashing into the opposite side of the ring.

Axel rose to his full height, looming over everyone in the room. His eyes burned with rage as he fixed his gaze upon Ryan. Lips curled back in a feral snarl, revealing rows of razor-sharp gleaming fangs.

Axel's great-grandfather leaned forward, his hands shaking with excitement.

"Extraordinary," he whispered. "Absolutely extraordinary."

"What's happening?" Deepa hissed, gripping Nastya's arm.

Nastya swallowed hard. "I've never seen a transformation like this before," she murmured.

Axel growled and launched himself at Ryan, quickly overwhelming his younger brother. He slammed Ryan into the floor of the ring, his massive fists pummeling the smaller wolf.

Axel needed to destroy him. He needed to reduce his enemy to dust.

All human guilt was buried under his new monstrous urges.

"Stop!" Deepa screamed, dashing across the ring to launch herself at Axel, shocking him out of his violent trance. "Please, you'll kill him."

Ryan's body lay bloody and limp on the floor. He'd shifted back into his human form, but a steady stream of blood leaked from the corner of his mouth.

"He's done." Deepa gripped Axel's arm. "Look."

A low growl reverberated from Axel's throat.

"Please." Deepa's voice trembled as she hugged Axel tightly. "It's over. You've won."

A shudder ran through Axel's transformed body, the animalistic ferocity slowly receding as he processed Deepa's words.

He reached down and scooped Deepa's petite frame into his massive clawed hands, cradling her protectively against his chest as he dashed out of the room.

CHAPTER 5

Deepa had watched Axel's monstrous transformation with stunned silence. It was like when they had sex, but he was larger and more terrifying than ever before.

And just the sight of it was enough to make her pussy clench.

It mortified her how watching him pound into Ryan's limp bleeding body had made her insides burn, but she had to step in before he did something that he'd regret.

But she didn't expect him to carry her away.

Deepa's body buzzed with electricity as Axel's large muscular arms held her closely. Her skin felt like it was on fire where his hands were touching her, and the sensation only intensified when she felt the hard press of his cock against her hip.

He dragged her out a door and across the lawn, throwing her down on the grass, his clawed hand tangling in her hair as his monstrous lips mouthed her throat and collar.

Deepa gripped his thick biceps, and his eyes snapped to hers, blazing and terrifying.

Deepa knew that Axel would never intentionally hurt her, but a tiny piece of fear gripped at her stomach when she saw his razor sharp teeth graze against her soft tender flesh.

He snarled, his gigantic cock pressing hard against her.

"Axel," she breathed, parting her legs to allow him to comfortably slot between them.

He blinked at her.

"Axel," she whispered, holding his shoulders as she locked her legs around his hips. "Don't stop."

The monster made a rumbling sound in his chest, his head diving forward, his lips meeting hers.

Deepa kissed him desperately, grinding her pelvis against his throbbing bulge as her pussy slickened and throbbed.

Axel's claws tore at her clothes, exposing her breasts and ripping off her skirt and panties. His rough tongue lapped at her nipples, sending hot flashes of pleasure down her body and making her breath quicken.

"Yes," Deepa gasped as Axel lined his engorged dick up with her entrance, slowly pressing inside.

Her walls clenched around his thick shaft as he bottomed out, stretching and filling her deliciously.

Deepa gripped his fur as he started thrusting in and out of her, grunting and snarling.

"Fuck," she breathed, holding him close as his pace increased, his large frame caging her to the ground.

The wolf inside her roared with delight. This was what her mate was supposed to be, a powerful beast that would destroy civilizations and fill her body with his spawn.

She could see stars as he plunged himself deeper and deeper into her slick core, her toes curling and her muscles quivering as a familiar pressure started to build.

Deepa whined as her insides contracted, gripping him tightly as his cock pulsated, thrusts growing desperate and sloppy.

His snarls grew louder as his knot expanded, stretching Deepa wide, and then the pressure was too much, her vision whiting out as ecstasy washed over her, sending her spiraling into a mind shattering climax.

He roared as his thick milky cum unleashed, pouring into her body as his cock filled every inch of her fluttering slit.

Deepa gasped, panting as she clutched at his fur, riding out the waves of pleasure, her chest heaving, and limbs numb as his knot continued to pulse inside her.

She hugged his neck tightly as his body slowly reverted back into his human form.

Axel's forehead rested against hers, his breath hot on her face. "Are you okay?" he asked softly.

"That was..intense," Deepa hummed, stroking his hair. "But not in a bad way."

Axel chuckled softly, gripping her tightly. "Good, because I plan on fucking you like that from now on."

Deepa slapped his back. "Pervert."

Axel nuzzled her neck, his lips gently sucking her collarbone. "You love it."

Deepa was certain that they were about to go another round on the lawn, when several harsh claps interrupted their moment.

Axel's great grandfather stood before them, a large smile plastered across his wrinkled face.

"Axel my boy," he wheezed. "What a brilliant performance."

CHAPTER 6

"The beast form is a transformation inherited by certain members of our family," Axel's great grandfather lectured as he led Axel and Deepa back through the halls. "Only achievable by keeping our bloodline pure. My father was partially gifted, as was I in my youth."

Deepa played with the sleeve of her borrowed dress, nervously walking behind Axel. She attempted to greet the elderly man once, but he immediately brushed her off and continued talking with Axel like she wasn't there.

Axel mouthed a quick *sorry*, but his attention was quickly stolen by the elderly man, who ranted about how great Axel would be once he became leader.

They emerged into a large dining room to a round of applause. All the elders had assembled, nursing champagne flutes and plates of food.

Reese clapped Axel on the shoulder. "Always knew that you had it in you man," he said confidently, even though he had stood behind Ryan during the duel.

Axel was soon swarmed by several elderly women. Deepa was left to drift towards Luke, who was sipping pineapple juice at a corner table.

"How's Ryan?" she asked.

Luke placed his drink down. "Still unconscious, but he'll live. Some of the elders are pissed that you stepped in, but if you hadn't, I don't think that Axel would have stopped."

Deepa nodded, biting her lip. Ryan was a deranged pervert, but she didn't want him to die. There were still people who genuinely loved and cared about him.

"Where's Nastya?" Deepa asked, glancing around the room.

"Most likely avoiding her mother." Luke gestured to Axel's mother who was sitting beside a young blond woman. The woman was the splitting image of Nastya, silently staring at the door as Latavia chattered in her ear.

Reese collapsed into the seat beside Deepa, raising an eyebrow when he spotted the juice in Luke's hand. "Seriously?"

"Not all of us use these events to get shitfaced," Luke grumbled.

"You'll regret it once they start throwing granddaughters at you again."

Luke sighed and pushed the juice towards Reese. "Fine, if only to keep my sanity."

Reese grinned, tipping half his champagne into Luke's glass. "Atta boy."

Axel's gaze met Deepa's. He walked towards them, but before he could reach their table, he was intercepted by his great-grandfather, who was flanked by two young blond women.

"Axel, my boy," the old man rasped, a feverish gleam in his eyes. "There are a few ladies I need you to meet."

Axel stiffened, his expression guarded.

"This is Elsa, the granddaughter of the Northern pack's leader." Axel's great-grandfather gestured to a curvy young woman in a red dress. "And this is Ava. The eldest daughter of the Western pack's leader."

Ava smiled coyly up at Axel, her pale hand brushing against his arm. "Hi, Axel. I've heard so much about you," she purred, her touch lingering.

Axel frowned but held out his hand, allowing Ava to take it and shake. "Nice to meet you." His tone was polite but distant.

Deepa tightly gripped her glass, her gaze fixed on Axel's interaction with the two women.

A part of her wanted to get up and join them, to assert her claim as Axel's mate, but Reese placed a hand on her arm.

"Don't," he murmured without looking at her. "It'll only make it worse."

"But-"

"Trust me," Reese murmured. "Just trust me."

Deepa reluctantly sat back in her chair, her teeth clenching.

"It's important to make connections," Axel's great grandfather hummed. "To make allies. To create strong children that will continue our bloodline."

"But I have-" Axel protested, gesturing towards the table where Deepa was sitting.

"Oh Axel," his great grandfather chuckled. "I have no plans on taking away your side piece, I'm not a barbarian."

"But she's-"

"Your mate, yes, yes." His great grandfather waved his hand dismissively. "And I am sure that you will make plenty of children with her. But the more wives you have, the stronger the chance that your future heir will be blessed with the gift."

Axel's shoulders sagged.

"There is no point in wasting all your time and energy on breeding with inferior stock," the old man continued. "Keep her as your plaything, but do your duty as my heir and spread your seed amongst our kind."

Deepa's eyes watered, her grip on the glass loosening. The delicate crystal slipped from her fingers, hitting the table with a sharp crack.

The sound of shattering glass echoed through the room.

Deepa's cheeks flushed with embarrassment at the unwanted attention.

"Sorry," she mumbled quickly, rising to her feet. "I just...I need some air."

"Deepa!" Reese hissed, reaching out to stop her.

But Luke placed a restraining hand on Reese's arm, shaking his head solemnly.

"Let her go," he sighed, gently pushing the pile of broken glass across the table. "There's nothing you can say that'll make her feel better."

"Fucking werewolves," Deepa muttered as she slammed one hallway door open after another, her body trembling with rage.

"Deepa!" a voice called out, and she turned to see Axel running after her, a worried look etched onto his face.

"Hey," he panted, coming to a stop. "Why did you leave?"

"Isn't it fucking obvious?" Deepa hissed, turning on her heel and storming away.

"Wait." He grabbed her arm, pulling her back. "Please talk to me."

"Let go!" she growled.

"I'm sorry," he breathed. "About what he said. He's...always saying weird shit like that...trying to force me to do what he wants."

"So that was all just talk, right?" Deepa pulled her arm out of his grasp. "You won't have to marry anyone else, right?"

Axel swallowed, averting his gaze.

"Fuck," Deepa laughed. "So I'm just supposed to sit back and watch you knock up the sister brides?"

"I won't have sex with them," Axel muttered. "I'll just cum in a cup for them or something."

Deepa glared. "And how the fuck is that any better?"

Axel sighed, running a hand through his hair. "It's not, but we can talk about that later, right now I have to go back there."

"Yeah," Deepa said sarcastically. "Because it's important to make *connections*."

Axel reached for her. "Please, let me-"

"Leave me alone," Deepa snapped, pushing him away. "Just fucking go."

She turned, tears welling in her eyes, and ran off before he could say anything else.

She knew that it was impossible to escape Axel. No matter where she went he'd eventually find her, but she needed to be alone with her thoughts for a moment.

CHAPTER 7

Parker surveyed the sprawling mansion grounds from the top of the hill. The party was still in full swing, with inebriated guests spilling out onto the lawn.

He rubbed his raw, chafed neck, wincing at the memory of his hour-long struggle to free himself from the car. He had twisted and gnawed at the leather restraints until his jaw ached and his skin was rubbed raw, but he had finally managed to escape.

Parker keyed his radio. "I count at least fifty vehicles," he reported. "These people are wasted. They're not going anywhere anytime soon. Over."

"Copy that," Craig's voice crackled through. "That's more than we hoped for. What's your assessment of the security situation? Over."

Parker scanned the perimeter, noting the positions of visible guards. "I've got eyes on four armed security personnel. Two at the main gate, one patrolling the east side, one near the pool area. Likely more inside. No dogs visible. Over."

"Understood. Varn's on his way with your gear. Once you're equipped, proceed with infiltration. Maintain radio silence unless absolutely necessary. Understood?"

"Understood, Base. I'll get it done. Out." Parker switched his radio to standby and tucked it away.

He began his approach, moving with practiced stealth through the shadows. His eyes scanned the surroundings, noting the positions of security cameras, when he was hit from behind and sent sprawling face first into the grass.

"Gotcha," Nastya laughed, pressing her knee between his shoulder blades to hold him down. "Somebody's been a naughty boy."

Parker thrashed, but she kept him pinned, a clawed hand tangling in his hair.

"And here I was thinking that we were friends," she mused. "Now what am I supposed to do with you?"

"Get off me!" Parker huffed, trying to wriggle out from underneath her.

Nastya laughed, tugging his head up. "And why would I do that? Especially when it's always so fun to feel you squirming beneath me."

"Fucking psycho!" he spat.

"Oh, you haven't seen anything yet," Nastya chuckled. "You should see me when I'm really feeling kinky."

The rustling of bushes drew Parker's attention.

Varn emerged from the shadows, his muscular frame covered in weaponry. Two rifles criss crossed his back, pistols hung at his hips, and ammunition draped his shoulders.

"Varn!" Parker cried out. "Get her off me."

Nastya cocked her head. A smirk played at the corners of her mouth. "My, my. Quite the arsenal you've brought. Compensating for something?"

Varn rolled his eyes, unslinging the rifles from his shoulders and laying them down on the grass. "It was a fucking struggle just to get this much. I had to rant on about going out alone on a suicide mission just to let me leave."

Nastya tutted. "Well, it'll have to do, I suppose."

The pieces clicked into place in Parker's mind, horror blooming in his chest. "You're... you're one of them.

"Ding, ding, ding!" Nastya's voice dripped with sarcasm. "Give the little boy a prize. Though I'm disappointed it took you this long to figure it out."

Parker stared at Varn, desperate to find some trace of the man he thought he knew, the friend he had trusted with his life. "How could you?" he choked out. "After everything we've been through..."

Varn's eyes met Parker's, a flicker of something, passing over his features before his expression hardened once more.

"I thought you knew already." Varn took a seat on a nearby rock. "Especially since I already told Deepa, but I guess that you were too busy giving her the cold treatment to listen to anything that she had to say."

Parker's fingers dug into the earth, rage and betrayal coursing through him. "You fucking-"

"Language." Nastya tugged at his hair. "That's not how you should address your new werewolf overlords."

Bile rose in Parker's throat. How could he have been so blind, so foolishly trusting?

"They'll kill you," Parker hissed. "Infection Control and the army have this place surrounded."

A grin spread across Varn's face. "Oh Parker, you simple, predictable human. You've played your part to perfection, drawing all our enemies into one convenient killing ground."

"What are you talking about?" Dread coiled in Parker's gut.

"While you were busy playing the hero, we've been setting the stage." Varn dumped the rest of his gear on the grass. "A grand finale, if you will."

A thunderous explosion rocked the earth. Fire and smoke billowed on the horizon, followed by the distant screams of men and the echo of gunfire.

"Right on schedule." Varn smiled.

Panic gripped Parker. "What have you done?" he shouted.

Varn's eyes gleamed. "We're rewriting the natural order, Parker."

Another explosion rocked the ground, followed by a third, and then a fourth.

"You're fucking crazy!" Parker hissed. "We trusted you. Craig trusted you."

"And now they're all going to die for it," said Varn.

Something primal awakened in Parker. In a burst of desperate strength, he wrenched free from Nastya's grip, his hand closing around the cold metal of one of the discarded rifles.

He pivoted, aiming the weapon.

Varn's eyes widened in shock as Parker squeezed the trigger. The gun roared, the recoil slamming into Parker's shoulder.

Varn twisted. The bullet tore a bloody furrow across his bicep as Varn dove aside. His form blurred and shifted, clothes shredding as fur erupted from his skin.

Where Varn had stood, a massive wolf snarled, muscles coiled to strike.

A guttural growl from behind was Parker's only warning before Nastya slammed into him.

They hit the ground hard, the gun skittering away.

White-hot pain exploded across Parker's cheek as Nastya's razor-sharp claws raked his flesh.

Parker tucked and rolled, narrowly avoiding Nastya's snapping jaws. He scrambled to his feet, heart pounding, only to face Varn lunging for his throat.

"Fuck!" Parker gasped, throwing his arm up in a desperate defense.

Varn's teeth sank into his forearm.

Parker thrust his knee up, catching Varn in the stomach, then twisted, using the momentum to flip their positions.

His fist connected with Varn's muzzle in a satisfying crunch.

The wolf yelped, momentarily stunned.

Parker's eyes darted, spotting the fallen rifle just within reach.

His fingers grazed the weapon, but Nastya's claws dug into his shoulders, yanking him back.

"Don't even think about it," she snarled.

Parker ignored her, raising the weapon and pointing it at Varn's head.

Parker's finger tightened on the trigger. The gun bucked in his hands, unleashing a round of bullets.

Varn's eyes went wide with shock, a choked whimper escaping his throat as he collapsed. Blood blossomed across his chest, staining the earth beneath him.

"No!" Nastya screamed. Her claws raked Parker's back as she lunged for the weapon. "You bastard! You killed him!"

They grappled for control. The gun twisted between them.

A thunderous crack split the air.

Nastya staggered back, her hand flying to her shoulder. Crimson seeped between her fingers, her face contorted in pain.

"I'll tear you apart," she hissed. "I'll make you suffer for this."

Terror and instinct drove Parker's actions.

He raised the rifle, his hands shaking violently as he squeezed the trigger.

The bullet found its mark. Nastya's body jerked, a strangled cry escaping her lips as she crumpled to the ground.

Silence descended on the clearing, broken only by Parker's ragged breathing and the faint whisper of wind through the trees.

The adrenaline drained from his system, leaving him hollow and trembling

He forced himself to look at the bodies, to really see them, as the monsters they truly were.

Varn's unseeing eyes stared at the canopy above, while Nastya lay crumpled nearby, her partially transformed body a grotesque reminder of her inhuman nature.

"They were werewolves," Parker whispered, his voice hoarse. The words were as much a justification as they were a reminder. "Just like all the others."

Images flashed through his mind, towns ravaged, innocent people torn apart, the chaos and destruction left in the wake of werewolf attacks. He had witnessed it all firsthand.

If he had allowed them to live they would have only caused more death.

He took a deep, shuddering breath, steeling himself against the doubts that threatened to creep in.

"This is how it has to be," he murmured. "They all have to die. All of them."

Parker swallowed, then shot another two bullets at Varn's head just to make sure that he was dead.

CHAPTER 8

Distant blasts sent tremors through the mansion's foundations. Crystal chandeliers swayed ominously, and windows vibrated in their frames, but champagne flowed freely, and couples twirled on the dance floor like they were immune to the carnage in the distance.

Deepa stood in the hallway, her trembling fingers splayed against the cool glass of a window. Her reflection ghosted over the apocalyptic scene outside.

Another explosion lit up the horizon, closer this time, causing her to flinch.

Was it the werewolves or Infection Control? Had the war finally arrived at their door?

A chill ran down Deepa's spine as cold fingers brushed against her neck.

She whirled around, heart leaping into her throat, to find Axel's mother, Latavia, standing behind her.

The older woman's face was a mask of eerie calm. "You may want to make your way down to the basement. Anyone with any sense is heading there now."

Deepa swallowed, her mouth dry. "And Axel?"

"Lost his shit the moment that the bombing began and started running around the mansion like an idiot looking for you. So do us all a favor and get down to the basement before he does something stupid and gets himself killed."

Deepa nodded. "Right, basement."

Latavia patted her shoulder, then glided off, leaving Deepa standing alone by the window.

Deepa swallowed, her hands clenching and unclenching at her sides. The urge to transform and seek out Axel was overwhelming.

Her wolf was restless, howling to be released, but she forced it down, turning and following after Latavia's footsteps.

A pack of werewolves burst from the upper floor, their massive bodies a blur of fur and muscle as they bounded down a grand staircase. Their claws scraped against the polished steps, leaving deep gouges in the wood as they raced towards the main entrance.

The air erupted with the sharp crack of gunfire.

Wolves yelped and howled in pain, their bodies jerking violently as bullets tore through flesh and bone. Blood splattered across the elegant wallpaper and dripped from the crystal chandelier overhead.

Deepa froze in horror, pressing herself against the wall. Her hand clamped over her mouth, stifling a scream that threatened to escape.

Strong fingers wrapped around her upper arm, yanking her sideways. She stumble as she was shoved through an open doorway.

The heavy oak door slammed shut behind her.

"Parker?" Deepa gasped.

He looked like he had been through Hell. His body was caked with dirt and his skin was marred by numerous scratches. Blood trickled down the right side of his face and arm. He gripped a large gun tightly in his hands. Two more firearms were slung over his shoulders, accompanied by multiple rounds of ammunition.

Parker's eyes flashed with anger. "Why the fuck didn't you tell me about Varn?"

Deepa blinked. "What?"

"The werewolf," Parker snarled. "He was pretending to be on our side this entire time, and you knew!"

"I wanted to..." Deepa's voice trembled. "But you refused to talk to me."

"And whose fault was that?" Parker's fingers tightened around the gun in his hand.

Deepa's eyes darted to the weapon, her heart pounding. "What happened?"

"He's dead. Just like the rest of them should be."

"Parker, please-"

"No!" Parker's hands shook with rage. "They're monsters, Deepa! This is our chance, our only chance, to end this nightmare once and for all."

Deepa's palms grew slick with sweat.

She couldn't tear her eyes away from Parker's face. There was something wild in his eyes that sent a shiver down Deepa's spine.

He looked...feral.

"Help me Deepa," Parker croaked. "Help me kill them all."

Deepa stepped back. "But I-"

"Infection Control is gone," Parker said. "There's no one left. If we don't do this now, then they're going to win."

"Parker," Deepa breathed. "I can't... I'm one of them now."

"No you're not! You'll never be one of them. They think you're below them, a piece of human shit that's only good as that monster's fuck toy."

Tears stung Deepa's eyes, blurring her vision.

"That's not true," she murmured, but deep down, she knew he was right. She had witnessed enough to understand her fate, to realize that there was no escape from Axel's twisted family unless they were all dead.

"If you won't help me," Parker whispered. "Then I'll have to kill you. Please don't make me kill you Deepa."

"Please Parker. Please don't do this."

"I don't want to hurt you." Parker's voice trembled. "But I have to end this. Now."

Tears rolled down Deepa's cheeks. "I'll help you," Deepa's voice shook. "I'll help you stop the others. Just... just promise that you won't kill Axel."

"Are you serious?" he snapped. "After everything he's done?"

Deepa nodded, wiping her tears with trembling hands. "Please. I'll do anything you ask. Just spare Axel."

Parker ran a hand through his dirty hair. He let out a heavy sigh.

"Damn it," he muttered. "Fine. But only him, Deepa. The rest have to go."

He reached into his jacket, pulling out a handgun and holding it out to her. "You remember how to use one of these?"

Deepa nodded, taking the weapon with unsteady hands.

"Alright then." Parker crouched down to reload his rifle. "Let's finish this."

CHAPTER 9

Deepa was surprised at how easily she fell back into the old routine of shooting alongside Parker. The weight of the gun in her hands felt familiar, and it brought back vivid memories of their nights spent patrolling the city's dark sewers.

They moved swiftly through the mansion, working together like a well-oiled machine. They ducked into doorways and alcoves, using the walls for cover as they advanced through the building.

Whenever a werewolf appeared, they reacted instantly, their guns barking out a deadly rhythm that filled the air with the scent of gunpowder.

"The basement," Deepa hissed as they shot up a pair of young blond werewolves. "All the leaders would have gone down there."

Parker nodded.

They followed the sounds of footsteps and screams. The trail led them to a large iron door. Two massive werewolves stood guard, hastily trying to usher everyone inside.

Parker and Deepa ducked behind a corner, their fingers hovering over the triggers.

"Ready?" Parker whispered.

"Yeah." Deepa darted forward.

They burst into the corridor, guns raised and ready. The air exploded with the deafening roar of gunfire as they unleashed on the unsuspecting guards.

The guards' eyes widened in shock as rounds punched through their bodies. They tried to shift, fur sprouting from their skin, but it was too late. One by one, they fell, their massive forms hitting the floor with heavy thuds.

The iron door was left wide open.

"I'll keep watch," Deepa said. "Go!"

Parker nodded and sprinted towards the door, but a massive white wolf slammed into him, sending them sprawling across the floor in a tangle of limbs and fur.

"No!" Deepa screamed, raising her gun, but before she could fire, two powerful arms encircled her waist from behind.

"Deepa," Axel's voice hissed in her ear, a mix of anger and disbelief. "What the fuck are you doing?"

She thrashed against his iron grip. "Let go of me, Axel!"

"Have you lost your mind?" he snarled, tightening his hold.

"Stop it!" Deepa cried, her voice cracking with fear and frustration. "Please, just stop!"

Axel yanked her backwards and threw her to the ground. The impact knocked the wind from her lungs, leaving her gasping.

Her gun skittered across the floor, far out of reach.

Bruno, Reese, and Luke emerged from behind Axel, the three of them pinning Parker to the floor.

"Why? Deepa!" Axel cried. "Why this? And with him?"

Deepa blinked hard, trying to focus her blurry vision on Axel's face.

"Answer me!" he yelled, gripping her arm and jerking her upwards.

"Because they'll never let us go," she choked. "As long as they're all alive we'll never be free."

The words hung in the air between them.

Axel's grip on her arm loosened as the full weight of her statement sank in.

His eyes widened, a kaleidoscope of emotions flashing across his face, disbelief, understanding, and finally, a grim acceptance.

"Can we kill him now?" Bruno growled impatiently, tightening his grip on Parker's arms.

Without a word, Axel turned and walked towards the iron door. His movements were mechanical, like his mind had gone elsewhere.

His footsteps echoed down the stairs, slow and deliberate at first, then quickening.

"I say that we just kill him," Bruno growled, his fingers elongating into razor-sharp claws. He raised his hand, ready to strike Parker.

A blood-curdling scream pierced the air, echoing up from the basement.

The sound froze everyone in place.

"Wait!" Luke hissed, grabbing Bruno's arm. His eyes were wide with fear.

More screams followed, full of terror and agony. Long guttural howls joined the chorus, only to be cut short by wet tearing sounds, punctuated by heavy thuds.

Deepa pressed herself against the wall, her whole body shaking. Her eyes were locked on the iron door, unable to look away despite the horror unfolding beyond it.

Each scream, each sickening rip, made her flinch.

"Is that... Axel?" Bruno whispered, his earlier bravado replaced by disbelief and fear.

"Shut up," Reese snapped, but his voice trembled. "Just... just shut up."

The violent sounds continued for what felt like an eternity. Then, abruptly, silence fell.

Heavy footsteps ascended the stairs, slow and measured.

The iron door creaked open, and Axel emerged, his entire body drenched in blood. It matted his hair, dripped from his hands, and splattered his face like a grotesque mask. His eyes, however, were clear and focused.

"Fuck," Bruno breathed.

Axel moved with unnatural grace, leaving a trail of red droplets in his wake as he approached Deepa. He gathered her into his arms, oblivious to the gore that covered him.

"It's okay," he said gently, nuzzling her hair. "Now none of them can ever hurt us again."

Deepa's stomach lurched. The metallic stench of blood and death clung to Axel, threatening to overwhelm her.

Yet the wolf inside her rumbled with satisfaction, pleased at Axel's display of devotion and raw power.

CHAPTER 10

Axel advanced, his massive werewolf form dwarfing the room. Wicked claws extended from his enormous paws, each one capable of slicing through flesh with ease.

"Please..." Axel's great-grandfather whimpered, shrinking back against the wall. "We're family. I always loved you... loved you more than my own children. You were the best... better than your brother... please."

In his human form, such words might have stirred something in Axel. But now, in this monstrous shape, they seemed meaningless. The beast inside him growled with savage delight, reveling in the fear radiating from the man who had caused him so much pain over the years.

If the old man died, then Axel could be leader. He could reshape and change the werewolf world into what he wanted.

The bodies of several other elders lay scattered around them, along with anyone who attempted to interfere.

Everyone else was huddling in the corners, except for his mother who confidently watched on, her eyes sparkling with excitement.

"Do it," she whispered.

"I'll give you anything," his great grandfather babbled. "You can have that girl. I'll never make you marry anyone else."

Axel growled, his claws scratching against the concrete as he advanced on the old man, ripping him to shreds as the whole room watched on.

CHAPTER II

"Can't you do anything right?" Bruno laughed as he shoved a foot against Parker's back, sending the human man and a basket full of fruit sprawling across the floor.

Parker silently took it, obediently collecting the fruit as Bruno and Reese took turns shoving him back down, the metal collar around Parker's neck clanking against the floor.

Axel's mouth curved up into a grin as he watched on from his throne.

Watching Parker get kicked around was one of his favorite forms of entertainment, even if Luke didn't approve. His kindhearted cousin had been loudly against enslaving the human.

Human society had crumbled in the weeks after the elders' deaths. Werewolves had taken their rightful place as the true rulers of the planet, and Axel had become their king.

He watched over his realm from the top of a tall skyscraper, spending most of his days in his large beast form, destroying what remained of humanity and asserting his dominance over any opposing werewolf tribes.

He had searched for Ryan amongst the faces of his enemies, but the twisted bastard had disappeared, no doubt fucking his days away on a tropical island.

Axel rose to his feet, taking a deep breath as he allowed the change to overtake him. His body began to shift and grow, muscles swelling beneath his skin as coarse fur erupted across his form. His limbs stretched and thickened, bones cracking and reforming.

Within moments, Axel had fully transformed into his beast form.

His claws scratched against the floor as he made his way to his chambers.

The scent of his mate was heavy in the air, making his dick twitch and swell to life.

Deepa lay on her side in the spacious king-sized bed, cradling their newborn son close to her chest. The baby's tiny mouth was latched firmly to her breast, eagerly nursing as Deepa stroked his soft hair.

A nurse moved across the room to remove the baby when he entered, quickly whisking it away to another room.

Milk flowed down Deepa's chest as she rolled over to face him, letting out a soft growl as she parted her thighs, hungrily eyeing the enlarged organ between his legs with blatant enthusiasm.

Werewolf Deepa was in control most days. Unlike her human self, wolf Deepa relished in the death and destruction that surrounded them, growing wet at the sight of his large beastly body. She loved being pregnant and eagerly accepted his seed.

Human Deepa said that he wasn't the same after unlocking his beast form. Human Deepa was upset about the way he treated Parker and the remaining humans.

She said that he was drunk on power and was turning into a dictator.

But what did she know?

This was what Axel had to do to protect her and his people. If he didn't turn the remaining humans and enslave the immune, then how could he ensure her safety? He needed to breed her as much as possible to surround her with loyal pack members.

Axel's clawed hands took hold of Deepa's soft thighs, pulling her to the edge of the bed. He rubbed his engorged cock through her slick folds, relishing in the intoxicating wet heat.

She whined, a mixture of arousal and impatience.

It was perfect.

Axel pushed forward and sank his cock deep within her silky wet walls, groaning at the way she tightened around him.

Fuck, he couldn't get enough of his mate. He couldn't wait to make her pregnant again.

Deepa moaned beneath him, her hands reaching up and gripping at his large muscular arms, digging her nails in and dragging him closer.

Axel snarled in response, lowering his muzzle and licking the bruised bite mark on Deepa's throat, loving the way that she shuddered under his tongue.

He increased his pace, filling her to the brim, every inch of his monstrously large length sheathing within her slick passage as his knot began to swell.

Deepa's body stretched beneath him, allowing the extra thickness without complaint, as his knot tied them together.

Her toes curled, back arching as they moved in sync, lost in pleasure, both panting and whimpering like animals.

His balls swelled, slapping against her plump ass with each powerful thrust, the tip of his monstrous length kissing the opening of her womb.

He buried his teeth in her shoulder, drawing blood, filling his senses with her addictive metallic scent.

Heat and passion exploded within him. His body stiffened, and he filled Deepa's silky entrance with cum, pouring everything into her.

Deepa's hot walls clenched around him, her own orgasm triggered from the knotting, milking him for all that he was worth, both of them moaning in unison.

Soon. He silently promised her.

Soon he would finish making the world perfect for the two of them.

Even if it meant becoming more of a monster.

Want more?

Download five hot bonus spicy scenes, plus an alternative ending where Deepa and the boys go live out in the forest as a foursome.

mated.beatrixarden.com/extra

SUBSCRIBE TO BEATRIX ARDEN

Subscribe to Beatrix Steam email notifications for future release updates, and get three free ebooks!

sub.beatrixarden.com

ALSO BY BEATRIX ARDEN

Find more hot stories by Beatrix Arden at

www.beatrixarden.com

Werewolf Breeding Academy

Newly turned Riley thought she could get her inner wolf under control by enrolling in a school for werewolves. However, it's nothing more than an elaborate mating ground.

Can she evade the penetrating glare of Elijah - a devilishly handsome pureblood werewolf who disdains people like her? Or will they succumb to the primal instincts that threaten to bind them together?

Download for free!

werewolf.beatrixarden.com/free

You're my Omega

Omegaverse story. Alpha girl Sara discovers that her school enemy is secretly an Omega. When he suddenly goes into heat and begs her to mate him, she finds it impossible to resist.

Download for free here!

omega.beatrixarden.com/free

Chained Omega

Omega Franklin lives in a world where Alphas are extinct, but that doesn't stop him from buying one for his bed.

Franklin thinks that he's in control.....until he suddenly isn't.

chained.beatrixarden.com